PRAISE FOR THE DUBRIC BYERLY MYSTERY SERIES

"A page-turning blend of fantasy and mystery, with touches of romance, action and the supernatural. A unique and compelling series."
—Kelley Armstrong, author of *Broken*

PRAISE FOR *THREADS OF MALICE*

"*Threads of Malice* is a dark, fascinating web of a novel; the kind of story that ties you up, sinks its claws into you, and never lets go. Tamara Siler Jones will keep you wide-eyed and terrified until the very last page." —Lynn Viehl, author of *If Angels Burn*

"A fascinating, if extremely dark, fantasy mystery, more than worth checking out." —*Locus*

"Keeps you guessing until the final pages . . . no one will be the same after this story—not the characters, and certainly not the reader." —*SFRevu*

"Jones is not a familiar name in fantasy, but I don't think it will be too long before she is."
—*Science Fiction Chronicle*

VALLEY
OF THE
SOUL

✝

Tamara Siler Jones

BANTAM BOOKS

VALLEY OF THE SOUL
A Bantam Spectra Book / November 2006

Published by
Bantam Dell
A Division of Random House, Inc.
New York, New York

This is a work of fiction. Names, characters, places, and incidents
either are the product of the author's imagination or are used
fictitiously. Any resemblance to actual persons, living or dead, events,
or locales is entirely coincidental.

Bantam Books, the rooster colophon, Spectra, and the portrayal of
a boxed "s" are trademarks of Random House, Inc.

ISBN-13: 978-0-553-58711-1
ISBN-10: 0-553-58711-0

Printed in the United States of America
Published simultaneously in Canada

www.bantamdell.com

OPM 10 9 8 7 6 5 4 3 2 1

For Sam—
I wouldn't be here without you.

I stripped Sweeny naked, tied her to the tree, and started a fire as I waited for her to wake. Once I knew she had no choice but to see, I began. Livestock first, from chicks to full-grown steers. I killed each one in sight of her and threw the carcasses on the flames, some in pieces. The livestock gone, I killed and burned her grotesque abominations, then everyone who worked for her, starting with the children, adding each body to the fire. Then her family. One by one she watched them burn. I burned her books, her papers, her furniture. Everything she had. Everything. When it had all burned down to ash and flame, I killed her and burned her with the rest. I waited, watching until there was nothing left, not even smoke or embers, nowhere for her filthy soul to go. Then, just to be sure, I burned the tree I'd tied her to.

I salted the earth and ash, released the villagers, and prayed for my sins and the innocents I'd slaughtered. Lastly, before sleep, I sent a messenger bird to Tunkek, telling him that Fayre Sweeny, the Butcher of Quarry Run, was dead.

—Oriana of Fallowes, from her journal
Dated 4 32, 2216

CHAPTER

I

†

"Mama!" Haydon called from near the window. "There's horses on the road! Fancy ones!"

"That's nice." Arien sat at her kitchen table, trying to make sense of the drawing in the old book before she had to leave to work at the sanatorium. She'd never learned to read, but she didn't think that mattered, at least not with this book. It was full of pictures, detailed illustrations in colored ink. Even if she couldn't understand the words, she recognized the things they represented.

"Mama!" Haydon pulled on her skirt and she looked down to see him on the floor, balanced on one hand while his legs dragged uselessly behind him. "*Horses, Mama! You have to come see!*"

She sighed as she stood and scooped him up. "Horses come by every day, Haydon."

Haydon wrapped his hot arms around her neck. "Not quarry horses! Nobles' horses! Three pretty ones, all brushed and shiny! With fancy saddles!"

Balancing him on her hip, she pulled the curtains. Sure enough, there were three fine horses prancing away down the road. "Well, I'll be."

The three noblemen pulled their mounts to a stop

3

and dismounted near Constable Marsden, who stood not far down the road. One was old and limped a little as he walked, but following him was a tall, slender young man with a purposeful stride. The third man dwarfed the other two combined and Arien sucked in her breath as he lumbered around the horses.

"Dien?" she whispered, leaning close to the open window.

"Who are they, Mama?" Haydon asked.

"Men from the castle," she said, watching the old man follow Calder Marsden into the ravine. The young man and Dien—she was certain it was him, even after almost six summers—stopped to talk to a nearby group of villagers and quarry workers.

"Can we go outside and see the horses? Please?"

Arien hesitated for a moment, then felt Haydon's forehead. Still too warm, but she hated to disappoint him. "Of course we can, sweetie."

* * *

Dubric knew the scent of death. He had known it for most of his life, the low stench that permeated his clothes, sometimes his very skin, settling into his pores like a thick oil clotted with grit and dust. Death's gassy breath was a stain he could never wash away, could never escape even if he wanted to, just as he could never escape his ghosts.

Below, on a flattened bit of ground, Calder Marsden, constable of Quarry Run, stood beside the burlap-wrapped remains, frowning. Marsden flicked away a swarm of flies then grimaced and spat. His pleasant face, stubbled from a long and trying day, looked slightly off color. To the best of Dubric's knowledge,

Marsden had never seen a mutilated corpse before, even if it was merely a sheep.

"It's here, Lord Byerly," Marsden said, glancing at the carcass as Dubric caught his breath. "At least the part I've found. Second one this phase."

Half hidden by an elderberry bush, a sheep's rump and haunches lay mostly intact, partially wrapped in burlap and tied with twine. Some of its flesh had been chewed away and parts of its intestines strung into the brush. Maggots roiled over the exposed meat and other insects crawled over the burlap and bloody wool.

Dubric ignored his arthritic knees as he knelt beside the remains. Up close, the reek from days of rotting in late spring heat made his eyes water. Flies landed on his face and he shooed them away. "Have any more sheep been reported missing since you sent word to the castle?"

"Yes, milord Castellan. Four of them."

"And you have found several like this?" Dubric pulled a pair of thin sheep-gut gloves onto his burn-scarred hands, positioning the stitched seams over his knuckles. He prepared to dictate his findings, then paused. Otlee, the boy who had taken his notes during two previous investigations, had stayed home at the castle.

"Yes, milord. Cut to the seven hells and tossed away, guts and all, but wrapped up tidy as a pin. Why, milord? If you're going to steal and butcher the lord's sheep and package it for storage, wouldn't a sane man keep the meat? I hated to bother you, milord, but I just couldn't make any sense of it."

Dubric looked up. "How well do you write?"

"Not very well, milord. I can make my mark and cipher a little, maybe read a word or two, but there's not much reason for a carpenter to learn to write. Since I became constable, I've been paying Philbe to do my official papers."

"Then fetch one of my men from the road," Dubric said.

Marsden nodded eagerly.

Dubric set to work, surveying the immediate area. He examined fallen leaves and looked under bushes and plants, but found no unexplained footprints, no knife, no apparent clues. Only the rotting back half of a sheep, partially wrapped in burlap. He wiped sweat from his brow and looked up to the arching branches of elm, sycamore, and maple. *By the King. I am too old for this.*

Someone broke through the brush above. "I am down here," Dubric said.

His elder page, Lars, skip-jumped down the steep slope. "I've taken a statement from the fellow who found it, sir. He was out hunting mushrooms when he stumbled over it. Dien's finishing up the spectator listings."

"That is fine," Dubric said, handing Lars his notebook. "How is he managing?"

Lars flipped through to an empty page. "He'll be all right, sir. It's just a sheep."

"I fear it is too soon to return to this gruesome type of work," Dubric said. Murders just a moon before had ravaged his team. His squire, Dien, had lost a child and young Otlee had lost his innocence. Lars had nearly died and even Dubric had . . .

Had what? he thought, pulling back the edges of the burlap and frowning at the torn flesh. *Had decided that I am not yet dead and had best resume living?* Dubric took a breath and let it free. The past was past. Only the now and the future mattered.

He began dictating his findings, describing the arrangement of the remains, then cursed. "It is not merely a sheep," he said, pushing wool aside to show Lars a shaved area near the spine. Two triangles were marked on the skin, one red and one black, and overlapping point to point.

"That's not Lord Brushgar's brand," Lars said.

Dubric let the wool fall. "No. It is a mage mark."

* * *

Dubric reached the road to find scores of villagers and quarry workers standing in loose groups. Most took a step back as Lars carried the sack of remains to his horse.

Dien left a woman with a little boy and walked over, raking his thick fingers through his shorn hair. Once a steady and solid brown, Dien's hair had become flecked with gray and his massive bulk seemed diminished. Dubric wondered if he ate much anymore, or slept.

Dien barely looked up as he spoke. "What are we looking at, sir?"

"Now is not the place to discuss it. We need to find the other pieces. Soon."

"Maybe I should have contacted you sooner, milord," Marsden said. "I almost did a couple of phases back when it became more than one or two at a time."

"How long has this been happening?"

"Off and on for a few moons. It started late last autumn, after the harvest. Kieran the blacksmith fattens a lamb every summer and someone stole it out of its pen. We looked high and low for it, then parts turned up, scattered around. I thought at first it was some kids causing trouble—Kieran isn't the most loved man in town and some of the lads taunt him—but it didn't stop. Couple of phases later we found a ewe without its back end, then a ram the same way. It was quiet all winter, but started up again a moon or so ago, after the thaw. Seems like every few days another one turns up, half a sheep or a whole one all cut up but still with their wool . . . So many have disappeared that folks are worried about paying their taxes and feeding their families."

"Were all of the sheep found in this area?" Dubric glanced up as Lars came close.

"No, milord," Marsden said. "They've turned up all over town."

"When was the last reported theft?"

"This morning. Woodley, a farmer up north of the pines, reported sheep missing."

Dubric added to his notes. "What did you do with the carcasses you found?"

"Burned or buried them," Marsden said. "No one wants to eat them, not after they've lain around spoiling. There's no telling if the meat's poisoned or tainted. I just can't figure out who around here would do such a thing to folks' livestock."

Dubric looked at the crowd gathered around them. "We need to speak privately," he said, "away from spectators and eavesdroppers."

"Of course," Marsden said. "We can talk in my office."

As the men turned toward the horses, Dubric touched Lars's arm. "Choose two men from the crowd to aid you. I want this ravine scoured for other parts. Tell no one we suspect a mage."

* * *

Marsden leaned forward, his arms on his desk. "You think I have a *what* on the loose?"

"A mage," Dubric said, shifting in his chair. "I saw a mark, two overlapping triangles, on the sheep's skin."

Dien paced behind him, muttering, "Not again. Goddess damned son of a whore, I've seen enough of this shit."

Marsden glanced up at Dien then returned his attention to Dubric. "Milord, mages are just monsters in tales parents tell their children to frighten them. Everyone knows they all died in the war."

"A few remain." Dubric flipped back through his notebook to his most recent case and handed the notebook to Marsden. "A bit more than a moon ago, we killed a mage in northern Faldorrah who murdered young men to use their blood to make dye."

Squinting, Marsden turned the book upside down, then upright again. "Dye? Like for coloring fabric?"

"Yes, dye!" Dien snapped, turning. "My daughter was murdered and good lads were raped and tortured to death. One of our pages barely survived. All for frigging dye!"

Dubric raised a hand to hush Dien. "Mages still exist and one has marked the sheep you found. I am hoping that Lars will locate the remaining pieces. Do you see the diamond-shaped mark on the bottom of the left-hand page?"

Marsden laid the book on the desk and pointed to the symbol. "This one? That looks like an eye?"

"Yes. That is a copy of the mage mark for the mage we killed." Dubric leaned forward and flipped the pages to the most recent entry. He pointed to the overlapping triangles. "And that is the mark I found on that sheep. It is a mage mark, one I have never seen before."

Looking horrified, Marsden slid the book to Dubric. "I've seen that before. On Kieran's ewe and some parts I found a couple of phases ago."

"You said these mutilations began last autumn. Did anyone new move into the community not long before then? Did anything strange happen?"

"Nothing strange, no, nothing strange happens around here, but we did have some new folks last autumn. Got a new physician, a man named Shelby Garrett. Philbe's boy married a girl from Strod, and Tupper Dughall came back."

Dien stopped pacing. "He what? I told him to stay gone."

"He's been dowsing here for moons, and hasn't caused much trouble other than an occasional fight at the Cypress." Marsden paused and looked up at Dien. "He works, he drinks . . . He keeps to himself. I haven't had cause to arrest him."

"He beat a girl nearly to death," Dien said. "Did it once, he'll do it again."

Dubric rubbed his eyes. "He completed his sentence and has earned back the right to his life."

"Anyone who beats a pregnant girl half to death with a hammer hasn't earned a thing except a trip to the noose," Dien muttered.

All three men glanced over when the door opened and Lars poked his head in. "Sir, I found your missing sheep."

Outside, Lars pointed to a muddy, burlap-wrapped parcel on his mare. At his feet, a scraggly brown pup with a sleek black head jumped on his leg, begging for attention. "It's the front half, sir. We found it next to the stream. Found two of the feet, too."

Dubric untied the burlap. "They were probably dragged off by scavengers. Did you find the head?" He brushed insects aside and searched through the wool near the exposed flesh, looking for a shaved patch.

Lars knelt to pat the dog. "No, sir, no head."

Dubric quickly found shaved areas near the spine at the neck and waist; both were marked with the same overlapping triangles. He covered the dead sheep and tied it to Lars's saddle again. "I want you to go back to the castle and take these to Physician Rolle. I need to know anything he can tell me."

"Yes, sir. Straight home," Lars said, smiling.

"Identify everything you can," Dubric said, meeting Lars's gaze. "Do you understand?"

The boy flinched, then nodded. "Yes, sir."

"It'll be dark soon. Maybe I should go instead," Dien said.

"I'll be fine." Lars climbed onto the saddle and reined about. "I'll stick to the merchant roads and be almost home by dark. Don't worry. I'll be careful. See you in the morning." He gave the other men a slight wave, then left, the dog following for a few steps before it stopped mid-road to scratch.

Dien clenched his fists. "Sir, he's too young . . . at night . . ."

"I seem to recall you riding alone to capture a cut-purse along the Deitrelian border at a rather young age," Dubric said.

"That was different. I was twice his size."

Dubric patted his squire on the back. "You still are and will likely always be. He is not a child anymore. Let him be a man."

The three men watched Lars ride away. "Why's the boy so glad to take a long ride back to the castle with a rotting sheep?" Marsden asked.

"Because my daughter's there," Dien said. "They've been courting a whole moon now. And they had plans for tonight."

Marsden looked over Dien's towering bulk, top to bottom. "Oh. Must be a brave boy."

Dubric smiled. "He is."

CHAPTER

2

†

"I dunno what good it'll do you to look," Woodley said, walking across the barnyard. "It's just a pen full of wooly sheep."

"But several are missing, are they not?" Dubric asked, breathing deep. No longer a hot wind from the south, the breeze had shifted and brought cool northerly gusts with the scent of rain.

"Aye. Four of them. Since folks'd been reportin' woolies gone, I do a head count every night when I pen 'em up, then again in the mornin' before I let 'em out to graze." A compact shepherd dog stood and bared its teeth as they approached, growling like a low rip in the evening air. Woodley called out, "Down, Buck. That's a good lad."

Buck wagged his tail and sat, his tongue lolling as he watched them.

They reached the sheep pens, a wide corral with a slat roof and frame walls attached to a high fence. Scores of common black-faced sheep milled together inside. A few turned to look at the men, but most seemed oblivious to their presence.

Dubric tried the gate and found it securely latched.

"Now, milord, woolies ain't the brightest of critters.

Hells, they'll walk right in front of a speeding carriage if given the chance, but there ain't no wooly I've seen what can jump a fence as tall as my chin, and the slats is too narrow for them to wriggle through. Then there's Buck here," he said, scratching the dog behind the ears. "He's on guard all night, him and Bess both after full dark. Ain't no strange man gonna climb in there and lift a wooly out without them takin' a bite out of his backside."

Dubric examined the latch and found it to be a simple mechanism; pulling a lever just within reach on the inside released the lock bolt. "How, then, do you believe the sheep disappeared?"

Woodley spat tobacco juice onto the ground. "Haunts. Them's what did it."

"You believe ghosts took your sheep?"

"Yessir. Happn'd before, you see."

"It did?"

"Yessir, lots of folks lose woolies whenever a haunt's loose. Always been that way. Hells, milord, I remember my daddy tellin' of a time when Sweeny's haunt done stole half the flock and left 'em lyin' about, dried up with no blood left in 'em atall."

"Sweeny's haunt?"

"Yessir. Sweeny used to rule these parts, way back b'fore I was born. My daddy and granddad used to tell us kiddies scary tales 'bout the dark times." He spat tobacco juice again. "Anyways, this here ain't no diff'rent, milord. I just hope the haunt don't take half my flock, leastways not before I sell 'em off at the faire. I got taxes to pay."

* * *

At her parents' suite in the Families' Wing of Castle Faldorrah, Jesscea Saworth struggled to make sense of mathematics with her hands clamped over her ears. Baby Cailin had colic and had not stopped crying for at least a bell. Unable to concentrate, Jess sighed and stood. "I can take her for a bit, Mam."

Sarea kept pacing across the sitting room, patting Cailin's back. "No. Study. I'm all right."

"You've got to be going deaf."

Smiling, Sarea kissed Cailin's head. "You get used to it."

"If you say so," Jess muttered, then turned as the door to their suite banged open. Her older sister, Kialyn, stomped through in a perfumed haze and shoved past her.

Sarea pushed the screaming baby into Jess's arms. "Kia, wait!" she called, following her, but Kia had already entered her room and slammed the door. Sarea sagged. "Kia?" she asked, knocking. "Can I come in?" Jess didn't hear the answer over the baby's cries, but Sarea turned and walked back to the sitting room and held out her hands for Cailin.

"I'm sorry, Mam."

"These past few phases have been hard for everyone. It's not your fault."

Part of it is, Jess thought, but she said nothing.

Sarea resumed patting Cailin's back. "You don't talk much either, you know. How are things? School? Lars?"

"Everything's fine," Jess said, shrugging as she sat at the table again. "There's nothing much to report."

The door opened again and Jess's younger sister Fynbelle ran through, her face red and blotchy from crying. She didn't bother to look at her mother or Jess; Fyn just hurried into her room, then closed and locked the door.

* * *

Dubric pulled his charger to a halt. "Do you smell that?"

"Something died," Dien said, dismounting. "Something big, by the smell." He pulled a battered lantern off the back of his saddle and lit it.

Marsden led his horse to a scraggly tree. "I didn't smell anything coming out."

"The wind has changed," Dubric said. He tied his charger beside Marsden's horse.

Dien held the lantern high and squinted into the evening. "I'm betting on that field, sir."

"Let us go see, then," Dubric said, climbing over the low stone fence.

Letting their noses guide them, they walked across a field of young oats as it sloped down toward a creek. The wind freshened, cool and damp, but the stench nearly knocked them back.

"It's been dead longer than a couple of days, whatever it is," Dien said.

They searched the creek bed but found nothing of interest, then climbed the bank to the next field, this one planted with sorghum. They continued on, the stench growing so strong on the far side of the field that it made Dubric gag. Beside him, Marsden retched.

A scattering of carcasses, dogs and sheep, lay in the rows of sorghum and the brush edging the field. The carcasses were dismembered, their limbs removed, their heads gone, their bodies cut in two. "How many, sir?" Dien asked, holding the lantern high as Dubric glanced back the way they had come. He estimated they were two furlongs or more from the road, far enough for winds to disperse most of the smell.

"I estimate ten dogs and a score or so sheep," he said, kneeling. The nearest carcass, the headless front portion of a half-grown pup, had rotted nearly to bones and dry, matted fur. Dubric checked along the spine but there was no skin there for a mage mark to be written upon and what little remained elsewhere was blackened and in patches. "This dog has been dead at least a phase," Dubric said, standing, "if not two."

"And the scavengers have got to them," Dien said. "There's not much left but wool and bones."

"But none have been completely consumed." Dubric turned to Marsden. "Have you found any dead scavengers? Coyotes? Raccoons? Weasels? Ravens?"

"Yes, milord, a few, but I never thought much of it. Some folks set out tainted bait. And I never thought much of a few missing dogs, either. They just run off sometimes. I hadn't seen any butchered like this before."

"The meat of these animals may be poisoned," Dubric said, pulling his notebook from his pocket. "But I have no way of knowing if the animals themselves died of poison." He sighed and sketched the arrangement of carcasses.

His sketch finished, he picked his way across the scattered carcasses, looking for anything out of place. Seeing a bit of dark glass reflecting the lantern light, he knelt and wriggled a vial out from beneath a legless, eviscerated dog. *What have we here?* He held it up to the light.

"What is it, sir?" Dien asked.

"A medicine vial," Dubric replied. "And there is a bit of fluid inside." He uncorked the vial and sniffed, then promptly replaced the cork and pulled an evidence bag from his pocket. "Laudanum."

"That's not something you can just pick up any-where," Dien said.

"No, narcotics usually are dispensed by a physi-cian." Dubric turned to Marsden. "Tell me about this physician who arrived last autumn."

* * *

Jess sat with some noble girls and pages in the castle library, relishing the quiet as she studied for the next day's mathematics test. Behind her, Clintte the librar-ian fell into a bout of coughing and other students made gagging noises. One said, "What's that smell?"

Jess just wrinkled her nose. It smelled like some-thing had died. *It's not that bad. Try cleaning a hen-house in the middle of six moon or changing a sick baby's diddy.*

A girl at Jess's table looked up and covered her nose with her hand. "He's here for you," she said.

Jess turned and saw Lars in the hall outside the door. Grinning, she jumped from her chair and hurried out of the library, reaching for his hand. "Where've you been? Are we going to the village?" Up close the stench was worse, but she didn't care.

"We can, if you want, but I'm still on duty. Get your books, and we'll talk."

She squeezed his hand before returning to her table. As she gathered her things, Deorsa leaned forward and said, "I don't know how you stand it." He lowered his voice. "The things he does. Why, just last phase, he went swimming in a cesspool. He swims in *sewage*. It's disgusting."

Jess buckled her book satchel. "That was two phases ago, for a case. It was only waist-deep, and the purse was floating. Sort of." She shrugged. Her father had worked under Dubric since before she was born. Sometimes they had to do disgusting things. Sometimes they got hurt. Sometimes they faced problems no one else would and, sometimes, they saved people. "It's just a job."

She returned to Lars. "If you're on duty, we shouldn't go to the Dancing Sheep," she said as they walked, hand in hand, past the scribe and the mapmaker to the back hall. "I'm surprised Dubric and Dad let you come get me at all."

"They didn't, but they're not here and I have some time before reports come back." Lars pushed the door open and stepped aside to hold it for the head accountant, Jelke, who coughed and covered his nose as he hurried past. "We'll have supper here, maybe do something, okay?"

"Sounds great," Jess said, questions dancing in her head. She knew Lars wasn't supposed to talk about active cases, but if he was working under his own supervision, it couldn't be too bad.

They climbed the west tower stairs to the second floor, passing nobles and servants who grimaced and stared. At Lars's room, clothes, armor, and clutter lay on every available surface as usual, and his three suitemates weren't home.

Jess smiled. They were alone. And unchaperoned.

Blushing, Lars knocked dirty socks off his bureau to make room for her books, then emptied his pockets. "Um, I need to get cleaned up. Give me a bit?"

"Of course." She looked away as he searched for clean clothes. She tried not to grimace at the rotten food and muddy clothes on the floor, the rumpled, stained sheets on the beds, or the mold climbing up the corner of the wall. She certainly did not acknowledge the frilly underdrawers tacked on the wall beside Moergan's bed.

Lars excused himself to the privy room, leaving Jess to her own devices. She thought about reviewing formulas again, but decided she'd had enough. The contents of Lars's pockets lay beside her books; his page's file, some coins, an intricate brass buckle, grimy burlap scraps, and a few folded bits of paper. Sighing, she picked up a library book from the floor and climbed onto Lars's bed to open it.

She had just settled in with the book on her lap when the door opened and Lars's roommate Serian came through, lugging armor and a wooden sword.

"Hey, Jess," he said, dropping the mess on the floor. "Hargrove working late again? That why you're frowning?"

She made herself smile. "No. He's taking a bath."

Serian peeled off his filthy shirt. "Ah. That's the new smell in here. Rumor is, there's a body in some pissant town. Dubric probably had Hargrove carry it. He always gets the shit jobs."

"I guess so." Jess shrugged and tried to focus on her book instead of Serian disrobing in front of her, but he was a big lad, nearly as big as her father, and he was difficult to ignore.

"Okay, Jess, out with it. What's got you so down?"

She looked up, then immediately returned her gaze to the book. Serian was discarding his pants. She prayed he'd keep his underdrawers on this time. "Down? I'm not down."

"Yeah, you are. Still having problems at home?"

She tried to focus on the paragraph but it kept blurring. "Some. Fyn and the baby both cry all the time and Kia's her same surly self." She chewed her lip then added, "And she's said some things."

Change jingled as Serian's pants hit the floor. "She still harping that bull piss about Lars using you?"

"Yeah."

"Don't listen to her, Jess. Shit, he's been head-over-ass smitten with you as long as I've known him. There ain't no other girl, anywhere. Never has been, never will be. Kia's just full of herself. *And,* I think our boy there has hogged the privy long enough."

Jess glanced up as Serian winked and, wearing only his underdrawers, strode to the privy room door and threw it wide.

Lars jumped back, startled, dropping his comb as the towel around his hips slipped. "What the hells?"

"Some of us have better things to do than entertain your girl while you primp, Hargrove."

"I'm not primping, and shut that damned door! For Goddess's sake, I'm not dressed!"

Serian's bulk partially blocking the view, he glanced back at Jess and grinned. "Like she cares about your dimply ass. You knew he has a dimply ass, didn't you, Jess?"

Jess giggled. "You're terrible!"

Serian's grin brightened and he wiggled his wide butt. "Hear that, Hargrove? She thinks I'm sexy."

Moergan came through the outer door. "No one thinks a moose like you is sexy," he said, noticing Jess. "But if you two eunuchs are comparing bits, I'm happy to take care of things out here."

"Oh, we're managing fine." Serian turned his back to Lars and blocked the privy room door. "How are faire inventories coming?"

Moergan flumped onto his bed. "Swimmingly. I got to count tankards for the ale tent, then pigs, then copper pots. A delightfully boring way to spend a day."

"Least you're not on security detail," Serian said. "Trumble and I have to spend the whole faire watching for drunks and thieves."

Lars pushed Serian aside and came out of the privy room with clean pants on, his shirt unbuttoned, and his feet bare.

"What torture has Dubric scheduled you for?" Moergan asked.

Lars finished buttoning his shirt then sat beside Jess to pull on his socks. "Nothing. I have faire day off."

"Lucky bastard. How'd you manage that?" Serian asked.

Lars grinned at Jess. "Told Dubric I needed the whole day."

"Really?" she asked.

Lars beamed. "Yep. Off duty till dawn the next morning. *And* I got your dad to extend our curfew. We can stay as late as we want at the dance."

Their gazes locked for a moment, but Lars winced and drew away as he had so many times before. Jess wished he'd tell her what was wrong.

* * *

"I want to speak with Physician Garrett, then we can rest for the evening," Dubric said, striding to their mounts.

"We're facing another nutter, aren't we, sir?" Dien asked as he untied his horse.

"Perhaps," Dubric said. "But the mage marks on the sheep worry me, as do all of the missing heads." He paused and forced his hands to unclench. "Only a few mages specialized in keeping or destroying heads, and those were the worst of a bad lot."

"It might just be kids killing livestock for thrills,"

Marsden said. "The marks you found might not have anything to do with that."

Dien muttered a curse. "What if it's Tupper, sir? It all started right after we released him, and we already know he likes to assault young girls. Maybe he just gets off attacking anything weaker than he is. Sheep. Puppies. Pegging bastard, maybe he's molesting the animals, too."

"That is a bit of a logic leap, and there is no reason to jump to such conclusions," Dubric said. "We cannot know for certain what is happening here or who is involved until we learn more about how the animals were killed and why. We have much random speculation, but few facts. Try to keep an open mind."

"There weren't any dead animals until after we let him loose, were there? Hells, he probably did it. So help me, if there are hammer wounds on that sheep, I'll open Tupper's frigging skull." Dien's voice grew low and gravely. "We should've hanged him when we had the chance. So help me, I won't let him beat another girl."

They rode in strained silence back to the village. Eventually Marsden asked, "Not that it's any of my business, but does that boy know you've got such a temper, seeing how he's courting your daughter and all?"

"Lars doesn't worry me," Dien said. "It's the other one."

"Your daughter has two lads courting her?"

"Not Jess. Her younger sister, Fyn, has a castle page after her. His father's a lecher and a sneak. The boy's no better."

"Oh." Marsden guided his horse down a narrow lane. "And does *he* know about your temper?"

"He's scared to death of me," Dien said. "Which is

probably the only thing keeping his filthy mitts off my baby."

* * *

Alone again, and he's barely looked at me. Jess slid down from the fence. "I'll help gather your arrows." She picked up the lantern while Lars set aside his bow.

"I only hit six that time. Out of fifty arrows. I'm never going to get promoted if I can't pass archery."

Side by side, they crossed the bow range. "That's better than the previous five quivers," she said, at a loss for anything else to say. "You'll pass."

He snatched a pair of arrows from the ground. "It's rotten, Jess, and I can't believe that you're willing to sit here and watch me waste my time every night."

Jess picked up half a dozen arrows and put them in a quiver, feathers up. "You're not wasting your time— you're practicing. Besides," she said, braving a glance, "it's one of the few times I get you to myself."

He smiled and really *looked* at her for the first time since supper in the great hall, and she felt suddenly warm. She forgot all about the arrows as he came toward her. The breeze picked up and ruffled his hair, tugged gently at her skirt, but she barely felt it—he was reaching for her, and maybe, just maybe, he would take her in his arms, maybe even kiss her, just like she'd hoped.

But he stopped before he reached her, his hands clenching into fists. She looked up, searching his eyes. He started to speak, then seemed to change his mind.

"Is something wrong?" she asked.

He started to reach out again, then jerked back. "No, nothing's wrong."

"Something is," she whispered. "I wish you'd talk to me."

He swallowed. "All right. What do you want to talk about?"

"How about why you won't touch me if we're alone?"

He glanced away. "Oh, Goddess, Jess, don't."

Her throat clenched but she pressed on. "We've been courting a whole moon and you won't even hold my hand if we're alone. There's *something* wrong."

"Nothing's wrong. I love you. I swear I do."

"Don't swear," she said. "Just talk to me. We come to the targets or the roof almost every night and we barely talk. You barely even look at me."

"Well, we're looking now, and talking," he said as he picked up an arrow from the ground. "Speaking of talking, has Fyn said anything to your mam?"

Jess held out the quiver for him. "No. Did Gilby talk to my dad?"

"I don't think so. I'd have had to clean up the mess. Besides, he's avoiding me. I think he's getting tired of me riding his ass about being responsible. She's thirteen, for Goddess's sake. Too young to do this alone."

Jess found two more arrows. "Well, they'd better do something soon. I'm tired of covering for them."

"I'm just worried about the baby." Lars sighed. "No one's making any plans for the baby. What are they thinking?"

"They're not. Not with their heads, anyway." She held out the quiver for Lars again. "Is that what's going on? Your worry over Fyn and Gilby and the baby?"

"Maybe. Maybe I just think too much. I think about us a lot, Jess. I'm just trying to do the right thing."

"I know," she said, smiling.

"Oh!" he said, reaching into his pocket. "I found

something today. Wasn't sure if you'd want it or not. I mean, it's nothing, really, just I know you like belts."

Jess grinned. She loved belts, especially unique ones. "That buckle?" she asked.

He sagged a little as he retrieved it from his pocket. "You saw?"

"Sorry," she said as he set it in her palm. "It was right by my books. It's pretty, with the carvings and all. Where'd you find it?" It felt heavier than she expected as she turned it in her hand, and still warm from his pocket. A nice solid buckle, perfect for a fabric belt.

"In the mud, actually," he said, "at the bottom of a ravine. Looked like it had been there for a while." He paused and met her gaze. "You don't have to like it."

"I think it's wonderful."

The moment stretched between them and he took a slight step toward her, flinched, then touched her hand before he bent to pick up an arrow. "The faire's in a few days. The dance, the dinner . . . Have you gotten your dress? Can you tell me what color it is, or is that a secret?"

"It's not a secret," she said. "It's yellow. And sleeveless."

He grinned. "Sleeveless? Well, I'll definitely be looking during the dance, then."

"That's the plan."

"It's a good plan."

*   *   *

Lights shone through Garrett's windows, but no one answered the door. Through the curtains, Dubric saw nothing besides a thin strip of wall and the corner of a table. He detected no movement within.

He walked to the back of the house and found the

lights lit, but the door locked. The silence was broken only by a neighbor's barking dog.

"Want me to break it down, sir?" Dien asked.

"No." Dubric walked to the horses. "We have no cause to burst into a man's home. I merely wanted to assess him."

"Do you think he killed those animals?" Marsden asked.

"I am not certain. The laudanum may have been there by coincidence, or it may have been dropped by accident. But a trained physician could surely perform the dismemberments we have seen, and would have access to the drug. He also arrived in town at the proper time. He is by far our best suspect." Dubric glanced at Dien. "More so than Tupper."

"Garrett doesn't do many surgeries," Marsden said. "At least that's what I hear. He's a tonic and powder man, more likely to make an elixir or an infusion than cut someone open, or stitch them closed."

Dubric hoisted himself up to the saddle "Alas, we will not be interviewing him tonight. It is late and I am fatigued. Where could we find lodging?"

Marsden mounted and reined about. "There's Vorrle's boarding house, but it's a filthy place, so I'd have to suggest Jerle's."

"Jerle Dughall?" Dien asked, his voice tight. "Tupper's father?"

"He's the largest landowner in town. Owns the worker shacks, the rental houses . . . Hells, he owns the blacksmith shop, the boot maker's, and the miller's, too."

"I've met the bastard," Dien said. "He tried to buy us off after Tupper's arrest. He wasn't happy that we weren't for sale."

And Tupper, however unlikely, remains on my suspect

list. "We probably should decline, if at all possible. If Tupper is involved it would be best for all concerned if we were not indebted to Jerle's hospitality."

"I'd invite you to stay with us, but with the kids there's barely room for Mari and me to sleep." Marsden tapped his fingers on the pommel of his saddle. "You know, Philbe has a couple of extra rooms. Her boy married off last fall, and her granddad passed on a while back. Philbe'd just as likely burn something as cook it, but she'll have a good bed and a clean room. Her shop's on the west end of town, by the miller. Don't you worry, I'll square it with her. She owes me a couple of favors."

"Thank you," Dubric said.

"I'm just glad you came," Marsden said. "And I'm sorry I didn't send for you when the first animals turned up. Honest to Goddess, sir, I thought it was just kids causing trouble."

"It still may be," Dubric said.

They rode in silence for a while, then Dien changed the subject. "How old's your boy now? He was just toddling around, last I remember. So you and Mari have had more?"

"Two," Marsden said proudly. "Ward's going on eight summers and the twins are five. Yours?"

Dien and Marsden chatted about their children while Dubric rode behind them, trying not to let his sorrow show. He had never felt the joys and trials of parenthood, never put his own child to bed or read stories or played. No one would carry on his name when he passed and few would grieve him. His only child had died in his wife's womb more than forty-five summers before. The pain of the double loss still burned.

Despite having love in his life again, he had little hope that fatherhood was within his reach at his age.

He would just have to resign himself to the company of other men, other fathers, and their children.

He looked up to the moon peeking through the clouds and sighed. He wanted to go home.

* * *

"Come in, come in," Maeve said, ushering Jess and Lars through the door. "Please excuse the mess." Pathways wound like eddies through the chaotic mess of looms, furniture, and boxed belongings in Dubric's suite.

"It's fine," Jess said.

"Let's show Lars the new sitting room," Maeve said. "They just finished plastering today."

Hand in hand, Jess and Lars shared amused glances as they followed Maeve through blankets hanging in the open archway.

No longer merely a narrow pair of rooms along the north-facing wall, the expanded suite engulfed two other suites and extended to the eastern castle wall. Windows were freshly glazed on two walls and the sprawling floors had been partially resurfaced with new oak planks. Everything smelled of linseed oil and plaster dust; Jess felt grit beneath her shoes throughout Maeve's tour. The suite was open and airy, bright and welcoming.

"The only enclosed rooms will be the bath chambers, Dubric's office, and my studio," Maeve said as she opened doors leading to a balcony near the corner. "Everything else will be open, or with wide archways in the support walls."

She leaned against the door frame. "What have you kids been up to?"

"Lars got me a new buckle," Jess said. "I'm going to make a belt."

"It's not new, exactly," Lars said, chuckling.

"It's new to me," Jess said, fishing it out of her pocket and handing it to Maeve. "I think it's an antique."

"I have some woven strips that would work perfectly for it, if you'd like them."

"I'd love that! Thank you!"

Maeve looked at Lars. "You didn't just come to see me at this time of night to tour the suite or show me the buckle, did you?" she asked, returning it to Jess.

"No, ma'am. I came to ask a favor," Lars said. "I'd like to use one of Dubric's, um, investigative tools for a minute. If I could."

Maeve straightened and frowned. "Has someone died? Again? Is that why he hasn't come home?"

"Not exactly," Lars said.

"Who? Where? How many?"

Lars swallowed. "We're not supposed to talk about case specifics. I just want to follow a couple of clues."

They looked at each other for a long time, long enough for Jess to fidget on her feet, but at last Maeve nodded.

"I don't like that thing," she said, her mouth tight. "It's not safe."

"I agree. I'll be careful."

"Thing? What thing?" Jess asked. "What's not safe?"

Neither responded. "Cover it when you're finished," Maeve said, and walked out of the room.

Lars squeezed Jess's hand. "You'd better go with her."

She searched his eyes. "What's going on?"

"You know I can't tell you," he said softly.

"Yes you can. If you're in danger, I need to know."

He led her toward the archway leading back to Dubric's old suite. "I'm not in any danger. Not here. I promise."

Jess bit her lip to keep from arguing. She knew his job entailed secrecy, especially during investigations, but, Goddess, Maeve seemed almost frightened. Jess looked around the suite, noting the carpenters' tools, the plaster trowels, the lumber, and finally the old mirror in the corner by the balcony with a plaster-dusted cloth draped over the glass.

"It's that mirror, isn't it?"

He stopped at the blanket-covered doorway. "It's my job, Jess. I'll be fine. Go on. You don't need to see this."

"Be careful," she said.

He smiled. "I always am."

Jess pushed through the blanket.

Maeve was at her loom with her back to the door. "I hate that thing."

Jess scooped up the cat and sat on a fabric crate. "What is it?"

"An old relic." Maeve passed another thread through, her voice strained. "It shows his dead wife."

"His *what*? How? Why?"

"I don't understand it, and I don't want to. But he put away all the other magic things, locked them away in the attic. Why not that mirror? Why can't he let that last bit go?"

* * *

Lars frowned at his reflection. How could he keep secrets from Jess? How could he keep his promises to her and maintain his duty to the Faldorrahn people?

Lars muttered a curse as he pulled a filthy piece of burlap from his pocket and presented it to the mirror.

He hated the mirror, hated looking at it, talking to it, realizing what it could show. "Show me." He half hoped it would fail.

The mirror shimmered, the image shifting out of the castle and through the night. Past field and farm he flew in the mirror's greenish glow, to the sleeping village of Quarry Run. The image moved downward, into a pool of golden light, then through the window of the Twisted Cypress Tavern to center on a man.

Oblivious to the mirror's watchful eye, the tavern keeper filled a flagon with ale, put it on a tray, then filled another.

Lars put the burlap away and his own reflection reappeared briefly in the mirror as he pulled the cleaner bit of burlap from his pocket. Expecting to return to the tavern, he set the mirror on its search, but the image flew past the village, across the ravine, to a large stone-and-brick building, then went no farther.

"It can't ever be easy," he muttered, reaching into his pocket again. He pulled out the slips of paper and unfolded them until he found the scrap he was looking for; a drawing of two triangles, overlapping point to point to create a diamond in the middle.

He held the paper up, facing the glass. "Show me," he said, uncertain if his query would work. "Show me who claims this mark."

His reflection wavered, then the mirror went black, dark and depthless. Not even lights in the room behind him reflected on the surface of the glass. It was an image of nothing. He sighed.

After putting the scrap away, he drew the cover over the mirror. He straightened the cloth, relieved to have the glass covered once again, then slowly drew his hand back as a sliver of reflection peered at him. A reflection not his own. Before he could make it out, the cloth fell with a sigh and covered the slice of dark face, the one wide eye.

His right hand on the hilt of his sword—not that it would be of much use against a mirror—he brushed aside the cloth again.

Just his own image, hard-eyed and unflinching.

CHAPTER

3

†

While Marsden made his nightly patrol, Dubric and Dien picked their way to a table in a quiet corner of the Twisted Cypress Tavern as dozens of eyes watched them. A barmaid brought tankards and a pitcher of ale and set two plates in front of them. The tavern fell into conversation and drink, the noise and tobacco smoke lulling Dubric into a drowsy haze. "So, what do you really think is happening here?" Dien asked, picking at his shredded pork.

Dubric frowned into his ale. "I am not yet certain. I have difficulty understanding why someone would spend so much time and effort slaughtering animals only to cast them away. It simply makes no sense to me. We are clearly missing a connection or it is too early to see it. Perhaps Lars will bring us some useful information."

He sighed. "The missing heads worry me, as does the continued slaughter. Troublemaking youths would likely engage in a frenzy of activity that would then taper off as they were intrigued by other things. Children are not doing this—it is too structured. I fear the killer is perfecting his methods, preparing himself for more challenging prey."

Dien stared at Dubric for a long time. "You think he's planning on dismembering people?"

Dubric thought about the mutilated animals, the wrapped and discarded pieces, the mage marks. "I do not yet know. It feels as if we have stumbled into the middle of a methodical process, with every piece planned and organized. That is not a logical opinion supported by evidence, merely a hunch. It could be anything at this point. Somehow, however, a mage is involved, even if only as historical inspiration. The marks leave no doubt about that."

Dien refilled their tankards. "Here's hoping you're wrong and it's some bored kids causing trouble."

"I can drink to that," Dubric said. He took a long sip and set down his tankard. "It is vital that we locate the heads, discover what they are being used for and what is being done to them. If a mage is involved and the heads are being used how I fear, it is very dangerous indeed."

"What's that, sir?"

"If our killers are collecting the heads and the placement of the mage symbols are accurate markers, we may be facing a death mage." He drained his tankard. "A death mage collects the dead and feeds upon them, especially the rotted brains. Some could kill with a touch."

"Shit, you're serious."

"I am afraid that I am." Dubric looked up from his plate to Dien's horrified gaze. "You did ask me."

"I won't make that mistake again."

They finished their meal in silence.

*   *   *

Outside, after the meal, Dubric said, "I must go home in the morning. I have to preside over civil cases tomorrow and meet with Lord Brushgar concerning the criminal Council, the faire, and the possibility of a mage gathering power here. You must continue the investigation in my absence and find the heads. I need to know what has happened to them. You have full authority to search wherever you deem fit and Lars is more than qualified to aid you."

"Bugger," Dien muttered.

"I could assign a different page. You seem reluctant to work with Lars lately. Is it because he is courting Jesscea?"

Dien shifted restlessly. "No, I don't think so, sir," he said with a heavy sigh. "Maybe. Hells, I don't know."

"Is he not comporting himself in a gentlemanly manner?"

"He's doing fine, as best I can tell," Dien said. "He minds his manners, Jess is practically swooning, and I did give my blessing. He always brings her home on time and is considerate of our rules. He's by far the best page in the castle."

"What, then?"

Dien shrugged as he untied his gelding, Sideon, from the post, but said nothing.

"Is it Alyson?" Dubric asked quietly. "I am certain the pain of her loss at such a young age stings, and will for some time."

"I miss her," Dien said, his voice shaking. "There's a gaping hole in my family where she used to be. Sarea barely speaks anymore, Fyn's never home, Kia won't leave her room." Dien sighed and climbed onto the saddle. "Even the baby does nothing but cry."

"You blame Lars for that?"

"No. Dammit, I know that the boy did everything he

could, probably more than anyone else could have managed."

"Then are you afraid he is growing up?" Dubric asked softly.

"Sir?"

"Lars has the restlessness of a man seeking his place in the way of things. The desire to make a home and a family, to put down roots, live his own life. Perhaps it is his courting of Jesscea that haunts you most, after all."

Dien looked away and muttered, "He argues with me, sir. That's not like him."

"I have noticed a definite change in his demeanor," Dubric said. "He rebels against me. He is quicker to take charge, more assertive, less likely to bow because it is expected of him." He neglected to mention that Lars had asked for a listing of available castle suites the phase before, or that the boy had made a practice of saving half his wage. Lars was making long-term plans and Dubric would confidently bet his best horse those plans included Jesscea.

"He is now as prone to questioning orders as you are, and as likely to keep his own counsel in private matters. Our boy is quickly becoming a man—you must learn to accept him as one instead of expecting him to remain a boy."

"You're right, sir. They just grow up so fast."

Dubric climbed onto the saddle and rubbed his throbbing knee. "That they do."

* * *

Jess walked hand in hand with Lars to her parents' suite. "You'll have to go back tomorrow, won't you? Because of what you saw in the mirror?"

Lars nodded a greeting to a passing nobleman. "Yes."

She wanted to ask what the mirror had told him, but she resisted. She tried not to let it bother her.

Lars stopped and leaned against the wall, still holding her hand. "I don't like keeping secrets from you. I hate it, Jess, I do, and it's so frustrating at times. But it's not just the oath I made to Dubric, it keeps people safe, too. Especially you."

"Me?"

"Yes," he said, offering a sad smile. "Sometimes the details are too gruesome to talk about. Even if I could discuss it, I'd want to protect you from having to think about it."

Her belly felt twisted and queasy. "That bad?"

"It can be. Sometimes I investigate some pretty horrifying things. Then there's the danger." His mouth tightened and his gray eyes grew hard. "Every now and then we track a criminal who threatens to remove anyone who might be a witness against him, including us. I hate to take the chance that some freak might think you know he stole the jewels or raped a little girl."

"I understand."

"I know you do, but it's just one aspect of the job I find frustrating." His gaze softened. "Even though I'm not supposed to, lots of times I want to discuss things, the cases, the clues, the suspects, with someone other than Dubric and your dad. Dubric tends to focus on a single solution and, I'm sorry, Jess, but your dad has blind spots."

"He is a softie for a kid. I remember a couple of summers back, when that boy was breaking into village houses and stealing money and trinkets. Dad was *sure* it was a grown man, not the boy."

"Exactly. He acts all gruff and mean, but kids can tell it's a bluff. And Dubric, he gets an idea in his head and it's tough to convince him otherwise until it slaps him in the face."

She dodged out of a lackey's way. Even this late, the Families' hall was well traveled. "What's your blind spot?"

"You," he said. "You could go on a rampage across the castle, leaving devastation in your wake, and I'd be oblivious to it."

"Now you're being silly."

"I know," he said. "I'm sure I have shortcomings, too, things I mess up, that I can't see. But I try to do my best."

"You do fine."

He swallowed as he gently gripped her waist. "Thank you for being so patient with me," he whispered, his voice cracking. His hand clenched, but this time he didn't pull away.

Jess stood still as his right hand came up and he touched her cheek with a single finger. She heard footsteps behind her, but she dared not look away, dared not take a chance of breaking the moment. Not when he was so close, touching her, holding her, his breath falling on her lips . . .

"You're on duty," Otlee said.

Lars groaned and rolled his head back to clunk against the wall. "What is it?"

"Rolle's autopsy report." Otlee held out a sealed packet of papers. "He was surprised you weren't in the office waiting for it." He glanced at Jess, then returned his stare to Lars. "Being on duty, like you are."

Lars took the packet of papers and broke the seal.

Jess stepped aside to give them a bit of privacy, but Otlee continued to stare, a smirk on his narrow face. Dubric's younger page was twelve summers old, bone thin, and redheaded, and he rubbed his wrists with ink-stained fingers as he talked. "I didn't even know you were back. You didn't check in."

Lars flipped to the second page. "Didn't know I needed to."

Otlee chirruped, "Procedure states that investigative team members are supposed to check in should assignments change or—"

Lars frowned at the page. "Did Rolle mention any of this to you?"

Furiously rubbing his wrist, Otlee glanced at Jess. "Uh . . . We're not in the office," he said, lowering his voice to a whisper. The ten bell chimed from the temple, the tones drifting through the hall, and Jess couldn't hear what else Otlee said.

Lars folded the packet and pocketed it. "Tell Rolle I'll be right there." He nodded his head toward the main stairs. "Go. I'll be right behind you."

Otlee hesitated, then walked away, glancing back often.

Lars walked Jess to her door. "Sorry."

"It's okay." Jess silently cursed Otlee's timing. "Someone has to catch the bad people."

Lars shrugged. "I guess so. There are days, Jess, lots of them, where I'd rather be a turnip farmer than look at another dead body or drag a mean drunk to a cell."

"Maybe so, but you're good at catching criminals and I sleep better knowing you and my dad are protecting us. Besides, if you were a turnip farmer, we never would have met."

"That's true." He smiled a little more easily. "I have to deal with this, but if I'm home tomorrow, would you like to do something?"

"Of course I would." She nudged him and grinned.

"Even if it's just shooting targets or stargazing. Whatever you want to do is fine."

"It's a date, then." He squeezed her hand one last time. "Good night, Jess."

"Good night." She watched him hurry down the hall, then, when he was out of sight, closed the door behind her.

"How's Lars? Did you have fun?" Sarea asked, yawning. She was walking up and down the sitting room, patting baby Cailin on the back.

"Yes, we did," Jess said. "He's fine." *And he almost kissed me.*

"Oh, good," Sarea said, as Cailin quieted. "Did he say when your father would be home?"

Jess kicked off her shoes. "Sorry, Mam. Sounds like they've got another murder. Lars just came home to have Rolle look over some evidence. He's going back in the morning, but maybe Dad will come home soon."

"Let's hope so." Sarea sighed. "Go on to bed. I think she's about ready to fall asleep."

Jess wished her mother good night, then went to her room, hesitating at the door. It had been Aly's and Fyn's room before Aly had died; Jess and Kialyn had shared the room across the hall. Kia, sixteen and the eldest, had demanded solitude and Jess had relocated to Fyn's room two phases ago. It felt empty without Aly.

Jess looked across the hall at her old room, Kia's room, and sighed. *One more try.*

Kia didn't answer the knock. She'd barely left the room since Jess had moved out, and her rare appearances were filled with cold silence. At most, she scowled and snapped rude comments, or slammed doors. Jess couldn't decide if Kia's newfound silence was an improvement over her usual troublemaking and jealousy, or if it was actually worse than the interfering pain in the backside she'd always been.

Sighing again, Jess pushed open the door.

Kia lay sprawled on her bed, her back to the door. As Jess stepped inside, her sister looked over one shoulder, grimaced, then turned away again to face the hand mirror propped up on her pillow.

"Hello," Jess said.

No response.

"How are you?" Jess tried again, stopping by the bed.

In the reflection, Kia raised one eyebrow, but said nothing.

"Did you do anything fun today?" *Like sit and stare at yourself in a mirror?*

Kia rearranged a lock of her dark hair so that it fell in a precise curve across one cheek, then examined the result with intense scrutiny, as if Jess weren't standing right there.

Jess dropped her book satchel on the floor and kicked the side of the bed, jolting Kia from her vain indulgence. "It wouldn't kill you to actually talk to us, you know."

Kia set aside the mirror and faced Jess with a tight smile. "Fine," she said silkily. "How was *your* day? Get kissed yet, or are bookworms still doomed to be spinsters?"

Jess tried to hide her startled gasp, but Kia's smile widened, triumphant.

"I didn't think so. Wonder why he doesn't want to kiss you? Maybe it's the same reason he hasn't bought you jewelry. Or anything else."

"I don't care if he buys me things," Jess said, gathering up her satchel and wishing she'd never come in. "I don't need to be bribed."

Kia sniggered. "What would you be bribed for? If he's not fey, Jess, then the only reason he wouldn't kiss you is if he just doesn't *want* you." She returned to the mirror, her reflected gaze cold and flat in the glass.

Jess tried very hard not to slam the door behind her as she left.

* * *

Lars reached the physicians' office to find Rolle waiting beside a sheet-covered examination table. "What do you have for me?" Lars asked. He had made Otlee remain outside, much to the boy's aggravation. Even if Dubric wanted Otlee involved in the investigation— which he had specifically stated he did not—Lars still seethed over the interruption in the hall. *I finally manage to touch her and Otlee ruins it. Can't I even have a quiet moment with my girl without work intruding? Just one?*

"Most of it's in the notes," Rolle said around a yawn. "Where would you like to begin?"

The stink of rotting flesh was overpowering. "How about the cuts?"

"The severings are slightly different in the way the tendons and muscles were cut. For example, they were cut from the left on the front portion, the right from the rear. It's masterful work, creating nearly matching halves from two different sheep. Whoever did this knew what they were doing."

"So we're looking for a butcher? A surgeon?"

"Not trained like one I've ever seen," Rolle said, rolling the halves onto their fronts. "Look here. These are hesitation cuts."

Lars stared at the cuts near the shaved areas, all running perpendicular to the spine. "They were cut apart from behind?"

"I believe so, yes." Rolle pointed at the severed spine on the rear half. "It took him three tries to get beneath the anterior process of the second lumbar vertebrae, then it was a fairly simple matter to sever the spine and slice straight through." He eased the pieces onto their sides again. "Not the method I'd have chosen, but oddly efficient."

"How about the neck? Same thing?"

"Yes. Spine cut from behind, then forward through the throat. I believe that's what killed it; the retracted muscles indicate it was alive when its head was removed."

Lars swallowed back a foul taste in his mouth. "Was the other sheep sexually assaulted?"

Rolle chuckled and shook his head. "Thought you'd ask. No, it wasn't." He flipped to the next page of his notebook. "The only physical anomaly I found was the loss of blood. I'm assuming that both were hung up to bleed out. Without the lower legs to show possible rope marks, I cannot say for certain, but it would make the most sense."

"Yes, it would."

"I'll check for cutting angles, see if there are any telltale blade abnormalities . . ."

"That'll be fine." Lars examined the cuts along the sheep's spines and severed limbs. They were clear and precise, from a sharp, smooth-edged blade. "So whoever did this knew what they were doing?"

"That's what the evidence suggests, yes."

"What about the mark near the spine?"

"It's common pigment, as far as I can tell."

Lars stared at the remains. "If you're butchering a sheep, why leave the wool on? And why toss it in the ravine at all? Wouldn't you want to keep the meat?" Lars sighed. "It can't ever be simple, can it?" He covered the remains, wishing he knew how to grow turnips.

* * *

Philbe lived in a stout stone house alongside a creek. The rhythmic grinding of the miller's wheel filled the air, and plants covered almost every available table, shelf, and window. As squat and sturdy as her home, Philbe chuckled and led Dubric and Dien past sprawling vines and towering potted ferns to a dark hall.

"Nice to meet you fellas," she said, shuffling down the hall. "And don't you even think about paying me. Calder's a good boy, and if he needs your help, I'm happy to give you a place to rest your head. We're sure not using the beds. Someone might as well."

She opened the second door on the left to a tall, narrow bed, a clean-swept wood floor, and a wide window with plants hanging before the glass. A bureau stood in the corner with a washbasin and another potted plant on top, and a wooden valet beside it.

"That's one," Philbe said. She smiled at them then continued down the hall to a door on the right. A smaller room, a bigger bed, and more plants. "And that's two. Take your pick, one or both. Whatever suits you." She pointed to the other doors. "That's my bedchamber, my folks', and my daughter's. They're already asleep, so try to keep it quiet, if you can. I've filled both washbasins, and there's a good square of soap and a towel for each if you need them. There's a well right outside the back door and the privy's out back and to the right, toward the mill.

"Calder's probably already told you fellas I can't cook a bit of meat without burning it, but I make a decent pot of tea and we've always got tinned biscuits. My girl loves the things. You're welcome to them, too, come morning. My mam can fry you up some eggs if you want, and she usually makes some sort of stew for supper. We eat 'round noonday and sunset, give or take."

"Sounds fine, ma'am. Thank you," Dien said.

"Heh." She grinned and shook her head before shuffling away. "Thank me by catching the rotten bastard. Cutting up folks' stock like that. Some dog dragged half a lamb to my garden this morning. 'Bout scared the daylights outta me. What's the world coming to?"

"You found a lamb?" Dubric asked.

Philbe turned back. "Right there in the carrots. Well, half of it, anyway."

"Do you still have it?"

"Hells, no. Tossed the nasty thing in the burn pile." She shook her head indulgently at Dubric. "If you'll excuse me, I gotta get back to work. It's wedding season and I have a pile of bans to write up before I'm done for the day. Guess there ain't no rest for the wicked." She winked and turned away, waving good night. "You fellas need anything, just holler."

"I'm going to sleep like a rock," Dien said as he lugged his gear into the nearer bedchamber.

"As will I."

Dubric's own bed was firm and cozy, the sheets smelling of grass and sunshine, and as he closed his eyes he almost escaped his worries. But with sleep came tangled dreams of dismembered animals and the ghost of a dead, crippled boy that looked like Lars but wasn't Lars at all.

* * *

"What's wrong? Why are you home so late and crying again?" Jess asked, looking up from her book as Fyn came in, her face red and puffy.

Fyn shrugged and pulled off her clothes, exposing her slightly rounded belly. "Nothing's wrong. Halind needed me to watch little Beffie and I stubbed my foot."

"My ass," Jess muttered. "Unless Beffie is Gilby's new nickname and you stubbed your foot on him." She set aside her book and crawled beneath the covers. "This has gone too far. You're crying all the time and sneaking out almost every night. You're going to get caught."

Fyn smiled ruefully, slipping into her nightdress. "We've had too much practice to get caught." She blew out the light and settled in. "Stop worrying."

"Practiced or not, you're not going to be able to hide the baby much longer. You're showing, you're upset, and you need to tell Mam and Dad. Now."

No one knew about the baby except Jess and Lars—well, no one else but Gilby and Fyn—but Fyn's rounding belly and inopportune burps, gurgles, and farts were becoming more and more common, and obvious. Many days she came home crying. Too many.

"We will, I promise, after everything's squared with Gilby's dad."

"It's never going to get squared with Gilby's dad. "You've been trying for moons and have a lot better chance with our parents than *Sir Newen Talmil*," Jess said sarcastically. "He's creepy and conceited."

"He's just Gilby's dad."

"I saw him forcefully grope a floor maid and he's downright rude to everyone. Including you."

"He'll change. After the baby."

Jess turned over to face her sister. "People don't change, not like that. Please, just tell Mam and Dad.

They'll help you. For Malanna's sake, you're only thirteen. You can't do this alone."

Fyn wiped her nose. "I'm not alone, I have Gilby. We'll figure this out. Good night, Jess." She rolled away and curled around her pillow. A few moments later, Jess heard a shuddering sob.

Jess slipped out of bed to sit beside Fyn, stroking her back gently. "Do you want me to tell them?"

"No," Fyn said, sniffling. "Gilby will. Soon. He promised."

"Good," Jess said, knowing that Gilby's word wasn't worth the air he used to speak it.

* * *

"Where the hells have you been?"

Gilby forced his jaw to relax. He calmly closed the door and faced his father. "Out."

"With her again, weren't you?" Newen Talmil spat, standing. "How many times have I told you to stay away from that Saworth brat?"

"How many times have I told you I love her?"

"Stop thinking with your prick, you know there's business to tend to. You were supposed to deliver the message."

Gilby pushed past and started toward his bedchamber. "Deliver it yourself."

Talmil grabbed Gilby's arm, wrenching him around. "You're my son and you're going to do exactly what I say. This delay could cost our benefactor precious time and thousands of crowns!"

"And I could lose my job, lose Fyn! I don't care about your benefactor. I can't keep running these errands for you."

"Yes, you damn well can. How do you think I keep

clothes on your back and food in your gut? It's business, family business. Now, get your ass back out there and deliver the message."

"Deliver your own damn message. I quit."

Talmil tightened his grip on Gilby's arm and shook him. "You can't quit. You're already in deeper than you know. And that Saworth brat will ruin us both. If you can't cut her out, I will."

"Keep Fyn out of this."

"I told you a summer ago to stay away from her. Her whole family's trouble. But what do you do? You disobey me and knock up the little bitch. Now that she has her claws in you, you're worse than useless. I won't let you muck this up because you're too busy boffing in the grain shed." Talmil smiled. "That's right, I know where you take her, I know what you do. I know where she has classes, who her friends are, even where she buys those blouses she likes so much. I can take her at any time—you might want to keep that in mind. The next time you disobey me, I will remove the Fynbelle Saworth distraction. Completely."

Biting back a curse, Gilby clenched his teeth and glared at his father.

Talmil said, "Do we have an understanding, or do I need to activate the stone?"

"I understand you're a shit," Gilby said before he turned and stomped away to deliver the message.

* * *

After a long shift tending patients and changing bed privies, Arien staggered into her yard while her fool dog barked its head off. "It's just me," Arien muttered, but Gidge kept barking, making enough of a racket to wake half the village. "Quiet!" Arien snapped, and Gidge went silent for one blessed moment before starting up again. Rubbing her tired eyes, Arien trudged to the house.

Haydon looked up as she entered. He sat propped in his chair at the kitchen table with his chalk color sticks carefully arranged before him. "I feel lots better, Mama," he said, coughing.

"I'm sure you do," Arien said, smoothing her son's unruly hair. He smelled of feces and piss and still felt feverish. She pulled a vial of medicine from her pocket and set it on the table. "Where's your grandmama?"

Haydon picked up a piece of chalk and returned to coloring his drawing of men on horses. "She went to get her whiskey."

"Drinking at the damn tavern," Arien muttered. "I should've been home."

"It's okay, Mama," Haydon said, looking up at her. "I know you have to work."

"Did your grandmama feed you supper? Feed Gidge?" Haydon shook his head.

Damn it, Mother. It's after ten bell. He should be in bed by now, not waiting to be fed. And you know he can't sit too long in a dirty diddy, especially not since he started having blood in his urine again. The filth will just make his sickness worse. "How long ago did she leave?"

"Before sunset," Haydon said. He coughed again.

No wonder you've messed yourself, Arien thought. She knelt beside the table and looked her son in the eye, feeling his hot forehead. She hoped Haydon wouldn't get sick again, but he'd been feverish for almost two phases. He'd had another lingering fever a summer or so before, with the same coughing and bloody urine as the fever got hotter and hotter. Then, for days, he wouldn't wake up. She drew her hand away. His brow felt hot, but not frighteningly so. "Let's get you cleaned up and I'll make us some soup."

"Sure, Mama." Haydon's grin revealed his missing front teeth and bright white bumps from the new ones. The teeth had fallen out only two days before and she'd spent the most of her saved money to put new colors under his pillow.

She ruffled his hair then smoothed it. He was worth it. He was worth all of it.

The door behind her creaked open and Arien stood, expecting to see her mother. She backed a single step away, toward Haydon, putting herself between him and the door.

Tupper looked her over, top to bottom, and leaned in, the muscles of his bare, tattooed arms flexing. He was lean and brooding; more than five summers in gaol hadn't aged him a day. "Damn, Ari, I can't believe you've gotten fat."

Arien stood her ground. She wasn't a scared little girl anymore. "What in the hells do you want?"

"Watch your mouth," Tupper said, stepping inside. "I just came to see what's mine."

"We're not yours," Arien said. "Not no more. Now, go on, get out of here."

Tupper stretched to his full height, his head nearly touching the saggy ceiling. He'd always been a fine-looking man, even wearing the stink of whiskey and pipe smoke. Blood flecked his shirt and Arien tried not to look at it, tried not to think of what it meant.

"You're mine if I say you are. Let me see my son."

"He's not your son," Arien said. "He's mine."

"Yeah, well, you told me he was mine six summers ago."

"He ain't no more and you're not supposed to be here," she said, shifting as he moved to the side.

"I saw your mama swapping favors for drinks, and she happened to mention he was here by himself." Tupper grinned and shucked up his pants. "Least I think that's what she said. She was busy at the time. I didn't want to think the boy was going without discipline so I thought I'd come over and see for myself."

"Well, he ain't here by himself, is he? And he don't need none of your discipline."

"Don't you backtalk me, woman." Tupper hit her across the mouth, knocking her aside, but Arien lurched back to stand between Tupper and her son.

"I ain't your woman no more, and you ain't touching my son!"

He hit her again, bloodying her mouth, knocking her to the floor. "I'll touch whatever I pegging want to touch. I spent five summers in gaol because of the little shit and I'll be damned if some mouthy bitch is gonna keep me from him."

"Don't you hurt him! I'll kill you if you hurt him!" Arien said. She tried to stand, but her legs weren't working right.

"You're not killing anyone, you worthless whore," Tupper said, kicking her belly. "Little bastard looks just like me. Guess you weren't stepping out, after all." He knelt before Haydon. "Hey, little fella. What's your name?"

Arien panted through the pain, putting it out of her mind, and crawled toward the nearest piece of furniture.

"Haydon," he said, covering his cough with his hand. He looked terrified.

"Why's he smell like piss?" Tupper asked, turning to glare at Arien. "Don't you ever give him a bath?"

She climbed up a chair, her knees threatening to buckle. "His spine's busted. He can't walk, can't hold his bladder. It's why they put you in gaol."

"I ain't never seen him before," Tupper said, standing. "How the hells could I bust his spine?"

"You did it before he was born," Constable Marsden said from the open doorway. "You all right, Arien?"

Ignoring the agony in her gut, Arien wiped blood from her mouth without taking her eyes off Tupper. "Yeah. I'm all right."

Calder entered the house. "C'mon, Tupper. You know you're not supposed to be here. Let's go."

Tupper snatched a dirty knife from the sideboard. "You crawling up her filthy skirts? That it? A man gets taken away and his best damned friend takes his woman?"

Calder's hand fell to the sword strapped to his hip. "I'm a married man, and you're coming with me."

"The seven hells I am. I'm not going back to gaol. Not tonight." He reached out and snagged Arien's arm, yanking her to him despite her struggles. His whiskey breath felt hot on her cheek and she fell still when he pressed the knife across her throat.

Calder drew his sword and moved forward, Haydon's cries flooding the silence between them.

Tupper dragged Arien toward the door, keeping her between him and Constable Marsden. "You'd better get out of my way, Calder, before I cut off her fat pig head."

"I can't move, Tupper. You know that," Calder said softly. "Let her go."

"Maybe I should," Tupper whispered in Arien's ear, his breath barely audible over Haydon's shrieks, "but then you won't see what I found." He kissed her cheek and the tip of the knife traced across the base of her throat—she whimpered as she felt the metal scrape her skin—then Tupper shoved her forward, toward Calder's sword.

Calder yelped. He scrambled back and away to avoid stabbing her, then fell backward through the open door and into the night.

Arien struggled for balance but her legs forgot their purpose and she followed Calder through, landing on her knees on top of him while the dog barked and snarled from the far side of the garden. Sharp and tortuous agony tore through Arien's shin, then something heavy and hard hit her back, knocking her onto her face.

"Goddess, Arien, get off me!" Calder tried to struggle out from under her, but she barely noticed over Haydon's shrieks, Gidge's frantic barks, and her own terror.

Calder pushed her off and scrambled away. She heard someone break through the brush at the back of her garden and go down into the ravine. Holding her bleeding shin, she staggered to her feet and called for Haydon to hush.

He quieted and she moved forward, hearing Tupper cursing as he reached the bottom of the ravine, hearing Calder Marsden, the man who had kissed her once on a drunken night so long ago, bellowing after him.

When she tripped and looked down at the thing at her feet, she barely heard her own scream.

CHAPTER

4

✝

Dubric and Dien rose early to find Marsden waiting for them in Philbe's sitting room, bleary-eyed and yawning. "Good morning," he said, standing.

"What happened?" Dubric asked.

"Tupper got liquored up enough to go see Arien," Marsden said, walking with Dubric and Dien to the door.

"Is she all right?" Dien asked.

"Other than a split lip, yeah, she seems to be. I tossed him in a cell to sleep it off."

Dubric followed the younger men around the house to the shed where they had bedded the horses. "If you have captured him, why did you come for us so early?"

"Yesterday, milord, you showed me your book and that mark you found on the sheep. I'd seen it before, just never really thought about it." Marsden shrugged. "So, last night, I thought. Stayed up half the night thinking. And I know where I've seen it. Even checked before I came to get you."

He paused and turned to look at Dubric. "The fence around the sanatorium."

* * *

Dubric smiled when he saw a familiar silhouette waiting in the intersection of the two main roads near the ravine bridge. Lars waved, leading his mare, Sophey, toward them, and Dubric nodded in reply. Beside him, Dien sighed.

"What do you have for me?" Dubric asked as he dismounted.

Lars handed him Rolle's report. "They were two separate sheep, sir, so we're still missing the rest. Smooth, sharp blade, right-handed assailant, and death by decapitation."

Dubric looked up. "They were bled?"

"Yes, sir. Rolle assumed they were drained like any animal after slaughter." He glanced at Dien. "There was no evidence of molestation. I asked."

Dubric skimmed the remaining notes. "No ruling on the marks?"

"No, sir, nothing definite. Just some sort of pigment on the surface, not a brand or tattoo. It'd probably wash off in time."

"That might explain why we didn't see anything on the others, sir," Dien said.

"I traced the other things, too," Lars said. "They're written at the bottom of Rolle's notes."

"Odd," Dubric said, frowning at the final notation about the mirror. "It was completely black?"

"Yes, sir."

Sharp blades, surgical precision, the symbol on the fence, burlap bags, and an absent physician. Dubric folded the notes and placed them inside his notebook. "Let us start our day with a visit to the sanatorium."

* * *

Her best loom assembled and passable pathways opened through the clutter, Maeve tried to decide whether to string the twill or the jacquard. Several of the castle ladies had recently expressed interest in her fabrics, particularly the jacquards. The flock of rich belles, perfumed and fanning themselves in the heat, had all asked about her finely woven goods even before the looms arrived. Maeve didn't trust their motives, but after a lifetime of self-sufficiency she couldn't imagine turning away work, either. The castle seamstresses and tailors were less gushing, but equally eager to pay exorbitant prices for whatever finery she could weave.

The village tailor, however, had examined the full range of her samples with a practiced eye and a firm grip on his purse. Palset had offered a fair price for much of her existing yardages and a marked preference for worsted twill and herringbone. After she told Palset she lived with Dubric in the castle, his price and business manner had remained constant. He immediately became her primary client.

She'd found Palset's wife, Cleanne, to be friendly and kind, the first friend she'd made since moving to the castle. They'd even shared tea and conversation when she'd delivered a box of tweeds to Palset yesterday, giving her a nice afternoon away from the moving mess. *The ladies can wait,* Maeve decided. *I'll make the twill.*

Maeve counted the warp bundles of worsted wool thread. Each sixty lengths long and containing fifty doubled strands, they lay carefully arranged in a crate with parchment sheets between them. *Seventeen and a partial,* she thought. *I'll need three more.*

Humming, she selected a spool of matching unmeasured thread from a box and tied one end to the warping reel. She spun the reel and silently counted each complete pass while the thread coursed up and down, catching the pegs. As she spun, she heard something clicking behind her, a random series of taps, and she frowned. *If Lachesis is playing with Dubric's medals again, he's going to get skinned,* she thought, sighing. *I'll shoo him away after I measure this bundle.*

Someone knocked on the suite door and the taps stopped. She finished the current pass then set down the spool. "Thirty-two," she said aloud, hurrying to the door as she repeated the number in her head. She'd had spells of forgetfulness lately, for only the second time in her life, but it was best not to think about that just yet. Not until she was sure.

She opened the main door to find her niece, Sarea, and Sarea's daughter Fyn. Sarea held a tray of tea and scones. "Are we too early?" she asked.

"Just measuring," Maeve said, motioning them in. "Sorry about the mess, but I need to get some work done, do something besides sort boxes and unpack."

"What are we stringing?" Fyn asked. She looked like she'd been crying.

"Twill today, on the four harness," Maeve said, following them to the loom. "A couple more bundles to measure, but the heddles are already in."

"Great," Sarea said. She set the tea and scones on a box then pulled a bundle of thread from the crate. "Fyn, take the back. I'll thread the heddles."

While Sarea and Fyn strung the loom, Maeve returned to measuring. She heard a quick series of four taps, then silence again. Her mind wandered, lost in the exchange of gossip as she planned her next project. *The jacquard next,* she decided, *in indigo.*

* * *

The sprawling stone-and-brick sanatorium sat on the crest of a hill facing the road, while the land fell away behind it, coursing downward to a marsh. Acres of grounds were fenced in with regularly spaced stone posts spanned by wrought-iron slats and rails . . . and the double-triangle symbol was a decorative element in the middle of each section. Dubric wondered how he could have failed to notice it on his previous trips to Quarry Run.

"It looks burnt," Lars said.

"It was, a long time ago," Marsden said. "It was just a ruined old manor when Jerle Dughall bought the land and rebuilt it, making a sanatorium. That was maybe twenty summers ago and there are still lots of folks who won't go near the place."

"Why not?" Lars asked.

Marsden chuckled. "The old-timers say it's haunted, that everyone who lived there died in the fire. The fire may be true, but there's no such thing as ghosts."

"I would not be so certain," Dubric said, turning his horse to walk through the main gate. But he neither felt nor saw ghosts as they rode toward the main doors. No one had been murdered here, at least no one who had not found justice for their death. *But what of a mage?* He tried to ignore the chill in his spine. *Could a mage kill but leave no ghost? Could people have died and I not know of it?*

They reached the stairs leading to the main doors and dismounted, tying their horses to a rail. Dien hesitated as they climbed the steps and Dubric looked back at him. "Is something amiss?"

"No, sir. I just hate hospitals. All the sickness and death." He shifted uneasily on his feet. "The nutters."

Lars scowled at him and stomped up the steps, entering the sanatorium and letting the door swing closed behind him.

Dien winced at the hollow bang.

Dubric sent Marsden ahead. Once he and Dien were alone on the steps, he said, "I thought we resolved this last night. Whatever is between the two of you, I want it stopped. Immediately."

"There's nothing between us, sir," Dien said, looking at his boots.

"Malarkey. You *know* his mother often receives institutional care for her mental affliction, yet you just referred to the insane as 'nutters.' You have barely looked at him since he arrived and you have been muttering under your breath every time he is mentioned.

"If you cannot work with him, then I need to know. I refuse to mediate your childish squabbles, whatever the reason behind them, and, with mages potentially involved in this case, I cannot afford the distraction of your bickering. I want it stopped. Do I make myself clear?"

"Yes, sir."

"Then you had best remain civil to the boy while on duty or one of you will be assigned to the castle for the remainder of this case."

Dien nodded and followed Dubric up the steps.

The sanatorium halls were narrow and dimly lit, thick with the stench of vomit and excrement. Dubric stepped aside as a skinny woman in a nightdress tottered by, babbling and waving her arms. She walked into a wall, bounced off, then continued her erratic trek in another direction.

VALLEY OF THE SOUL

Dien started to say something, then closed his mouth.

Lars and Marsden waited down the main hall, not far from the door. Lars was looking about, his mouth open. A short man with disfiguring lumps on his head and arms walked toward them. He kept one hand trailing along the wall and paused at Lars, felt across his chest, then maneuvered around him to touch the wall again. Before the man moved past, Dubric saw that his eyes were milky white and blind.

"What are we looking for?" Marsden asked, dodging out of the blind man's way.

"Your secretive physician," Dubric said. "I also want to see where the burlap is kept."

"Office and treatment rooms are this way, I think," Marsden said, leading them down the hall. "Do you think the burlap came from here?"

"It may have," Dubric said, reluctant to tell Marsden about the mirror. "I thought it best to check."

The hallway widened and a middle-aged nurse came through an open door, carrying a bedpan. She nearly walked headlong into them. "I'm sorry!" she said, taking a quick step back as the pan made a sloshing sound. "Didn't see you. How can I help you, gentlemen?"

"We are looking for Physician Garrett."

The nurse smirked. "Randy Goat Garrett? His office is down this hall, past the next two intersections, then fourth on the left." Shaking her head, she walked on, taking the bedpan and its stench with her.

As they walked on, Dubric looked away from the floor, where a thin, scraggly-haired man knelt on all fours beside a puddle of vomit, lapping it up like a dog.

Two women, one thin and toothless, the other one-legged and obese, waved at them and batted their eyes.

"Gol, Mert, there's four of 'em," the obese woman said. "Two apiece."

"C'mere, li'l boy," Mert coaxed, reaching out a bony finger to touch Lars's backside. "I ain't gonna hurt ye none."

Both women giggled as Lars skittered away.

The group continued on, past a man yelling at people who weren't there and an old woman masturbating. A middle-aged man drooling and mindless. A pregnant young woman strapped to a bed and screaming. A boy with a head so huge Dubric didn't know how he remained upright. A leper. Two children joined at the hip. A woman with arms so small and shrunken they looked like baby bird's wings. Countless people sagging in their chairs who stared with bland, hopeless boredom.

They reached the fourth door and Dubric knocked.

"One moment," came from within.

A few seconds later, a flushed young nurse opened the door and slipped out, giving them an embarrassed smile. She smoothed her hair and disappeared around a corner.

The door opened wider. "What can I do for you gentlemen?"

Dubric hoped he was able to hide his astonishment. The man in the doorway was young, very young, perhaps twenty summers old at most. *He is too young to be a physician; he has pimples across his brow, for King's sake!* "Are you Physician Shelby Garrett?"

"I am," the man said with a cordial nod. "And you are?"

"Castellan Dubric. These are my associat—"

"Gracious Goddess! Castellan Dubric!" Garrett

grasped Dubric's hand with both of his own. "It's an honor, sir, a glorious honor to meet you! I've heard so much!"

Dubric withdrew his hand and took a step back. "You have?"

"Of course I have. The grand library in Fliskke has a multitude of historical bans and records about the war, and you, sir, are a prominent name among the grandest stories."

"They are hearsay and rumor," Dubric said, "facts stretched so far they could cover a pavilion. There is nothing grand about war."

Garrett smiled and stepped aside, motioning for Dubric to enter his tidy examination room. "Humble, I see. I hope that someday you will grant me the pleasure of hearing the tale of how you defeated Guinniel the Toad. The story sounds fascinating."

Dubric had faced Laoch the Black's personal mage deep in the caves of Morant, where Guinniel had nearly set the mountain to collapse upon them all. It was not a battle he wanted to revisit, nor were any of the others. "I assure you, it was not. Merely one battle among many."

Garrett frowned. "What of Jidderlit? Near the Serle coast?"

"I mainly remember that it rained a great deal while we were in Serle. There is little else to tell," Dubric lied. Despite the rain, Jidderlit had set afire the grassland Dubric's army had marched across. Nearly seven hundred soldiers had been hopelessly maimed or burned to death, including Dubric's personal clerk and his mage killer, the second he had lost in the war.

Perplexed, Garrett looked at Dubric's men then back at him. "You are Lord Dubric? Lord Dubric Byerly? The man who pressed the armies north to claim the Lagiern mainland from the Alhegayne River to the Casclian Mountains?"

"I am."

"And you personally killed a dozen mages?"

Seventeen myself, plus forty or so by my men, Dubric thought. "My armies did, yes."

"My lord! That's an astounding number!"

"It was not enough. Now, if I may ask—"

"Weren't they fascinating?" Garrett asked, hopping up backward to sit on an examination table. "The mages? All the types, the traits, the signature attacks?" Garrett's face broke out in a grin, like a child who has discovered a puzzle. "Which was your favorite?"

My favorite? Dubric stared Garrett in the eye. "A dead one. Now. Please. Have you heard about the missing sheep?"

Garrett waved his hand dismissively. "Sheep? Who cares? Mages are so interesting. What's the first thing you do when faced with a fire mage?"

"Kill it," Dubric said through gritted teeth. "It is the same with a mind mage, bone mage, death mage, any mage. Find it. Kill it. I do not know who convinced you there was something romantic and wonderful about the war or facing mages. The war was brutal and bloody, and the only good mage is a dead mage. They were vermin that needed to be exterminated. I did everything I possibly could to bring about that state as rapidly as possible while limiting the loss of innocent lives and the lives of my men." Dubric frowned. "There. I have just given you my entire philosophy and recollections of the war."

Garrett swallowed.

"The sheep, if you please. Have you heard anything about missing or harmed sheep?"

"Only that we've lost much of the flock here," Garrett said. "The administrators are concerned over having enough for food, let alone taxes and income."

Dubric retrieved his notebook from his pocket. "Do you perform many surgeries?"

"I offer occasional surgical services as part of my duties here."

"Occasional?"

"Yes, milord. Many physicians are too quick with the knife or leeches. I prefer to treat illnesses with less drastic measures whenever possible. It's amazing what the proper ointment or tincture will do."

"But you do surgeries? On occasion?"

"Yes, milord. Why? Are you in need of medical treatment?"

"No, not today. What specific surgeries do you do?"

Garrett shrugged. "Whatever I must."

"Does anyone else provide surgeries? Other physicians? Midwives? Anyone?"

Garrett hopped down from the table. "There are no other physicians here, but a few of the nurses deliver babies. Several members of the staff manage routine treatments and minor surgeries so I can focus my attention on more-involved cases."

"Like that girl who left before we came in?" Dien muttered.

"Lisette?" Garrett said, smiling as he walked to a washbasin. "Her treatments are a bit involved, yes, but very enjoyable."

He glanced back at the others as he scrubbed his hands. "Why the stern looks, gentlemen? The pleasures of the flesh are for all to enjoy. Doesn't the

Goddess command us to procreate and spread our joy with others of like mind?"

"I know scripture," Dubric muttered.

Garrett dried his hands and hung his towel on a hook near the washbasin. "Is there anything else I can do for you? I should return to my duties."

"I think that will be all, for now," Dubric said. "We can let ourselves out."

Pausing in the hall, Dubric added a few last impressions to his notebook. "He gave us no helpful information."

"He certainly didn't want to talk about sheep," Lars said.

"Lord Byerly! Constable Marsden!" a man called from behind and Dubric turned.

Jerle Dughall, the third largest landowner in Faldorrah, strode to them with efficiency as precise as his impeccable attire and salt-and-pepper hair. His gaze fixed on Dubric, Jerle thrust a pile of papers at a harried-looking young man beside him as if the fellow were a table or a file box. "Thank goodness you're here," Jerle said. "My son did not report for work this morning, nor did he come home last night. I want men assembled immediately to search for him. I fear foul play."

"There is no need," Dubric said. "Your son is safe and in good health."

"Well, he might have a broken nose," Marsden said. "Maybe a sprained ankle. He *was* limping."

Jerle's authoritative expression faltered for a moment. "Excuse me?"

"I found him assaulting Arien last night," Marsden said.

"You what?"

"I saw him strike her and hold a knife to her throat. I arrested him on charges of assault and locked him in a cell until he sobered up."

"You locked up my son? Again?" Jerle asked, his voice lowering.

"It's my job," Marsden said.

Jerle took a deep breath then slowly let it out. "Despite moons of searching, you cannot manage the time and effort to locate the blackguard who stole scores of my sheep and return my property to me and my tenement farmers, but, in a single evening, you just happen to 'come upon' my son drunken and dangerous?" He glanced at Dubric. "I suppose you are behind it. Again."

"Actually, I knew nothing of it until this morning," Dubric said. "I came here because of the peculiar situation with the livestock."

Jerle crossed his arms over his chest. "And it led you here? Do you think a patient stole them?"

"I have not yet decided."

"Of course not," Jerle said. "You are too busy arresting my son to actually look for my sheep. Which I need to pay my taxes. Which, in turn, pays your salary, and yours, Calder, whereas incarcerating my son does nothing except make me want to have you both replaced."

Recalling the mage symbols in the fence, Dubric sighed and flipped to a clean page in his notebook. "Since you are here, I do have some questions."

"And I have answers. Who will supervise the demolition workers if Tupper's in chains? No one, that's who. What will happen if he's not released immediately? I'll have both your backsides served to me, that's what. What will Lord Brushgar say when I inform him—?"

"I understand you purchased and rebuilt this building even though it was in ruins. Would you care to tell me why?"

"Investment potential. Do you know how many sanatoriums are in the northern territories? Three. One in Jhalin, one in Serle, and one here. Mine. We have almost one hundred patients, yes, one hundred, many bringing in a stipend every moon or phase. Few of my patients are destitute, although I do house a few charity cases. It keeps the clergy happy."

He paused to smile. "You see, poor people usually care for their own sick, dying, and deranged. The rich pay me. For a nominal fee, I can care for them for you and keep them out of your sight and off your conscience. For a few crown I can wipe your drooling father's ass, treat your tender sister's hysteria, or even hide your dirty little secret." He smiled, looking Dubric in the eye. "But you already knew that, didn't you, milord?"

Dubric stared back. "And the fence outside? Is it from original construction, or did you have it installed?"

"It was already here. Well made, I must say."

"And who owned the property before you?"

"It was unclaimed public land. No one here wanted it, everyone considered it haunted and cursed. Pah. So a woman and her staff died in a fire. All I care about is profit potential."

"If there was no owner, how did you purchase it?"

"I petitioned Lord Brushgar and offered a reasonable price for the land. He agreed." Jerle paused and raised an eyebrow. "Perhaps you should release my son before I find need to petition our lord on Tupper's behalf again? Hmm?"

Dubric snapped his notebook closed without taking his attention off Jerle. "Constable, what is the customary punishment for public intoxication and assault in Quarry Run?"

"Happy drunks get to spend the night in the cell, mean ones two or three days," Marsden said.

"There is your answer, Mister Dughall. Barring serious injury complaints from Arien, Tupper will be eligible for release in two or three days. Is there anything else I can do for you?"

Jerle flicked his fingertips over the front of his jacket as if removing dust. "If he's in that cell one bell longer than dawn the morning after tomorrow, I'll hold you responsible." A formal nod, then he returned to the young man with the papers.

"That went well," Dien muttered, crossing his arms over his chest.

"At least he didn't try to bribe you this time," Lars said.

Dien grumbled an expletive under his breath.

"We are losing precious daylight," Dubric said, "and I am overdue for my return to the castle." They walked back outside. "I want to know precisely what surgeries young Physician Garrett routinely performs, as well as which ones he does not."

Lars knelt to pat the black-headed pup that had been waiting beside his horse.

Dubric untied his charger and looked back at the sanatorium. "Find out about his surgeries. Track down the burlap. And find those heads." He climbed up and reined about. "I will return as quickly as I can."

CHAPTER

5

†

After Marsden left to tend to Tupper, Dien squinted through a crack in the tavern's shutters. "Got that burlap scrap?"

"They're both in my notebook." Lars tried the tavern door. Locked. "Looks like they're closed. It's not even mid-morning yet. Should we go around back?"

Dien started to say something, then took a deep breath and looked away. "Never too early for a cool ale on a hot day," he said, then banged on the door as if he wanted to bust it down.

The black-headed dog circled around them, its back half wagging. Lars sighed and knelt to scratch it behind the ears. "You need to go on home, boy. I'm not your owner."

"Picked up a pup?" Dien asked.

"He started following me while I searched the ravine yesterday," Lars said, standing. "He must belong to someone." The dog sat adoringly at Lars's feet, its tongue lolling out.

Dien banged on the door again. "An ugly, scrawny mutt like that? Probably a stray. Didn't feed it, did you?"

"I had a couple of stale biscuits in my jacket pocket."

Glowering, Dien stepped back from the door. "Yup, you got yourself a dog. Big responsibility, a dog."

Lars sighed as the dog jumped on his leg and begged. "I don't want a dog. I can barely take care of myself."

"Then you shouldn't have fed him," Dien muttered as the tavern door opened to the limit of the latching chain.

"We're closed," a man's voice said.

Dien showed the gold marker on his collar. "Squire Saworth and Page Hargrove from the castle. We're here on official business. You can let us in or we'll break the door down. Your choice, but a busted door probably won't be good for business."

A heavy sigh. "I 'member you from yesterday. All right."

The door closed, rattled, then opened again. A hunchback let them into the common room. He had muddy feet and wore only trousers. "What's your business?" he asked, rubbing his eyes.

"We're here to talk to Gunth," Dien said.

"He's sleepin'. We're all sleepin'. Mosquitoes on my ass, man, this is a tavern. We're open half the night!"

Dien dropped his hand to his sword. "Get him. Now."

The hunchback muttered and shuffled off.

They didn't wait long. Yawning and unshaven, Gunth came in from the back hall. "Is there a problem?" he asked.

"We just have some questions for you," Dien said. He pointed to the nearest table. "Have a seat."

Gunth sat. "Questions? Me? Why? What's going on?"

"That's what we're here to ask you," Dien said as Lars pushed the bit of burlap across the table. "This look familiar to you?"

Gunth squinted at the scrap. "It's a piece of burlap."

"We found it wrapped around a dead sheep," Dien said, "and we have reason to believe it belongs to you."

Gunth shoved the scrap away as if it were diseased. "Me? Why in the seven hells would you think this belongs to me? I don't know anything about any dead sheep."

"Why so jumpy? We're not accusing you of anything," Dien said.

Gunth swallowed and leaned forward, lowering his voice to a whisper. "Look, I don't know anything about the sheep, can't stand them myself, but I hear things. Folks get a little ale in them and they want to talk."

"What sort of things do they talk about?"

"There's more missing than just sheep."

Lars and Dien shared a glance. "Oh?" Dien asked.

"Missus Hathers put up a couple of pecks of spiced beets last autumn, and they've all disappeared."

Lars noted the information. "Someone stole her beets?"

"Just the jars," Gunth said. "They dumped the beets right there in her cellar and took the jars. Eleven of them. And she weren't the only one. Other folks lost fruit jars this past winter."

"Is there anything else missing besides canning jars and sheep?" Dien asked.

"Yes, sir," Gunth said. "Ain't no one supposed to know, but the sanatorium's missing medicines, the things they keep under lock and key. And some things called scalp ells. Not sure what they are, but I've heard they're dangerous."

"They can be," Lars said as he wrote.

"Anything else?" Dien asked.

"No, sir. But I'm happy to keep my ears open for you."

Dien picked up the sample. "What do you know about this?"

"Only burlap I get is from bags of potatoes and carrots and turnips. I buy them from Hillsgrant's farm every few days."

Lars noted the information and Dien asked, "Have any of your deliveries been short? Any bags of vegetables missing?"

"Deliveries are always fine, and no, none of the vegetables have come up short. Edgur would've told me."

"Edgur?" Lars asked.

"My cook and washer. He let you in."

"What do you do with the empty bags?" Dien asked.

"Just pile them up outside the outhouse. Folks can use scraps to wipe, or whatever else they want. I sure don't need 'em."

"By the outhouse." Dien sighed.

"Yes, sir," Gunth said. "I can show you." He leapt from the chair and hurried toward the back of the tavern. Lars and Dien shared a tired glance and followed him outside.

Sure enough, a thigh-high stack of burlap bags stood beside the outhouse door. "We put a busted knife on the wall here," Gunth said. He dragged a bag over the chipped blade, roughly cutting it. Another swipe and he held a forearm-sized scrap of burlap. "Lots easier to keep burlap handy than corn shucks or leaves."

Dien grumbled and turned around. They stood in a common area behind several shops, with open and easy access to the road.

"Has anyone asked for bags?" Lars asked.

"Asked? Hells, boy, there's no need to ask. Everyone knows they can just take the blasted things."

* * *

"Okay," Jess said, rooting through the box. "Looks like kitchen utensils and towels. The other one's tins. Of what, I don't know."

Maeve climbed over a stack of boxes overflowing with clothes. "Just put them anywhere in the back room." She reached solid footing and wiped damp hair from her brow. "Have you seen my pack of shuttles? I know I saw Dubric move them yesterday morning before he left."

Jess stood, lifting the heavy box of tins. She'd promised to help her aunt before her afternoon classes, but hadn't thought it would be so chaotic. "Um. Over by the armoire? I think?"

"Thanks," Maeve said, maneuvering through the clutter as she made her way to the armoire beside the bed. With all of Maeve's and Dubric's things crammed into his old suite, and the dust and grit from construction as they expanded the space, the place was a mess.

Jess squeezed between an old bureau and a rack of shelving to what had once been Dubric's sitting room. "Did Dubric say when they'd be finished?"

Jess heard a bang behind her and Maeve cursed.

"Ow! No, he didn't. He didn't even say what they were investigating, only that he had to go. You and Lars have plans for tonight?"

"Always do." Jess smiled as she shoved the box of tins onto the already substantial stack of boxes in the corner. She pulled a piece of pressed graphite out of her pocket and wrote *TINS* on the outward-facing side. "Probably watch Lars shoot targets again tonight, most likely," she said. As she left the room, she glanced at the battered crate of books beneath the window. The crate was piled high with a busted lamp, a box of old, tattered socks, and a ruined pair of boots—but surely they weren't planning on throwing books away. Surely.

Jess carried the box of kitchen things in and put it on top of the tins, trying to not think about the books forlorn and forgotten beside rusty weapons and old, worn clothes.

Maeve came in with a basket of cloth scraps and stained linen. She pulled a dagger and a pair of pewter goblets off the top, handed them to Jess, then upended the basket on the crate of books, covering them. She glanced at Jess. "Is something wrong?"

Jess swallowed. "Those books . . ."

Maeve's brow furrowed. "Books? Oh! Those old things? They're Dubric's. I don't even know what they are, but he said he didn't need them anymore and he put them in the toss pile. Just some moldy old books." She shrugged. "See if you can find a good place to put those other things. I know Dubric wanted to keep them and not put them in storage."

"Of course." The goblets were beautifully carved with dragonflies and fish, while the simply styled dagger in a worn leather sheath seemed plain and utilitarian in comparison. Maeve left and Jess cleared off some space on a shelf for the goblets, then, curious, pulled the dagger from its sheath. The narrow, double-edged blade was etched with holy symbols, gleaming like freshly minted silver, and long enough to run a man through. Unlike the pretty little ornamental daggers noblewomen wore sometimes, Dubric's dagger was razor-sharp and vicious-looking; a killing weapon, not a toy.

It has a nice weight to it, Jess thought, putting it away.

* * *

As they returned to the horses, Dien asked, "Why didn't Dubric ask about the burlap while we were at the sanatorium?"

Lars heard a rumble, a low vibrating hum, from the north. "I think Jerle annoyed him enough that he just forgot," he said, squinting and trying to pinpoint the sound. "Do you hear that?"

"Hear what?"

"That," Lars said, seeing the cloud of dust rise above the buildings as the rumble became a low thud. "It's at the quarry." The ground beneath his feet shook, gravel rattling against the road, and he swore.

Lars scrambled onto Sophey's saddle and kicked her to a gallop, Dien following close behind on Sideon.

It was eerily quiet as they rode through the town, the villagers in a daze—but as they neared the quarry, Lars heard screams. Three men stood at the edge of the pit, gesturing downward and yelling. Lars and Dien pulled up their mounts and Dien's big gelding reared back for a moment, hooves churning in the dusty air. Lars whipped Sophey's reins around the saddle pommel and dismounted.

Far below, men writhed and bled among boulders and slabs of granite, lost beneath a flood of stone and rubble. "What the hells happened?" Lars asked, looking about for a way down.

"Landslide," Dien said as the man ran to the right. "This way, pup."

Lars started to follow, but one of the men grabbed his arm. "You can't!" the man said. "Don't you see those cracks? The walls aren't stable!"

Lars ripped his arm free and followed Dien down a

curving ramp of compacted stone chips to the quarry floor. "Don't waste time on someone with no chance," Dien said as they ran. "Save who you can."

Boulders and cubic slabs lay alongside the path in tidy rows, some marked with numbers written in char. As Lars and Dien ran, coughing, toward the screaming men, the organized arrangement of stones turned chaotic and the footing treacherous. A grit-covered quarryman stumbled through the mess, tripping over loose stones and someone's arm. The right side of his face and shoulder were drenched with blood.

"Sit down," Lars said, scrambling to him. He grabbed the man by the shoulder and made him sit on a stone so he could better see the injury. The man's scalp was flayed open in two strips from the crown, one slicing down the side of his head to split his ear, the other curving to his forehead, through a gaping eye socket, and to the corner of his mouth. Lars could see bone and muscle through the blood pulsating from both gashes and the ruined eye, along with chips of stone. The muscle of the man's right shoulder was punctured by a vicious shard of granite. Lars pulled it out and flung it aside, nodding as blood oozed gently from the wound.

"What happened?" the man asked, his head rolling back as he looked up at Lars with his one remaining eye.

"Landslide." Lars rummaged in his pocket for an evidence sack. "What's your name?"

"Yaunel," he replied. "What happened?"

Lars folded the sack into a tidy square about twice the size of his palm. "A landslide. Okay, Yaunel, it looks like you got hit in the head." He gently laid the folded sack on Yaunel's scalp, then lifted the man's hand to hold it there. "I want you to stay right here and hold that there, on your head. All right?"

"Yeah, sure," Yaunel said, lifting the sack away and bringing it down to look at it. "Is that blood? What happened?"

Lars put Yaunel's hand and the makeshift bandage back on his head. "Landslide, Yaunel. Keep that right there. Okay?"

"Sure. Okay," Yaunel said. Lars ran on.

He passed two men, one flailing while blood streamed from his half-crushed chest and a gaping hole where his arm used to be, and another who sat, legs splayed before him, with his skull split open and his forehead completely gone. Another stone fell, bouncing down the loose pile of debris and knocking up a new cloud of dust. Lars coughed and looked around. *Goddess, what do I do?*

"Pup! Over here!" Dien called.

Lars scrambled over rocks and past two dead men— one with his head crushed to pulp—and a third man screaming for help, everything below his waist lost beneath a massive slab. Lars followed Dien's cries and found him kneeling beside a man with one leg pinned mid-thigh under a stone, a smear of blood spreading out from beneath it.

"Take off your belt," Dien said as Lars skidded to a stop. "Mine's too thick and I can't get my hand under there."

Lars unbuckled his belt and ripped it off, kneeling as Dien stood. He tried to squeeze his belt under the man's leg, but it was too tightly clamped to the stone ground. Lars looked up at Dien. "I can't, either."

"Then I'll have to move this frigging thing."

"I can't feel it anymore." The man struggled to sit, but Lars pushed him back down. "I can't feel my leg!"

"It'll be okay, Sevver," Dien said. "This is Lars, he's going to put on a tourniquet."

"Save my leg!" Sevver begged, grabbing Lars's shirt. "I'm getting married in a moon! Please, save my leg!"

"We'll try," Lars assured him, but he doubted there was much chance. The stone was waist high and roughly cubic, and it lay almost flush against the ground. "I need you to lie still, okay?" He glanced up at Dien, who was crouching by the edge of the rock, ready to lift, and taking a few deep breaths. "It's gonna hurt something fierce when I move your leg. But I need to, so you won't bleed to death."

"Oh, Goddess," Sevver said, covering his eyes with a scratched and scraped arm.

"Ready?" Dien asked.

Lars leaned toward the leg, belt ready. Sevver just nodded, his eyes still covered by his arm.

"One . . . two . . ." Dien heaved, Sevver screamed, and Lars yanked the leg aside enough to slide the belt under, snatch it tight, and drag the leg out of the way before Dien pushed the rock onto its side. There was little left but mangled flesh and bone from just above the knee to Sevver's toes, but at least he wouldn't bleed to death.

"I got him, pup," Dien said. "Go!"

Lars stood and ran farther into the chaos, coughing and wiping muck from his mouth and nose. He heard others behind him, villagers, coming to help. "I need a stretcher down here!" Lars yelled as he unearthed an unconscious but breathing quarryman from a pile of loose rock. A man in a baker's apron hurried to him and Lars left the unconscious man in the baker's care.

"Somebody help me!" a man called to Lars's left. One battered quarryman was struggling to pull another out from the rocks, with no success. "Kid! Help me!" he cried.

Lars ran close. The man jutted out of the rocks faceup, but he hung crookedly downward from the waist, blood leaking out of his mouth. He dazedly raised his head, apparently oblivious to the other man pulling on him. One rib poked through his shirt and blood spread across his chest, soaking him. His mouth worked noiselessly and he gurgled through the blood, blowing splattering bubbles.

"Kid! Pull your head out of your ass and help me!"

"He's dead," Lars said. "There's nothing to be done."

"Goddess damn you, kid, help me pull him out! He's my brother!"

"He's dead," Lars repeated. "I'm sorry." He turned away, then grunted in surprise when a heavy body hit his back and knocked him to the ground.

Hands gripped his throat and lifted his head. Lars twisted and rolled, thrusting the man off him, but before he could get his feet beneath him the man dove at him, wrestling him back to the ground.

"You're gonna help me get my brother!" he screeched, pummeling Lars's chest and face. "He's not gonna die!"

Lars shoved the man well away from him. "His back's broken and his lung's punctured. He's already dead."

"Liar!"

Lars struggled to his feet and pointed. "Look at him! I'm sorry, but—"

The man lunged at him, screaming. Lars stepped aside, letting him charge by and crash against the rocks. The dying brother gurgled his last and fell limp. Lars sighed and pulled the man to his feet. "I'm sorry. There was nothing you could have done."

"I'll get you, you bastard," the man snarled. He sunk to his knees and cradled his brother's bloody head, smoothing hair away from his brow. "If you'd have helped me . . ."

"There was nothing to be done," Lars said, staggering away to find someone he could help.

* * *

Jerle Dughall started as Dien carried in the man with the crushed leg. "What happened?" Behind Dien, Marsden and other villagers helped injured men up the sanatorium stairs. Lars pushed a cart with three unconscious men up the path.

"What the hells does it look like? Your quarry collapsed," Dien said, setting his charge on a wheeled table.

Jerle took a step back, startled. "My what?"

"I counted eighteen dead and we've brought eleven injured. There are more, but their injuries aren't as serious and they are being treated on-site."

Jerle looked at the filthy, injured men. "That's just not possible," he said. "Which facing? Why wasn't I told?"

"Was the east facing, boss," a man with a mangled arm said, staggering in. "And splitting a shear off the east's been on the schedule for a good phase."

"Who authorized the shear?" Jerle said, his voice hardening.

The man winced and lowered his gaze. "Tupper, sir."

Jerle took a step toward him, looking back and forth over the injured men. "And who supervised the shear?"

"Rhand, sir."

"And where is Rhand?"

The man looked up. "Dead, sir."

"Tupper should have been there. This never would have happened if he'd been there." Jerle stomped to Marsden, who was helping an injured man into the sanatorium. "This is your fault," Jerle said, then punched Marsden in the mouth. "Men have died! How dare you arrest my son!"

"Hey!" Dien said, lunging past the men to reach Jerle. He pulled him off Marsden and slammed his back against a wall. "Knock it off!"

Beside them, Lars grabbed hold of Marsden and held the struggling constable away.

"Let me go!" Marsden said. "I'm just doing my damned job! I'm gonna toss his mangy ass in the cell with his drunken thug of a son!"

Jerle struggled harder but couldn't break Dien's grasp. "This is my town, you ungrateful lackwit! I practically handed you your post and this is how you thank me?"

"Okay, boys," Dien said, looking back and forth between them. "We've got eleven men here who need urgent medical care. Immediately. You can have your pissing contest some other frigging time. You get me?"

"Fine," Jerle snapped, and Dien let him go. He huffed, squaring his shoulders and smoothing his jacket. He gave them one final glare then stomped off, yelling out commands for the sanatorium staff to help the injured men and prepare for surgeries.

Lars released Marsden. The three men stood aside as sanatorium nurses and orderlies rushed through to aid the injured. "You all right?" Dien asked Marsden.

"Yes," he said, then muttered, "Pompous ass."

* * *

Arien and Peigi burst into examination room four to see Celisse laying a pungent cloth over a man's face as blood flowed out of gashes across his head and shoulder. "What the hells happened?" Arien asked.

"Landslide, at the mine," Celisse replied as the man fell limp.

Arien gently probed the cranial gash with her fingers. "Piss. Peigi, get me some bleached linen. I need to get this cleaned out. Fetch me a number six—" she leaned forward and squinted into the gash "—no, a number eight applicator. Also a needle and thread, and I want him strapped down, just to be sure."

Peigi whipped open a cupboard door.

Arien looked at Celisse. "Hot water, mineral spirits, and tincture alcohol. Now."

"Yes'm," Celisse said, then bolted from the room.

Piss! Arien thought, barely looking up as Peigi shoved a folded bit of clean linen into her hand. She gently flicked shards and dust out of the bloody mess, nodding as Peigi attempted to rinse some of the grit away. "He's lost one eye, might lose that ear," Arien said, clearing out the gashes. "See if you can get that shard from his eye socket."

Celisse ran back in with a steaming bucket in one hand and two bottles clenched between her body and her forearm. She set the bucket on a long, narrow table and put the bottles beside it before reaching into the cupboard for a basin.

"Aw, piss!" Arien exclaimed, lifting out a thin, curved bit of bone. "I've got open skull here. Where the hells does this piece go?"

"Ari . . ." Peigi said, turning her head aside as blood

burst out from the ruined eye socket, splattering her. "Got a bleeder." She glanced down then grasped his arms. "He's convulsing!"

The three women hurried to strap leather strips around his limbs and clean and close his wounds, but there was nothing to be done. Minutes after reaching the sanatorium, the patient was dead. The three covered him, gathered their equipment, and hurried to the next room, where a man was screaming for them to save his leg.

* * *

Dubric could see the castle about a quarter of a mile ahead when he felt a ghost fall, icy and heavy, behind his eyes. He winced, leaning forward over his charger's neck, and took a startled breath. *A murder,* he thought, sitting upright again. He pulled his charger to a halt.

A young man's severed head floated in front of him. Cut cleanly at the throat, it didn't bleed ghastly green gore, and it had no body. None. Nothing but a head. Dubric had never seen a partial ghost before.

The young man's ghost looked about, confused, but did not scream. It turned its face toward the castle, then floated backward, toward Dubric.

What the hells? Dubric thought, trying to duck out of the way before the severed head went straight into him. He nearly succeeded, but coldness passed through his shoulder as the ghost floated by. He turned around to look at the ghost and saw its mouth working silently and its eyes wide, as if startled.

This is odd, he thought. *Ghosts scream, they bleed, they ignore everything but other ghosts and the weapon that killed them, especially at first. How can—*

Then he lurched back again. The ghost had floated

close, peering at him, his glowing green gaze piercing and aware as if he had been dead moons instead of a few moments. Dubric felt a chill slither down his spine and he heeled his charger to hurry back to the castle.

CHAPTER
6

✝

Dubric was painfully aware of his tardiness and grimy state as he stepped into Lord Brushgar's office. He mumbled an apology and shoved an armload of papers and knickknacks off a chair. Sitting, he tried not to sneeze. The office smelled like moldy paper and weevils, as it did every spring.

"Where the hells have you been?" Partially obscured by the mountain of papers on his desk, Lord Nigel Brushgar leaned back in his chair. Once a massive, muscular man, seventy summers of life had weathered him until flesh hung loose on his thick frame. Although they were nearly the same age, Dubric hoped he did not look so old and decrepit. "Do you think I want to twiddle my thumbs until you wander in?"

"I apologize, my lord, but matters in a nearby village have required my attention."

Brushgar looked Dubric over and raised an eyebrow. "What sort of matters?"

"We may have a mage loose near Quarry Run."

"We *what*?" Brushgar stood. A few papers fluttered to the floor.

Dubric flipped through his notebook. "There have been scores of dismembered sheep, several slaughtered dogs, and I found this," he said, handing the notebook to Brushgar. "It was written in red and black on the skin of dead sheep."

"Who?" Brushgar asked, brandishing the book. "Who claims this mark?"

"I do not yet know." Dubric paused, waiting for Brushgar to look him in the eye. "None of the sheep had heads, and I believe that a man has already been killed."

"That's simply not possible. We routed the mages."

"Stolen heads, a mage mark, and murder, milord. What else would you call it?"

Brushgar paled, his ruddy skin turning sallow. "What do you expect me to do?"

"A great deal." Dubric grasped his notebook before Brushgar dropped it. *Let us begin with simple matters.* "First, do not tax the people of Quarry Run these seasons. Many have already expressed concern over their finances after the loss of their flocks."

Brushgar sat, his hands shaking. "No taxes? I do not know if I can do that. You know we've been having budgetary difficulties. There are income projections to meet—" He looked up at Dubric's stare, then swallowed. "All right, no taxes."

"Prepare for the possibility that we may need to relocate the population. Better safe than dead. All moving costs should be covered and adequate housing supplied."

"What? Have you gone mad? How many people live in the area? Hundreds? *Thousands?* You can't possibly expect—"

"The people of Faldorrah depend on you to protect them."

"Protection is one thing, but relocation? With *housing*? Do you have any idea what that will cost?"

"Less than if we have a mage running loose."

Brushgar flinched and looked downward. "The budget may never recover, but all right."

Dubric checked it off his list. "Delegate faire organization and today's civil cases to someone else. I do not have the time."

Brushgar almost smiled as he looked up. "Done."

Dubric paused before mentioning the delicate matters. "I do not want my men worried about covering their backsides when they should be focused on the task at hand. There must not be even the slightest possibility of reprimands or charges against myself or any of my staff as we pursue these matters, and I need your assurance that we have free rein to do whatever we must. Jerle Dughall has already threatened us because we have stepped on his well-shod toes. Placate him however you must, but I do not want his complaints or any others to distract us from what must be done."

"You do realize Jerle's one of my most prominent landowners? Ignoring him won't go over well."

"That is not my concern," Dubric said. "I also need my men properly outfitted with full approval to use magic as required."

"What?" Brushgar asked, looking up. "You ask the impossible. Outfit your men, fine. You have keys to the armory; take whatever you want. But turn a blind eye to what? Flame slayers? Eraser stones? A stelan-seula? Something worse?"

"To admit to possessing any of those items is treason."

"Balls!" Brushgar said, slamming his fist on his desk.

"What the hells have you been up to these fifty summers?"

"Protecting your people."

"If you have a soul-stealer in Faldorrah, we'll both hang," Brushgar said. "You let it loose to kill this mage and they'll feed us to it as well."

"I do not have a mage killer! If this is a bone mage or a blood mage, what choice do I have? Even with a stelan-seula, at *best* we could slow it down for a few bells. At best!"

"Maybe it's just a mind mage who keeps trophies," Brushgar said, coming around his desk. "Or a death mage gloating over its kills."

"Did you see either of those conditions during the war?"

"Well, no. But I did meet up with a fire mage who collected charred ears."

"Ears? Dammit, Nigel! *Heads* are missing. That leaves me two reasonable options, neither of which I have any hope of defeating. I will know more once I find the heads, but to do that I may need to use some illegal methodology. I do not want to hang for simply trying to save people."

"Sheep heads? You're risking getting hanged for corruption, possession, and Goddess knows what else for a few missing sheep heads? Maybe they've just been turned into head cheese."

"And maybe I have a damned bone mage planning to raise the dead or a blood mage preparing to control half the northern territories! Perhaps it is a few children causing trouble for thrills and we have nothing to fear. Until I find the heads, I cannot be sure of *anything* other than scores of dead sheep and dogs, one man dead, and that symbol."

"Do you really think it might be troublemaking louts who don't know any better?" Brushgar asked hopefully.

"Anything is possible, but my gut tells me it is a mage. I hope I find the heads desiccated and it is merely a death mage, but I fear it is much worse." He looked at his ghost, the severed, bloodless head. "Much, much worse."

* * *

Dubric entered his suite to find Maeve working at her loom.

"Ah, you're finally home," she said, coming to him. "You look tired."

He set aside his gear and drew her into his arms. "I am. It has been a long pair of days. Did the package arrive yet?"

She leaned back and draped her arms around his neck. "No, not yet. What's happening?"

"Someone is dismembering sheep in a nearby village."

"Sheep? So it's not a murder?"

"It is," he said. "I received a ghost on the way here." He paused, not wanting to look her in the eye as he answered. "A young man."

"Oh, no." Maeve shook her head, looking pale. "Not again."

"I will catch whoever is responsible. Please, let us not dwell on such things while I am home for such a short while. How are repairs coming?"

She smiled up at him. "Let me show you."

Hand in hand, they wandered through the rooms and Dubric tried to imagine a settee here, a four-posted bed there, a table in the sitting room, and his mirror—

He pointed to the far corner. "What is that doing here?"

His old, battered mirror stood alone in a featureless drift of plaster dust, facing the corner like a punished child. Made during the War of Shadows by the sage Sett Nuobir, the full-length mirror had stood near his bed for two decades. It belonged there, not cast aside in an empty, unfinished room.

"Didn't you put it there?" Maeve asked, her brow furrowing. "I've never touched the wretched thing. I saw it near the balcony yesterday. Then, when I came home today, it was in the corner."

"It must have been the carpenters," Dubric muttered. "This is the first time I have been home today, and I certainly never moved it before I left."

He reached for it, intending to carry it back to the old suite, but when he noticed Maeve's forlorn face, he wondered if it might be better to leave the mirror where it stood. Maeve feared Nuobir's old glass because she knew Dubric had once used it to commune with his deceased wife, and because he could use it to look upon anyone without their knowledge.

Nuobir had created the mirror to help others watch over their families when they were far from home, but few had wanted to look fondly upon their loved ones. Most wanted to see the secrets, the betrayals, the sordid, private matters that no one else should witness. Abuses. Adultery. Theft. Debauchery. They had lined up to see their spouses in the arms of another, their children carousing, or folks simply taking a bath. Nuobir's customers only wanted to see whatever would garner a laugh, a snigger, or disgusted shock.

Sickened by the blatant voyeurism, Nuobir had supposedly destroyed the mirror and all its twisted desires.

Instead, he had hidden it, and Dubric had found it after Nuobir died.

Knowing that the mirror was too powerful and too important to destroy, Dubric kept it hidden and secret. Only he, Maeve, and his staff knew of its existence. Dubric considered it a tool and Otlee found it fascinating. Dien and Lars, however, had decreed it highly disturbing. Perhaps they were right. At times, Dubric himself feared what he saw in the glass. *Disturbing* was too gentle a word some nights.

Still, regardless of its unpleasant qualities, the mirror was valuable beyond measure, a rare and powerful find, and it deserved better than an empty, unpainted room. Dubric reached for the wood frame and turned the glass to face him, the only safe way to carry it.

Then he took a startled step back, astounded at the image of his recently arrived ghost in the glass.

A reflection of its missing body shimmered pale and translucent green beneath its severed head. Average of build but a bit on the short side, the young man wore a corporal's uniform with a sword strapped to his hips and a canteen and pack flung over his shoulder. Dubric could discern no uniform colors from the pale image, but the symbol on the lad's shoulder belonged to Lord Fevver Nanke, a prominent general of the war and a man who had died of a failing heart more than twenty summers before.

How is this possible? Dubric thought, staring as the ghost lifted its hands and gazed at them in amazement. *The war ended fifty summers ago. How could a soldier's ghost arrive today?*

"Are you all right?" Maeve asked.

Dubric rubbed his eyes and the ghost's body faded

away, leaving just the severed head again. "I am fine. Merely examining my ghost."

* * *

Jess sat on the floor beside Dubric's office door, polishing her new buckle and trying to study the history notes spread across her lap. She was finding it hard to focus and her mind kept wandering to Lars and her father. She hoped they were all right. Serian had told her that Lars had gone to bed late after meeting with Physician Rolle, then left again around four bell in the morning, far too early to tell her good-bye.

Please come home, she silently prayed, not really seeing her notes about the battle of Felder Flats. *Please, Goddess, let them come home.*

She looked up as footsteps approached and her hopeful smile faded. It was only Otlee. Again.

"I've told you that you can't sit there," Otlee said, scowling.

"And I've told you I don't care. It's a public hall."

"A hall that you're blocking. What if there's a fire?"

"Then I'd go outside or to some other safe place," Jess said, rolling her eyes. "I'm not an imbecile."

The young page's voice turned cold. "I know what you're doing, hanging around like a blood-sucking harpy, and it's not going to work."

Jess set her notes down beside her, her face flushing. It was getting harder to remember the sweet boy Otlee had been just two moons ago. "Excuse me?"

Otlee snapped his mouth shut, took a step back, and bowed slightly.

"Is there a problem?" Dubric asked, approaching.

"Of course not, sir," Otlee replied as Jess gathered up her things and stood. "Rolle has additional notes for you concerning the case in progress and I've taken the libert—"

"I need you to research this symbol," Dubric said, handing Otlee a piece of folded paper. "I also want to know about Lord Nanke and his army's involvement with any wartime activities in Faldorrah. Anything you can find for me, no matter how minor it may seem. I need it immediately."

"Yes, sir," Otlee said, trudging off.

"And you, Jesscea." Dubric pulled a set of keys from his pocket. "I am afraid that Lars is still working at the site."

Jess sighed. "That's all right, sir. I'm here to see you."

"Me?" Dubric asked, unlocking the outer office door. He opened it and held it for her.

"Yes, sir," she said, entering. "See, I've been helping Maeve organize boxes and find things to put in storage or throw out." She followed Dubric across the office waiting area. "I just have a question, is all."

"What sort of question?" Dubric asked, unlocking the inner office door.

She entered and sat on the chair nearest to the door. "There's a trunk of books, sir, that Maeve said were to be tossed on the refuse heap."

Dubric walked around his desk and sat to open a low drawer. "Yes. They have been in my back closet since I moved here and I have never opened them, let alone read them. I see no reason to keep them any longer." He pulled out a box and a sheaf of papers, dropping them on his desk.

"Yes, sir. But they're *books,* sir. Do they have to be destroyed? Couldn't they be given to Clintte or something?"

Dubric chuckled as he rummaged through the

drawer. "Actually, they are journals, but I appreciate your point. You are welcome to them if you want them."

Jess leaned forward. "Really, sir? A whole trunk of books?"

"There are other things in the trunk," he said, pulling out a tiny brass box with an odd set of gears on the top and one side. "You can keep whatever you like. I no longer have need for any of it."

He turned the gears, one after the other, and Jess heard a slight *click*. Dubric lifted the lid and removed a silver key, which he pocketed. He stood, put the brass box away, and closed the drawer. "Is there anything else?"

Jess grinned. *A whole trunk of books!* "No, sir, other than wondering when Lars might come home."

Dubric walked with her to the hall. "I do not know. Complications have arisen in the investigation."

* * *

Lars blew his nose for the umpteenth time and grimaced at the gray, goopy muck in his handkerchief. "Okay," he said, putting it away as he looked at the injured men waiting among the fallen stones. "Who's next?"

"I want someone else to stitch me up."

Lars looked over and saw the man who had fought to get his dead brother saved. He stared at Lars, glowering, and spat a mouthful of tobacco juice on the ground.

Lars patted the stool. "You're stuck with me. Everyone at the sanatorium's busy with worse injuries."

"Hewl shoulda been there with them," the man said. "And you know it."

"Do you want your forehead cleaned and stitched up or not?"

"What, and have you kill me, too?" The man turned and stomped away.

Lars shrugged, and the next man came up and sat, holding out his arm. Lars sopped the numerous gashes clean with hot water and a rag, then handed his patient a cup of whiskey before he readied a needle.

Dien stood nearby, also stitching up injuries. "What was that all about?"

"The guy's brother was snapped in half, had compound fractured ribs and a punctured lung. He was gurgling blood when I got there and died only a few moments after." Needle and thread in one hand, Lars picked up the whiskey bottle with the other. "Ready?" he asked his patient.

"Yep." The man grimaced as Lars poured whiskey into the wound. "Verlet never had anything but his simpleton brother," Lars's patient said, turning his head away as Lars stitched. "If he's blaming you for Hewl dyin', you might wanna watch your back, kid."

"Thanks for the warning." Lars made a second tidy X-shaped stitch then tied it off, just like Rolle had taught him.

* * *

"Where is it?" Just as Maeve sat down to work, a woman's voice sounded behind her. She turned from her loom, her heart thudding. No one was there. Lachesis hissed and fluffed up on her lap, then he let out a low growl and dug his claws into her thigh.

The carpenters and plaster workers had finished the day's labors a bell or more before and Dubric had left to gather some things from the office. Maeve had thought she was alone.

"Who's there?" she asked. She stood, dropping a growling Lachesis to the floor.

No response, but Maeve heard a shift, like grit grinding into the floor, beyond the archway to the new suite. She lifted the blankets to peer inside. "I'm Lord Dubric's companion and he'll not like an intruder in our suite."

"What have you done?" the voice said from behind her, so softly Maeve could barely hear.

She turned and saw a beautiful woman staring at her from across the room. "Where is it?" the woman asked, her hazy image flickering and fading as she moved closer.

Maeve took a deep breath, then another, as she struggled to control her rising panic. "Oriana?"

The spectre's mouth moved silently, then she disappeared, leaving nothing behind but a waft of perfume and cold.

* * *

Empty knapsack over his shoulder, Dubric climbed the east tower stairs and nodded to a pair of floor maids clattering downward with mops and buckets. He reached the third floor and walked the halls as if he were going home, but strode to a different door and unlocked it to a set of dusty stairs. Dubric climbed up to the north wing's cluttered attic, wiping cobwebs away from his face. The last footprints to use the stairs appeared to be his own, from about three moons before. He reached the top and the dim attic spread out before him. Here, family heirlooms slowly rotted alongside yellowed correspondence and moth-chewed garments disintegrated over battered trunks bearing family crests. The attic and its contents were old, desolate, and forgotten.

At a wall at the far end of the attic, near the jutting end of the north wing, Dubric paused at a barred door and fished the silver key from his pocket. After unlocking the bar and the door behind, he stepped inside and paused to light the lamp hanging beside the door, then closed and locked the door behind him.

Rows of boxes, oddities, and gilded trinkets stretched to the outer wall, filling the air with the rotten-sweet scent of their own slow decay. The lantern cast strange shadows as he walked across the attic, illuminating old books and relics: strange creatures floating in jars of amber fluid, a gilded desk, a ragged woolen robe, countless weapons, a scarlet-colored hat with strings of blackened bones hanging from its rim, rusty artifacts from the ancients, even a whirring machine.

He reached the far wall and paused to wipe dust off three sealed jars. Two held only dust and decayed remnants of silver-green carapaces, wings, and segmented legs. The misshapen nightmare of a locust in the third peered up at him and lunged, its phallic stinger slamming forward to leave a smear on the glass.

Dubric sighed, uncertain if he felt relief or disgust. One stelan-seula, a filthy beast known as a soul-stealer, still lived, even after nearly fifty summers trapped and starving in a blessed jar. A stelan-seula could kill a mage as easily as it could kill a common man—once the stinger broke the victim's skin, the stelan-seula injected a poison that dissolved blood, turning it into a transparent fluid that would kill yet leave him upright and walking—but how many innocents would it kill before Dubric could catch it again? *If* he could catch it again. If it did not turn on him instead of attacking the mage.

He pushed the stelan-seula aside to look at the silver-gilded cage behind it. A pair of jewel-colored nippers slept curled together like kittens. They were tiny lizards, about the size of his palm, with black needle teeth and claws. The vicious miniature demons were created by the dark mage Nenter to pass through solid rock and attack living flesh. A swarm of nippers could consume an unarmored man in less than two minutes. These two, who had not eaten since he caged them during the war, could likely kill in a mere heartbeat or two. Only a blessed weapon held any real hope of slaying a nipper, or any other magically created beast. Could he stop them from slaughtering innocents? Was he still fast enough? Strong enough?

As if it could hear his thoughts, the emerald-colored nipper raised its head and chittered at him, a demonic giggle that sent a shiver down Dubric's spine. The blue raised its head as well, chittering in reply, and a bit of saliva dripped off its teeth. They both seemed to smile, their glowing red eyes brightening and inviting him to unlock the cage door and reach in to touch their bright, pebbled skin. Just once.

He pushed the stelan-seula jars in front of the nippers' cage again and rubbed his tired eyes. Even under perfect circumstances, he had no real hope of controlling a soul-stealer or a nipper. His flame slayer had perished decades before, as had the easy-to-control blood toads and the sight wren, which might have proven useful.

Not the beasts, he thought, turning away. *Not unless I have no choice.*

He pulled his knapsack off his shoulder and opened

a nearby trunk. Polished marble spheres lay inside, cradled by wadding. He collected ten, wadding and all, and placed them in his pack. The trunk closed and latched, he moved on to a nearby crate and removed two vials of pinkish fluid. He considered taking the old cloak that the castle murderer had used for concealment and protection moons before, then decided against it. The cloak might make him invisible to a common man, but it would be a glowing beacon to a mage.

He worked his way back toward the door, pausing occasionally to add an item to his pack, then stopped at a bureau in the corner. He opened the doors and flinched at the burst of light, then gritted his teeth as he selected three solid silver bracelets. Barely looking at them, he shoved the bracelets in the front pocket of his knapsack and snatched the pocket closed. He checked the marble spheres—still well padded in their wadding—then closed the main portion of the sack as well. He hefted it to his shoulder and strode to the door, pausing only long enough to grab a sword and, after a slight hesitation, an axe.

* * *

Sickened by the Goddess's putrid reek mixed with the sickly sweet scent of dark magic emanating from the bag over his shoulder, Dubric returned to his suite. As soon as he opened the door, Maeve leapt from her loom with a knife clenched in her hand and her eyes wild. She sagged with relief when she saw him. "Thank goodness you're back."

He set down his burden and held her tight. "What happened?"

"Oriana," she said, her face buried against his chest. "She was here. I saw her."

Dubric frowned. "Oriana is dead, almost fifty summers now. Dead and gone."

"She's here!" Maeve pointed toward his old sitting room. "She stood right there and asked me where something was. Her ghost was *here,* not a bell ago, and she spoke to me."

"Ghosts do not speak," he said, drawing her close again.

"She did. I saw her and I heard her. Don't you believe me?"

Dubric had endured numerous ghostly visitations since Oriana's death summers before. He wanted to assure Maeve that of course he believed her, but he *knew* ghosts, and not once had one spoken to him.

"I believe you saw something," he said, brushing wisps of hair from her brow. "Perhaps it is fatigue."

She frowned at him. "It wasn't my imagination."

"Minds wander," he said. "You barely leave these cluttered rooms. It could have been your imagination."

"It was real. She spoke."

"And you have been worried that I still love Oriana. Is it not possible, even remotely, that you dozed off while working and dreamt the whole thing?" He kissed her gently. "When will you believe that I love you and I have put my past behind me?"

"When you get rid of that mirror."

He sighed and stepped back. "I cannot. You know that."

"It scares me and it whispers to me, whether you believe me or not. It's dangerous."

"It cannot harm you."

Maeve sighed and stared at the floor.

"I love you. You. Not any ghost. And I want to marry you, if you will have me."

"I'm thinking about it," she said, still looking at the floor.

He toyed with her fingers. "Then I will ask again. Will you marry me?"

Her silence was answer enough.

* * *

Jess sat in the library, engrossed in the old journals Dubric had passed on to her. Oriana had been pressed into service to Tunkek Romlin's army at thirteen. She had killed her first mage four moons later at the battle of Yidderlang, her second two phases after that at the village of Glinderhold, then the third along the Klandian coast.

Oriana wrote of the marching and the combat and the food. Of blisters and a broken wrist and her first glimpse of the ocean. Of falling in love with a soldier, only to see him die. Fear that she carried his child, then relief and sorrow that she did not.

She was my age, Jess thought, enthralled. Oriana's early journal entries were filled with ordinary observations and musings Jess understood and had experienced herself. Feeling different from the other girls her age, complaints about clumsiness and being too awkward and tall, a poem about the butterfly she saw on the apple blossoms, and her secret desires for a village boy. But after the soldiers came, after Oriana was taken away, the poems and wistful thoughts trickled away and were replaced by murder and cold determination.

Oriana practiced killing by stabbing living pigs that were trussed up and held vertical like men. Her dagger, which she simultaneously loved and loathed, was hungry, starving, constantly screaming for blood. Sometimes her journal entries disintegrated into rabid ramblings about the desperate need to consume dark magic. Other times she wrote of mundane matters, like the quiet simplicity of a walnut grove. Most of the entries detailed combat statistics, magical devices found and destroyed, or the rotten sweet smell of mage blood on her hands.

Memories of that rancid nutmeg scent chilled Jess's spine. She had smelled it while running from a dark spectre in the rain, then again when her grandparents had died. She hoped she'd never smell it again.

"Whatcha reading, Jess?" Serian asked, sitting down across the table from her.

She jumped and tried not to appear as startled as she felt. "Just some old books."

He leaned back, his bulk making the chair creak. "It's a wonder you're not blind, all the reading you do." He groaned and stretched, tipping the chair farther back. "And, damn, I do not want to be on guard duty tonight." He leaned forward again, the chair feet clunking on the floor. "Don't suppose you'd want to work my shift for me?" he asked, winking. "Let me get a little sleep?"

Jess laughed and shook her head as she stuffed the journals in her bag. "Can't. I have plans. Assuming Lars comes home."

* * *

His clothes tacky with dust and blood, Lars frowned at the sky as he and Dien rode back to the ravine bridge. *Late again.*

The sanatorium stood on the far hill, its brick structure imposing and observant, shadowing the road that ran before it. Just looking at it turned Lars's stomach into knots. His mother stayed at a Haenparan sanatorium for moons at a time. He'd always assumed it was a clean, tidy, and healthful refuge, full of caring physicians and sunshine, not like the place he'd just left.

He looked at the rambling building. *My mother? In a place like that? It's like a prison.*

"Which side do you want?" Dien asked. "West bank is steeper, but we found the pieces on the east. We could flip for it."

Lars shifted in the saddle. "I don't suppose we could come back and do this tomorrow? I'm late again. Jess is gonna kill me."

"She knows the job," Dien said. "She'll understand."

Lars looked across the rusted bridge, where a woman trudged toward them and a heavily laden stone cart thundered away. "Yeah, I guess she will." He thought of the scent of Jess's hair and the feel of her hand in his. Dreams were the closest he would get to her tonight.

Dien cleared his throat. "About Jess. Anything you want to talk about?"

Lars cursed himself for mentioning her. "Not really. It's awkward enough around you lately."

"I'm not trying to make things awkward."

"I know." Lars stared down the bridge while the dog looked up at him. "And I know you're my friend, but you're also Jess's dad. There are some things we just shouldn't talk about."

"We can talk about anything, pup. You know that. Especially the important stuff. The . . . hard stuff."

Lars winced at Dien's lie. They could never again talk about what had happened to Aly. Some words could not be unsaid. But Jess wasn't Aly and Lars had his future to think about, not just the mistakes of his past. "Not this, okay?"

"Yes, this. I need to know something. About you and Jess."

Lars closed his eyes. He thought of the tilt of Jess's head when she laughed, the curve of her throat, and how she twirled her hair with her fingers. The imagined feel of her belly, her breasts, her thighs. How he ached to touch her, kiss her, make love with her, make a home with her. Happy thoughts, of Jess, of love and warmth.

But the vision in his head shifted, as it always did, to raped children and beaten old men. Slaughtered girls Jess's age with their insides pulled out. A young man ravaged and shredded. An infant, burned crisp in a fire.

The reality of his life.

He opened his eyes and forced himself to breathe. *How can I explain this? I try to touch her, kiss her . . . but I see intestiness steaming in the snow. Rotting bodies. Corpses. Pain. I want to touch her so badly it hurts, but every time I do, all I see is blood. How can I have a normal life with this damned job?* Lars clenched his jaw and relaxed it before turning to look at Dien. "What?" he asked, sharper than he intended.

Dien cleared his throat. "Are you afraid of me?"

Lars turned back to the bridge and stared at the nearest set of rivets. One was missing from the cluster and had been for decades, judging by the rusted hole. "Not especially."

"Then I can't figure out why in the seven hells you won't come to me. You're so damn wound up, she's . . ."

A nervous laugh escaped Lars, and he was powerless to stop it. "I really don't want to talk about this."

"Yeah, well, I do. I'm your friend and you're worrying me, pup. You both are."

"It's none of your business."

"Not my business? Dammit, boy, will you please talk to me?"

"What do you want me to say?" Lars snapped, turning his head to look at Dien. "What in the bloody hells do you want me to say?"

Dien said softly, "I want you to talk to me, to someone, and admit what's going on. You don't have to face this alone."

Lars looked Dien in the eye. "There is nothing going on."

Dien stared at him for a long time without speaking. "All right. Deny it, then. You can't keep these things secret forever."

Another rock cart rattled past them and Lars returned his stare to the bridge. The woman walking toward them was closer now. "I love her," he said. "Let the rest go. Please."

"If you need to see Physician Rolle about . . ."

Lars gaped at Dien. *Does he think I'm deformed or something? That my goods don't work?* "Everything is fine. Stop worrying."

"I can't stop worrying. It's my job. Deny it all you want, but everything is not 'fine.' You're so damn wound up, the littlest thing has you jumping out of your skin, and Jess . . ."

Lars's hands clenched and unclenched. "What about Jess?"

Dien dismounted. "Dammit, I heard her talking to Fyn. I know. Guess I just hoped you had the balls to tell me yourself." He gave Lars a withering glare then walked across the bridge to meet the approaching woman.

Lars frowned. *What the hells just happened?*

The woman halted, fidgeting shyly as Dien approached.

"Arien," he greeted her warmly, shaking her hand.

"Dien," she replied, smiling. "It's good to see you." A tallish, big-boned woman, her plain face clouded over. "What brings you back to Quarry Run?"

"Arien, this is my associate, Lars. I'm glad we ran into you. We'd like to ask you some questions," Dien said.

Lars dismounted and smiled at Arien. The dog jumped up on her, muddying her skirt.

"All right," she said, her voice sounding a little nervous. She shooed the dog away and swallowed. "It's about that sheep head, isn't it?"

Lars felt Dien tense up beside him, but they both kept their faces calm.

Dien nodded and opened his notebook. "Tell us everything."

Arien released a rush of air and started babbling. "It was in my garden. See, I got home late last night, had to work and all, but Tupper came—"

"Marsden told us. Why do you think he came?" Dien asked.

She flinched and touched her mouth. "He wanted to see Haydon. I tried to stop him, but he knocked me down, then Constable Marsden came—"

"Tupper assaulted you?" Lars asked, his voice low.

"He hit me and kicked me a couple of times. But, like I said, Constable Marsden came, and Tupper held a knife to my throat but they fought—"

"Tupper and Marsden?" Dien asked.

"Sort of. Argued, I guess, and Tupper said I needed to see it—"

"See what?" Lars asked.

"I'm getting to that. Tupper told me I needed to see 'it,' then shoved me out the door. I landed on Calder and got cut, too, see?" She lifted her skirt to show them the bandage on her shin. "It was just an accident, but Tupper ran, then Calder chased him."

"And that's when you found the sheep's head?" Lars asked.

"Yes. Was lying right there in the middle of my yard." She shuddered. "I'm guessing you want it, right? I mean, I put it in a sack in the shed. I didn't know what else to do."

"Do you know where the head came from?"

She glanced back and forth between them. "Tupper must have put it there to scare me. Is he going to come back and hurt me again? Is he going to hurt Haydon? Someone who'd kill an animal like that, dump it in someone's yard . . . They'd do *anything*, no matter how bad it was, maybe even kill people, to get what they want. Wouldn't they?"

"Yes, ma'am, they might," Lars said. "What do you think Tupper wants?"

Arien clenched her fists. "I think he wants my son."

CHAPTER

7

†

Dien and Lars escorted Arien past a row of pitiful shacks. A cluster of crude dwellings made of scrap wood and filthy canvas, the workers' homes stank like chamber pots. Blank-eyed women ground grain in stone mortars and the sound of children screaming and tussling filled the air. Lars guided Sophey over the worst of the sewage trenches, and looked up as the dog at his heels yelped. A grimy little boy stood beside a shack, laughing and throwing rocks at the dog. "Stop that!" Lars said.

Arien scowled at the boy's obscene gesture. "That's Raffin. He does it to everyone."

Arien's house stood a quarter mile or so north of the bridge, in a cleared patch of land bordered on the west by the ravine and the north and east by sparse trees and pasture. The lilies blooming in her front yard helped erase the stench that followed them from the road. Lars wondered if Arien would let him pick some flowers for Jess and if he could get them home in good condition.

"It's in the shed," Arien said, sighing as a dog started barking.

Lars and Dien tied their horses then followed her

around the house. A sleek brown bitch was chained to a post, barking in a ceaseless clatter and staring at Lars, Dien, and the black-headed pup. The back door of the house opened and a scraggly-haired old woman squinted out at them. "Who the blue bells are you? What do you think you're doing upsetting Gidge when I'm trying to sleep? And why the hell'd you bring that fool pup back here? We got rid of all the little bastards moons ago."

"Squire Saworth and Page Hargrove from the castle, ma'am. We're conducting an investigation," Lars said, bowing slightly as Arien quieted her dog. "The pup just followed me. I didn't know he used to be yours."

The old woman spat tobacco juice onto the dirt. "Why don't you investigate why my daughter never comes home on time and when she does she's almost as filthy as you."

"You know I have to work," Arien said. "Tending patients is good money."

"You just want me to change his damn diddies. I've got better things to do, you know!" the woman snapped. She turned back to the house, slamming the door behind her.

Arien mumbled an apology as she unlatched the shed door, stepping aside to let the men enter.

Flies buzzed around a ragged burlap sack on the dirt floor. Dien pushed aside a hoe and some other clutter, then knelt to open the sack. Lars coughed at the reek of spice and rotting meat. "I think it's a little slimy," Arien said.

Dien grimaced and closed the bag. "A little." He stood. "We can't keep Tupper in Marsden's goal forever. Can you lock your doors and windows, maybe keep the dog in the house? Might be safer for you and your boy."

Arien stepped back as Dien and Lars left the shed. "You think Tupper will come back?"

"I'm sure of it."

Dien handed the sack to Lars. It felt damp and heavy, and hung off balance, the stinking head resting crookedly in the burlap.

"All right," Arien said, nodding hesitantly at first, then with more conviction. "I can start locking up."

"Is there somewhere else you can stay? Somewhere he doesn't know about?"

Arien shook her head. "No, there ain't nowhere else." Behind them, the door creaked open.

A little boy of four or five summers dragged himself onto the stoop, his legs following limply behind him. "Mama?" he said, his dark eyes huge. "There's horses in our yard!"

Arien brushed past Lars. "The horses belong to these men," she said, lifting the little boy. He wrapped his arms around her neck to hold on, but his hips and legs swung free and loose below. He stared at Lars and Dien in amazement.

"Haydon, this is Dien," Arien said, nodding toward Dien, "and this is Lars. Right?"

Lars bowed his head in greeting. "Yes, ma'am."

"They've come from the castle to get something."

Haydon grinned. "And you brought the horses?"

Lars smiled back. "You like horses?"

"Yessir!" Haydon said. "And those are real pretty ones. All shiny with fancy saddles."

Lars looked at Arien before asking, "Would you like to meet them?"

Haydon coughed, his face turning a dangerous red before he asked. "Can I, Mama? Can I?"

Arien looked between Lars and Dien. "I, um . . ."

"It's all right," Dien said, yanking his notebook from his pocket. "He'll be fine and it'll give us a chance to talk."

Lars set the sack on the ground and reached for Haydon. "C'mere, little guy. Let's go see those horses."

Arien hesitated for a moment, then allowed Haydon to latch on to Lars. The boy's hands felt hot against Lars's neck, feverish, but he was excited and giddy. Charmed, Lars introduced the boy to both mounts, let him stroke Sophey, and took him on a ride around the house.

"Maybe I can ride one all by myself someday," Haydon said, his hands gripping the saddle while Lars climbed up behind him and wrapped his arm around the boy.

"Maybe," Lars said, but he didn't see how. Haydon had no strength below the waist. His legs didn't function at all; they seemed to be little more than bones with skin stretched over them.

Haydon grinned, patting Sophey. "Mama says I'll get better someday. Even be able to walk. She's sure of it."

"She is?" Lars tried not to frown. So much false hope could only lead to disappointment.

"Yessir," Haydon said, certainty in his voice. "She says that if you want something bad enough, and work hard enough no matter what, you can do anything."

"That's good advice."

"Yeah, and I work hard, real hard, just like Mama says." He wove his fingers through Sophey's mane, marveling at it. "When I learn to walk, can you show me how to ride?"

Lars smiled. "I'd be happy to."

* * *

"Why would Tupper want the boy?" Dien asked.

"How should I know?" Arien watched Lars ride with Haydon around the house. "Maybe he wants to kill him, finish what he started. Who knows what he's thinking. Why'd you let him loose?"

"We had to, Ari, you know that. His time was done."

"Well, you could've given him more, at least until Haydon's able to walk. Until Haydon can get away from him."

"He's not going to walk. His spine's busted. You know that."

She turned. "Busted or not, my boy's going to walk. He's not going to end up strapped to a chair sitting in his own filth, you hear me? That's not going to happen to my son."

"I hear you fine," Dien said, "but facts are facts. I was there when Rolle looked him over."

"Pah! Damn castle doctor. He don't know nothing."

"He's a cripple, Ari. There's nothing to be done."

"There's always something to be done."

"How? Even if you went all the way to Waterford, to the University, facts are facts."

"I won't accept that. I can't." She looked Dien in the eye. "He'll grow up, become a man, have a family. He's an artist, a damn good one. He might even go to that University in Waterford someday, become a painter. Anything he wants to be."

"Ari," Dien said, shaking his head.

"These cases and things you do. Can anything stop you from finding the truth?"

"Of course not. But this is different. His *spine* is busted. That isn't something you can fix, no matter how much you want to. You're just lying to him, and to yourself."

"*Lying?*" she snapped. "Look at me. I'm twenty-one summers old and I'm used up. An old woman. Tupper lied, took my dreams, everything I had, and the one damned thing he gave me he broke. Haydon's the best thing that ever happened in my life and I'll be damned if anyone, even you, will take his hope away."

She slammed the shed door closed. "Sometimes, when you're poor, hope's all you got. You'll do anything to keep it alive, anything to see that dream come true. Don't you take my dream from me. Don't you dare."

Dien changed the subject. "Do you know anything about these missing sheep? Heard any rumors?"

"Not that I can think of."

"What about that new physician? Garrett?"

"What about him?" she asked, crossing her arms over her chest.

"I'm not the enemy here, Ari," Dien said softly. "I'm just doing my job."

"Garrett's an idiot," she said, sighing. "His cure to every complaint is some elixir or tonic or bit of bitter powder under the tongue. I've worked in that sewage pit for the better part of six summers and he's the first physician I've seen who balks to set a limb or put in a stitch. If his ignorance ain't killed anyone yet, it will."

"You're joking. What about all the injured quarry-men today? Didn't he patch them up?"

She craned her neck to watch Lars take Haydon around the house. "Some, but I do most of the treatments now. Manipulations, examinations, minor sur-geries, including a lot of the accidents today. Do I get paid extra for it? Hells, no."

The dog started barking again, pulling on its chain,

and they turned to see Marsden coming to them with Lars and Haydon following behind.

Marsden nodded a greeting to Arien then looked at Dien. "Woodley found his missing sheep. *Inside* the pen."

* * *

"They was there this morning," Woodley said, walking with the men to the sheep pen as dusk closed around them. "Two of 'em, anyways."

"Two of the missing four?" Dien asked.

"Yessir," Woodley said. "Couldn't tell you which ones they were, but I had fifty-seven last night when I penned 'em up, fifty-nine today when I let 'em loose. Go ahead and count 'em yourself, if you want."

"Who else might have walked through your barnyard today?"

Woodley tilted his head as he frowned. "Ain't nobody been here but us."

Dien shoved the lantern at Lars. "Run a circular search."

"Whatever you say." Lars took the lantern and walked away, looking downward, and his pup followed.

"What's he doing?" Woodley asked.

"Looking for footprints or something the thief might have dropped," Dien said. "Did your dogs bark at anything last night?"

Woodley squinted at Lars. "Yep, sometime late. But by the time I got my pants on, they'd quieted down. I thought it might be a coon, or Gurley's dog running loose again."

"Did you go outside and check?"

Woodley watched as Lars knelt. "What's he doing?"

"Working. Did you go outside and check on the dogs?"

Woodley shook his head and looked back at Dien. "No. They'd quieted down."

"He came from the ditch," Lars said, returning to them. "I found sheep dung and a path broken through the weeds. The ground's too dry for definite prints, but I did find some chewed-up bones." He showed Dien a gnawed leg joint. "I'd say he bribed the dogs."

"Can't bark if they're eating," Dien said.

"They wouldn't bite, neither," Woodley said, glaring at Buck. The dog whined and cowered.

"Where's the ditch go?" Dien asked.

"Down to the creek," Woodley said.

Dien smiled. "Where there might be some mud."

* * *

Maeve looked up from her weaving and sniffed. The air smelled damp and slightly rancid. Stagnant. It had grown dark while she worked, and she'd lit a lamp without thinking about it, but now, alone in the dark, she felt her heart flutter against her ribs.

"Where is it?"

She swallowed and stood, reaching for the lamp. Raising it, she looked behind her, toward the source of the voice. "Who's there?"

Tap tap clack clackclack, then a creak of shifting wood.

Maeve turned, shaking her head. The clacks and creaks came from the new suite. She took one step toward the blanket over the door, then another, the lamp shaking in her hand.

Behind her again. A whisper. "Find it. Get it back."

Then silence, punctuated only by her breathing.

She stood in the midst of boxes and stacked furniture for what seemed a long time, the shadows and trembling lamplight casting an illusion of movement against the walls. It was only her imagination. Fatigue and worry and the fear of having a magical relic in her home. It was nothing, nothing at all.

* * *

Dien, Lars, and Marsden followed Woodley's ditch to the creek, leading the horses, and found smears of mud on the grass from where someone had stepped up. "Watch the muddy banks for footprints," Dien said, taking the right bank while Lars took the left.

"I don't see anything but animal tracks," Marsden said, walking alongside Dien. "And not many of those."

"Same here," Lars said. "It's too dark for this."

"We've searched at night before." Dien walked slowly, looking for breaks in the vegetation on the upper bank, as well as tracks. "They had to come this way."

"Unless they came from upriver instead of down," Marsden said. "They could've turned partway around to go up the ditch."

"Piss." Dien stopped and looked back the way they'd come.

"If they stayed in the water, we'll never see their tracks." Lars shrugged. "That's what I'd do. Make sure any traces would be washed away."

Dien ran his fingers over the top of his head. "Goddess damned son of a whore. Do you know where this creek goes?"

"Into a bigger creek," Marsden said. "Then another. It finally meets up with the stream that runs down the ravine."

"Then they came this way," Dien said, sighing. "But we're not gonna see a damn thing in the dark. Piss!"

"That's what I said," Lars muttered.

"We can come back in the morning," Marsden suggested. "If a track's stayed here this long, it'll be here in the morning."

"Unless it rains," Lars said. "But I don't think there's anything to see."

Dien sighed and turned his horse to the bank. "Let's go, then."

* * *

Jess lay in the sitting room with her head propped on one arm of the settee while her mother consoled the baby. Jess was in the midst of Oriana's fourth journal and reading about the aftermath of the battle of Ferns Wood Creek.

I get so tired of the smell of blood. It reeks all the time, no matter how hard or how often I scrub. I've scoured lye into my skin until it's almost as red as the blood I've washed away. I just can't get away from the mess.

We made camp about a quarter mile away from the battlefield, and we were upwind, but the wind shifted and every breath now stinks of decaying corpses and exposed guts. No different from any other day, I guess. I killed seven soldiers and one stinking mage today—I don't think he'd bathed for a season—before I got my arm cut up. The doc says it's all right, only needed thirty-seven stitches. Be just fine in a week or so. Tunkek's put me on light duty— again—not that that'll make much difference if we run across another damn bone mage. At least it's my left arm. I can still write, still use that damn dagg—

The door opened and Jess looked up, hoping to see Lars, but it was just Fyn, red-faced and shaking.

"Fyn, wait," Sarea said, but Fyn ran past, into their bedroom, and slammed the door.

Sarea sighed and turned away.

"I'll check on her," Jess said, closing the journal.

She knocked quickly on the door before she opened it. "Hey," she said, closing the door behind her. "You okay?"

"Yes." Fyn sniffled. "No. I don't know. It's just . . ."

Jess sat beside her. "Just what?"

"It's just I keep asking Gilby to talk to Dad, and he says he will, but he doesn't, and he's always in trouble with Fultin or his dad's needing him to do this or do that."

Jess squeezed her sister's shoulders.

Fyn wiped her nose. "It's nothing. He just wants . . ." She hitched a shaky breath. "Never mind."

"It'll be okay," Jess said. "You can tell Mam. She knows something's going on. She'll listen."

"She'll kill me. Dad'll kill us both. Maybe Gilby's right."

"Right? About what?"

Fyn's lower lip curled in, then she looked away. "Nothing. Forget I mentioned it."

"Fyn. Talk to me. Talk to someone."

"I can't," she said, standing. "If I tell Mam and Dad, Dad'll kill Gilby, and even if he doesn't, it'll never be okay because Dad'll just blame him and say he wasn't man enough to be responsible and all." She walked to her bureau and ripped open a drawer. "You know how Dad is."

"Yeah, I know how Dad is."

"And he hates Gilby already. The only way Dad'll ever accept him is if he's the one who tells them."

"Right," Jess said. Of course, Fyn telling their parents about the baby was worlds better than no one telling them at all.

"So he has to, but he can't. And I can't because if I do it'll just all fall apart and . . . Hells!" Fyn slammed the drawer. "He's got all this other stuff, stuff I can't talk about."

"Who? Gilby?"

Fyn nodded. "And, because of that, he can't tell Dad. But I can't tell Dad either, and I just don't know what to do!"

"Someone has to tell them," Jess said. "Someone has to prepare for this baby. It's going to come whether you tell anyone or not, and what are you going to do then?" She took a breath. "Lars and I can tell, if you can't."

"No," Fyn said, shaking her head. "That'll be worse than anything." She sat on her bed again and looked at Jess. "You're already the responsible ones, officially courting and all. Heck, Lars even asked permission to court you. If you tell, that'll make us look that much worse."

"You're almost five moons pregnant. You can't hide it much longer. Mam and Dad have to know, and soon. Babies need things. Clothes, diddies, somewhere to sleep . . . You can't provide that." Jess paused and tried to give her sister an encouraging smile. "And neither can Gilby. Our folks are going to have to help."

Fyn turned away. "I don't want to talk about this anymore. Gilby and I . . . We'll figure something out."

* * *

After bells of worry, Dubric saw his men walk into the Twisted Cypress Tavern, and let out a relieved sigh. "Where have you been?" he asked. "And why are you so bloody and filthy?"

Dien fell onto a chair and sagged. "We've been to Woodley's farm. Two of his sheep were returned." He glanced up at the barmaid. "Ale now. And whatever's hot when you can."

She nodded and scurried off.

"Returned?" Dubric asked.

"Yes, sir," Marsden said, reaching for the bowl of fried pork skins. "He found them in the pen this morning."

"We found a partial track leading to his ditch, and down to the creek," Lars said. "But we couldn't see in the dark. Have to go back tomorrow."

"That does not explain the dirt and blood."

Dien smiled his thanks to the barmaid as she set a flagon of ale in front of him. "There was an accident at the quarry today." He took a deep drink, emptying the mug, then raised it, gesturing for another.

"I have heard people discussing it," Dubric said. "What happened?"

"Landslide. Eighteen men died, that we know about," Dien said. "We helped who we could, and got the rest of the injured to the sanatorium." He shook his head. "And we tracked down Arien. When Tupper threatened her, he also left her with a little present." Dien met Dubric's gaze. "A sheep's head."

"Where is this head?" Dubric asked.

The barmaid set plates of mutton and boiled turnips in front of them. Lars grunted happily and started shoveling in food. "On my saddle," he said around bites.

"What condition was it in?" Dubric asked, gripping his mug so tightly that it hurt his hands.

"Wet," Dien said. "Even after a whole day in Arien's shed, it was slimy wet."

"And it smelled funny," Lars said, chewing. "Like, um . . ." He looked upward for a moment then back to Dubric. "Like spices, but not anything you'd want to eat."

Dien nodded. "Like rosemary or thyme that'd been pissed on by a skunk."

Dubric pushed away his mug of ale and stood. "Wait here."

He turned and left the tavern, walking quickly to Sophey. As he reached for the fly-crusted bag tied behind her saddle, he let out a sigh of relief. It stank, yes, but not with a scent that tugged at his memory. He opened the sack to find a sheep head, still sticky with slime, reflected lamplight glistening in its open eyes. It looked freshly killed, not slaughtered days before, and the cuts at its throat appeared every bit as clean and precise—and bloodless—as those of his odd ghost.

He looked up as Dien approached. "Everything all right, sir?"

"Fine," Dubric said, closing the sack. "We will talk more after you eat, and I want to return home tonight."

"Why, Lord Dubric!" a man said from the road, and Dubric turned to see the physician, Garrett, hurrying toward him and dragging a young woman by the hand. "What a delightful surprise!"

"Yes, it is," Dubric said, forcing a smile. He nodded to the young woman, a different girl from the one they had seen with Garrett earlier that day. "Milady."

She nodded a return greeting. "Milord."

Garrett grinned. "I was just telling Mirrabelle about

the Keep of Hoddern Trail and how you—and Lord Nuobir, was it?—handily defeated Quincet and his army of walking dead."

"You have an enormously distorted view of the war. Do you know how many men died at Hoddern Trail? How many innocent women, children, and farmers struggling to feed their families perished? Yes, Nuobir and I routed and finally killed Quincet. We did not do so 'handily,' but with great toil and loss of life." Dubric shook his head and turned away, intending to return to the tavern and supper.

"But, milord, the records are clear. You did indeed defeat him, did you not, and open the primary route into Felder?"

Dubric sagged and turned back. "Facts in a ledger are nothing compared to the reality of battle. Surely, as a physician, you have a greater compassion for the value of a life than the simple numerical figures and dates in a book."

"It wasn't a book, milord, but official banns and tribunal records. They showed, without a doubt, that your armies—"

"We fought more than two thousand walking dead on the fields of northern Hoddern. Doing so ruined the people's grain crops, cabbages, and grazing grounds. Countless souls starved that winter because they, and their few sheep that survived, had nothing to eat. Not only that, but hundreds of soldiers lost their lives and limbs, nearby villages were demolished and burned to the ground when the dead swarmed through, and Nuobir's wife and young son were slaughtered by Quincet and his followers while we were busy fighting the primary battle.

"Do not tell me about what the damned banns and

tribunals reported. I was there. There was nothing heroic or fascinating about holding a fourteen-summers-old soldier's head while he bled to death in a burnt wheat field, nothing pleasant about rotting corpses walking across the land destroying everything in their path, and nothing the least damned bit glorious in seeing a five-summers-old child and his mother gutted alive and staked out for the crows."

Mirrabelle swallowed, looking like she might be sick.

Dubric took a step toward the couple. "I apologize for my bluntness, but war is seemingly endless days of mind-crushing boredom separated by fiercely brief periods of death and pain and suffering and terror. Pray that you never have to experience it for yourself, or see its aftermath firsthand."

He paused to take a cleansing breath. "Now, tell me how the men who were injured today are faring."

Garrett's smile faltered, then strengthened again. "As well as can be expected, milord. One perished while in surgery, the others are resting and healing."

"Good." Dubric walked with Garrett into the tavern. "So many injured all at once. That must have been hectic."

Garrett chuckled. "Not as much as you might think, milord. Unlike making war, medicine is an organized endeavor. Most of the patients merely needed bandages, ointments, and other simple procedures. My day was not at all hectic, merely an enjoyable practice of my training and skills."

Dubric glanced at his ghost, the precise severing of his throat, and thought of the dismembered sheep, as well as Garrett's reputation for preferring pharmaceutical treatments. "Do you enjoy surgery?"

"It has its merits," Garrett said. "Why all the questions about surgeries, milord?"

"Idle curiosity."

"Perhaps we could make a trade? I could tell you about surgery and you could tell me about mages?"

"Perhaps," Dubric said. "Tell me, however, as you are so interested—which type of mage is your favorite?"

"Why, the most feared, milord. There's just something remarkable and deliciously dangerous about a blood mage." Garrett paused and leaned forward to whisper, "I hear they found the miracle of eternal life. That, milord, is a feat worthy of admiration."

CHAPTER

8

†

Dubric followed his men into Marsden's office and waited for the constable to lock the door behind them. "Can Tupper hear us from his cell?" Dubric asked as he gently set his knapsack beside his chair.

"No, milord," Marsden replied, sitting behind his desk. "Not unless we shout."

"Garrett concerns me a great deal," Dubric said, "particularly his continual questions about mages. I cannot tell if he is attempting to get an estimate of the scope of my knowledge, perhaps in an effort to discern what I do not know, or if he is merely a history-hungry fool." He pulled his notebook from his pocket and opened it. "Physician Rolle informed me that the evidence suggests the sheep were dismembered with a surgical knife. He also confirmed that laudanum was in the vial we found last night, and traces were found in the sheep's stomach. Also, the sheep's head reeks of a medicinal concoction." He looked up at Marsden. "Are there any local sources for laudanum other than the sanatorium?"

"No, milord."

"How many butchers live in the area?"

"Two, milord," Marsden said.

"I want both questioned tomorrow, as well as the tracks leading from Woodley's farm followed, should they exist. I also want all of his sheep checked for shaved areas along the spine. If you can identify which sheep were returned, I want them separated from the flock and brought in for examination. Purchase them if necessary."

"Yes, sir," Dien said, adding to his own notes.

"Did you have any luck locating additional heads? Did you question Tupper?"

"No, sir, never had a chance," Dien said. "The quarry took up most of our day." He sighed and looked up. "I heard what Garrett told you earlier, but when I talked to Arien this evening she said that he's a piss-poor physician prone to shoving tonics down some-one's throat when they'd be better served with a splint or a few stitches. She also said that she and others do most of the nonmedicated procedures, including patching up the injured quarrymen. That doesn't mesh well with Garrett being our man."

"Perhaps he is purposely trying to confuse us," Dubric said. "Perhaps one of the butchers delivers to the sanatorium and has opportunity to steal the med-ications. I want the connection to the sanatorium pin-pointed and secured before we find dismembered people cast about to rot."

"You really think our sheep thief is going to kill peo-ple, milord?" Marsden asked.

Dubric glanced at his ghost. "Yes, I do."

* * *

While Marsden checked on Tupper and locked up for the night, Dubric waited outside with his men. "I received a ghost while riding to the castle."

"Great," Dien said, his hands balling into fists. "Who?"

"A young man I have never seen before. I received only his head, severed cleanly at the throat."

"Like our sheep," Lars said.

"Yes. But while at the castle, I visited my mirror and it showed me the rest of him." Dubric paused, unsure if his men would believe him. "He wore the uniform of a foot soldier, a corporal, with Lord Nanke's army."

"What?" Dien asked, his brow furrowing. "That's not possible. Nanke kicked the goat when I was just a boy."

"And the war," Lars said. "It ended almost fifty summers ago. How can a soldier just die, today? And how can he still look young?"

"I do not know." Dubric opened the front pocket of his pack. "There is no blood on the ghost or the sheep's head, and very, very little on the pieces of sheep we found yesterday. I have a partial ghost. Not once in all these summers has that ever happened before. Magic is involved whether we like it or not, and someone here knows what is happening. Someone is involved. Immediately after I return, we will question Tupper about that head. Until that time, let him rot in the cell. I do not want him to know that we suspect magic."

"Yes, sir," Dien said.

"Return?" Lars asked. "Where are you going?"

"Back to the castle. There is a favor I need to call."

"I can go, sir," Lars said, stepping forward. "You've been riding all—"

"You're here," Dien said. "That's that."

"But Jess and I had—"

Dien scowled, and Lars fell silent.

Wincing, Dubric reached into the knapsack pocket and pulled out three bracelets. "These were blessed by King Grennere's high priest and should grant you some protection, should the mage show itself." He handed Lars and Dien each a bracelet. "Wear them. That is an order. And insist Constable Marsden wear one as well."

"Protection from what?" Dien asked.

"If there is a mind mage, like the one we faced in the Reach, the blessed silver should protect you from control. It may also aid you should you face something more powerful. I have also brought blessed weapons, but I have no idea how strong their remaining magic is." He reached into the pack and removed the two vials, handing one to Lars and the other to Dien. "Drinking these should counteract any magical poisons. They are the last two vials I have. Try not to waste them."

"Yes, sir," Lars said.

Dubric handed his knapsack to Dien. "There are ten blast spheres in there and some other items. Handle the spheres carefully—they explode on impact."

Dien and Lars looked at each other. "Sir," Dien said, "I don't feel qualified to—"

"You must. I need to find out exactly what was used to preserve this head. It is not desiccated, so the chances of us facing a death mage are almost nonexistent. Mind mages are known for their physical roughness, not this precision, and I do not like the remaining options. We may need to relocate the village before countless innocents die."

"You're serious," Dien said, staring.

"Yes." Dubric removed the fly-covered sack from Lars's saddle and tied it to his own before climbing up. "I will return in the morning. Continue the investigation. Should you run into trouble, fight if you can, hide if you must. And stay alive. That is an order."

* * *

Yawning in the saddle, Dubric rode past the castle and to the village beyond. He reined up at a squat little shop and dismounted. Pungent sack in hand, he stepped onto the wooden walkway and pounded on the door.

There was no answer, and he could hear no movement within. Scowling, he walked a few doors up the road to the Dancing Sheep. Marlee, the head bar matron, smiled and tapped her used pipe ash into a bowl as he walked in. "Evening, sir," she said, filling a mug with ale as he approached the bar. "I gather you're not here to drink." She slid the mug down the bar to a patron, then pulled a pouch of tobacco from her apron pocket and proceeded to reload her pipe.

"I'm looking for Inek."

Marlee rolled her eyes and lit the pipe. "He's in back."

Dubric nodded his thanks and walked across the room, the scattered patrons coughing at the stench he left in his wake. Without pause, he opened the door to the back room and strode in. Five men looked up from the table and laid their cards facedown in front of them. "We're just having a friendly game, milord," a young man said. Dubric thought his name was Paolle and that he worked for the miller, but he was not certain.

Willfer the shoemaker took a drink of his ale, his hand shaking. "Nothin' wrong with a few hands of jesters."

"I have never claimed there was." Dubric stared at Inek, a pockmarked toad of a man on the far side of the table who wore an annoying smirk and clothes that were more stain than fabric. "If you gentlemen will excuse me, I have a private matter to discuss with our local herbalist."

The four men fled the room without bothering to take their cards.

Inek raised a grimy eyebrow and reached for Willfer's discarded hand. "Well, you saved me a couple of crown," he said, tossing the cards to the table. "I thought he was bluffing."

"I need a favor."

Inek looked up and sneered, a snot bubble flaring where the left half of his nose had once been. "Like I give a sow's ass what you need."

"What will it take to convince you otherwise?"

"Bring Ri back, you coldhearted bastard." Inek stood and shoved his chair away.

"Rianne was murdered," Dubric said. "We caught and killed the man responsible. No matter how I wish otherwise, I cannot change the past. You, however, can aid me in protecting—"

"I'm not doing bollocks for you." Inek pushed another chair aside as he stomped to the door.

"Your case for urinating in the public cistern arrives before Spring Council in a mere two phases. Are you aware that your crime is the worst currently facing judgment?"

"For pissing in public? You've lost your feeble old mind."

"Ah, but I have not. You see, it is all a matter of degree. You polluted the water that hundreds of people drink. When the next ranking criminal case is the theft of a few turnips, your little indiscretion looks much worse by comparison. And, my friend, you know how our glorious lord enjoys his public punishments."

"I'm not your friend, you old shit."

Dubric released a sigh. "What do you think it will be? Flogging? Branding? Castration, perhaps?"

"I was overcome with grief and you know it. You might be a brass-balled prick, but there's no damned way you'd sentence anyone to be flogged for grieving, no matter what they did. Even you have your scruples."

Dubric smiled. "I may, but Lord Brushgar does not. And I swear to you I will stand aside and let him assign sentencing as he sees fit. Requests for leniency will not leave my lips."

Inek drew a breath, then huffed it out, crossing his arms over his thick chest. "Pegging bastard. What do you want?"

Dubric lifted the bag. "I want to know *precisely* what concoction is on these partial remains. Ingredients, percentages, potential applications, everything."

Inek's eyes narrowed as he sniffed the odor from the bag. "What sort of remains?"

"A sheep's head."

"And in return, if I cooperate?"

"I will ensure you have a light sentence. Fines, at worst."

"No. You take my case from the listings, let me walk out of here an innocent man."

Dubric hesitated, merely for appearances, then held out the sack. "I want the complete identification of the substance by this time tomorrow, if not sooner, or you are facing Lord Brushgar alone."

Inek snatched the sack from Dubric's hand. "Done."

* * *

A short while later, Dubric quietly closed his suite door and removed his sword and boots, trying not to wake Maeve. He started toward the bed then detoured. *Perhaps I should remove the mirror, after all.*

The mirror stood facing the wall in the far corner of the new suite, its cover lying on the floor. Without looking at the glass, he carried it to the small room they had set aside for bathing. Plaster grit crunched beneath his feet and a tapping sound creaked from the frame, but Dubric maneuvered the mirror around the tub and washstand. The painters had laid a canvas over the tub to protect it from spatters. Dubric retrieved it and draped it over the mirror, hoping that securing it away would ease Maeve's worries. Plumbing would not resume until after the faire, leaving the mirror locked away for at least three days. Long enough, perhaps, to take Maeve's mind off it. Satisfied with his plan, he locked the bath chamber door.

Yawning, he found his way to bed and crawled in beside Maeve, wincing as he felt the ghost's chill against his skin.

"I'm sorry I'm such a ninny," Maeve said as the bed shifted under his weight.

He reached for her. "And I am sorry that I am a belligerent old fool."

She snuggled close. "You're forgiven."

"As are you," he replied. He kissed her and, despite the presence of his ghost, it was a long while before he remembered that he needed to sleep.

* * *

"Where do we start?" Lars asked, picking at his egg. Across the table, Dien glowered into his tea and remained silent. Lars sighed and pushed his plate away. He wanted to go home, wanted to see Jess. The castle faire was tomorrow, the lord's dance, and, as he looked out the window to the morning, he doubted he'd be able to go. He'd disappoint Jess, all his plans would be for naught, and he'd spend the whole day scraped on the edge of Dien's anger.

And I haven't done anything wrong, Lars thought. He sighed and stood, turning away from the table. *At least I can go clean my boots or—*

"Sit your ass down," Dien said.

Lars sat and wished he were somewhere else, anywhere else, rather than in a crummy town, in a plant-filled house, across the table from Dien's brewing fury.

Dien looked up, staring into Lars's eyes. "You ready to talk to me yet?"

"There's nothing to talk about." Returning the stare, Lars leaned back in his chair and crossed his arms over his chest.

"So you're still telling me nothing's going on."

"Nothing I want to talk to you about."

Dien reddened, his hands clenching. "Piss!" One final glare, then he stood and stomped away. "Get your gear together. We're starting with Woodley."

* * *

"Come-bye," Woodley coaxed the dog from the far side of the sheep. "In here, that's a good lad, now drive him easy." Buck skirted the herd, peeling off one sheep and driving it toward Lars. The sheep saw Lars and turned to bolt, but Buck was there, staring it down, keeping it still. As Lars approached the sheep, the dog crouched, still staring, his tail wagging.

"Ho there," Lars said, running his hand down the sheep's spine. It quivered, wanting to run, but stared at the dog and remained still.

"All clear," Lars said. At Woodley's command, Buck

lunged to the side and directed the sheep away to the open field.

All the while, Dien and Marsden stood by Woodley, watching. Lars sighed and waited for the next sheep. He'd checked seventeen so far, each one with the same weather-matted wool as the one before. *Only forty-two to go*, he thought.

Number eighteen stood quivering like the rest as Lars approached. He glanced at Buck and the dog crouched, his eyes riveted on the sheep, then Lars leaned over to check the spine. A shaved spot, about twice the size of a gold crown, was on the sheep's neck halfway between the base of its skull and its shoulders. Inside the shaved area he saw the telltale pair of triangles, and he looked over to the men.

"That's one," he said.

"Walk up!" Woodley called out and Buck sprang forward. The sheep backed away so fast it stumbled, then, dog zigzagging on its heels, trotted across the pasture to an open gate leading to a small pen.

* * *

"Found them both, sir," Dien said, walking up to Dubric. "Pair of rams. I've paid Woodley for them and his trouble, and I've had the sheep sent to Marsden's house. We were about to check the creek."

"Then I have perfect timing." Leading his horse, Dubric followed his men to the ditch and down to the creek. They easily found their tracks from the night before, but no others.

Watching the ground and the banks, they walked downstream and talked of mundane matters while Lars's pup bounded ahead, sniffing and splashing in the water. The creek fed into another, then another, widening as it worked toward the ravine. As they walked alongside a pasture, Dubric swallowed. He could delay his news no longer. "While at the castle yesterday, I sent Otlee to research a few things," he said, patting the pocket where he had stored Otlee's report.

"What'd he find, sir?" Dien grunted as he climbed up the bank. He pulled something from the edge and put it in an evidence sack. "Just a bit of hair," he said coming back to the creek. "Looks like lynx, but it won't hurt to check."

Dubric nodded and resumed his search, trying to keep his tone light even though his belly felt twisted and sick. "The triangular symbol belonged to a group of mages from the Casclian Mountains, or at least the shape did. Otlee found three versions, all colored differently, none matching the symbol we have found."

"But all were Casclian?" Lars asked.

"Yes." Dubric picked his way around a fallen tree. "Supposedly it represents two mountain ranges and the valley between. All were . . ." He paused to rub his aching eyes and settle his heart. He did not want to tell them, did not want to speak the words aloud, but what choice did he have? "All three of the symbols Otlee found belonged to blood mages." Dubric glanced at his ghost and added, "Two were removed by Lord Nanke's mage killer. She and a group of scouts disappeared while tracking the third. They were never found."

All three men stopped searching to look at Dubric.

"Two more generals sent mage killers to remove the mage. Again, they and their support soldiers disappeared. An entire army was sent, supposedly to central Faldorrah. Seven hundred men led by Lord Galdet."

"And?" Dien asked when Dubric didn't go on.

"They received their orders and were never seen again. After that, Otlee found no record of the mage's symbol."

"So you're telling me this thing survived the war?" Dien asked, his voice rising. "And it's been here, right in our own damned back garden, for fifty frigging summers?"

Lars looked around, his face paling, and his voice shook as he asked, "What do we do?"

"We find it. And we kill it." Dubric looked at Marsden. "Once we return to town, I want you to prepare a list. Get organized. We will need to relocate your people."

"How can we?" Dien asked. "How can we relocate a whole village? And, dammit, sir, what if we move the mage with them? If it's hidden this long, it knows how to blend in."

"How can we kill something that seven hundred soldiers couldn't kill?" Marsden asked. He swallowed, wincing, and looked as if he might vomit. "I have family here. My folks, my kids, for Goddess's sake. You're standing here telling me we're all going to die?"

"There is always hope. If we can—"

"Seven hundred men, a whole frigging army, disappeared, and you say we have a chance?" Dien asked, nearly screaming. "There are four of us! Four!"

"There is a *chance*," Dubric said. "All records of the mage disappeared after Galdet came to fight it. It is possible it died in the battle or shortly after. It is possible it died of natural causes at any time during the past five decades. It is still possible that this is someone's idea of a sick prank and there is no mage, only the illusion of one."

"Maybe that's all it is," Marsden offered. "Up until

last autumn, we'd never had a bit of trouble with this sort of thing." He looked back and forth between Dubric and Dien. "It's probably some kid," he finished weakly.

"It could still be Garrett," Dien said. "He has access to the medicine, access to the surgical knives, and last night he talked about blood mages as if they were a bucket of kiddie toys." He looked at Dubric. "If he thinks this is some kind of joke, I'm going to bust his frigging legs, so help me."

Lars had sat quietly, his head down. "What exactly do blood mages do, sir?"

"They gather their power by draining their victims of fluids. Sometimes it happens quickly, like sucking the juice out of a grape, and the victim falls dead. However, they typically kept their victims in flocks, as a farmer keeps milk goats, taking a bit at a time. Either way, the draining was reputed to be extremely pleasurable, often equated with . . . romantic sensations. The kept flocks quickly became addicted to the bliss of draining and would happily submit to every whim, follow every instruction, do whatever their master asked of them. Once trapped and under the mage's control, there was no saving them."

"So we might not be facing a single mage, but a flock of its followers as well?"

"That is a possibility, yes. Our best hope is, for appearances' sake, to keep the investigation focused on slaughtered sheep and appear to be solving a mundane crime, not a magical one. That should garner us a little time. If we can find the mage before it realizes what we know, we may be able to use innocent pretext to trap it, and, once trapped, kill it." Dubric looked at Dien and Marsden. "I hope."

Dien sighed and led his horse forward again. "It's not like we have much choice. Do we?"

"There is always a choice," Dubric said. "However, those choices may be severely limited."

* * *

Maeve removed a swath of folded cloth from a box and measured it, trying not to sneeze at the linseed oil and turpentine burning her nose. Noting the length on a bit of paper, she folded ten yards of bird's-eye in finely spun cream and gray wool.

"Where is it? What have you done?"

Maeve turned, trembling. She could hear the painters chatting in the new suite, but saw no one else. "Hello?" She craned her neck but saw no one. "Dubric sees ghosts, not me," she mumbled, her heart hammering. "It's just my imagination."

"Where is it?" a woman's voice whispered in her ear, a voice without breath, without warmth. "If you have care for the child you carry, you must find what she wants and give it back."

Maeve turned, startled, struggling to see whoever was whispering to her. "I can't be pregnant," she said. "I'm thirty-four—"

"Young enough."

Maeve lurched around to track the sound. "But I'm not even late yet. Not really," she said, knowing it was a lie. She'd been as regular as the seasons for as far back as she could remember. She was late, barely a phase, but late just the same. And the ghost knew it.

"You had it," the voice said. "You must get it back."

Cold hands gripped her shoulders and wrenched her around, forced her to face the archway leading to the new rooms, and the blanket fell to the floor. Dubric's old mirror stood across from her, the mirror he promised he'd locked in the bathing room, and she saw her own hazy reflection rippling in the glass. Beside her stood the ghost she'd seen before, a beautiful young woman, her reflection crisp and clear.

"You must find it," the ghost said, then she faded away.

Maeve struggled to remain calm, her gaze riveted to the mirror. She looked like herself, only different. Thinner. Her hair a little straighter, her eyes more green than brown. Her image shifted as if lost in water, bright then dull, sharp then muted. Then it wasn't her reflection at all, but someone else's. Someone dead and burnt.

Maeve screamed.

CHAPTER

9

✝

Dubric led his horse down the creek bed, his nose wrinkling as he detected a low, rotting stench. He picked up the pace. Dien and Lars trailed behind, silent even when Marsden tried to coax them into conversation. Dubric frowned and glanced back at his two men. Dien and Lars had always been close and Dubric now realized he depended on their familial camaraderie, like father and son yet trusted friends. He found the quiet animosity distressing.

They had best settle this soon. If not, I will have to knock their fool heads together until they see reason. If we indeed face a mage I will need them functioning as a unit, not as two opposing forces.

Dubric paused at a muddy ditch and looked up to the sorghum field. He heard buzzing flies and the stench had thickened into a palpable force. "I have footprints here," he said. His knees creaked as he knelt.

"I'll head up," Lars said. He walked downstream a bit then led Sophey up a shallowly pitched section of bank, the pup following all the way.

"Looks like prints from a common boot," Dien said. "Smooth sole, low heel. Crack in the right heel, but nothing else remarkable about them that I can see."

Marsden pointed to a section of flattened, muddy grass. "And they've been up and down several times. It's the same field from a couple of nights ago, milord."

"I have dead sheep up here!" Lars called out. "And dogs."

Dubric led his horse up the ditch. Once at the top he stopped and reminded himself to close his mouth.

Scores of severed heads lay piled near the ditch. Most were sheep, but he saw several dogs, goats, and chickens as well. None were particularly decayed. A few looked quite fresh, but all were covered with flies and the same slime as the head he had given to Inek, if the stench was any indication.

"What's this mean, sir?" Lars asked, picking his way over the corpses rotting between rows of sorghum.

"I am not certain," Dubric said. "How can the bodies be rotten and decayed but the heads appear fresh? They look as if they were left here a day or two ago."

"About the same time Tupper left that head for Arien?" Dien asked.

"Perhaps. Again, we have virtually no blood." Dubric pulled a sheep-gut glove from his pocket and drew it on, then opened an evidence bag. "We will take one back to the castle to compare to the first head. I wager the slimy substances will match." He chose a damp and dripping specimen, the head of a goat, and put it in the sack.

Behind him, Dien muttered a curse. As Dubric turned, Marsden bent over and vomited.

"What?" Dubric asked, the head partly in the bag. "What is wrong?"

Dien and Lars pointed. Dubric turned back to the pile of heads, then scrambled to his feet and away from the pile. Beneath where the goat's head had lain was a rooster's head, severed mid-neck and completely sub-merged in a glistening puddle of slime. It was blinking, its eye rolling as if in fear, and its mouth opening and closing. As Dubric watched, it jumped, flipping like a fish, then resumed its silent crowing.

* * *

Jess searched through the trunk of books, trying to organize the contents. She stacked a pile of journals by her side, reached in for a few more, then paused at the small wooden box sitting on the next few journals. The top and sides advertised combs for purchase and the contents shifted as she lifted it. Curious, she opened the hinged lid.

It contained trinkets and little mementos. Buttons. Strips of carefully rolled lace. A seashell. A tarnished silver spoon. Three wooden matches in a tiny box, the sulfurous ends flaking off.

She sniffed the matches, her nose wrinkling at the sharp tang. Sulfur was uncommon at best, a rare al-chemic powder the ancients had used. The officers of the armies had seldom had the luxury of flint and steel and dry tinder, so they had been assigned precious matches. Jess had learned about it in War History.

She put the matches back then noticed something dark below the trinkets. She furrowed her brow as she moved aside bits of paper and lace.

It was a flat card of metal with a brownish sheen, roughly the size of her hand.

"Oh, my," she marveled aloud as she lifted it from the box. It was cool to the touch and heavy for its thinness, slick on one side and rough on the other. "A ferrotype."

She knew that ferrotypes were thin sheets of iron

with expensive images burned onto them by machines from the ancients. Her father had brought an image of himself home after a great Council, summers and summers before, as a gift for her mother. Jess had seen it but had never been allowed to touch it. It was too precious, too dear.

She turned the ferrotype over and wondered what image she'd find. Surely someone, or something, marvelous and grand.

A young couple in military uniforms smiled in the image. Her hair was long and flowing and black, her eyes narrow and slightly angled in a heart-shaped face. A southerner. He was dashing and sturdily handsome, with short curly hair of a lighter shade and eyes that were sparkling and fierce. Even without his burn scars and with a grin teasing his usually stern lips, Dubric's face was unmistakable. Jess touched their faces and smiled. Dubric and Oriana looked so young, so happy.

He's happy again, with Aunt Maeve. When they're together, he smiles just like this.

Jess carefully returned the picture to the box, tucking it beneath the laces and papers, as she wondered how Dubric had become so scarred and what had happened to Oriana.

* * *

"How in the seven hells is that possible?" Dien asked, pacing.

"I have no idea," Dubric said. "Get me a damned jar. Now. Before it stops moving."

Lars ran to them, empty-handed. "Sorry, sir, we don't have any jars. The closest we have are specimen bottles, and they're too small."

Marsden sat on the ground, staring blankly ahead. "I

need a drink, maybe a whole bottle of whiskey. I don't care that it's still morning, chicken heads don't do that. They don't." He looked up at Dien and laughed. "There's really a mage here and we're all going to die. All of us."

"I think we've lost him, sir," Dien said, shuddering.

"Wish you'd lose me," Lars said. "What do you need me to do?"

Marsden stared straight ahead again. "Sheep were missing, farmers were concerned. Call the castle and ask for help. Made perfect sense at the time. But now, now . . ." He fell back into the sorghum and laughed. "We're dead."

"Take care of him," Dubric said to Lars. "Perhaps get him up and walking. There is a bottle of brandy in my saddlebags."

Lars nodded and ran for Dubric's horse.

"Talk to me, sir. I need to know what the plan is," Dien said.

Dubric ripped the sheep-gut glove off his hand and blew into it, opening it like a small sack. "If we cannot find where the tracks originated, I know someone in the sanatorium," he said softly, glancing up at Dien. "A patient. I do not know whom else to trust. My best hope at this moment is that she has heard a rumor, seen something useful . . . something." He scooped the rooster head and a good measure of goop into his glove and lifted it from the mess of heads, holding it up to the morning sky. The head floated inside, still moving.

Dubric tied the wrist of the glove closed, then put the whole sticky thing in an evidence sack. "We have to find the mage, and soon." He stood and looked Dien in the eye. "We have to save the people of Quarry Run."

"And you think some sanatorium patient can help

us? Even if she does know something, how do you know you can trust her?"

"I had better," Dubric said, walking to his horse. "She is my goddaughter."

* * *

Maeve tried to keep from shaking as she knocked on the Saworths' door. Lachesis was in no mood to be carried—he had been yowling and struggling to get loose most of the trek from her suite—but she held him tight and prayed that Sarea was home.

Sarea opened the door, her hands full with a wet and wailing baby. "Sorry," she said, ruffling Cailin's hair dry, "it's bath ti—" She stopped, gaping. "Watch your sister," she said, thrusting the baby at Fyn.

Sarea helped Maeve into the sitting room and closed the door. "Are you okay? What's wrong?"

A ghost. I saw a ghost. Oriana. Me. Burnt. In the mirror. Maeve tried to talk, but no sounds came out.

Sarea smoothed Maeve's hair. "Everything's going to be fine. Let's put the cat down, and we'll go back to my bedroom and talk. All right?"

Maeve dropped Lachesis, who ran beneath a chair and hissed. Dumb and staggering, she let Sarea help her through the suite.

* * *

Dubric led his men down the creek bed and ravine floor, pausing only at ditches and broken paths as they looked for tracks. Nearly every house and field had access to the creek and, as they neared Quarry Run, the paths down became frequent. Some were lined with stone, others used tree roots as makeshift stairs, and most were merely smoothly packed earth. Many showed signs of recent travel, leaving countless potential pathways for the killer to take.

"That one's torn to the seven hells," Dien said, looking up a line of broken brambles and weeds. He stepped toward the mess and pulled a scrap of fabric from a prickle bush. "And what do we have here?"

"Probably a piece of my shirt," Marsden said. Though his voice still shook a little, he looked and sounded much stronger. "It's where I followed Tupper down from Arien's place."

Dubric looked farther down the ravine. "Garrett's house is not far ahead. Let us check that area, then find a way to get the horses out of here." He took a few steps forward then stopped as a cold, heavy weight fell behind his eyes.

"Oh, no," he mumbled, slumping as the pain of a new ghost slammed through his head.

Dien touched his shoulder. "Sir? You all right?"

Dubric took a cleansing breath, then another, before standing upright again. "Someone has died," he whispered, then took a step back as he saw the ghost. Another severed head, also that of a young man, hovered near the first ghost. The ghost's head was bruised and battered, covered with scabbed-over gashes, some with stitches, and a patch of his hair had been ripped away to leave an oozing wound.

"I believe it is one of the injured quarrymen," Dubric said to Dien, his voice low. "Decapitated like the other."

Dien raked his hand over his head. "Shit."

Dubric looked over to where Lars stood with Marsden, a short distance away. "Find us a way out of here," he called out. "Now."

"Yes, sir." Lars handed his reins to Marsden and ran back the way they had come.

He returned a short time later. "About a hundred yards back," Lars said, pointing, "I think the pitch is shallow enough to lead the horses thr—"

Behind Dubric, from far down the ravine, someone screamed. Dubric let his reins fall. "Lars, take the horses. Dien and I will handle this."

*　*　*

"She was burnt," Maeve said. They sat on Sarea's bed, behind a closed and latched door, and Maeve stared at a laundry basket of folded socks and undergarments sitting beside the bureau as she tried to explain what had happened. The basket was so normal, so sane, she couldn't bear to look away. "I saw myself in the mirror, saw *her,* and she was burnt!"

"How can your reflection look burnt?" Sarea asked. "You look fine."

Maeve balled her hands and pounded her knees. "I don't know! And it wasn't me, not really. It was *her.*"

"Her who?"

"Oriana," Maeve spat, hating the venom in her voice. "Dubric's dead wife." She took a breath, closing her eyes to the laundry, then opened them again as she exhaled. "It's complicated."

Sarea smoothed Maeve's hair. "Evidently."

"She was there, right beside me, then she vanished and I wasn't myself, I was her, and I was burnt." Maeve sighed and looked at Sarea sitting beside her. "That sounds crazy, doesn't it?"

"A little." Sarea smiled and patted her hand. "Maybe you just need to relax. Do something you enjoy. After all that's happened the past couple of moons, it'd be enough to drive anyone a little crazy." She stood. "I'm going to get you a cup of tea, all right?"

Maeve nodded. Trying to calm herself and breathe properly again, she began to carefully scrape black, sooty grime out from the edges of her fingernails.

* * *

Dubric, Dien, and Marsden rounded a curve then skidded to a stop, slipping on rocks and mud. "Goddess, is that someone's leg?" Marsden asked.

"Yes." Dubric also saw an arm caught in the stream, wedged between two rocks just beyond the severed lower leg and foot. The woman's screams came from above. Ignoring the pain in his knees, Dubric climbed, grasping trees to aid him as he dragged himself to the road.

He staggered out of the brambles to see a clot of people at the edge of the workers' shacks. Two ashen-faced women dragged a panicked woman away, and, as the men saw Dubric approach, they parted.

"She found it in a sack, milord. Right there by the fence."

"Found what?" Dien asked, right behind Dubric.

The men pointed and Dubric stepped through to kneel by a muddy burlap sack. A man's head lay inside, wide-eyed and staring. The face of the first ghost. It smelled faintly of soap, along with the familiar scent of the slime he had found on the other heads. Dubric noticed no taint of decay, either in the scent or appearance, and the clean, dry skin looked rosy and alive. He half expected it to move, perhaps gasp for air as the rooster had done, and wondered why it had been discarded. "Search the area," Dubric said to Dien. He drew the sack closed and stood. *Two murders in two days.* "Who found this?"

"Ellbeth," a bent, middle-aged man said. He pointed to the left. "She was putting out her wash."

A pile of wet washing lay on the ground not far from the head, half spilling out of a tipped basket. Some of the gawkers were treading on the clothes as they whispered and stared.

"Has anyone been about this morning?" Dubric asked. "A stranger? Someone from a different part of the village? Anyone you do not usually see?"

Several people in the crowd said, "No," and Dubric did not notice anyone who appeared suspicious.

"I don't see anything, sir," Dien said. Beside him, Marsden shook his head.

Dubric gathered up the sack, thanked the bystanders, then led Dien and Marsden back to the road. "Are you willing to look at this?" he asked Marsden. "Identify the remains?"

"All right." When Dubric opened the sack, Marsden flinched, but examined the man's face. The constable shook his head. "I've never seen him before."

* * *

Jess came home from class and flopped onto her bed to read the next journal. She skimmed through Oriana's telling of the skirmish at Hepplebrow, flipped past the journey to Fyre Gate Pass, pausing long enough to read Oriana's one-night romance with a goatherd she met along the way, then forward through the journal again until the next romantic encounter. And again to the next, then the one after that.

Jess closed the journal and stared at the ceiling. *Is*

that all there is to mage killers? Kill, maim, torture, walk forever, lay with some local boy, then do it again?

Yes, the killing was dreadful. Yes, the lusty bits got her heart racing as she wondered if Lars would ever want to do those things. Some she'd never heard of, let alone considered, and a few intrigued her in a delightful way. But there had to be more. Something worthy of all the myth and rumors.

Setting the journal aside, she sighed and reached for the next. It began with a battle in a village, followed by carousing and a tryst in the storage room of a tavern. Then Oriana wrote:

11 13, 2214
Tunkek was waiting for me when I staggered out. My shirt was half off, my trousers unfastened, and I had my chemise in my hand. Tunkek had seen me—hells, he'd seen all of us—in worse shape.

He told me I had new orders, then he handed me a scroll with Nuobir's seal on it. He said nothing, just waited while I read.

It said:
Report to Sett Nuobir at his private offices at midday, 11 17, 2214, for reassignment. Mission expected to take four days; after which, assignment immediately reverts to General Romlin.

It was signed by the King, Byreleah Grennere himself.
I can't believe they pulled me from the line. It makes no sense. I have the best record of any killer I know of and we've nearly reached Albin Darril's team in central Lagiern for the combined push north. Why pull me out now? For four days? What's the point?

When I showed it to Tunkek, he told me there aren't mages in Waterford, so we couldn't figure out why they'd

want me. Still can't. It's supposed to be a temporary post-
ing, though. Four days. What kind of posting lasts four
days? I guess it could be worse.

Tunkek returned the scroll and told me to button my
shirt before I met with Nuobir. Then he bought me an
ale to warm my gut for the ride. I'm drinking it now and
trying to make sense of this. Why in the hells does
Nuobir want me? He has his own mage killer. If I leave
tonight, I'll arrive at Nuobir's on time. Barely. Another
night without sleep in the dead of winter.

One of the things Jess found fascinating about
Oriana's journals was the way she mentioned so many
renowned generals in such a casual way. King Tunkek
Romlin currently ruled Lagiern. Sett Nuobir had been
the King's high sage before the war, and had created the
weapons that ultimately defeated the mages. Byreleah
Grennere was, of course, the King during much of the
Shadow Wars—and Lars's great-grandfather.

Oriana had mentioned Albin Darril only once before.
The King's rapier—possibly the King's chief assassin—
had commanded a small contingent of soldiers and a
mage killer. They had specialized in removing mages for
interrogation, or killing them with minimal peripheral
bloodshed. Oriana had met Albin while tracking a pair
of mages the summer before. Both mages had ultimately died, but no soldiers had lost their lives, thanks
to Albin Darril's precision.

Oriana had written about his grace and blinding
speed with a blade. Efficient and cold, Albin could
drop a man in an instant, leaving him helpless but alive
and able to talk, or he could remove a small but vital bit
of flesh and be on to the next victim before the dead
even knew they had died.

Oriana admired Albin Darril greatly, preferring his precise approach over the bloody battles Tunkek fought, but Jess knew little about him. History texts mentioned him only in passing.

Maybe I should learn more about him. She flipped to Oriana's next entry. *He lived here, in this castle, after the war. Surely he stayed in Faldorrah for a reason.*

Then she stared at the words on the page and sat up, swinging her legs off the edge of her bed.

11 17, 2214

I stepped through Nuobir's mirror into a house in Casclia. My first target, Lieutenant Swelldin, sat marking a map with his back to me. He raised his head, sniffing, and I wondered if he smelled the same thing I did, an odd mix of myrtle and plum. Fruity and sharp. Pungent. The mirror's scent clung to me, but I slit his throat before he could turn. I tried not to get much mess on the map. Once I secured the location, and retrieved the items Nuobir required, I stepped out into the storm and found shelter in a hog shed a quarter mile or more away. I'll stay here until the storm clears. I have shelter, plenty of fresh pork, and there's enough dead brush nearby to keep a smokeless fire burning for days.

Jess stared at the words, her mind churning. *Casclia's in northern Lagiern. It's north of Faldorrah, more than a two-phase ride from Waterford in good weather, let alone in winter. How could she cross the kingdom like that?*

She stared at the first sentence: *I stepped through Nuobir's mirror into a house in Casclia.*

Dubric had a mirror, the old one with strange markings on the frame that Lars and Aunt Maeve were afraid of. Could it be the same mirror? And if so, what was it doing in Faldorrah?

* * *

His knees too sore to kneel much longer, Dubric was about to ask Lars to help him search a tangle of juniper bushes for the last part of the dismembered body, but the creaking jingle of tack and a threatening whinny from the road silenced him.

"That's Sideon," Dien said, reaching for a sapling to help him stand. He climbed the ravine slope like a bear breaking through the underbrush.

Struggling to hold several burlap sacks, Marsden helped Dubric to his feet.

From the road, Dien bellowed, "Get your filthy hands off my horse before I tan your hide!"

"We should hurry," Dubric said. He grabbed a sack and hoisted himself up the ravine. Lars hurried past him and disappeared over the edge.

"It's probably a kid, sir," Marsden said. "Some of the worker brats can't keep their fingers in their own pockets."

A child shrieked. By the time Dubric and Marsden reached the road, Dien was holding a little boy by the scruff of his shirt and staring down at a small tattooed man who stood in front of Dien, hands on his hips. Lars stood nearby, trying to keep back the crowd of quarrymen armed with picks and shovels.

Marsden set his sacks in the weeds. "Raffin, can't you ever keep your fool hands to yourself?"

Raffin twisted in Dien's grip and gave Marsden an obscene gesture. Then he spat.

"My boy ain't no fool," the lone worker said, staring

up at Dien. "And his hands ain't, neither. You tell this ox to let go a him b'fore I kick his mangy ass."

"Simmer down," Marsden said, slowly approaching the man. "He's a castle squire, on the lord's business, and you don't want trouble with the lord, do you? We've talked about Raffin before, remember? About how he likes to look at the pretty, shiny things? Look at them up close?"

"Pegging steal them, you mean," Dien muttered.

The man's fists shook. "Let my boy go. I'm warnin' you."

"Be happy to, once he gives back my pouch."

"I ain't got no stinkin' pouch!" Raffin said, squirming.

"Yes you do," Dien said. "Right front pocket. I can see the bulge, and its lacings are sticking out."

"It's my money!" Raffin cried. "Had it for phases."

Dien sighed. "It's not money. You pilfered tins of soft wax, print dust, soap, saddle grease, and aromatic mint. Might be a packet of headache powder or dry ink in there, too."

"Show him," Marsden said softly. "If it's a pouch of money, show him and we can all go home."

"He'll steal it," Raffin said.

"Show the bastard, Raf," his father said, his voice low and even. "Show him you're not a liar."

"Piss," the boy muttered, twisting in Dien's grip. He reached into his pocket and pulled out a rumpled pouch of worn leather.

"Lemme see that," his father said, snatching it away. He opened it, squinted inside, then closed it. "You're right, milord," he said, handing the pouch to Dien. Then he struck Raffin across the face. "Lying little shit."

"Ho there." Dien pulled the boy away and stepped in front of him. "No harm done. There's no reason to hurt him."

"Mind your own children," the man said. "Raf, get your backside home and pick a switch."

"Yes, Pa," the boy said. He ran through the crowd and slipped past Dubric, his hands stealing down to cover his backside.

The man gave Dien a firm nod, then stomped away. The spectators soon drifted into the evening and Lars climbed back down into the ravine

"Sorry about that, sir," Dien said. "I knew the pouch wasn't worth anything and I didn't mean for the boy to get a beating. I just wanted to scare him."

Marsden dragged a sack from the weeds and set it beside the others. "He needs more than a scare. I can't count how many times I've pulled that brat out of someone's shed or garden, how often I've had him empty his pockets or dragged him home after he's given another boy a black eye or hurt some damn dog."

"He hurts dogs?" Dubric asked.

"Killed a dog a moon or so ago. Little ratter pup. Strangled it then lit it afire. A couple of other boys saw the whole thing but were too scared to stop him. He's always throwing rocks, spitting on people. The boy's just trouble."

"Reminds me of Tupper. But he's not who we're looking for, is he?" Dien asked as he carried a sack of body parts to Dubric's horse.

Dubric tied the sack to the saddle. "Tupper? Not as the killer, no. But he could be involved. I want you and Marsden to question him about where he found the head. Lars and I will go to the sanatorium."

"Yes, sir."

"Here's the last leg," Lars said as he came through the brush at the edge of the ravine. "Should be the last of it, but it's pretty torn up."

"From an animal?"

Lars opened the sack. "No, sir. Crushed, it looks like. Maybe from the accident yesterday?"

Dubric examined the pulpy mess of bone, muscle, and torn skin. Although the lower leg was irreparably mangled, the thigh was severed cleanly above the knee with the same smooth incisions he had seen on the dismembered animals and the man's other remains. "Tie it to my horse," Dubric said. Why was that limb alone severed mid-bone, when all of the others were separated at a joint?

* * *

Dubric strode down the sanatorium's west hall with Lars beside him. The double triangle symbol was inlaid on the floor, etched on the corners of glass panes, even molded on the door latches, and he chided himself for never noticing them before. "Open the bonding on your sword," he whispered.

"But, sir, we're in a public place, a hospital . . ."

"Do it."

They passed through a set of double doors and startled a brown-skinned woman at a desk. "Lord Byerly! Is it you?" she asked, beaming. "You're moons early. What brings you here today?"

He wanted to say, *Death*, but instead he forced a smile. "Business." He wished he could remember her name.

"Of course," she said, quickly stacking some papers and setting them aside. "We've been most appreciative of your stipend every moon."

Dubric cleared his throat, and the woman—*Weirta?*—stood.

"If you've come to see Elena, I'll take you to her, but don't expect a friendly welcome."

"I would not expect to be welcomed." *At least Elena will tell me the truth. I hope.* He resisted the urge to look at Lars. "Take me to her."

Weirta turned down a side hall to a heavy door, which she unlocked to let Dubric into a dim hall.

"We've had to separate her from most of the other patients," Weirta said, pushing aside a cart of soiled linen.

"Are her seizures still severe?"

"Yes, milord, and she's also become quite violent."

"Who's Elena?" Lars asked.

"A woman I tried to help, a long time ago."

Weirta continued down the hall in her brusque gait, to a set of double doors. She pushed them open, and the scent of porridge and toast mingled with the foul sanatorium stench as Dubric followed her into a wide, open room where several patients were eating, tended by a few nurses and orderlies.

Weirta stopped and indicated a table with three women in patient gowns. One dark-haired, one blonde, and one gray, all thirty summers old or so. The three ate without talking to one another. The blonde was twitching, her left hand curled into a twisted clench and jumping upward in random spasms. The dark-haired woman jerked her head to the side over and over as if constantly startled. The gray-haired woman merely ate her porridge with her back to them.

"Elena?" Dubric said, approaching the table.

The gray-haired woman turned and licked her lips. She had no teeth, or eyes, and scabby gouges streaked her face. "Who's come to see you, El?" she asked, sniffing. "Smells like a man."

The blonde's eyes widened for a moment, then she frowned and returned to her breakfast. Her left hand leapt up, then slammed down again, rattling the dishes. "Just the bastard who brought me here. He's too old for you. Probably can't get it up no more."

"Pah!" the eyeless woman said. "What good's that?"

"None," Elena said. Her head and left shoulder twitched back in a violent series of sudden jerks.

"I would like to talk to you," Dubric said softly.

"Well, I don't want to talk to you," Elena said. She jerked to her feet and staggered away, limping.

"Stay here," Dubric said to Lars. He followed Elena across the room, wincing every time a spasm wracked her body. "Please," he said, reaching for her. "It may be important."

"Get your pegging hands off me, you old shit," she snarled, turning. Her right hand whipped out and grabbed his throat above the larynx, her fingernails barely digging in, then she leaned close to snarl in his face. "I was fine, perfectly pegging fine, until you decided to come find me."

"You were a child, a prostitute," Dubric said, holding out his hand to stop Lars, who had immediately stepped forward to assist him. "I tried to help you."

"You lying shit. It's your fault I have these seizures." She squeezed, her nails gouging his flesh. "You dumped me here almost sixteen summers ago, old man. Left me here to rot. Why should I talk to you instead of ripping out your lying throat?"

Attendants came toward them but Dubric barked out, "Stay back!" He felt tremors shudder through her body, saw the rage in her slate-gray eyes. "Because your father would want you to," he whispered. "And I never forgot you. Have I ever missed your birthing day?"

She growled, baring her teeth, then pushed him away.

Four attendants rushed past him and shoved Elena against the wall as Dubric struggled to keep his balance.

"Sir, are you all right?" Lars asked.

"I am fine." Dubric strode forward. "Release her. Now."

"But, milord!" Weirta winced as an attendant slumped to his knees, the corner of his mouth split by deep scratches. "She's dangerous."

Dubric dropped his hand to his sword. "I said, release her!"

"Let her go!" Weirta commanded. The remaining attendants, all bleeding, backed away.

Her back against the wall, Elena panted, glaring. "What do you want?"

"Where can we talk?" Dubric asked.

Her gaze shifted to Lars, resting on him for a long moment as her expression eased into calm boredom. "All right," she said, looking to Dubric again. "We can talk in my room."

Without waiting for his response, she turned and limped away, her left side shuddering.

* * *

Elena led them to a whitewashed private room with a single bed on a plain stone floor. In the corner, an assortment of toiletries were spread over a tall bureau topped with a chipped mirror; a small chest by the bed held a tin of tobacco, a stained china cup, and a comb on top.

"Home sweet home," Elena said as she sat on the bed. She scooped a finger of tobacco from the tin and tucked it behind her lower lip. "Talk," she said as she reached for the cup.

"We are investigating matters that may concern the sanatorium."

Elena leaned back against the wall and spat brown fluid into the cup. "Why should I care?" Her right knee came up and she rested her arm on it. The left kicked forward, twitching, and she drew it up as well.

Dubric could see everything to her navel. He sighed. Sixteen summers off the Waterford streets had not changed a thing. "At least cover yourself."

She smirked, and glanced at Lars before returning her attention to Dubric. "The kid's a quiet 'un." She spat, then licked tobacco juice from her lower lip. "Won't even look at me. I could be a busted wheel or a cooked cabbage, for all he cares."

Lars said, "I'm not here to gawk at naked women, ma'am."

"Ah," she said, an amused smile twitching on her face. "And I bet you're housebroke, too." She spit again. "So, Byr, ol' boy, now that we've all met, why'd you ruin my day?"

"I need information about what happens here."

She smiled. "Every day's full of revelry and song. We play jesters on holy days, dance naked in the halls, and put kittens in frilly dresses."

"This is not a laughing matter, Elena. Two people have been murdered."

She smoothed her sleeping gown demurely and pulled her knees together. "Why you asking me? I ain't killed no one." She gave him a bright and twitching grin. "Lately."

Dubric said, "Have you met Physician Garrett?"

"Randy Goat? Hells, yes. Any woman here who isn't

chair-busting fat has met him, probably been groped by him."

"He gropes his patients?" Lars asked.

"Any skirt he can, and I hear there are a lot of them."

Dubric asked, "What medical procedures does he perform?"

She spat into her cup and chuckled. "There you are, asking me tricky questions." Grinning, she looked up at Dubric and Lars. "You see, there are procedures, then there are *procedures*."

"Would you care to explain?"

She shrugged. "He does all the regular things physicians do, as far as I can tell, especially if it means he can dump a vial of nasty tonic down your throat or pinch a bosom."

"Does he do surgeries? Set bones? Put in stitches?"

"What good would he be if he didn't?"

"I am not asking what good he is, I am asking what he does."

She leaned forward. "Word is, he medicates some of the female patients, sometimes they're so limp they piss themselves. He's laid with nearly every female member of the staff." She looked at Lars and winked. "Rumors say ol' Randy Goat's great with his hands, leaves a lot to be desired in the sheets. All tease, no delivery. Where's the fun in that?" She leaned back again and shrugged. "That's what he does. He tried his game with me and I quoted my price. He hasn't bothered me since."

Dubric sighed and rubbed his eyes before continuing his notes. As much as he hated to admit it, murders and potential mage presence outweighed possible rape and coercion. "Has he performed many surgeries that you are aware of?"

"Some," she said. "I heard some nobleman's son had a rupture in his guts. Garrett patched him up, *then* made him swallow the tonic." She fidgeted uneasily. "Damn, he loves his tonics."

"Does anyone else do surgeries?" Lars asked.

Elena shifted her gaze to him. "I suppose so. I hear there's a group of nurses who do the routine injuries, sores, things like that. Probably so Randy Goat can chase his skirts." She looked back at Dubric. "He kill one of his girlies?"

"I do not yet know," Dubric said, then closed his notebook and looked at Lars. "Find the administrator. Ask about the injured workers, and learn if any have died mysteriously. I will find you shortly."

Lars nodded then left, closing the door behind him.

"Are you doing well? Is your care adequate?" Dubric asked once he and Elena were alone.

She spat in her cup and shrugged. "Could be worse." She drew a heavy breath. "That him?"

Dubric met her stare. "Yes."

She licked her twitching lips and looked away. "You raise him as your own?"

"No. He was adopted into a family."

"He looks like my brother Marcus."

"And your father, when he was that age." Dubric sat on the edge of her bed. "He does not know."

"Good," she said. "Maybe it'll keep him alive." She sniffled, wiping her nose with the back of her shuddering hand. "That's why you had to speak to me, ain't it? So I'd see him? You'd have learned about Garrett easily enough without me."

He bowed his head. "Actually, my reports on Garrett

have conflicted and I trusted your insights into the truth. I also thought it a good opportunity to see you, milady."

"You always were a charmer," she said, her eyebrow lifted in sarcasm. "What else you want?"

He opened his notebook and showed her the double triangle symbol. "Have you seen this?"

"You're joking, right?" She rolled her eyes and pointed to her door. The brass latch had the symbol molded in.

"No, no," he said. "Have you seen it anywhere that is not architectural? On a person, perhaps? A vial of medicine?"

"Not that I can think of, but I see it so much I might not notice."

"What of rumors?" he asked. "Have there been any whispers? Any unusual happenings?"

Elena stared at the ceiling for a long time. At last she nodded. "One thing, but I dunno if it matters, or if it's even true."

Dubric prepared his pencil.

She spat tobacco in the cup. "Couple of phases ago I heard that one of the mental patients woke up missing his arm. Was there when they sent him to bed, was gone the next morning. Nothing there but a bump."

"His arm?"

She nodded. "It wasn't the first thing like that I'd heard. One of the girls upstairs, few moons back, the same thing happened, only it was her foot. Least that's what I heard. Was just gone, removed about mid-shin. They say there wasn't even a scar."

"You might as well tell him," Marsden said, leaning his shoulder against the wall. "Save us all a lot of trouble."

"There isn't anything to tell!" Tupper's voice faded to a squeal and his feet twitched, swinging free.

Dien held Tupper against the wall, his hand wrapped around Tupper's throat, supporting the smaller man by the underside of his jaw. "Don't lie to me." Dien smiled as he raised Tupper a little higher. "You told Arien you'd left that head for her. I want to know where it came from." He glanced at Marsden. "You think a couple of busted fingers might help him remember?"

Marsden frowned as if considering the idea, then nodded. "They might. I'd start with the thumbs. Can't grip anything without a working thumb. Can't eat, can't piss like a man . . ."

Dien reached for Tupper's shackled hands. "Thumbs, it is."

"No, wait!" Tupper squirmed and struggled to keep his hands away from Dien. He looked at Marsden and squealed as Dien grabbed a thumb, then choked out, "Calder! Remember, back when we were kids, how we used to dowse for caves, and found that one to twiddle off in, down by Sutter's pasture?"

Marsden pushed away from the wall and stood beside Dien. "Yes."

Tupper flinched as Dien bent his thumb a little farther. "It was there. They all were. Buckets and barrels of the damn things. I just took one to scare her. I swear, Calder, you have to believe me! You never gave me a chance to tell you before!"

Dien gave Tupper's thumb a firm press, just to the edge of snapping the joint, and glanced at Marsden. "You know this place? Where it is?"

"Yes, I do," Marsden said.

"And, and . . . you're not going to believe this," Tupper said, frantic, as he looked between the two men, "but it's absolutely true. Swear on my mam's life."

Marsden crossed his arms over his chest. "Your mother died summers ago."

"I know, it's just a saying, but . . . eeehh!"

Dien felt the joint start to give and he eased up, just a hair.

"But I tell you, I *swear*, most of those heads were alive! I swear! That sheep head was still moving when I got to Arien's. I swear!"

Dien released his grip on Tupper's throat, then, once Tupper was on his feet, forcibly threw him into his cell.

* * *

"You're wasting your time," Kia said. "He's not coming."

Jess tore her gaze from the window to see Kia standing by Cailin's crib, holding the baby. Without bothering to acknowledge her sister, Jess turned back to her view of the coming evening. Still no riders, no Dad and no Lars—just people scurrying about, preparing for the faire. She had no intention of reasoning with Kia, not after her last attempt. If Kia couldn't be polite, why endure the aggravation?

Patting Cailin's back for a burp, Kia came up behind Jess. "If there's some sort of horrible job to be done, he'll do it rather than come home to see you, you know that."

Jess ground her teeth, trying to hold her tongue. Eventually her irritation won. "Doing a good job isn't something to be ashamed of," she said. "It's the same as Dad does."

Kia snorted and stepped away, rocking the baby in an oddly protective manner. "He's not worth your time," she snapped. "He acts like your brother, not your suitor. And if there's a choice, you know he won't pick you." In her arms, Cailin burped and looked around, her plump little fists waving about.

"Why don't you just go back to your room and sulk?" Jess suggested helpfully. She looked out the window again, trying to ignore the mocking words. She wished Kia would get her own suitor and stop worrying about her and Lars.

"He's using you," Kia said. "You think he'll settle for you once he gets what he wants? Once he sucks up to his father enough to go home, he'll take his title and leave you behind. He doesn't even want you. He won't kiss you because you don't do it for him. And besides, nobles never, ever settle for commoner girls."

Cailin twitched, asleep at last. "We'll prove you wrong," Jess said. "He loves me."

"High nobles do choose commoners," Maeve said as she came from the hall. "Dubric chose me."

"See?" Jess said.

Kia laid Cailin into her bed with a smug smile. "That's different. Sorry, Aunt Maeve, but Dubric is old, and he doesn't even have any real power around here, not even his own lands."

"Ah, yes." Maeve sat and smoothed her skirt. "But Dubric was young when he first married, and she was a commoner, too."

"That's right," Jess said. "She came from a Klandian village. Her father was an indentured field worker, almost a slave."

Maeve looked at Jess. "How do you know that?"

"I've been reading her journals for a couple of days. From that trunk of books Dubric gave me." Jess glanced at Kia. "See? It's not impossible."

Kia scoffed. "Whatever. Don't disturb the baby with all your pointless pacing." She swept out of the room, her head held high.

"Since when do you care about the baby?" Jess muttered.

"What else do you know about her?" Maeve asked. "Dubric's wife, I mean."

"When she was about ten, a bard came through the village and took her as an apprentice. If he hadn't, she probably would've been a field worker, too. She was thirteen when she joined King Romlin's army, fourteen when she killed her first mage—"

"Not her history," Maeve interrupted. "Her."

Jess hesitated. "She wrote odd poetry, maybe they were songs, I dunno. She liked bugs, especially crickets. Apples made her sick, so she never ate them. Her favorite color was blue. She always wore pants, absolutely hated skirts. She was pretty, in a southerner sort of way. Tall and skinny; long, almost black, straight hair; exotic eyes, sort of tilted—"

"That can't be right," Maeve said, leaning back and shaking her head. "She was blonde, fair . . ."

"No she wasn't," Jess said. "Honest. I've seen her."

Maeve's hands clenched into the arms of the chair as if she were trying to rip them off. "What? How? How could you have seen her?"

"There's a picture, a ferrotype, of her and Dubric. It was in the trunk with her journals and things. I can show you, if you want."

"You're sure, Jess, *certain*, that she's not blonde?"

"Yes. She's definitely a southerner, just like Trahern, Lord Brushgar's carriage driver. Have you met him?"

"He drove us to Falliet to get the last of my things."

"Same coloring, same tilted eyes, same tall, skinny frame. A southerner."

Maeve pushed up to her feet and bolted for the privy room.

Before Jess could follow, she heard Maeve retch, then vomit.

* * *

Dubric walked down the main hall, looking for Lars, while patients milled about or languished in their wards.

"Where am I? Who are you?" a young dark-haired patient asked, struggling with a pair of nurses in a ward. He looked about, frantic, then screamed as they shoved him back onto the bed and strapped him down.

"Sir!" Dubric turned to see Lars hurrying toward him. "We brought eleven men in with severe injuries yesterday. Nine are still here, plus two more who came in earlier today to get their infected wounds looked at. I had Arien and another nurse, Peigi, take me to them all. Most are sleeping. I didn't see a reason to wake them."

"What of the two missing?"

Lars consulted his notes. "Records show they both died of head injuries. Yaunel Derk shortly after arrival, and Thom Higgle today. Supposedly passed on in his sleep. I asked about that, and Arien said no one had expected him to wake. His head was too damaged."

"And their bodies?"

"Neither man had family, so they were taken to the pyre in the cellar. I had them show me the oven, and it's sealed, still burning."

Then there are no remains to examine. "They are the only two missing? You are certain?"

"Yes, sir. Just the two. I've confirmed it."

Dubric looked at both spectral severed heads, especially the facial injuries of the newest ghost. "Despite his grim prognosis, Mister Higgle may have been murdered. Who authorized the rapid disposal of his body?"

"Jerle Dughall, sir." Lars closed his notebook. "And Garrett was his surgeon."

* * *

"How far are we from that sorghum field?" Dien asked, pulling a lantern from his saddle before descending to a creek bed to visit the cave Tupper had directed them to.

"It's just over there." Marsden pointed across the creek and over the far bank. "The field on the other side of those trees."

"Have we been down this creek before?"

"No. It feeds into the bigger creek a bit past where we climbed up to the sorghum field." He looked at Dien and shrugged. "We have a lot of little caves and old storm cellars around here. I didn't even think about this one being so close."

Dien sighed. "The road's right there and the town's, what, maybe a quarter mile away?"

"As the crow flies, yes," Marsden said. "Maybe half a mile south by road. It crosses over there with the road we took to Woodley's, and we dismounted maybe fifty, seventy lengths farther up when we smelled all the dead animals that first night."

"All nice and cozy," Dien said, sketching the basic map while, beside him, Marsden lit the lantern. He led Dien a few steps away to an overhanging mass of old roots and knelt to peer into the shadows beneath.

Dien knelt beside him. "No time like right now," he said, pushing roots aside. Lantern lighting the way, he crawled in and down to a stone-and-mud-lined pit, about fifteen lengths on a side. It was just tall enough to stand in, with roots and mossy strands hanging from the ceiling. Three half barrels and several old buckets lay empty and overturned, slick with slime that had spread to coat much of the floor.

Marsden slipped and grabbed a root to catch himself. "We're too late. Everything's gone."

"Looks like it." Dien knelt and filled a specimen vial from a puddle in an upright bucket. "You have a cooper in town? Someone who might have made these?"

Marsden flipped a barrel over. "Yes, we have a cooper, but these aren't his. They've got the lord's mark."

"And there are thousands of them around the province." Dien walked about, searching, and found footprints that seemed to match those in the ditch leading to the sorghum field. He found a pair of empty bottles, which he placed in evidence bags, and, beneath an overturned barrel, he saw a shimmer of metal reflecting lantern light.

He knelt, wiping mud away, then yelped and yanked his hand back. Cursing as he wrapped his bleeding fingers with his kerchief, he nudged the metal thing with the toe of his boot until he unearthed it from the mud.

A surgical knife.

* * *

"What's all this about?" Jerle Dughall burst into Garrett's treatment room. "One of my nurses informed me you barged in here with your sword out."

Dubric glanced over his shoulder. "Your physician had his sword out. I did not."

Garrett fastened his trousers and scowled at Dubric. "I am off duty and my personal affairs are none of your concern. As I keep telling you, they have nothing to do with this Mister Higgle you insist on asking me about."

"Higgle?" Jerle asked, closing the door to a cabinet Lars was searching. "What does this have to do with him?"

"I understand that he died," Dubric said.

"Yes," Jerle said. "From injuries sustained in the accident." Frowning at Lars's continuing search, Jerle pushed the boy aside and slammed a drawer closed. "Is this just an excuse to snoop?"

"You may not have heard," Dubric said, "but partial human remains were found today. Remains that showed evidence of medical attention."

Jerle glanced at Garrett. "What sort of medical attention? Bandages? Stitches? A splint?"

"Surgical dismemberment," Dubric said.

Jerle coughed. "Surgical dismemberment! That's a term I've never heard before." He chuckled, shaking his head. "Go on home, Shelby. I'll handle this."

"He cannot leave. I am questioning him."

Jerle strode between Dubric and Garrett. "I am his

employer and I decide when he can leave." He paused to motion Garrett toward the door. "If you have questions, you ask me, no one else. I won't have you badgering my staff the way you do my son."

Dubric seethed as Garrett slipped away.

After Garrett left, Jerle closed the door and leaned against it. "Whoever's remains you found, they're not Higgle's. He died this morning and I had his remains incinerated not long after lunch, along with some of the other deceased victims of the accident. If rumors are accurate, your 'surgically dismembered' remains were found well before his death, if not his incineration. You're chasing smoke and getting no closer to finding who has stolen my sheep."

"Why were you in such a hurry to have his remains destroyed?" Dubric asked.

"Higgle was a shoddy worker at best, a drunk, and had no one to mourn him. He stank up my quarry. I saw no reason for him to stink up my sanatorium. To be frank, I was astounded he lived till morning with the damage to his head. We can't save everyone, and severe injuries kill people sometimes. That's the nature of this business."

Dubric noted the information. "Among your staff, who performs surgical procedures? Even minor ones?"

"Every nurse is trained for simple wound care and repair within her first season of service. A few expand their skills for minor surgeries, such as removing boils or gangrenous flesh, and we have several who aid in emergencies, like yesterday's. Planned and internal surgeries are strictly the responsibility of my physician."

* * *

"Where is it? What have you done?"

Maeve rocked Cailin and tried not to flinch. She felt

cool breath in her ear, heard the words like a whisper in the middle of her head. She wondered if she was going mad. *This is ridiculous. Whoever or whatever that ghost is, it's not Oriana, I should just go home. Let Sarea's family settle in without my madness. They have enough problems of their own.*

Though the loss of her son was still a fresh laceration across her heart, with Dubric's help Maeve had been able to function, to stop herself thinking about Braoin all of the time. But her sister's family hadn't healed from Aly's death. Their suite no longer rang with the dramatics of adolescent girls that she had become accustomed to over the summers—Fyn and Kia, especially, and their mindless squabbling over dresses and baubles and hair and boys. Instead, Fyn was distant and quiet, Kia sullen and occasionally malicious, and Jess, usually by far the quietest of the three, paced restlessly about the rooms, full of nervous energy. Even Oriana's old journals could not hold her attention for long.

Jess had shown Maeve a passage where Oriana had written a rambling grievance against her straight black hair and bronze skin, and another against the restrictions of corsets and skirts. Even without the proof of the ferrotype, Maeve realized that Oriana was nothing at all like the beautiful, finely dressed female ghost she had seen in their suite.

Maeve rocked in the chair, holding back tears. *Dubric was right all along. The whispers in my head, the spirit that I've seen, it's not Oriana. It's me, just me, going mad.* She looked down at baby Cailin, so innocent and sweet, and tried to smile. But she remembered rocking her own child, and his sweetness hadn't saved him from being murdered by a madman. Maybe the wounds were not healing so well, after all.

She wondered if she truly was pregnant again. Perhaps that, too, was madness, or grief over her son.

Then the voice came back, in her ear, in her head. "You have to get it back!"

Her hands shaking, Maeve stood. "I think I'll go back home," she said as she returned Cailin to her crib. "See if I can get some work done."

Jess, who had been lying on the settee and staring at the ceiling, sat up. "You're welcome to stay."

Maeve looked down at the sleeping baby. "I should go."

"Mind if I come along?" Jess asked, bouncing to her feet.

"Of course not," Maeve said. "The company might do me good."

* * *

Jess struggled to hold Lachesis, yowling and squirming in her arms, and she noticed her aunt's hand shaking as Maeve opened her suite door. "Want me to go first?"

Maeve smiled. "No. I'm all right."

Jess smelled fresh plaster and paint in the air as they stepped inside. "Smells like they're almost done." She let Lachesis slip from her arms.

"Yes. There's some plumbing to finish after the faire, and the furniture to arrive, but the carpenters should be nearly finished."

Jess peeked into the new area. "It's going to be gorgeous."

Maeve sighed. "I've been such a fool. The mirror's probably locked in the privy room, right where Dubric left it."

"I'm sure it is," Jess said. "You've had so many changes lately, and Dubric can't be the easiest person to live with."

"He's fine," Maeve said, looking away. "I've been a fool about that, too."

"About Dubric?" Jess asked, worried. They'd seemed so happy.

"He's asked me to marry him four times," Maeve said. "And I won't answer him even though I know full well how improper all this is, how it must affect his reputation." She pulled a handkerchief from her sleeve. "Here I go again. What's wrong with me?"

"Nothing." Jess put her arm around Maeve's shoulder and led her to a chair. "It's been hard, I know, since Braoin died, then coming here, with Dubric, and everything."

"He's a good man," Maeve said, dabbing at her eyes.

"Yes, he is."

"I love him, and I know he loves me."

Jess just nodded, letting Maeve talk.

"But, see . . ." Maeve sniffled and stared at the doorway to the new suite. "I thought . . . I thought he still loved her, too, Oriana, even though he said he didn't. Then when I saw her, thought it was her . . . Goddess!"

"He loves you," Jess said, hugging her aunt. "Everyone can see it and we've all been so happy for both of you."

"Not everyone," Maeve muttered with a wry smile. "I heard a rumor that Lord Brushgar refers to me as Dubric's rag maker."

"Lord Brushgar's an ass," Jess said. "He thinks women aren't fit for anything but birthing male children and that commoners should all kiss his scabby feet."

Maeve chuckled, stealing a sideways glance. "Scabby feet?"

"Yep. I've seen them. Sometimes I run errands for Dad and I had to deliver our illustrious lord some papers once. He was sleeping in his office with his bare feet up and oozing on his desk." She rolled her eyes. "Have you seen his office? It's a pigsty of papers and junk. It's as awful as his feet." Jess shook her head. "It's just the way he is. Don't let him bother you."

"I'll try," Maeve said. She blew her nose, looking a little cheerier. "Do you want to see what the carpenters did today?"

"Of course," Jess said.

Each carrying a light, they walked into the new suite. Jess spun around, holding the lantern high, amazed at what a difference new plaster and paint could make.

"Kia's jealous of you and Lars," Maeve said as they walked to the main entryway.

"I wonder about that sometimes." Jess picked a bit of plaster from the floor and tossed it aside. "Before we started courting, she used to throw herself at him. I'm pretty sure she wanted him for herself."

They continued to the sitting room and admired the light reflecting in the polished floor. "Not just that," Maeve said. "She's jealous of your happiness because she'll never have it. Few do. Cherish it, Jess. It's rarer than you might think. That boy loves you with every breath of his life. Everyone sees it, even your sister. Give him time. I'm sure he'll make you very happy."

Jess felt her face get hot, remembering Lars flinching away every time he got close. "Time? Time for what?"

"Time to realize it's all right to relax, mostly," Maeve

said as they moved to her studio. "I knew when Bray was struggling with love. Lars is struggling, too, I think. Sometimes it's scarier for young men than they let on."

"I just wish he'd kiss me," Jess said. "We've come close . . ." She shrugged. It seemed so hard to explain.

"He will. Don't rush him." Maeve nudged her and winked. "He did pick you, after all, not Kia."

Jess laughed. "That's true." She walked on to the bedchamber area, her lantern held high so she could see the ceiling. She looked up to the almost completed mural, rolling hills and sky, then stopped when she heard Maeve's gasp.

"What? What's wrong?"

Maeve pointed past Jess.

The mirror stood in the far corner, reflecting their images and lantern lights back at them. Jess saw movement in the depths of the glass, a reflected shadow, probably from the swing of her lantern, then it was gone. She took a step toward it, squinting. Something made a noise, a rapid series of clicks, like a spider spinning a beetle in its web, then it fell silent.

"Don't you see it?" Maeve asked.

"Just you and me," Jess said, moving closer as she examined the worn frame, touching some of the figures carved onto the surface. *Is this Nuobir's mirror? The one Oriana walked through?*

"Look, Jess. For Goddess's sake, step away and look!"

"What?" Jess asked, looking into the glass, at her own reflection.

Her eyes glowed white.

CHAPTER

11

Maeve ran ahead and opened the bath chamber door. "Goddess, Jess, be careful."

"I am," Jess grunted, waddling forward blindly. As tall as she was and wider than her shoulders, the mirror was heavier than it looked. She took a few steps, then set it down to catch her breath. She took a couple of breaths, waiting for the quaking in her arms to subside, then she gripped the mirror again and inched forward.

Her cheek pressed against the glass, she smelled the faint aroma of plums, mint, and wet ash.

Might be my imagination. She set the mirror down again. *But I doubt it.* She tried to ignore her reflection. Seeing her eyes glow as if a lantern burned behind them made her dizzy. She had no idea what the light meant, if it meant anything at all, or if the mirror was trying to trick her. But she was convinced the thing had to be locked away before Maeve broke down completely.

Jess finally wrestled the mirror into the bath chamber, then she stepped back to assess her image. The whites of her eyes still glowed, and her pupils reflected every glimmer of light, as bright as a beacon.

White-eyed or not, it was her. Too tall, dark curly hair and fading freckles, long dark blue skirt and tan blouse. Her chin, her brow. Her.

And behind, near the archway, Maeve's terrified face.

Jess slammed the door, then locked it with a key. She tried to lift the latch. Definitely locked. "Get a chair," she said, glancing at Maeve.

She heard a soft clacking sound that rapidly increased in volume.

clackclackclackclack clackclack

The latch jiggled. Jess held it still, bearing down, then skipped out of the way in horror as swampy water seeped out from beneath the door. The clacks turned to a low, chattery hiss, then became louder again. The key started to turn. Jess yanked it out, her hands sweaty. "I need that chair!"

clackclack clackclackclackclack clack

Huffing, Maeve hurried to her with the chair, an ornate carved monstrosity. "All the others seemed too tall," she said.

Jess slammed the chair beneath the latch and backed toward Maeve. The door jiggled, but held.

clackclackclackclack

Then silence.

"Get what you need," Jess said. "You're not sleeping here tonight."

* * *

"How many people are left to question?" Dubric asked, finishing off the last mouthful of his supper.

Lars chewed as he flipped through the notes. "Just two, it looks like. The butchers."

Dubric pushed his plate away. "I hope they are not a

waste of our precious time. The surgical knife in the cave leads us back to the sanatorium, not butchers, but I dare not leave any lead untended." He sipped his ale and looked at Lars. "Tomorrow morning, while Dien and I talk to Garrett's female companions, I want you to meet with the first butcher on the list."

"Can't do it, sir." Lars stabbed a chunk of pork with his fork.

"Why not?"

Lars swallowed. "Because I'm going to be at the faire."

"We are in the midst of a murder investigation, potentially involving a mage."

"I know that, sir."

Dien and Marsden looked at each other but said nothing.

"You are not attending the faire."

Lars kept eating. "Yes I am."

"I think I need another ale." Marsden pushed his chair from the table and walked to the bar.

Dubric tried to remain calm. *Insubordination? From Lars?* At last he said, "I know you look forward to the festivities every spring, but we have other obligations."

"Actually, sir, I've never attended the faire. I'm always working. Gathering drunks, most often, sometimes cutpurses. Once, you had me patrol the livestock, just in case someone decided to steal a sheep. This will be my first real faire." Lars set down his fork. "I know this is important, but I made a promise. You'll have to manage without me."

"You are a vital part of my team," Dubric said, "and your first duty, your only duty, is to me."

"Sir, I've been your page for six full summers. Not once in all that time have I asked for a single indulgence.

Not once have I taken a holiday or shirked my duties. I've risked my life countless times, have done every deed asked of me. I've been injured and exhausted and worse, all for you and Faldorrah and my duty, but I made a promise to the woman I love that I will spend all of tomorrow with her. Before I made that pledge, I asked your permission and you gave it. You made a promise to me, sir."

"Circumstances were different when I made that promise."

Lars stared Dubric in the eye. "I know that when you agreed, we had no murders or mages, and now we do, but that's not my fault. I've busted my ass out here since this started. I haven't spent one moment with Jess for two days. *Two days,* sir. You and Dien will get to sleep beside your women tonight. Jess and I don't get that. There's no chance I'll be home by ten. Today is gone from us, forever. I won't lose tomorrow, too."

"Lars, we have at least two dead people. Murdered people. We may face a blood mage, for King's sake. I need assistants who are trained to recognize and connect whatever small clues the killer may let slip, who are trained to face whatever madness will come. I need *you.*"

"I know that, sir, but it doesn't matter."

Dubric glanced at the two ghosts. "Does not matter?"

"Not this time, sir. I'm officially off duty from midnight tonight until dawn the morning after the faire, as per our agreement." He looked at Dien. "That's the curfew you set for Jess. You said she could stay at the dance until it ended at dawn."

"I remember," Dien said, glowering.

Lars looked back at Dubric. "It's not just the dance,

sir. It's keeping my word. I will not disappoint Jess. She has a dress for the dance, I've made arrangements, have plans . . . all because you swore I could have the day. You are not a liar, sir, and neither am I."

"I should have trained you to be an advocate," Dubric muttered, staring into his ale. "But it is not a matter of lies or truth."

"You're right, sir. It's not. It's a matter of life and death. Mine. As long as I've worked for you, whenever you talk about the war you mention the boys that died under your command. Fourteen-, fifteen-summers-old boys. I'm one of them, sir, and it's quite possible that I'll die while serving you. I know that, and I can face that. But what of my life? What life, what joy have I ever had?"

Lars's hands shook as he stared at Dubric. "I love Jess, sir. I intend to marry her, make a home, raise a family. If we keep stumbling across mages, I might not be able to do that. If that happens I won't lose it all, I can't, and I won't let you or anyone else take one little faire away from us. One dance. One damned kiss. For Goddess's sake, sir, I've never even gathered the courage to kiss her. At least let me do that. Let me have one day of my life for myself, for us. One chance to show Jess I love her."

Dubric lowered his head and nodded, unable to speak.

Dien opened and closed his mouth a few times. "You've never *kissed* her?"

Lars looked at Dien as if he had just realized he was there, and shifted nervously in his seat. "No. I . . . We . . ." He swallowed. "We've been courting long enough and I thought, surely, at the dance, with all the other couples, it would be okay to—"

"It's fine," Dien said, his fingertips digging against the wood of the table. "I should have known, damn it to the seven hells, I should have known."

"Known what?" Lars asked.

"Never mind." Dien stood and fished a few coins from his pocket to dump on the table. Grumbling, he walked to the door and out to the night.

Lars swallowed, watching him go. "What did I do?"

"Nothing," Dubric said. "Nothing except command our respect and force us to look at what is important."

Lars sighed. "It's just one day, sir."

"Yes, it is." Dubric just hoped it would not be one day too long.

* * *

Lars came outside and saw Dien leaning against the tavern wall, glowering. "Did I do something to upset you?"

Dien looked to the sky. "No. Forget about it."

"Not sure I should," Lars said. "You've been trying to get me to admit to something, but I can't figure out what." He walked in front of Dien and tried to catch his gaze. "I've done everything I can to obey your rules and curfews, remain a gentleman, be good to her, and if you have a problem—"

Dien winced and turned his head away. "No problem."

Lars moved back into Dien's line of sight. "If I've done something, said something, hells, even *thought* something—"

Dien clenched his fists and turned away. "Not now."

Lars followed. "Yes, now. If you have a problem working with me, I need to know. I can't do this anymore.

"You've barely looked at me since Aly died. Barely talked to me, even while we're working. You think I failed you, failed her. Fine. I can respect that. You hate looking at me, that's fine, too. But it doesn't change how I feel about Jess."

Dien started to say something, but Lars cut him off.

"Let's assume we survive this mage. If I'm going to someday have to support Jess and our family, then, honestly, I'm not willing to deal with your temper at work all day *and* in our personal life. One or the other is bad enough."

"It's not that," Dien said.

"Then what is it? Every time I mention her you get angry. What in the seven hells do you want me to do?" Lars pointed to the alehouse door. "Want me out of your sight? I'll go right back in and resign. I'll do any damned thing you want, except stop seeing Jess."

"I don't want you to stop seeing Jess."

"Could've fooled me," Lars muttered. "You want to hit me? Want to knock my teeth in because I admit to loving your daughter? Or is it because you still blame me for what happened to Aly?"

"No. And it's not Aly either, not really. I know you did everything possible, probably more than anyone else could."

Lars felt his throat tighten. "I would've died to save her."

Dien bowed his head, his eyes glistening. "I know. I remind myself of that most days, that you, of all people, would have moved the heavens to save her. It wasn't your fault. I miss her, but it's not your fault and I don't blame you."

"Then, what?" Lars asked. "What did I do?"

"Nothing," Dien said, sighing. "I thought you had,

but I was wrong. I should've known better, but I was thinking as a father, not as someone who knows you."

Lars frowned, confused. "What did you think I did?"

Dien grumbled under his breath and ran his hand over his head. "I thought you were afraid to tell me she was pregnant."

What? Lars took a step back, shaking his head. "Why would you think that? I've never even touched her."

"I know, pup, I know," Dien sighed.

"And even if I had, even if *we* had, I'd take responsibility for our child and marry her."

"I'd expect nothing less." Dien shook his head. "I heard something, Jess and Fyn, talking . . . I must have been wrong." He frowned, a thick furrow forming between his eyes.

Lars swallowed. He could see Dien was thinking through the idea testing the logic. If he'd been mistaken about Jess, then maybe . . .

Fyn. Lars wished that he could tell Dien—he was a good father and he deserved to know the truth—but it wasn't his secret to share. Lars took a step toward him, hoping to distract Dien and make his own intentions clear. "I'm going to ask Jess to be my intended tomorrow, and if Dubric doesn't get me killed, we'll get betrothed, get married, and, Goddess willing, have children. That means that I'm going to kiss her and, someday, we'll do more than hold hands."

Dien nodded, staring at Lars's knees.

"I love her and parts of our life will be private. Knowing that, are you going to be able to work with me?"

Dien raised his eyes and met Lars's steady gaze. He looked slightly sick, but his eyes no longer held the anger Lars had seen in them the past few phases. "Yes," Dien said at last. "You're a good man, the best I know, and there's no one I'd rather have as a son-in-law. Just . . . not yet, all right? Let her be my baby a bit longer?"

Lars relaxed, smiling slightly. "I can do that."

Dien grasped Lars's offered hand, then pulled him forward, into a quick embrace. "We're all right, pup. I promise."

Lars hugged him back. "Good."

"Just one thing," Dien said, releasing Lars. "If Dubric's right and it all goes wrong out here tomorrow, don't come looking for us, and don't try to be a hero. You take my family and get out of Faldorrah."

"What?"

"You heard me, pup. You take them and you run. Swear to me."

"Dien, I . . . I can't. I have a duty, I made a promise."

Dien looked him in the eye. "If Dubric and I are dead, your duty is to our family and your promise is to Jess. You protect my girls. Get them somewhere safe."

Lars nodded, hesitantly at first, then more surely. "Okay."

The door behind Dien opened and Dubric and Marsden stepped through. "Is there a problem?"

"No problem, sir," Dien said, patting Lars on the back. "Just settling some things."

* * *

It was late when Dubric and his men arrived at the castle stables. Yawning, Dubric dismounted and reached for the bag of parts behind his saddle.

"Lord Dubric?" someone called from the dark. It was Werian, the lead archer. "Can I speak with you and Lars?"

"Of course," Dubric replied.

"I've wanted to discuss this for several days," Werian said, "but this is the first I've seen either of you."

"Matters in one of the villages have required our attention," Dubric said as Dien took their mounts' reins. "What can we do for you?"

Werian glanced at Lars. "Milord, you know I've trained the lads to the bow for a good decade. All the pages have to pass."

Dubric nodded. "Yes, competence in archery is a requirement for merit promotion to squire."

"I'm sorry, sir. I know Lars has been trying, putting in long nights at the targets, but I can't pretend it's getting any better."

"It *is* getting better," Lars said. "Night before last, I hit six the final batch. My average is four."

"Six? Out of fifty arrows? That's barely ten percent." Werian shook his head. "And the *final* batch? How many times did you go through both quivers?"

Lars looked down. "Three."

"Three. One hundred and fifty shots. How many hits?"

Lars fidgeted.

"Answer him," Dubric said.

"Twelve."

"On halves?"

"Yes, sir."

Dubric held back a sigh. He had not known that Lars had stalled on halves. A whole target was the size of a man's torso. Each level split the previous target in half. Wholes became halves, halves to quarters, quarters to eighths, and so on, teaching the students precision while weeding out those unable to achieve accuracy.

"You're a good lad, no doubt about that, and you're

doing your best, but the rest of your class completed sixteenths—"

"Sixteenths? That's barely the size of my palm!"

"Son, they've finished sixteenths and are on thirty-seconds. All but three have already passed the course. I've got two lads starting the advanced class and participating in the demonstrations tomorrow. Hitting eight percent on halves isn't going to cut it. You're just too far behind."

Lars sagged. "I know. I'll put in more practice."

"Only four days remain in the term. If you're not shooting a solid fifty percent on eighths by the day after tomorrow, I'll have to fail you. You have to shoot *something* on sixteenths, just to pass, and I'm not setting up sixteenths for practice until you master eighths."

"Yes, sir," Lars said softly.

Werian looked at Dubric again. "This is his last chance, sir. He's taken the course three times. I'm sorry, but unless he shows a marked improvement at the next class, he fails."

"I understand," Dubric said. "Thank you for telling me."

As the archer walked away, Lars stomped to his mare and yanked the sack off the horse's back.

"There's still a chance you can pass, pup." Dien handed off the horses to a stable boy.

"A chance? To be proficient at eighths by the day after tomorrow, especially with everything else that's happening? I can't shoot a stinking half! Hells, I barely managed fifty percent on a whole."

"Not everyone is meant to be an archer," Dubric said, flinching as soon as the words passed his lips.

"It's supposed to be in my blood. My father's an archer,

my grandfather, my great-grandfather. Grenneres are archers."

"It'll be all right, pup. We'll figure something out." Dien glanced at Dubric, who lowered his gaze.

Lars stomped toward the castle. "I can't be promoted to squire without passing archery. I'll disappoint my father yet again, and I'll disappoint Jess."

"No one's disappointed in you, least of all Jess," Dien said, walking alongside Lars.

Dubric hurried to catch up and groaned, his knees protesting the strain of jogging after two much younger men.

"She'll be mighty disappointed when we can't afford to marry," Lars snapped, pulling open the west tower door, "and my father's barely acknowledging me as it is. He'll probably disown me for failing my bloodline."

"There are other ways to achieve promotions," Dubric said.

"Last time I checked, I'm not proving my worthiness on a battlefield or kissing some lord's ass for a couple of parcels of land. Face it. I'm done. This is the best I'll ever be." Sack in hand, he stomped through the tower door, slamming it behind him.

Dien turned to Dubric. "We should tell him the truth, sir. Archery isn't in his blood any more than it's in mine. He doesn't have to live up to unrealistic expectations of being Bostra's son."

"It is not our secret to tell," Dubric said.

* * *

After sending the two rams to the head shepherd, delivering the parts and pieces to Rolle, and insisting that Dien get his fingers stitched, Dubric had just grasped the handle of his private office door when the door behind him opened. Inek the herbmonger sauntered through. "Our deal still on?"

"If your information is accurate, yes."

Inek tossed three vials to Dubric. "You're a tricky old bastard. Thought I'd never separate that one out. There were three concoctions on that head, and they're all similar."

Dubric held the vials in his palm. Each contained greenish yellow fluid in varying hues. "What are they?"

Inek flopped onto a chair. "Plant-based, primarily tree sap. Some sort of evergreen, but after that, I'm at a loss. It's not a pine, spruce, or fir. That's all I have to compare to. Might be redwood, cypress . . . cedar, maybe. Nasty shit, whatever it is."

"How so?"

"It's caustic, but in an odd way. The dark one's the purest of the three and mixed with some common herbs, like skunk cabbage and goldenrod. The shit wanted to melt my fingers together."

Inek held up his grimy hand, showing Dubric his bandaged fingers. "I had to cut the bastards apart, and still they wanted to seal back up. Most of that mess was the pale one, and it contains tincture alcohol. It counteracts the sap. I tried it on my finger. Hells, I'm already cut, right? It quit hurting immediately. It tingled halfway up my arm, but I felt everything I touched. All it did was take away pain." He shrugged. "Not sure why anyone'd want to keep a mangy old sheep from pain, but I figured that was your problem."

"And the third sample?"

"The last one's cut with liniment oil and spotted cowbane. I found just flecks of it here and there. Not sure what it does, but it's as toxic as arsenic. The other two aren't toxic at all."

The poison that has killed the scavengers. Dubric examined the three vials. "How do you know they are not toxic?"

"I fed them to mice. Always do, when I'm working with new concoctions. One died, two are happy as could be."

* * *

A quarter bell later, while checking over his notes at his desk, Dubric looked up at a knock on his door. Dien entered the office and closed the door behind him, shifting uneasily. "Sorry to be the bearer of bad news, sir."

Fear twisted in Dubric's gut and tainted the back of his mouth with dread. "What is it? What happened?"

"It's Maeve, sir. She's at my place. With her cat."

Dubric choked out, "Is she all right?"

"Appears to be, sir, other than some crying. At least as best as I can tell. She, um, had an incident with your mirror. She says it's haunted, that she saw someone in it. And when Jess tried to help her put it away, the reflection scared them both and the mirror made noises then leaked water all over the floor."

What? Noises? Water? Nonsense. Dubric frowned. "How can it make noises or leak water? It may be magical, but it only shows reflections. I have done everything I can to reassure Maeve that I no longer love Oriana."

"I don't think that's it, sir. She looks scared. It's not a jealous snit."

"How can you be certain?"

"Honestly, sir, I can't, but I'm telling you this as a friend. You need to get rid of the damned thing. Sell it. Break it. Lock it up in the attic. Something."

"I cannot," Dubric said. "I have wracked my mind to find a solution. I have no one to trust it to and cannot store it in the attic. It must be kept away from enchanted items that Nuobir did not create, especially shadow magic. He was very specific about that."

"Then destroy it, sir. The things it shows . . . it's evil."

"It is not evil. It is simply an enchanted mirror."

"One that lets you spy on private moments? Using it to find a criminal is one thing, but it shows *anyone*, sir, without their knowledge. Some things aren't other people's business." Dien lowered his voice and asked, "What if I watched you and Maeve in the sheets? Or sat back with an ale and chaperoned the kids? Followed Jelke the accountant through his day until he opened the secret coffers? Jerked off while watching cleaning maids bathe?"

Dubric's hands clenched. "I do not do those things."

"Perhaps not, but someone will. Someone with far less principle than you. It would be very easy to get addicted to watching, spying . . . seeing the darker bits of innocent lives. And, frankly, sir, considering all the tussles we get into, whether we have a mage in Quarry Run or not, I doubt you'll live another decade. What then? Who can you pass it to? If there's no one while you're living, who in the seven hells can be trusted with it after you're gone? Because neither Lars or I will take it, that's for sure."

"I will think of something," Dubric said.

"While you're dead? Dammit, will you listen to yourself? No secret is safe. You know Lord Egeslic's collecting magic and plotting war. If he got it, there'd be no stopping Pyrinn. They'd know where our armies were, how many men, armaments, weaknesses . . .

They'd find coffers and caches, know where the officers slept—"

"Do you not think I know this?" Dubric snapped.
"How do you think we defeated the mages? We were
outnumbered twenty to one when we began the cam-
paign north. Nuobir controlled the spies, the flow of
information to and from the armies. We never would
have survived beyond the first battles without precise
details of where to go and whom to remove. And how to
get to them. It is an observational *tool*, nothing more,
nothing less, and we are lucky to have such a tool at
our disposal. Four men, including Nuobir, knew he lied
when he told the Council he smashed it. He told Albin,
Siddael, and me that he destroyed it after the war
ended, along with the rest of his magic. Summers
passed before I discovered it had survived. Officially, it
does not exist."

"It doesn't matter. Our enemies will come for it, sir.
We're inviting trouble just by having it."

"They will not come without my foreknowledge."

Dien stared at Dubric a long time, realization growing in his eyes. "How many spies do you have, sir?"

Dubric stared back. "That is confidential information of a sensitive nature."

"Sensitive, my ass. It's treason to have spies. We're
a peaceful province, populated with farmers, for
Goddess's sake. We're not at war with anyone."

"We have never ceased being at war," Dubric said.
"The battles may have ended, but the war continues."

"The war ended fifty-some summers ago."

Dubric leaned forward. "Just over a moon ago, in
the Reach, we faced a mage who stole young men. Late
last winter we tracked a killer—a man aided by a magical device—who slaughtered young women. Two sum-

mers ago, in Pavlis, you helped me stop a group of men who took children. Do you remember?"

"Of course I remember. They were kidnappers stealing kids for slavers on the coast."

"They did not intend to sell those children," Dubric said. "They chose them for sacrificial blood. They were not kidnappers, they were acolytes of a mage named Moddil the Tooth."

"Bull piss. They were bandits. Thieves and cutthroats."

"Why would I concern myself with bandits in Pavlis?"

Dien crossed his arms over his chest. "Because they were stealing kids and it was the right frigging thing to do."

"How would I know where they were? Did we ever see, or speak to, a Pavlis official? Did we talk to any Pavlis natives beyond simple politeness? Did we ask directions? Seek rumors? Did we do anything that resembled an investigation?"

"We went in, killed four men, took six or eight kids to the nearest village, then came home."

"We killed four acolytes and saved eight children from sacrifice. Because of items I received, and the use of that mirror."

Dien frowned, silent.

"It is our purpose here in the north," Dubric said. "We seek and kill magic as it appears. We contain it, destroy it, whatever we must, to ensure the mages have no chance to rise again."

"Our purpose, sir, is to protect Faldorrah."

"*Above all else,*" Dubric said. "As you said, we are at peace. Our army is small, our borders open. We are obviously not protecting Faldorrahn farmers from an invasion from Deitrel or Haenpar or Jhalin. There is no reason to. They, too, are peaceful. The oath I had you take did not mention protecting Faldorrah against an invading army or keeping the peace amongst its people. We are not political. I may serve on Councils and speak for Nigel in Waterford, but my office is not a political one. I focus on the preemptive removal of threats, and the threat we focus on is mages, *above all else*."

Dien scowled. "So we track killers and rapists and thieves for laughs?"

"We went to Quarry Run to find a sheep thief, and found a mage. Do you think that is coincidence? We capture thieves, rapists, and murderers because that is part of our duty, but sometimes they are but the leading symptoms of a mage's power. The magic gathering in Quarry Run is far more serious a concern than Maeve's worries."

"If it's so damned important, why didn't your spies notice it and inform us? Why did we have to frigging wait until Calder Marsden found a sheep rotting in a ravine? Why the hells aren't we using your mirror to find the bastard responsible?"

"Only Nuobir could focus the mirror with merely a name or a question. I need an item to trace, and nothing we have found shows me the mage's identity. As for spies, I have none in Faldorrah," Dubric said softly. "Here, I use my own eyes. They are old and beginning to fail me."

"Is that why you have the lads? Have *me*? To be your frigging eyes?"

"My fortitude, my heart, my intellect," Dubric said. "Each of you fills a precise niche. After I am gone you must—"

"No. You kick off, I'm not doing one frigging thing

with that mirror other than smash it to shards and splinters."

"It is the single most powerful enchanted item ever created and is a vital tool for defeating mages. It is priceless."

"You're right, sir. Spies or no spies, no one's going to want to pay a penny for a pile of broken glass and wood."

Dubric stared at his squire. "You must not break it."

"I will, I'm telling you that now. I don't want that filthy thing near my family. It's dangerous."

"You are mistaken. It is a tool, a vital, powerful tool."

"I understand fine," Dien said as he reached for the door. "I understand you spent almost fifty summers alone with that mirror, losing your life and your perspective while you stared at your dead wife. I understand that after all this time you've met a woman who loves you, and, frankly sir, you're no catch. I understand you're frigging lucky to have her. I understand that you're about to throw her away for a piece of glass and wood that's done nothing for you except steal your youth, your life, and your sanity. You're choosing a *thing* over a woman who loves you. And that, sir, is simply insane."

He yanked the door open and looked back. "Get rid of it. While you can."

CHAPTER

12

✝

Dubric sat at his desk for a few moments, fuming, before reluctantly following Dien's path to the third floor. They entered the dimly lit suite to find Sarea pacing with the baby and Maeve dozing on the settee.

"How's Cailin?" Dien asked.

Sarea yawned. "She's finally asleep, thank goodness. I'm exhausted."

"Is something wrong with her?" Dubric asked.

"Colic," Dien said, taking the baby. "Had it for days." Cailin wailed fitfully, half awake, as he rested her against his shoulder. He patted her backside, and she quieted. "Let's go," he said to Sarea. "They have a lot to talk about."

After Sarea and Dien had left the room, Dubric watched Maeve sleep for a moment. Just looking at her tore at his heart.

Perhaps Dien and Lars are right, Dubric thought. *Perhaps my priorities are misplaced. Perhaps I have just been angry over her refusal to marry me.*

He swallowed, reaching out to touch her cheek. *Perhaps I have forgotten what truly is important.*

She stirred at his touch and opened her eyes. "You're home."

"What happened?" he asked, grasping her hand.

"I saw that ghost again. But she's not Oriana," Maeve said softly. "She's someone else. I'm sorry I doubted you."

"It is all right," Dubric said, cradling her. "What does the ghost look like?"

"She's my height and finely dressed in a grand gown. She has blonde hair, and long earrings that touch her shoulders."

"That is Brinna Brushgar," Dubric said, relieved. In the dark reaches of his heart he realized he had worried that perhaps Oriana was haunting them, after all. Or that Maeve had truly begun to see things. But Brinna was real. A special ghost, she had haunted him so long she had become autonomous. Brinna was able to touch things and to appear to others besides himself, as she had proven once before when she had sent Lars to Dubric's aid when he had most needed it. "I never found her killer. She has walked these halls for more than thirty summers, but she has nothing to do with my mirror."

"What is she trying to tell me?" Maeve asked. "And why me?"

"I do not know, but Brinna would never harm anyone."

"It's like she's trying to warn me, and after Jess—"

"What happened to Jesscea?"

"Her eyes. They reflected white in the mirror."

Dubric stared at her. "White? You are certain?"

"I saw it," Maeve said.

"Did you see anything else while Jesscea was there? Feel anything else?"

"After Jess locked it in the bath chamber . . ." Maeve shuddered.

"What happened after she locked it away?"

"There was a clacking sound, and something tried to

get out. I know it sounds crazy, but the door latch jiggled, so Jess put a chair against the door, then water gushed out all over the floor. We were both terrified."

"When you first returned to our suite, was the mirror in the far corner of our new bedchamber, as it was a few nights ago?"

"Yes, the same corner as before."

Under my attic, like I found it yesterday, Dubric thought, swallowing past the lump in his throat. *Under my magic.* "And you did not put it there?"

"I've never touched it. I can barely stand to look at it. Her eyes didn't reflect white before, when she visited me with Lars."

Of course they did not, Dubric thought. *She must have touched the dagger afterward.* "Everything is fine," he said, kissing her. "You are safe, Jesscea is safe, and tomorrow I will move the mirror to my office."

"You will?" Maeve asked.

"First thing. I promise. Let us stay in a different suite tonight," he said, holding her close.

She kissed him. "Where can we stay? I thought all the suites were full with visitors and performers for the faire."

Dubric smiled and reached into his pocket. "There are always a few suites left empty, and I have the keys."

* * *

Jess sat near the window and worked on a braided ribbon belt while waiting to hear her father's snores. They began and she sat quietly, listening, for a couple of minutes before she stood and tossed the belt onto her bed.

"You're gonna get in trouble," Fyn yawned.

Jess pulled on her shoes. "So? I haven't seen Lars for

two days and he's out there practicing. Maybe you're a bad influence on me."

Fyn rolled away. "Well, have fun, then."

Jess slipped from the room and crept out of the suite, closing the door silently behind her.

Then she ran.

She sprinted down the hall to the tower and down the stairs, bursting out to the courtyard and startling a pair of caged geese.

The courtyard was full of people. Carnival workers smoking around their fires, livestock tenders with their animals, pages and soldiers patrolling, everyone talking in low, hopeful voices. The sky was full of stars, the air with eager excitement.

At the archery grounds, Lars stood alone in a circle of light, another lantern beside his target at the far end. He shot arrow after arrow, his stance and form practiced and perfect, yet he continually missed his shots. Some hit the form outside of the marked target, some the straw bales behind. Others hit the ground or the post. Only three had hit the target. Each miss made him sag, but he'd pull another arrow, stand straight, and shoot again.

It broke her heart to watch him, his steadfastness in the face of failure. She opened the gate.

* * *

Sounds of faire preparations all around him, Lars nocked an arrow and settled his mind, pushing away thoughts of death and failure, of being a disappointment, of murderers and rapists and torn, ravaged girls. He took a deep breath, then pulled the bowstring, bringing his drawing hand to beside his ear.

His father was a master bowman. His father before him. And his father as well. And so on, back through the line of Grennere kings. This was easy. It was in his blood. His destiny.

He closed his eyes and released his breath, then opened them again. He focused his aim and let go of the string.

The arrow struck the straw bale about a length and a half below and to the left of his half target, burying itself nearly to the fletching.

Lars sighed and drew another arrow from the quiver. *At least they fly fast and hard. Even if it's just right into the ground.*

Arrow in, nocked. A deep breath . . .

Someone came through the gate and he turned, loosening the tension on the arrow. His dog wuffed and Lars grinned as Jess came onto the range. "Why are you up this late?"

"Couldn't sleep. I heard Dad come home and I saw you practicing." She knelt beside the dog and ruffled his ears. "I heard you'd gotten a dog. He's um . . . kind of odd-looking."

"Yeah, I know." Lars sighed. "Just a mutt."

The dog licked Jess's face and she laughed. "Seems friendly, though. What's his name?"

"He doesn't have one yet," Lars said. "I'm thinking of calling him Kedder, maybe."

Jess stroked the dog's fur, hesitating as her hand moved from his slick head to his scraggly back. "He's a good dog."

"He is," Lars said, kneeling beside her, his fingers touching hers in the dog's fur. They wove together and he drew his thumb along her fingers. *I want my life, my future,* he thought. *There has to be a way to win. To live. I'll find it, somehow. I have to.*

She twisted to face him. "And you are, too. A good man, I mean."

He looked into her eyes. "I've messed things up. I'm sorry, Jess."

"Messed what up?"

The dog jumped on her, breaking their grasp, and they stood. "I'm not going to pass archery," he said.

"Not everyone's meant to be an archer."

"That's what Dubric said. But I need this promotion. We need it."

"We'll manage. There's always a solution. You've probably just got too much on your mind. Maybe I can help."

Jess grasped his hand and led him to the fence. She climbed up to the top rail and sat, facing him. "Now, come here," she said, knees apart under her long skirt and her feet curling behind a lower rail.

He looked at her spread knees and the inviting dip in the fabric between them. "You're going to get us in trouble."

"No I'm not. The height's for leverage. Come here, let me rub your shoulders."

He hesitated then stepped between her knees with his back to her. Her skirt hiked up as he moved close, up to her mid-shin, and he felt the warmth of her leg against his forearm. She didn't seem to notice. She hummed, kneading the muscles of his shoulders and neck. It hurt at first, but a good pain, deep and soothing.

"You need to relax more," she said.

He grinned. "Not likely with you around." She rubbed his neck until his head drooped to the side. It felt glorious. "I've never had a backrub before."

She moved on to his upper shoulder. "Mam gives them to Dad all the time. He says she has magic fingers."

"Oh, you do, too."

Another muscle loosened. "Lift your arms," she said. "Put them over my legs. It'll help relax them."

He hesitated, but did as she asked, sighing happily as she worked deeper, her thighs alongside his ribs.

"Maybe we need to do this every couple of days," she said.

He sagged under her hands, letting her legs support some of his weight. "Goddess, Jess, I'd let you do this forever." He raised his head as footsteps approached and he felt Jess turn to look.

"Dammit, Hargrove, you have to be the luckiest bastard I know. No girl ain't never given me a backrub."

"Then you're missing out." Her bare shins felt like the perfect place to put his hands. "This is heavenly."

"I bet." Serian leaned on the fence beside them. "Hey, you guys seen Gilby? He's supposed to be watching the livestock pens, but I can't find him."

"Sorry," Jess said. "Fyn said he was working tonight." She danced her fingertips up the back of Lars's neck.

"You might try Flanningan's," Lars said, rolling his head back to rest against Jess's belly as she worked on his shoulders. *To the hells with archery and mages*, he thought, smiling up at her.

"Piss. I forgot about the damned dice games. Bet him and Norbert both are there."

"Yeah, probably." Lars's voice faded into a contented sigh.

"Keep up the good work," Serian said to Jess. He punched Lars playfully on the shoulder before striding away. "Lucky bastard."

Quiet settled around them again and Lars tilted his head to glance up at Jess. "You're too good to me."

She worked her fingertips into his scalp. "Oh, I don't know."

The tingle flowed clear down his legs. "You are." He felt relaxed, his muscles pliant and warm. At ease. Calm.

"I like touching you," she said.

"Me, too." His right hand slid up her shin, and she unhooked her right foot from the fence as he cupped her calf, massaging it as her leg came around him. *It's late, past her curfew, and we're delving into dangerous territory. I should take her home.*

But, Goddess forgive me, I don't want to.

Releasing her legs, he turned to face her. He grabbed the top rail on either side of her hips then hoisted himself up. Her fingers curled into his hair at the nape of his neck, sending delightful shivers through him.

"Don't let me go too far," he whispered, easing closer, feeling the warmth of her calves against the back of his thighs.

"I won't," she replied, her breath a promise on his lips.

And I can't let myself. Horrific memories of the things he'd seen flared in his mind, but he forced himself to think only of her, so close, so warm. He leaned in to kiss her, but hesitated again as he worried he'd do it all wrong. He rubbed her nose with his own. "It's late. I should take you home."

He felt her smile against his cheek. "You should kiss me."

Maybe I should, he thought, but by then he already was.

Their teeth bumped, and they giggled, but she folded into his arms as if he'd held her a thousand times. She was warmer than he'd expected, her breasts against his chest softer, her lips sweeter. He kissed her and, for the first time in memory, had no thoughts of death or pain.

* * *

Maeve's head rested on Dubric's chest as she slept, spectral goo speckling her skin, but Dubric stared at the ceiling, his mind churning over the case.

He needed at least one page to assist tomorrow, preferably two. More than that, he needed brave lads well trained to a sword, who could take notes and follow orders and make sound leaps of logic should the need arise. Who could he trust to carry that load?

Lars, he thought. *I can trust Lars. He is trained, dependable, self-sufficient, and he has spoiled me. Damn that boy. But he is right. Regardless of ghosts or mages, I cannot deny him one moment of happiness.*

Dubric cursed the Goddess for setting the grim task before him, and he cursed himself for being unable to see the connections that surely existed in Quarry Run. The dismembered bodies and animals were, in part, predictable. Organized. The outward traits were obvious, but the nuances mattered, the telling details. What common thread drew them together? Someone was responsible—and if he could just discern who and why, before matters spun out of control, they might have a chance at success, at survival.

He reached for sleep, lulled by Maeve's soft warmth, and kissed her shoulder. Just as he started to drift off, he jolted awake again, startled by a deep chill falling heavily behind his eyes.

Dubric looked up to see his newest ghost: the boy who had taken Dien's pouch, his severed head screaming in confusion and terror.

Dubric cursed, covering his face with a pillow. He did not want to see any more.

CHAPTER

13

†

Three ghastly heads staring at him, Dubric rose early from the borrowed bed and kissed Maeve good-bye before lugging his gear and evidence to their suite.

He entered to silence and walked through the cramped chaos of the old suite, pausing at Maeve's smaller loom strung with thread for an indigo jacquard. He saw a single yellow strand pass through the heddles to disappear in the fabric—her mark, a thread so few would see—and his heart clenched.

Dien was right. Maeve's safety and happiness was much more valuable than Nuobir's old mirror. Perhaps Tunek would take responsibility for it. Nuobir had always said that dark magic would be drawn to the mirror like a moth to a flame. In all his summers as the mirror's caretaker, Dubric had not witnessed that particular phenomenon, but perhaps the King's castle in Waterford, the only place dark magic reputedly could not grow, would be the best resting place for it and Oriana's old dagger, after all.

He walked through the archway, then paused. An old carved chair lay broken in a puddle and the bath chamber door stood ajar.

Dubric approached the door, water squelching beneath

his boots. Peering warily, all he saw was a freshly painted room awaiting final plumbing, the tiled floor wet with puddles of pooled water, just as Maeve had said. It smelled of old ash and swamp, not paint and oiled wood.

The mirror was gone.

A break-in? A thief? Maeve said she and Jess left the mirror locked inside.

The main door had been locked by key. The new suite, too, was locked, and barred from the inside.

No water flooded the entryway or hall, but smaller puddles led past the bath into the new suite. Hand on his sword, he followed the wet trail.

The curtains were drawn, shrouding the room in deep shadow. Maeve always preferred to leave them open and let in light, even starlight. The balcony doors were locked from the inside, as was the window beside them. He snapped open the curtains to the coming dawn. As his eyes adjusted to the light he recognized a dark shape in the far corner and muttered a curse. His mirror.

"Blasted thing." He threw the curtains wide.

The shadows retreated, and the room took on a bluish cast from the brightening sky. He knelt to retrieve an old marsh weed from a puddle. Grimacing, he flung it into a waste bin.

He turned the glass to face him and saw the three ghosts, two floating heads and the soldier with his hazy body. *At least there are no others,* he thought, lifting the mirror to carry it toward the old suite.

He heard faint clacks behind him, like a twig stuck in a wheel sprocket. He set the mirror down and turned, but saw nothing. The corner was empty; even the shadows had gone. He detected no chill, no rancid nutmeg stench of shadow magic, nothing but the still quiet of a nearly empty room.

Dubric carried the mirror away.

* * *

Lars woke at his usual time then rolled over. He didn't have to get Jess until after seven bell. Plenty of time to doze. Besides, he'd only had about three bells of sleep and he had the room to himself. All of his roommates were still on duty. A rare treat of solitude, silence, and sleep.

Then the door opened and Serian thundered in, grumbling. "I'm gonna kill that little shit, so help me."

Lars sighed, wondering if he'd ever get a chance to sleep in. "What happened?"

"Three drunks, one lecher peeping in the women's privies, and a stolen goat, that's what happened." Serian unbuckled his sword and tossed it aside. "The drunks, the lech, fine. That's what we were there for. Hells, I'll even add in the crooked gambling and the old whore selling blows behind the pottery shed."

Lars sat upright and rubbed his face to wake up, then licked his chapped lips. He smiled, remembering how they had gotten sore. "And the goat?"

"Your pegging brother-in-law," Serian snapped. "He was supposed to watch over the livestock, remember? Trumble and I had to track down his scrawny ass three frigging times."

Gilby rarely completed a duty shift without a reprimand, most often for not being at his post. "He's not my brother-in-law."

"He's bedding your girl's sister. I sure as the seven hells don't want to claim him." Serian sat on his bed and slammed his fists on the rumpled mess. "Fultin chewed my ass and docked my pay to cover the damned goat. I was lead man on duty, so it's my fault."

"Was he at Flannigan's?" Lars stood and stretched.

"No. Norbert was, and I slapped his lazy ass back at the main door. He stayed put after I threatened to bust his legs. Your frigging brother-in-law, though . . ."

Lars ambled to the privy room. "We're not related. Probably never will be."

"Right. You and Jess might as well talk to Friar Bonne, and if Fyn's not knocked up yet, she soon will be. Face it, you're family. So, anyway, *your pegging brother-in-law* didn't take the hint. I actually knocked his ass to the ground the second time, but he still kept wandering off. He's lucky I didn't kill him."

Lars finished in the privy and came back, yawning. "If he wasn't at Flannigan's, what was he doing?"

"Lazing off. First, I found him dozing by the kitchen. The second time he was talking to a vendor, a ferr-oh-type-ist, whatever the hells that is, and the third time, after the goat disappeared, we found him goofing off at the well."

Gilby was always anywhere but where he was supposed to be. At seventeen, he was the oldest junior page in the castle. Most pages his age were training for squire, not waiting for their very first promotion. "There's a ferrotypist? Here?"

"Yeah. He's got a machine that puts pictures on iron cards."

"Where's his booth?"

"Along the east wall. Stall thirty-seven."

Would Jess like a ferrotype? Do I have enough money saved? "Did Gilby say why he kept going to the east side of the castle?"

The door opened and Trumble sulked through. "I

haven't had my ass chewed like that since I was a junior page." He, too, ripped off his sword belt and flung it in the corner. "You're gonna have to talk to him," he said to Lars.

"He's not my problem, and I'm off duty."

"Someone has to bust his ass, and you outrank all of us."

"Not for long, I won't," Lars said. "I've reached the pinnacle of my career as a castle official."

"Bull piss," Serian said. "Squire pips get assigned next moon. You must be heading the list."

"Nope. Failed archery again. I'm done."

"Aw, shit, I'm sorry," Trumble said, sitting on his bed.

"What? You outshone all of us in blades, unarmed combat, *and* concealed weapons. How can Werian keep flunking you in *archery*?" Serian asked.

Lars shrugged. "Because I stink at it?"

Serian's face fell. "Piss. I know you've been counting on that promotion. What are you gonna do?"

"Jess wants to apply for University next summer, and start the spring after that. I can keep squirreling away money, then before classes start, we can get married and move to Waterford. I should have enough saved for a few moons' rent, and I'll get a job, maybe with the city guard. She wants to teach. Her classes will take a couple of summers, and I'll support us while she studies. That's what I'm hoping, anyway."

Trumble shook his head but Serian leaned forward and asked, "You decided this *last night*?"

"I've been thinking about it for a while, sort of. Me losing a chance at squire focused the plan."

"You're really gonna leave us?" Trumble asked.

"Maybe. It's all up to Jess." Lars paused. He had worried that they'd need to stay in Faldorrah because of his job, or that Jess would have to leave him behind to go to University, but what once had seemed like a failure was actually a gift. "It feels like the whole world just opened up. We can live our own lives, not the ones planned for us." Lars grinned. "We'll be free."

* * *

Arien trudged to work, yawning and picking dirt from her fingernails. Near the workers' shacks, she stopped, tripping over her own feet. Men were crashing through the ravine. They bellowed furiously, the words lost to brush and leaves, the sound growing closer as they climbed toward her, ripping their way up the ravine wall. Arien scrambled to get out of the way when suddenly four men, all quarry workers, emerged on to the road from the ravine.

One, a compact man with black lines tattooed on his arms and chest, looked furious and scared. He stomped toward her. "You! You seen my boy? Raffin?"

Arien backed away, holding her hands out before her. "No," she said. "Not for a couple of days."

"He took off last night and ain't come back."

Arien shook her head. "Sorry."

"Blast! You see the little shit, tell him if he don't get his ass home he ain't never gonna sit again."

"Be happy to," Arien said.

The men grimly descended into the ravine again.

* * *

Dubric was refolding the last piece of burlap when he heard a knock and Dien entered the suite.

"Any luck, sir?" he asked, glancing at the mirror.

"Three of yesterday's burlap pieces came from the tavern, one from a poultry farm, and the rest of our gathered evidence, including the bottle and scalpel, came from the sanatorium. I found a hair that belongs to a sanatorium kitchen worker, and a corn kernel and feather that came from the same farm as the bag they were in."

"That's two people to question, at any rate," Dien sighed. "But I doubt the poultry farmer's involved."

"I doubt it as well." Dubric paused to toss the burlap into a box. "You may be relieved to know that I have decided to store the mirror and dagger in the office until I can make arrangements to send them to King Tunkek. He can take responsibility for them."

"Thank you, sir," Dien said. "Have you picked Lars's replacements for today?"

"I am at a loss. Serian and Trumble worked all night and Deorsa has no field experience. None of the others seem likely candidates. Who do you think we should press into service?"

"Hells, sir, I don't know. Most of the pages are drunken louts."

Dubric pulled a blanket from the bed. "I would not label them all as louts, but I have little confidence most could handle the particulars of today's duties." Blanket in hand, he walked to the mirror. "I acquired another ghost last night; the boy who stole your pouch."

"A kid? Goddess damned son of a whore." Dien helped Dubric cover the mirror and lash the blanket down. "Why the hells would he kill a kid?"

"Likely for the same reason he killed the two men, whatever that reason may be. We have to learn why. Soon."

* * *

Dubric unlocked the outer office door and pushed it open, standing aside so Dien could carry the mirror in. From inside, he heard Otlee say, "Good morning, sir!"

Dien glanced back at Dubric but kept walking.

"Why are you here so early?" Dubric asked, closing the door. "Your shift does not begin for more than a bell."

Otlee stood beside one of the waiting room benches. "Yes, sir, I know," he said, pushing a blanket back with his foot. "But I'd hoped to catch you before you left."

Dubric walked around Dien to unlock the inner office door. "You cannot sleep here, Otlee. It is not safe. We have told you."

"Sleep? I wasn't *sleeping*. I just came really early so I'd be sure to catch you, and it was chilly, is all."

Dubric opened the door for Dien. "What can I do for you, then, since you have been waiting so long?"

Otlee swallowed and stretched a bit taller. "I heard that Moergan's on the squire list and I'd—"

Dubric followed Dien in far enough to toss the dagger onto his desk. "There is no squire list. Even if there were, promotions are privileged information."

"Yes, sir, I know, sir, but, see, if Moergan is promoted, he can be assigned a private suite. He's eighteen, the eldest one there, and if he moves out, or Serian does, that'll leave an open bed and . . ."

Dubric looked over as Dien leaned in the doorway, shaking his head. "Otlee," Dubric said, "I know that you want to relocate to Lars's suite, but I cannot allow it. You are a senior page. As such, you can room with other senior pages in the dormitories or you can reside with your parents. You have been assigned a dormitory, one with another open bed, no less. I will not reassign others on a whim, and I see no good reason to break apart four young men who have roomed well together for summers and are good friends. Besides, you have two roommates, whereas all of the other lads have three, *and* you have one of the larger rooms."

"Yes, sir, I know," Otlee said, lowering his head, "but it's Deorsa and Jorst. They hate me."

"They do not hate you. They may be disgruntled because you outrank Jorst, but I seriously doubt—"

Otlee's face turned red. "They despise me, sir. Because of what that man did to me." His lower lip curled in a moment as he looked up. "Please, sir, let me room with Lars. I know he doesn't hate me."

"Have they hurt you?" Dien asked.

Otlee shook his head and furiously rubbed his wrists. "No. They just say things."

"Do you want me to talk to them?" Dien asked.

"No! It'll just get worse. They'll tell everyone . . ." Otlee sagged. "It'll get worse."

"If you are unharmed and will not return to living with your family, then we have little choice," Dubric said. "The past is behind you. Stand tall, lad. You are a senior page now."

Otlee nodded, looking at the floor. "What are my duties today, sir? Will you be needing me to help you in Quarry Run?"

And possibly send you to your death? I believe you have endured enough. "No," Dubric said, "you do not need to accompany us and I have no pressing research. Your day is your own. Enjoy it."

Otlee sighed and gathered up his blanket. He left without looking back.

Once Otlee had gone, Dien said, "You ought to reconsider, sir. He's having enough problems without having to deal with constant taunts from the other boys about his abuse. Lars would put a stop to it."

Dubric locked the inner office door. "And how would that aid Otlee? We cannot undo the molestation, but would his fears disappear if we deflect the strife from his life? If he does not learn to stand up for himself, to believe in himself instead of relying on Lars to save him, how will he manage as an adult? How will he survive if something happens to Lars? Who will watch out for him then, if not himself?"

"Otlee's twelve summers old, sir. It's only been a moon. He needs time to come to terms with what happened."

"I agree, but he cannot do that if he puts his burdens on Lars. He needs to find his own way. I preferred that he remain with his family—"

"They treat him like a freak. What happened to him wasn't his fault."

"They are still his family," Dubric said, following Dien to the hall.

"I think we're all the family he has."

Dubric locked the outer door then turned to head to the physicians' office with Dien. He had barely taken two steps before stopping at the sound of his name being called.

Lord Brushgar's personal squire stomped up the hall, fuming. "I've tried, sir," Fultin said, "Goddess knows I have, but if you don't dismiss that boy, I will."

"What boy?" Dubric asked.

"That blasted Gilby," Fultin said. "I've given Serian and Trumble a tongue-lashing over this mess, but how many times do I have to punish Gilby? He's not fit to be a damned page!"

"I know his conduct is less than exemplary—" Dubric started.

"Less than exemplary?" Fultin snapped. "I've caught the little shit lying and stealing and I've had leaky boots that were more dependable. No matter what reprimand I slap on him, he still refuses to remain at his post or even arrive on time. He has the lowest rank possible, even lower than the little lads who've just started their training. I can't demote him any further. I've run out of options and I want him off my roster. I can't do that without your signature."

"His father is an influential member of Lord Brushgar's court," Dubric said patiently. "Certain concessions—"

"Concessions, my ass. You know Nigel's oblivious to everything except his comforts and antiques. Let Talmil have his tantrum; I'll knock his primping ass on the floor. That boy is a disgrace and a detriment to the rest of the staff."

Blast it, Dubric thought. *Talmil will badger me to my grave.* "Fine," he said at last. "Reassign Gilby to me. Effective immediately."

"What?" Dien asked, his eyes wide.

"Thank you," Fultin said. "I'll have him report to you this morning, assuming I can find him." He gave Dubric a grim nod, then turned and walked away.

"You've lost your frigging mind," Dien said.

Dubric ground his teeth and continued to Rolle's office. "The decision is made."

* * *

Rolle sat at his desk, snoring, his head on his crossed arms. Dubric rapped a knuckle on the door frame and Rolle started, sitting upright. He had drool smeared across his cheek.

"Is it dawn already?" he asked, fumbling for his spectacles.

"I am afraid it is," Dubric said. "What do you have for me?"

Rolle handed Dubric the report. "Death by decapitation on the head, and clamped blood vessels on the body postmortem," he said, stretching as he walked around his desk. "The head and crushed leg don't match the rest or each other. You brought me three victims."

"Three victims? Clamped blood vessels? Are you certain?" Dubric asked, following the physician out of his office and to his examination tables.

"Positive." Rolle uncovered the head and carried it to the next table. Pulling back the sheet to expose the dismembered body parts, he set the head next to an upper torso where reason dictated it should go. "This head was separated alive, the torso was not. Look here," he said, motioning Dubric to look closely and compare the severed area of both pieces. "On the torso, the neck muscles are flaccid, but they are retracted on the head. Throat diameters are vastly different. Major anatomical points do not match, and the head belonged to a much smaller man than the body. They also both possess their fifth and sixth cervical vertebrae."

How, then, could I have acquired only one ghost before the pieces were found? Three victims, three ghosts, but one is a boy. None of these parts belong to a boy, and we found them long before I received the boy's ghost. Dubric shook his head, trying to settle his thoughts. "You said the blood vessels were clamped?"

"Only on the torso side of the neck," Rolle said, pulling flesh aside to show Dubric distinct indentations near the ends of the exposed vessels. "There is no clotting on exposed features or incisions, no retraction of muscles, and no blood aspirated into the trachea. He was dead when he was dismembered. I did, however, find a good measure of dust and grit in his throat and lungs, as well as some odd fluid."

"So he was a quarryman?" Dien asked.

"That is my assumption," Rolle said. "He has not been dead long, roughly a day or two at this point, and that fits well within the time frame of the accident. I found no evidence of trauma or disease that would have killed him, and can only assume that he died of head injuries."

"You found fluid?" Dubric asked.

"Yes." Rolle handed Dubric a vial with a sample of dark sludge, which had been tucked beside the corpse's arm. "I have no idea what it is other than some sort of pungent, viscous material. It was spread over the cut and exposed areas of both men's throats. None was aspirated. The head was also washed; I found traces of soap in the hair and the folds behind the ears. I found no soap residue on the body or leg."

Dubric noted the information. "Was this done by the same person who dismembered the sheep?"

"Likely, yes," Rolle said. "There were few if any hesitation cuts, the incisions are precise, and all incisions on the body and lower leg originated from behind, just as with the sheep."

"So our killer is becoming more certain?" Dubric hoped he did not sound relieved. Surely a mage, even one living quietly for fifty summers, would not refine his surgical skills as he progressed from sheep to people. Mages had little care for precision, and no reason to perfect it.

"It appears the killer is improving with practice," Rolle said, sliding the main pieces toward one another.

"Other than the head and mangled lower leg, all parts and pieces match. They are one body. I found a deep puncture in the joint of the right shoulder that occurred premortem," he said, pointing to the torso side of the dismembered joint. "I did not realize the victim had suffered an injury until well into my examination; the severing ran through the injured area, and the precise, delicate workmanship concealed it."

Dubric noted the victim's injury, hoping to match it to one of the quarrymen. "What else?"

Rolle looked up from his notes. "The head, I'm afraid, was cut in one slice, from the side, not the back, and the blade was much longer than a scalpel."

"So we may have two killers? One with a sword?"

"Possibly," Rolle said. "I cannot say for certain."

"And the leg?" Dubric asked. "You said it did not match either of the victims?"

Rolle moved down the table, to the lower extremities. "I thought at first it matched the head. It was removed while the victim was alive—whereas the thigh was severed postmortem—but the head has dark hair, the leg has light hair. It's *possible* they're the same victim, but I doubt it."

Dien cursed and Dubric nodded, frowning. There were three victims on the examination table. How could he be missing two of their ghosts?

"The leg may have been amputated because of medical necessity," Rolle said. "The overall trauma to it is quite severe, with the bones being crushed to slivers and the muscles torn apart. If a patient was brought to me with a leg like this, I would certainly amputate." He shrugged. "There is a possibility that it is surgical waste and whoever once had this leg is alive and well."

"An amputee," Dien said, nodding. "Lars and I pulled

a man out from beneath a boulder with a leg crushed like this. Maybe it's his leg, tossed out after amputation. We should check to see how Sevver's doing."

"We shall," Dubric said, adding to his notes.

"One more thing," Rolle said. "I found your triangle marks. Three of them."

"Oh?"

"The nape of the neck on the head, base of the cervical spine on the torso, and the back of the thigh just above the severing." Rolle showed Dubric each. "Only the head is inked. The other two are scraped into the skin with a sharp object, perhaps a pin or slender awl, and filled with the same pigment as the sheep."

* * *

As Dubric left Rolle's office, Fultin came toward them, pushing a slight, cowering page to the hall as if he were tossing scraps to a garbage heap.

"Ow, hey! Let me go!" Gilby said. One last shove and he stumbled forward, his arms flailing for balance.

"He's all yours," Fultin said. "Goddess help you both." He shook his head and walked away.

Gilby's unkempt uniform looked as if it had been put on wet three days ago, and Dubric doubted if the boy had polished his boots at any time within memory. *At least he does not reek.* "Welcome to my personal staff. You will find that my tasks and training differ greatly from Fultin's."

Gilby glanced at Dien, who glared back with alarming intensity. Gilby swallowed. "I've been on duty all night, so, um, I'm gonna get some sleep—"

"No, you will not." Dubric turned on his heel. "We have a full day ahead. Come with me." He continued down the hall.

"Hey, look, I haven't bathed or eaten. Can't I—"

"Shut your fool yap," Dien said. "You're ours now. We're going to have lots of fun today, aren't we, sir?"

Dubric smiled. "Yes, our duties are always delightful."

Dien said, "Just think, we'll start with a long ride to a village where you'll get to search a ravine for corpses and missing body parts."

"Body parts? As . . . as in *human* body parts?"

"Give the laggard a shiny apple!" Dien said. "You figured that one out right frigging quick."

Gilby coughed, covering his nose and mouth with his hand. "There must be some mistake. I run errands, occasionally stand guard duty, not gather body parts."

"Your duties have changed." Dubric reached the east tower door.

Gilby coughed again. "Dead bodies? In parts? Goddess, sir, you can't be serious."

"I am deadly serious." Dubric pulled the door open. "Which weapons classes have you excelled in?"

"Um. Uh. *Excelled?*"

"You're just as useful as a frigging bug crawling up a wall," Dien muttered, nudging Gilby outside. "Did you *pass* any combat classes, bug?"

Gilby stumbled, nearly running into Dubric. "Pass? Um. Swords. Nearly."

"Nearly?" Dien sighed. "Oh, it's going to be a grand day."

They reached the armory and Dubric unlocked the door. "What type of sword?" he asked, entering.

"There's more than one kind?"

"A *grand* day," Dien muttered.

Blast! Dubric frowned at Gilby. *I cannot take an unarmed child to Quarry Run. He is going to get us killed.* "I require my staff to be armed whenever on duty."

"Um. All right," Gilby said, shrugging.

Muttering a curse, Dien plucked a sword from the rack. Standard military issue, the blade was slightly longer than a shortsword and in need of a good polish.

"Plain, no-nonsense weapon," Dien said, shoving the sword into Gilby's hands before picking a scabbard. "You manage not to kill yourself or either of us with that, maybe you can step up to a real sword."

* * *

"Is Jess about ready?" Lars asked as Sarea invited him in.

"Almost," Sarea said, stumbling back to the settee. She looked tired, exhaustion shadowing her eyes.

"I'll take Cailin for a bit," Lars said, taking her from Sarea's arms. She wailed, squirming, but he draped her over his shoulder and patted her back. "She still colicky?"

"Yes." Sarea sighed as she sat. "Something I eat doesn't agree with her, as best I can tell. It's got her all gassy. If she toots, she quiets right down. I thought it might be potatoes, Fyn had trouble with those when she was little, but I haven't eaten a potato for almost two phases."

Cailin squirmed, crying, but Lars held her close and patted her with his free hand.

From the depths of the suite he heard the girls quarrel, something about a hairbrush, and he smiled. He hadn't realized how much he missed the sounds and relationships of family. He'd spent more than a phase as their honorary brother a moon or so ago, and even Kia's belligerence reminded him of home.

He looked over as Kia sulked down the hall and to

the main door in a perfumed cloud. Without comment, she walked out, slamming the door behind her.

Sarea sagged, leaning back against the cushions, and covered her eyes with her arm.

Jess came down the hall a few minutes later in a simple cotton blouse and skirt, with her hair pulled back from her face and hanging loose and curly down her back. She looked fresh, comfortable, and gloriously happy.

Lars returned the baby to Sarea. "Good morning," he said, reaching for Jess's hands. He drew her to him and gently kissed her, then rubbed her nose with his. Unlike her sister, she smelled clean, no perfumes, no rouge, nothing but her. His love, his Jesscea. "You ready?"

She beamed. "All set."

"Do you have enough money?" Sarea asked, blinking blearily as Cailin quieted and fell asleep.

"I've got it covered," Lars said.

Jess checked her purse at her hip. "And I have a few crown. We're fine."

"I'll have lunch out by the west gate around noon. You kids be good and have fun. I'm going to try to take a nap while I can."

Sarea stumbled away as Lars and Jess left the suite. He kissed her again and hugged her, lifting her as he turned around. "What do you want to do first?"

"How about the shops?" she asked, laughing as he set her back on her feet. "Then maybe the carousel? I've never ridden one before."

"Me, either," he said, taking her hand before kissing her again. It was going to be a grand day.

CHAPTER

14

✝

Dubric, Dien, and Gilby reached Quarry Run to find Marsden waiting at the outskirts of town. "Where have you been?" he asked. "I expected you a bell or more ago. And who's the boy?"

Dubric introduced Gilby. "Preparations took longer than expected. Have there been new developments?"

Marsden reined about to ride alongside Dubric. "One of the shack boys has gone missing. The workers are up in arms and I have damn near every able-bodied person in town searching for him. Do you think he's been taken by our killer?"

"It is possible, yes." Though Marsden seemed a good man, Dubric had no intention of mentioning his fore-knowledge of death in front of him or Gilby. After so many summers of holding the secret to himself, it still felt strange having shared it with Lars, Dien, Otlee, and Maeve.

Marsden tightened his grip on the reins. "How can I tell his father? Especially after what happened in the road yesterday?"

"What happened?" Gilby asked, then cowered as Dien glared at him.

"You cannot. Without proof, he will not believe his

225

son is dead, especially so soon after he has gone missing." Dubric paused to glance at Dien. "And he will not believe we are not involved."

"What do we do, sir?" Dien asked.

"We help him look for his son."

* * *

They reached Marsden's office to find Jerle Dughall pacing on the walkway outside. "Ah, there you are," he said, scowling. "Late. I should have expected as such."

Marsden dismounted. "What can we do for you?"

"You can release my son, as you promised."

"We cannot," Dubric said, dismounting as well. "Complications have arisen in our investigation."

"My son is not involved in that and I demand he be released. Immediately."

"You may demand all you wish," Dubric said. "I will not release him."

Glaring, Jerle stomped close. "We had an agreement."

"A man has been murdered and his body found in the ravine. That supersedes any agreement."

"You mean to tell me you have discovered a connection between my missing sheep and that body?"

Dubric said nothing.

"How? What connection? How can you possibly believe my son is involved when he obviously was locked up at the time the man died or was left in the ravine? And how can you expect my crew to locate shear lines without Tupper's expertise?"

"If you will excuse us," Dubric said, "we have a missing child to locate."

Jerle pushed Dubric back. "I'm not excusing anything. You gave me your word you'd release my son."

Dubric dropped his hand to his sword. "Touch me again and I will drop your intestines on your polished shoes. I am in the midst of an investigation and your son will stay precisely where he is until I deem him worthy of release. Do I make myself clear?"

"Perfectly," Jerle said. "And I am certain Lord Brushgar will be delighted to hear that you threatened me."

* * *

Kedder trotting on their heels, Lars and Jess sipped ciders and held hands as they looked over wares. They wore matching kerchiefs around their necks, second-place prizes from the three-legged race. Second place was just fine, as far as Lars was concerned. After Jess scrunched up her skirt so he could tie her bare ankle, knee, and lower thigh to his, then let him undo everything after the race, last place would have been worth it.

After examining carved staves, they moved on to a confectioner's booth. They found slivers of marzipans and caramels and hard candies, all artfully arranged on silver platters and offered for sampling, if the customer appeared to be in the mood to buy. Jess showed a definite, almost swooning, preference for caramel-covered nougat, especially with pecans. Lars bought a half-box assortment for two crown. He received a kiss on the way to the next booth, where the vendor was selling a wide and colorful selection of hats.

Not utilitarian or dress hats like Jess's grandparents used to make, but jester hats, bard hats, silly hats, and oddly shaped monstrosities, all in brilliant colors. Hats with ribbons streaming behind. Hats with bells. Hats with bouncy feathers. They tried a few on for size, laughing at each other's selections and their own reflections in mirrors.

"That's so manly," Jess said, giggling as she arranged droopy belled flaps in purple and yellow over Lars's shoulders. He shook his head and jingled.

"That style has been very popular this morning," the proprietor said. "I've sold four of them already."

"It is comfortable," Lars said as he shook his head again, jingling the bells at Jess. She squealed and ticked his nose with a bright pink feather.

"Only four and a half crown," the proprietor said. "And each hat is unique. There are no others of that style in those colors."

Lars couldn't imagine actually wearing the odd thing. "I can't. Thanks." As soon as he set it on its perch, a farm boy snatched it up and tried it on.

Jess broke a nougat in two and they shared it as they left the hat shop. She took two steps toward the next stall and her breath fell out in a rush. "Ferrotypes? Here?"

Lars grinned. "Looks like it." Nobles, castle officials, and well-to-do farmers lined up to sit before the camera with stiff postures and stern faces. Lars nodded hello as he walked with Jess to examine the sample pictures on display.

Some of the samples were pocket-size but most were as large as a half target. Two were nine sets of the same image on a single rectangle of metal. At fifteen crown apiece, Lars figured he could manage a pair of the small ones. One for each of them.

Jess admired the samples as the ferrotypist seated his next subject, head accountant Jelke, positioning him into a grim and haughty pose. Lars blinked at the bright light that flashed over Jelke with a *pop,* then the ferrotypist pulled a slim box from the back of his camera and set it on a growing stack. A new box slid in and the next subject came forward, money in hand, while Jelke wandered away, blinking dazedly.

"These are just amazing," Jess said.

Lars checked the prices again. "Would you like one?"

Jess grinned as the camera popped again. "Can we? Can we really?"

"I brought a little extra money this morning, just so we could." They took their place in line, Jess leaning against him while he wrapped his arms around her waist. He marveled at the difference a single day had made. He barely remembered not touching her, kissing her. The horrible images that had haunted him for phases now seemed just a foggy and fading dream.

"I want to smile," Jess said, looking back at him. "Laugh. Not be all stern and serious."

"If he'll let us."

They took another step forward and Jess squeezed him tighter. "He will."

They watched an older couple pose for their portrait, the man sitting, the woman standing behind, both as dour as vinegar. Next, a farmer proudly put his rooster on the chair and stepped back. The rooster didn't seem to mind the bright flash of light. The farmer collected his bird, then it was Lars and Jess's turn.

Lars paid for the ferrotypes then followed Jess to the chair. She knew exactly what she wanted, and it wasn't stiff or dour. Lars sat on the chair and Jess perched happily on his leg. His arms around her waist, she snuggled close and kissed his cheek.

The ferrotypist was a middle-aged man in a fine suit, with a rounded belly that told of many ales. He frowned. "Miss, it is not proper for the couple to sit together."

"I don't care about proper." Jess asked Lars, "Do you?"

Lars didn't care if they stood on their heads, as long as it made her happy. "No," he said. "Sitting together's just fine."

"It's your money." Muttering about headstrong children, the ferrotypist stepped behind his camera. He made a few adjustments to the lens, then *pop*. The bright light blinded Lars for a moment.

The ferrotypist fumbled at the lens, dropping the slim box that held their image. "Oh, my," he said, picking it off the ground. "I cracked the case. That picture is surely ruined."

"Do I need to buy another one?" Lars asked.

The ferrotypist slid a case into the camera. "It was my mistake. You paid for two ferrotypes and shall receive both."

"Let's take off the kerchiefs," Jess said, untying hers. "So we'll just look like us. Regular."

"Sure." Lars pocketed his kerchief while the ferrotypist made additional adjustments. They grinned cheek to cheek for that picture, then the ferrotypist put a new case in and took another one. Lars blinked as he stood, trying to clear the spots from his eyes. The ferrotypist pressed a paper card in Lars's hand and herded them toward the exit.

Once his vision cleared enough to read, Lars noted the instructions to return in two bells' time. He pocketed the card, then, tying his silly kerchief around his neck again, he escorted Jess to stall number thirty-eight.

* * *

Dubric had lain awake half the night planning his tasks for the day, none of which included searching for a missing boy. After a bell or two of hunting through the ravine and looking down wells and into cellars without luck, he pulled Dien aside.

"I must go to the sanatorium," he said. "Continue searching with Marsden. Perhaps you will find something useful."

Dien glanced over his shoulder at Gilby fiddling with his sword belt. "I doubt it. What about the bug?"

"He will come with me. I need someone to aid me and I cannot trust him to remain on task alone with Marsden, nor am I about to leave him alone with you."

"Sir, I wish you'd assign him to me. I'd be *delighted* to knock some sense into him," Dien said, winking.

"If you did that, his father would see us both gelded."

Dien and Dubric walked toward the porch Gilby looked beneath. "You still think a mage is involved, sir?"

"With all that we have seen? It is likely. Whoever it is, he is connected to the sanatorium."

* * *

Maeve smiled as she poured herself a fresh cup of tea and meandered back to her loom. The mirror was gone, the suite quiet, and the solitude was a pleasant change. Even Lachesis was dozing on the windowsill.

She felt a bit of guilt that Dubric had been forced to remove the mirror, but that feeling was vastly overshadowed by relief. The glass's presence no longer plagued her, and for the first time since coming to the castle, she felt as if Oriana were truly gone. Working steadily, she lost track of time. When someone knocked on the door she jumped nearly out of her skin.

A courier stood outside the door, harried and sweaty in his purple uniform. He held a long wrapped parcel and a signature form. "Milord Dubric Byerly, castellan," the man said. "Please."

"He's not here," Maeve replied.

The courier squinted at her. "This is last suite, third floor, north wing, of Castle Faldorrah? Lord Brushgar's demesne?"

"Yes, you've come to the right place," Maeve said.

"Then I must speak to Lord Byerly."

"He lives here, but he isn't home. He's tending to business in a local village. Is there something I can do for you?"

"Are you his wife?"

"Not exactly."

The courier removed his cap to wipe sweat from his brow. "I'm sorry, milady, but I come from the King's Holy Church of Waterford, with instructions to hand deliver this parcel to Lord Byerly. I cannot leave without an approved signature."

From the church? For Dubric? "I'm his companion," Maeve said, "and I'd be happy to sign for it."

The courier squinted at his form. "When will Lord Byerly return?"

"I have no idea," she said. "Perhaps later today, perhaps tomorrow, perhaps next phase."

"A phase? Milady, I have already ridden two full phases to deliver this, far longer than I anticipated. As it is, I will not return home for a moon after my departure. I cannot lounge about for a phase waiting."

"Then let me sign for it."

"Is there someone else, another titled religious official who can be entrusted to accept the package? The castle priest or priestess, perhaps?"

Maeve gave him an amused smile. "Dubric and Friar Bonne rarely speak and I have no idea where he might be. It is faire day, and I believe Bonne is enjoying various festivities."

"A friar? I cannot leave this with a friar."

"Then you may leave it with me. I'll put it right here, by the door. I'll give it to Dubric as soon as he comes home, and you can resume your return journey without delay."

He looked her over top to bottom and back again. "This is a very important church matter. How can I be certain you're his companion and not a swindler?"

Maeve stepped past him to the hall. She saw a pair of cleaning maids nearby. "Girls!" she called out. "Could you come here, please?"

"Is there a problem, miss?" the taller maid asked as they curtsied.

"Of course not," Maeve said. "Would you please tell this gentleman who I am?"

"Of course, miss," the taller maid said, looking confused. "You're Mistress Maeve, Lord Dubric's intended."

Maeve thanked them and the courier shifted uneasily. "You can give me the package," she said. "Or you can come in and wait until he returns."

Frowning, the courier handed her the parcel.

* * *

Gilby following close behind, Dubric walked down the sanatorium halls until he found a nurse who looked vaguely familiar. "I need to see a patient named Sevver," he said.

"He's not one of mine, milord," she replied, shoving

an armful of dirty linen into a cart. "Is he a terminal? A mental?"

"Injured," Dubric said. "He was hurt in the quarry landslide."

"A few have been sent home, milord, but the rest are down the main hallway, wards five, seven, and eight," she said, pointing. "You might try there."

"Have we met before?" Dubric asked, squinting at her.

She blushed. "Not exactly, milord. You, um, interrupted Shelby and me a couple of days ago."

Ah! "I apologize. I was not aware he was occupied at that particular moment." Dubric paused, then asked, "If I may inquire, milady, surely you are aware of his philandering reputation. Why do so many lovely young women agree to such treatment?"

She pulled her head back, startled. "Excuse me?"

Dubric gave her a consoling smile and eased a bit closer. "Forgive my ignorance, but why, milady? Why be romantically involved with such a man? Why endure clandestine meetings with a man who readily admits he will be in the arms of another a bell or two later? A man who, by all reputation, is not talented at lovemaking?"

She glanced at Gilby standing close behind Dubric, and scowled at them both. "How dare you?"

"I dare because it is my business to do so, milady," Dubric said, backing her against the wall as he watched her eyes. "What is the attraction? The addiction?" He lowered his voice to a whisper and asked, "Does he bite you? Draw blood? Is that what you enjoy?"

"You, sir, are a filthy, nasty man," she snapped. "Shelby is a fine man, a physician, and unmarried. Do you have any idea how many young men of means are available here? Yes, I know what he does, but it's a small price to pay for the chance to marry a physician. Now, get out of my way."

Dubric bowed his head in agreement then stepped aside to set her free.

Gilby watched her stomp away. "Um, milord, do you often do that sort of thing?"

"No. I do not care who beds whom or why," Dubric said as he opened his notebook and wrote her comments. "I required the information, and some secrets are difficult to obtain. At worst I have tarnished her self-image, at best I have encouraged her to stay away from a potentially dangerous man." He smiled as he closed the book and walked down the hall. "Plus, I doubt she has been bitten. That one insight gives me hope."

"Bitten?" Gilby asked, trotting to keep up.

Dubric did not answer but, following the nurse's directions, quickly found ward five, which contained five patients. Two were awake. "Do either of you know where I might find Sevver?"

"Yah, I saw 'im this mornin', toddlin' 'round the hall on crutches," one of the men said, his voice muffled by bandages.

"He come in and said hey," the man in the next bed said. His right arm and chest were encased in a plaster cast and he shifted, wincing.

"Do you know what ward he is in?"

Both men claimed they did not.

"What do you know of a man named Higgle?"

"Heard 'e died."

The man in the cast nodded. "Yeah, last I saw him, half his head was smashed. I knew he didn't have no chance, even when they took him for another surgery."

"A *second* surgery?" Dubric asked, glaring at Gilby,

who had stretched out upon the only empty bed, filthy boots and all.

"Yessir. After the accident, he come in right behind me. Was still talking and all, even with his head tore to the seven hells, and they took him right in to get stitched up. He slept there in that bed behind you till yesterday, when he started shaking the whole bed."

"Do you mean he had convulsions?"

"Yessir, that's it, cun-vul-shuns. Couple of nurses'd been trying to get him to wake up, but he wasn't gonna. He was a goner, you could just tell. They took him out to the surgeon again, but he never come back."

The other man adjusted his bandages as he leaned back onto his pillow. "Wish they woulda brought 'im back, dead er not. The other guy kept me up half the night."

"The other guy?" Dubric asked.

"Yah. Ain't never seen him b'fore. Kept askin' where he was and who we was and spoutin' off his name and some nonesense numbers."

"What sort of numbers?"

"Was the same dang thing ev'ry time they'd ask him who he was. Klammer Felk four seven two six major two Galdet first d'vision. Just gibberish, milord. He'd say it o'er and o'er, like they never heard him. Hells, we all heard him."

A major? For Galdet? Asking where he was? Dubric nearly snapped his pencil in half. *I may have seen that man yesterday and did not give him a second glance.* "Where is this man now?"

"I dunno, milord. They took him away during the night."

*　*　*

Evidence bag in hand, Dien climbed out of slimy muck and handed the bag to Marsden. While looking for the missing boy, he, Marsden, and two quarrymen had followed the ravine downstream to the marshy swamp that covered much of the lowlands. Instead of the boy, they had spied a man's mangled head caught in a tangle of weeds near where the stream fed into the swamp. It was grayish and puffy, and had probably been submerged in the water for a couple of days.

"Who is he?" Dien wiped the worst of the mud off his trousers then rinsed his hands in the marsh.

Marsden showed the contents of the bag to the two quarrymen. Both paled.

"It's Yaunel," one choked out. "Yaunel Derk. That's his head."

At least someone has a name. Dien pulled his notebook and pencil out of his jacket pocket. "When's the last time you saw him?"

"Day before the accident. I heard he'd got hurt, but never saw him." Beside him, the other quarryman nodded.

"He have family? Someone who might know how badly he was hurt or what happened to him afterward?"

"No," the first quarryman said. "He didn't have no one."

Dien glanced at Marsden and frowned, wondering how the dead boy fit in with the murders of a soldier and a man with no family.

* * *

"You are not permitted to lie down while on duty," Dubric snapped as he and Gilby walked down the hall.

"But I'm tired," Gilby said. "I haven't had any sleep, nothing to eat . . ."

Dubric stopped and turned to face the boy. "You are

a member of my staff and sometimes this job requires that you remain awake for days at a stretch. Sometimes we miss meals. Sometimes we must endure unpleasant and exhausting circumstances to fulfill our duties to the Faldorrahn people. We do so without complaint, and without succumbing to weakness. And we absolutely do not lie on beds while on duty because we are 'tired.' Fatigue is an illusion. Convince yourself that you are not tired and you will not be."

"But sir, I've been up all night!"

"As have I, many, many times, often for several days and nights at a stretch. As have Dien and Lars and Otlee. We never lie abed while on duty and neither will you." Dubric stepped closer, nearly nose to nose with Gilby. "If you cannot do this simple task, then perhaps you should resign your post and go home."

"My father would disown me if I quit."

"Are you striving to be dismissed?"

"No, sir."

"I am certain that you know your rank and reputation are abysmal and that you have been placed in my care because there simply is no one else who will be responsible for you."

Gilby winced, but his gaze on Dubric's held. "Yes, sir."

"You will find I am a different sort of taskmaster than those you have had before. I have no pity, and no compassion for laziness, tardiness, or sloth. I also have no fear of Lord Brushgar's wrath or your father's, and unlike Fultin and Borlt, I will not hesitate to dismiss you from your post should you fail to meet my standards of conduct."

"Yes, sir," Gilby said, standing a little straighter.

"You will not receive another warning," Dubric said.

He handed Gilby his notebook. "You shall take my notes for the remainder of today. I expect a thorough record of witness testimonies." One last glare, then he turned to go and saw Arien carrying a sprawling armload of soiled bed linen.

"Good day, milord," she said, jostling her laundry to keep from dropping it. "By the way, milord, thank you for keeping Tupper locked up. Haydon and I are sleeping a lot sounder now." She glanced behind her, then leaned close to whisper, "I'm just trying to stay out of Mister Dughall's way. He's even more angry with me than usual."

"You are quite welcome," Dubric said, bowing his head. "I am relieved to hear that you and your son are all right."

"Thank you, milord." She relaxed a bit and smiled. "Is there something I can help you with?"

"I am seeking a man named Sevver."

She beamed and pointed behind her. "Right down the hall, milord. Can't miss him." A final nod and she hurried away with her soiled linen.

Dubric continued down the hall and rounded a corner, nearly knocking over a man on crutches.

"Oh! Sorry, milord," the young man said, struggling to stay upright even as Dubric grabbed his nightshirt to help. "Still getting the knack of these things and I didn't expect you just then."

"You have my apologies." Dubric looked the man over, noting the cast that covered the man's leg, leaving only his toes exposed. "You would not happen to be Sevver, would you?"

"Ayup, sir, I am," Sevver replied, looking confused. "Is there a problem?"

A nurse hurried up to them. "Sev, are you all right?"

"I'm fine, Peigi." He grasped her hand and pulled her close for a kiss on the cheek. "Just practicing my new three-legged walk so I won't embarrass you next moon."

She blushed and lowered her eyes.

"Isn't she lovely, milord?" Sevver asked. "And to think she agreed to marry me."

"Yes, she is," Dubric said. "I understand your leg was injured in the accident."

"Ayup, sir, it was. Flattened beneath a stone. Thought for sure I'd lose it, but I told that surgeon fella I wanted to keep it, no matter what."

Peigi smiled. "We're just lucky it was repairable. When I first saw it, I was sure there was nothing to be done."

"You saw the injury?" Dubric asked, motioning for Gilby to take notes.

"Yes, milord. I was there when he came in." Peigi said. "His leg was crushed, just bits of bone and burst flesh all mashed together. But we kept the tourniquet on, cleaned it up as best we could, and prayed."

"Must have worked," Sevver said, looking downward. "Hurts like a snarling bastard from my thigh to my foot, but I could wiggle my toes as soon as I woke up. Never thought I'd ever do that again."

Dubric looked down and, sure enough, Sevver's toes flexed and straightened, just as any toes would. "Who repaired your leg?"

"That there surgeon. What's his name?" Sevver asked Peigi.

"Garrett," she said. "Shelby Garrett."

* * *

"Aw, shit," Dien muttered under his breath when he saw a familiar little buckskin tied beside Sideon. "Otlee!"

"Right here," Otlee said, putting away a book as he walked out from between the horses. "Glad I found you. I rode all over town looking for Lars."

Dien untied Sideon. "He's not here. And you're not supposed to be, either. Didn't Dubric tell you to stay home?"

Otlee grinned and rocked back on his heels. "He said he didn't *need* me, and that my day was my own. I thought about it, then decided to volunteer. Because that's what I want to do. With my day." His grin brightened. "So, where's Lars?"

"At the faire."

Otlee's smile fell. "The faire? Why's he at the faire?"

"Because he is. And you should be there, too, enjoying yourself."

"Too many people," Otlee said, his voice cracking as his fingers stole under the cuff of his sleeve. "You sure that's where he is?"

"Yes." Dien introduced Otlee to Marsden and the two quarrymen.

"What's the crime?" Otlee asked. "What's in the sack? What can I do to help?"

"We're searching for a missing boy."

Otlee paled and took a step back. "A missing . . ."

Dien climbed into the saddle. "We told you to stay home, but now that you're here, I can't send you back alone. Mount up. We're assigned to search a field just east of town."

* * *

Garrett handed an elderly patient a vial of powder and ushered him out the door. "Yes, I tended a crushed leg."

"What, precisely, did you do to repair it?" Hoping he

could commit Garrett's words to memory, Dubric scowled at Gilby. The boy dozed against the wall, the notebook sagging in his hands.

"I wanted to amputate but the patient refused. He insisted on keeping his leg. So, after assuring him I could repair it but it would be a long, difficult surgery, I sedated him and amputated it."

"You what?" Gilby asked, opening his eyes. "But I just saw him and he had a leg."

"I removed the leg," Garrett stated, scowling. "If I had not, he would have died. Someone was playing a prank on you, or you are attempting to play one on me. I do not have time for such nonsense."

Garrett pointed toward the door. "If you will excuse me, sir, I have many treatments this afternoon."

"I have a few more questions about surgical procedures." Dubric knew full well that the leg was certainly present. A surgeon had clearly reattached a limb, possibly taking it from the dismembered corpse.

Garrett leaned a hip against his examination table and crossed his arms over his chest. "As do I, milord, but you continually refuse to converse with me about the war. I see no reason to be accommodating if you cannot."

Dubric watched Garrett's eyes. "Perhaps we could discuss mages, then."

"So that I may continue to hear your vitriol about how horrid and evil they are? How they all must die? Even though I clearly find them fascinating, you have insisted that all mages must be exterminated like vermin. Have you come to believe otherwise?"

"No."

Garrett opened the door. "Then we have nothing more to discuss."

Dubric walked to the door and paused. "I am in need of a piece of burlap. Do you know where I might find some?"

"The kitchens always have an ample stack near the outer door. Burlap and other rags are free for the taking."

Dubric thanked him and turned to go, stepping out to the hall. "Oh! Do you know a boy named Raffin? Roughly seven summers old, lives in the workers' shacks?"

"That filthy child who likes to throw rocks and break my windows? Yes, I know him. The little wretch needs his backside paddled."

Before Dubric could say another word, Garrett slammed the door in his face.

* * *

Dubric examined Gilby's notes and cringed. "When I set you to take my notes, I require you to pay attention." He added his own recollections of the conversations with Sevver and Garrett before they were lost. "*Every word* a witness or suspect utters must be noted. Not counted, not alluded to. Specifically written with the precise phrasing they used. You may shorten words and make notations for my statements and questions, but *every single word* a witness utters must be written down. 'Lord B. asked a question, the man answered' does not tell me anything."

"But why?" Gilby asked. "And how? They talk so fast."

"Garrett did not talk quickly," Dubric muttered.

"I'm sorry, sir."

"Sorry does not fix my notes," Dubric said. "People are dying. That should matter."

Gilby looked downward. "Yes, sir."

Dubric willed himself to remain calm. "I am not going to allow you to work without direct supervision until you can show me, prove to me, that you are trustworthy." He shook his notebook. "These notes are abysmal. Do you take class notes like this?"

Gilby shook his head. "No, sir."

"Then why in the seven hells would you think it is acceptable to take mine this way?"

"I didn't know how else to do it, sir."

Did not know? Dubric drew in and released a breath. "Do you take class notes?"

Gilby shook his head.

"Do you have such a memory that you do not require notes?"

Another head shake.

"How, then, do you pass your classes?"

Gilby shrugged. "I don't. Usually."

Dubric stared at the boy for a long time, struggling to find something, anything, to say. At last he said, "That, too, will have to change."

CHAPTER

15

†

Despite questioning several members of the staff, Dubric had no luck locating Klammer Felk, the amnesiac soldier. No one had seen him, no one had heard of him. It was as if he had never existed at all.

While searching in vain for Elena in the hope that she might know something about Klammer Felk, Dubric tried three times to begin a conversation with Gilby, but could not get the boy to utter more than the simplest of pleasantries. Determined, he tried again. "I like to know a bit about the lads who work for me. What do you like to do for recreation?"

"Nothing, milord," Gilby said.

"What about Dien's daughter, Fynbelle? Do you do enjoy doing things with her? See the village minstrels, perhaps, or play jesters? Go fishing or on picnics?"

"No, sir."

"Do you have any questions about the job?"

Gilby just shook his head.

They searched in silence for a time and the quiet began to grate on Dubric's nerves. "Do you have any questions at all?" *Something? Anything?*

The boy looked at Dubric. "You're a high noble, right?"

Dubric had had no choice in his birth parents. Luck alone had delivered his first title, and he had always found his status mildly embarrassing. He could just as easily have been born a merchant or a slave. "Yes," he said.

Gilby's hands clenched, turning his knuckles white. "And you helped make the laws, right? Not just for Faldorrah, but all of Lagiern?"

"Yes," Dubric said softly.

Gilby looked up. "How old, sir? How old until someone doesn't have to obey their parents anymore?"

"It depends on various factors," Dubric said. "For example, a typical girl of sixteen must follow parental guidance, by law if not by actual practice. But if she is married, her parents no longer have a say."

"And a young man?"

"Armies are traditionally filled with men as young as fourteen. Once they make their mark at conscription they no longer answer to their parents. Marriage severs parental rule. Servitude and apprenticeship. Induction into the clergy. Even as young as nine summers, a child can be autonomous from their parents."

"How old, sir? Without joining the army or becoming a priest?"

"A man may purchase land at seventeen," Dubric said, "and marry without consent. He also may vote in public elections and various referendums, should the opportunity occur."

"Seventeen?" Gilby swallowed. "You're sure, sir?"

"Yes."

"Thank you, sir."

After searching two more wards without luck, Gilby said, "May I ask another question, milord?"

"Of course."

Gilby stopped and touched a double triangle symbol etched in a door latch. "This thing. What is it?"

"Why do you ask?"

"It's just . . . Well, it's everywhere, sir. All over this place. And it's even on that man we talked to. Just wondered if it meant something."

Dubric hoped he did not look as surprised as he felt. "What man?"

"That physician. The rude one."

"Describe to me, exactly, how and where you saw that mark on him."

"It's under his hair, sir, behind his ear. It's red with a black center. Saw it when he scratched. What do you call it . . . a tattoo?"

Dubric turned, his heart thudding, but he saw no one suspicious nearby who could potentially hear their conversation.

"Sir? Are you all right?"

"I am fine," Dubric said, ushering Gilby toward the main doors. "We had best find the others."

* * *

"Haydon?" Arien called out, walking into the house.

Her mother sat at the table, smoking as she scraped her fingernails with a knife. "He's sleeping."

"How long?" Arien took a step toward the bed then hesitated. He was lying so still.

"Bell or two." Her mother flicked her scrapings on the table. "Still running that fever."

Arien's heart fell. She continued to the bed, sat on the edge, and felt Haydon's warm brow.

"Mama?" he asked, rolling his head to look at her.

She smoothed his hair. It felt damp and tacky with

sweat. "I'm here, sweetie. Grandmama tells me you're not feeling well."

Haydon shook his head.

"Does it hurt somewhere? Or just a sick feeling?"

"Just sick, Mama." He rolled toward her, leading with his shoulders, and his legs followed, lagging behind. *It's just momentum*, she reminded herself. *Not real movement, but, someday . . .*

"I brought ointment," she said, unlacing his shirt, "and medicine. From the sanatorium."

" 'Kay," Haydon said, drowsy. He lay still while she spread the ointment on his skin and his sores, then she broke a pressed willow bark tablet into quarters. She propped him up and helped him swallow the medicine with a bit of water.

He settled back down, curling on his side. "Know what, Mama?" he asked, yawning, his eyes drifting closed.

She smoothed his hair, and tucked the blanket close. "What, sweetie?"

"I dreamt my feet were cold."

Arien smiled and kissed his cheek. "They're covered. I promise."

* * *

Dubric paced across Marsden's office, his mind churning as he tried to decide what to do about Garrett.

"No sign of the boy, sir," Dien said, breaking the silence. "We looked all over hell and back. The ravine, fields, the cemetery, the marsh, every damn yard and garden in the village. We didn't find any sign of him, but we did find another head. A man, identified as Yaunel Derk. He'd been in the water a day or two."

Otlee rocked on the floor in the corner, hiding behind his knees and writing furiously in his notebook. He winced when Dien mentioned the head. *He was supposed to stay home on holiday.* Dubric thought, *not search for bodies.*

Marsden leaned against his desk. "I got scores of terrified people jumping at shadows. I need to tell them something."

"Tell them we are doing the best that we can," Dubric said. "I only wish we had time to relocate them."

Dien frowned at the door to the cellar stairs. "Damn that Gilby," he said. "How long does it take to feed a prisoner?"

"Maybe he's wiping Tupper's ass," Marsden muttered. He shook his head. "This business was bad enough when it was sheep, or that man no one knew. But that kid lived here. Even if he was a troublemaker, he had a family, a history in this town."

"Every victim has a family and history," Dubric said.

Dien banged on the cellar door. "Hurry your ass up! We've got work to do!"

"I know, milord," Marsden said, "but a child? From my town?"

"There is something you should know," Dubric said. He looked Marsden in the eye. "Garrett may have the mage's mark tattooed behind his ear. If he does, then we need to subdue and capture him quickly."

"Garrett did this?" Marsden asked. "Are you sure?"

"He performed surgeries on the known victims. A man has both legs, even though one was amputated. And Garrett has been taunting me about blood mages since I first arrived here."

Otlee made a squealing noise, but kept rocking and writing.

Marsden nodded slowly. "Garrett. All right. Surely we can capture him."

Cursing, Dien yanked the cellar door open and thundered down.

Marsden sighed. "He really hates that boy."

Something crashed downstairs. Dubric hoped Dien could keep a handle on his temper. "Do not underestimate Garrett. He may be far more powerful than he seems, and I have no way to know how many he has corrupted to aid him."

The men turned as Dien dragged Gilby up the stairs and shoved him through the door. "The little shit was talking to Tupper."

Gilby fell against Marsden's desk. "He was eating. I thought I'd wait for his dishes—"

"By telling him all about our case?" Dien loomed over the boy. "That piss-brained bastard didn't need to know about the head we found, what Garrett said, or that he had that mark by his ear. I heard you telling him about what we know."

"Stop it," Otlee mumbled from the corner.

Marsden threw his hands in the air and started pacing.

"You what?" Dubric stomped across the room and shook Gilby's shoulders. "This is a murder investigation, we are facing a mage, and you gossip about our case to a *suspect*?"

Gilby scrambled away. "I didn't know he was a suspect, I thought he was just a prisoner!"

"Suspect, prisoner, Goddess damned ditch digger, or your best pegging friend, they're all the same. You don't mention cases to anyone!" Dien bellowed, knocking Gilby against the wall.

"No one told me that!"

"I did not think I needed to," Dubric snapped.

"Stop it!" Otlee said, louder this time.

"I was just trying to be friendly. Pass the time. I never meant any harm."

"Intent is immaterial," Dubric said. "Only the damage matters. At least three people are dead, a boy missing, and you may have shown our hand. I do not care who they are, prisoners are never, *ever* our friends. The next time you forget that, I will cut out your tongue."

"Stop it stop it stop it!" Otlee screamed.

Everyone stopped and turned. Otlee was pressed into the corner and stabbing his own thigh with his pencil, punctuating each anguished scream with a downward stab. Blood flicked onto the wall with each strike.

"Don't hurt him!" Otlee wailed, his hands pounding his thighs.

Dubric and Dien abandoned Gilby and hurried to Otlee. Dubric pulled the bloody pencil from Otlee's fist as Dien crouched beside him, drawing Otlee's thin shoulders beneath his own sturdy arm. "Hush now," Dien said. "You're safe. Everything's okay."

Otlee cowered back, panicked, his right hand smeared with blood. "Don't cut out his tongue! Please! Don't. Don't . . ."

"We will not. I promise." Dubric glanced up to Marsden and mouthed *Get bandages.* "Everything will be all right."

"Where's Lars? I just wanted to see Lars!"

* * *

Maeve stood and stretched, her neck cracking. She ached between her shoulder blades from leaning over her work for most of the afternoon without a break. She rolled her head and shoulders to loosen the muscles as she walked to the window. Evening was approaching and the faire was still in full swing, with wandering minstrels and acrobats and hundreds of people looking at wares and livestock.

Too big of a crowd for me alone, she thought, turning away. *And my nieces are likely having fun on their own. Better to get some more work done.*

Lachesis wrapping around her ankles, she opened the main door and waved down a harried lackey to request a supper tray. That done, she rubbed her aching neck and walked into the new suite to stretch her legs, as she had several times during the day. She stopped a few steps past the archway. The air smelled like swampy water and char.

The room had smelled fine a couple of bells ago. *It must be the faire. Perhaps I left a window open.*

The curtains were drawn wide, but the sun had long moved past and the rooms were deep with shadow. The bath chamber door stood open, as she had left it, and the room was clean and sparkling. She walked through the suite, squinting into the shadows, but she couldn't see anything out of the ordinary at all.

As she stepped across the waxed and polished floor, Maeve slipped, wrenching her knee as she fell. She struggled to catch herself, but her palm skid on a puddle of water and sent her flat onto her belly.

Wincing at the pain and her clumsiness, she carefully stood again. She rubbed her sore knee and peered down at the puddle she had slipped in. She saw more small puddles leading to the far corner. They were vaguely greenish against the polished oak planks.

"You have to get it back!"

The whisper had come from the old suite. Maeve shivered, terror rising inside her, but she swallowed and tried to stay calm. "Brinna?" she asked, taking a tentative step back. "What are you trying to tell me?"

No answer, nothing but the stench of bad water and ash.

She heard a faint crackle—*clackityclackityclack*. She turned, her nose wrinkling at a strong scent of rot.

Gurgling, green-gray fluid trickled from the corner toward her, spreading like a stain. She backed away quickly.

Brinna's voice, in her head, "Get it back get it back get it back!"

The water suddenly drew away, retreating to the corner as if it were a piece of silk being drawn into the dark. A shadow rose from it. A woman. Her eyes were swamp green and faintly glowing, but her body was black, flaking and charred and burnt. She opened her mouth as though to speak, her head tilting on a stiff and broken neck as she reached forward, begging, but all Maeve heard was her bones and skin cracking like burning sticks, *clackclackclackclack*.

Paralyzed, Maeve drew a breath to scream. Then the apparition was gone, the floor dry, the air sweet with early summer breeze along with the faint essence of paint and plaster and oil. Letting out her breath hesitantly, Maeve crept forward, but the corner was empty, dry, and clean. Nothing there at all.

* * *

Dubric managed to remove Otlee's trousers despite the boy's shrieks and struggles. Five clustered punctures bled freely among rows of fresh and scabbed gashes. Similar cuts marked the opposite thigh. "What happened to your legs?" Dubric asked.

"Nothing! Let me go, you bastard!" Otlee shrieked, trying to kick Dubric. "Don't you touch me!" Dien and Marsden held him down on Marsden's desk, but the boy fought like a wild thing.

"Hold still. If I do not bandage these, you could lose a great deal of blood."

"I don't care! Let me go!"

Dubric bandaged the wounds. "I care. Have you been harming yourself?"

Otlee shrieked, "A boy's missing, and there's a mage just like before! Lars can kill him! I want Lars!"

Dien looked at Dubric, his expression stricken. "He needs to go home, sir."

Dubric tied off the first bandage then walked around the desk to tend the other thigh. He met Dien's gaze and nodded.

"Not again! Not mages again! *Lars!*" Otlee took a breath and screamed loud enough that Dien and Marsden turned their heads away.

"I need you to calm yourself," Dubric said as he bandaged the gashes on Otlee's left thigh. "Look at me. Take a breath. No one is going to hurt you here."

"You tore my pants off!"

"Only to tend your injuries," Dubric said softly. "Look at me, Otlee. I would never harm you. You know that."

"You shook Gilby," Otlee spat. "And you hit me, back in the Reach. Put a bruise on my face, then . . . The dark. That man!"

"We are no longer in the Reach. You are safe here," Dubric said, finishing the bandages. "Calm yourself, and we will let you go."

Otlee stared at him, his brown eyes furious, but he stopped struggling.

Dien mouthed *One, two, three,* then he and Marsden stepped away.

Otlee scrambled off the table and backed into a corner. Dubric held out the bloody trousers and Otlee snatched them from his hand.

"Can you stay in here while I talk to the others outside?" Dubric asked.

Otlee yanked his pants on. He nodded as he fastened them, then sat on the floor, hiding behind his knees.

Dubric and the others stepped outside and shut the door quietly.

"That boy is a mess," Marsden said as Dubric closed the door. "What happened to him?"

Dien said, "He was severely hurt a moon or so ago, during an investigation. He had no business helping us search for that boy. No business being here at all."

"I know. I had no idea he was harming himself," Dubric said. "Or I would have taken measures to ensure he stayed home."

Gilby stared at his feet and shrugged.

"What is it?" Dubric asked as Dien scowled at Gilby.

"He's been doing it since he came back," Gilby muttered. "I heard some of the pages talking about it. He cuts himself, pisses the bed. Mutters." He shrugged. "Other things."

Marsden cursed.

"What do we do, sir?" Dien asked. "I can't take Otlee

back to the castle, not if you intend to capture Garrett tonight."

Dubric glanced at his ghosts and rubbed his aching eyes. *We cannot catch him with Otlee having hysterics. Marsden is untrained. Gilby's ignorance will get us all killed, and I cannot manage alone. Blast!* He gritted his teeth. "Tell me the truth," he said to Gilby. "Can you safely and efficiently ride home without supervision?"

"No," Dien said, stepping between Gilby and the office door.

Gilby glanced nervously at Dien and pointed east. "Yes, sir. I follow this road east to the paved crossroads, then north to the castle."

"Can you take Otlee home? And not lose him, harm him, or frighten him?"

Gilby nodded. "I'll go straight there, sir."

"And take him to Physician Rolle?"

"Yes, sir. I can do that."

"You're insane," Dien said. "After everything that's happened, you're trusting our Otlee to the bug?"

Gilby winced. "I promise, I *swear*, I'll get him home."

Dubric stepped toward him. "You had better," he said, "because if you fail, I will track you to the ends of the earth. No matter where you hide, how you plead, you will not survive my wrath. Do we have an understanding?"

"Yes, sir," Gilby said. "Straight home, and I'll take him to Physician Rolle." He drew the four moon phases over his heart. "Swear to the Goddess, I'll get him home."

"Never mention that bitch in my presence," Dubric said, then stepped around Dien to open the door to Marsden's office.

CHAPTER

16

✝

Lars checked himself in the mirror one last time. Freshly bathed. Clothes pressed. Hair combed. Teeth clean. Even his shoes were shined. He patted his pocket. Gift in place. All set.

"Hargrove, would you quit primping already?" Serian staggered out of bed. He and Trumble had been allowed four bells of rest before they were back on duty. "You're gonna be late."

"Maybe I should wear my dress uniform instead."

"Moergan borrowed it last phase and it's stained." Trumble yawned, walking to the privy room. "Stop worrying. You've caught her. Jess won't care if you wear rags and bare feet."

Lars smoothed his collar again. "We've been waiting for this dance for so long, I want it to be perfect."

Serian scratched himself before reaching for fresh pants. "Hate to break it to you, Hargrove, but you're not perfect." He yanked the pants on and motioned toward the door. "Relax. Dance her feet off, maybe sneak a feel. Go. Have a good time."

Lars nodded at his reflection and took a deep breath. "Okay, I'm gone. See you guys tomorrow."

Serian grinned. "Yeah, you lucky bastard. Remind us

again how she doesn't have a curfew tonight. Kiss her once for me, willya?"

Trumble laughed from the privy. "If you're passing out favors, tell Jess I'll take a good long grope."

"Over my dead body," Lars said, grinning as he left. He hurried up the stairs to the third floor and her parents' suite. He took a breath and settled his heart before knocking.

Sarea answered. "Oh, Lars," she said. "You look so handsome." She opened the door wide so he could step in. "Jess is almost ready."

Lars paced. *I hope I'm not overdressed. Or underdressed. Or making too much of this. I mean, really, it's just a dance, right? Not a big—*

Then Jess came into the sitting room, nervous and smiling.

She wore a gown of shimmering yellow that clung to her, highlighting the promising curve of her waist, while simple straps over her shoulders left her arms completely bare. Her eyes and lips looked bright, and her hair hung in rivers of dark, shiny curls down one shoulder.

She looked so beautiful, and so happy. *I must be the luckiest man in the castle.* She took his hand, her fingertips dragging along his palm. He bowed slightly to kiss her knuckles.

"You like the dress?" she asked, blushing.

"Very much." He glanced down at the gown then back to her eyes. "I brought you something," he said, pulling the package from his pocket.

"You didn't need to get me anything," she said, untying the ribbon.

"I know." He watched her face, her eyes as she opened the box.

"Oh, Lars," she breathed. "It's beautiful." Jess lifted the necklace to admire the delicate filigree ball. It shimmered around a white stone and floated along a fine silver chain.

He took it from her hands and undid the clasp. Sarea watched them with her hand over her mouth as Jess turned her back to Lars and lifted her hair.

"It's a blessed moonstone in a silver moon orb." He fastened it around her neck and let his fingertips stroke her skin.

"It must have cost you a fortune," Jess said. Then she gasped, "It's engraved!"

My Love, My Always.

Jess leaned against him and he held her close, his arms around her silken waist.

"You didn't need to."

"I know." Goddess, he wanted to kiss her, touch her skin. He tilted his head, gesturing toward the door, and she nodded.

"We'd better get going," she said. "Before we're late."

"You kids have fun."

"We will."

Alone in the hall, Jess wrapped her arms around his neck. "You shouldn't have."

He glanced down to the hollow between her breasts and the fragile silver moon against her throat, then he looked into her eyes. "Oh, yes, I should," he assured her. He kissed her, one hand moving up her arm, caressing her bare skin while the other pressed her close. Sighing happily, he drew back. "Now, let's dance before we get into trouble." One last kiss, then he tucked her hand on his arm and escorted her to the Lord's Spring Ball.

* * *

"What do you need us to do, sir?" Dien asked.

Dubric checked his weapons then looked at Marsden. "Does Garrett visit the Twisted Cypress frequently?"

"Most evenings," Marsden said. "But not all."

"I want to catch him unawares and take him quickly, preferably from behind." Dubric looked at Dien. "I need you to subdue him. He must not be able to move his hands or talk."

"I can kill him, sir. Snap his neck before he even knows I've touched him."

Dubric debated his answer for a moment. If he was wrong, it would be murder. Could he live with that? But if Garrett was a mage, they could all die if they did not kill him first. "If you can, yes," he answered at last. "You may not get the chance."

* * *

Soft chamber music filling the air, Lars nodded to several castle officials as he escorted Jess into the ballroom. He smiled at her astonishment over the crystal sconces draped with ribbons, the flags hanging above, and the grand paintings on the walls. "Never seen the ballroom before?" he whispered in her ear.

"No. I've lived here my whole life and I've never seen it other than a glimpse through the door. It's always been locked, or off-limits or . . . Goddess, is that bird made of *ice*?"

"Looks like it." The bird, a swan, was carved from ice, with its base surrounded by sweets and bits of fruit in tiny silver cups. While Jess stared at the swan, Lars plucked two glasses of wine from a passing server's tray.

He pressed a glass into her hand and encouraged her to sample the treats.

Lars sipped his wine, happily watching her as she nibbled on a delicate square of cake and tried to take in the room.

"Do you do things like this all the time?" she asked as she set the silver cup in a ribboned basket with other empty dishes.

"Never, actually," he said, selecting his own treat. "Dubric always has me working. This time of night, I'm usually out in the game area looking for drunks and pickpockets."

Her eyes glistened with mischief over the wine as she raised it to her lips. "So this is a first for both of us?"

He swallowed his pair of sugar-crusted berries and discarded the cup. "I guess so," he said, reaching for her. She giggled and her lips opened, just a breath, as he leaned close to kiss her.

"This is supposed to be a somber affair," a man said from behind Jess. "Not an adolescent romp."

Lars raised his head to see Sir Newen Talmil select a pair of cups from the assortment. He swallowed one treat, letting the cup fall from his hand to land where whim took it, then raked his gaze down Jess's back. "I'm surprised to see you here, Lord Hargrove. Aren't you usually getting vomited upon by drunken farmers or fetching old ladies' purses from pigs' wallows?"

"Occasionally," Lars said as Jess turned to stand beside him. "But not today."

Talmil munched his second treat. "Yes. I see you have more luminous pursuits in mind," he said, smirking. "I don't suppose you could tell me where I might find my son?"

"I haven't seen him."

"Pity." Talmil raised an eyebrow as he looked at Jess, his gaze lingering on her chest before returning to her face. "And your sister? Where might she be? Alas, I couldn't locate either of them in their usual haunts."

Lars felt Jess's back stiffen beneath his hand. "At home. She hasn't seen Gilby, either."

"Of course she hasn't." A chilly smile frozen on his face, Talmil nodded at Lars then turned to go, soon disappearing into the crowd.

"He makes me feel filthy," Jess said, shuddering.

Lars's free hand rested near his hip as if balanced on the sword he had long been accustomed to wearing. *He makes me wish I were armed.*

* * *

Dubric and Marsden stood in the dark, leaning against the western wall of the Twisted Cypress. Dien hid on the other side of the road, between the boot maker's and the coppersmith's, Dubric guessed. The lack of illumination made Dien's actual location difficult to determine.

"I don't think he's coming," Marsden said.

"Where is he likely to be?" Dubric asked.

"Not sure, sir," Marsden said. "He associates with several women, all of whom have homes and beds he could be in. Maybe he's still at the sanatorium."

"And perhaps he is walking down the road right now," Dubric said, pushing away from the wall as he saw a familiar figure. "Remain calm. We must attempt to keep him at ease."

Garrett strolled toward them, a tipsy young woman on each arm and a delighted grin on his face. He whispered in one girl's ear and she giggled while the other appeared to grasp Garrett's backside. He wriggled forward, laughing, and kissed her.

One girl gasped and the trio slid to a halt. "My Lord Byerly!" Garrett said a bit loudly. "What an unpleasant surprise!"

Dubric walked toward them, Marsden at his side, and was struck by the unmistakable scent of gin, almost as if the three had bathed in it. "How are you this evening?"

"Absolutely lovely, as you surely can surmise from my delightful companions," Garrett said. "And I assume you are your usual curmudgeonly self?"

"Of course," Dubric said, bowing his head as he saw Dien moving toward them. "May I have a moment of your time? I have a private matter I wish to discuss."

Garrett laughed. "You jest, sir. You merely wish to berate me again for my interests, perhaps question my talents as a surgeon. I've had enough of that, I assure you." Arms around his women, he turned and led them toward the tavern.

The woman on Garrett's left tripped, stumbling to her knees, then, as Garrett bent to help her, the other woman squealed and scrambled away. "What the bloody—" Garrett said, turning, and he squawked, falling back and out of Dien's grasp.

Tunkek's blood, we are all dead. Dubric rushed forward. The woman who had fallen jumped on Dien's back and scratched at his face, while the other backed away, screaming. Garrett wailed like a trapped pig and tried to get his feet beneath him, but Dien, with the crazed woman still clawing at him, stumbled into Garrett and knocked him flat on his back.

"Leave him alone!" the woman on Dien's back

shrieked, trying to get a grip around the big man's throat.

Dubric reached down to grasp Garrett, then grunted as the other woman started pounding his back with her clasped fists. She lunged at him and he grabbed her shoulder and swept her off her feet with his leg.

Marsden pulled the screaming woman off Dien's back and held her aside while Dien flipped Garrett onto his belly. The physician squealed and struggled, but Dien held him down, his hand crushing the side of Garrett's face into the road and his knee on the small of his back.

"What'd I do?" Garrett screeched, his voice a muffled squeal under the pressure of Dien's weight. Garrett's eyes grew wide as Dien flicked his dagger out of its sheath and flipped it in his hand right in front of the physician's face. "For Goddess's sake! Please!"

No magic. He has cast no magic. He should have slaughtered us by now. "Hold!" Dubric said. He knelt and swept Garrett's hair away from his ears. Nothing.

"I've got the girls," Marsden said, his voice shaky. "Do what you need to do."

"I need to see the other side," Dubric said, and Dien obliged, yanking Garrett's head to face the other way.

Garrett whimpered, tears streaming down his cheeks. "Please. Please don't kill me."

Dubric released a hiss and, beside him, Dien cursed. The mark, two red triangles with a black diamond center, was tattooed behind Garrett's right ear at the top of his neck. "I will slit your throat right here in the road if you do not answer my questions correctly," Dubric said.

"Yes," Garrett said. "Anything."

"How did you get that mark behind your ear?"

Garrett swallowed, his upward-facing eye rolling back to glance at Dien's dagger. "I've had it a couple of summers. Just thought it'd be interesting. It's nothing, just a tattoo. I swear!"

"What does it represent?" Dubric asked, leaning close. "Specifically?"

"It's . . . it's just a mark used by some mages. It's all over the sanatorium. I never meant any—"

"What mages?"

Garrett cringed, tears leaking out of his eyes. "The three sisters."

Dubric looked up at Dien. "Remove his nose."

"No! No! Wait! They were blood mages, from the Casclian Mountains! Glynte, Fayre, and Selle Sweeny. I just . . . I just found them fascinating!"

The mages Otlee found? Dubric looked up at Dien again. "Perhaps this is not the best location for this conversation."

"All right." Dien rolled back, creaking Garrett's spine, then yanked the physician to his feet. "C'mon, shit heap. We're taking a little walk." Garrett's wrists in one hand, his own dagger in the other, Dien shoved the man down the road and into the dark.

"Where's he going?" one of the women asked, struggling in Marsden's grip.

"Somewhere quite painful," Dubric said. "You may join him, or you may go home. Immediately."

* * *

"Gilby? Where in the Goddess's name have you been? I've been looking all over for you," Serian said, Lars's mutt trotting beside him as he patrolled along the castle walls.

Gilby glanced at Fyn and stretched, letting the east

tower door swing shut behind him. "Been gone. All day. Reassigned to Dubric and I just got home."

Gilby looked exhausted, and he stank of horse and sweat. "Nobody told me," Serian said, walking behind a row of vendor tents with the couple. "The old bastard back, too? Dien's gonna have your ass if he sees you two out here."

Gilby draped his arm over Fyn's shoulders. "Nah, they're still at the town. Had me bring Otlee home. He had the hells scared out of him so I left him with his folks." He kissed Fyn's head then said, "I'm off duty. See you later."

"*Otlee* had the shit scared out of him and you took him to his folks? Is that what Dubric told you to do?"

Gilby turned, wincing in his usual manner. "Dubric said to take him home, have Rolle look him over, then get him to bed. Well, Rolle wasn't in, so I left a note then changed Otlee's bandages, gave him a bit of my father's laudanum, and took him on home."

Serian wanted to pull his hair out. Instead, he cursed. "Otlee's *home*, you pegging idiot, is in the pages' quarters. After what happened last moon, some well-meaning ass told his mam that molested boys molest other kids, especially their siblings. She *beats* him to keep him away from his little brother and sister, you shit, and his father's too drunk to stop her. And laudanum? An opiate? Goddess, he's a kid! Pull your fool head out of your ass and think, for once. And if you can't think, ask!"

Cursing, he shoved past Gilby and stomped into the castle, with Lars's dog on his heels.

* * *

Dubric followed Dien into Marsden's office and watched as Dien flung Garrett into a chair.

Dubric stood before the young physician, staring down at him while Dien fastened his binds. "If you lie to me one time, I will kill you. Do you understand?"

"K-kill me?"

"As I have told you many times, I kill mages. On sight."

"The only good mage is a dead mage," Dien muttered. He finished tying Garrett then drew his sword. "Took the head off the last one I met."

Garrett squealed at the sleek hiss of steel on sheath then breathed in rapid gasps as he looked between Dubric and Marsden. "You know me!" he cried, his shaky gaze on Marsden. "Tell him! Tell him I'm no mage!"

"I can't tell him anything," Marsden said. "Right after you came here, sheep began disappearing. That mark behind your ear matches one we've found on the dead sheep."

"That's not possible!"

"But it is true," Dubric said. "We have found your patients dead in the ravine. The boy you said you wanted to paddle is missing, probably dead, and you insist, against all sanity or reason, to be intrigued by blood mages. If you are not a castor of shadow, you are surely a follower, a blood bond."

Garrett shook his head. "No! I'm not, I swear!"

"Why did you come here?" Dubric asked. "Why Quarry Run?"

"A job! They offered me a job!"

Dien tapped him on the back of the head with the hilt of his sword. "Horse piss. No one offers a slimy slip of a lecher like you a job caring for the sick. You had to come looking for it."

"Why?" Dubric asked again.

"Because of the sisters," Garrett said, frantic. "They found the secret, the Valley! Two died, but one lived, and she came here, came to Quarry Run." He swallowed and leaned forward. "Please, I just came to look for the Valley. It's here, somewhere!"

"We don't have a Valley," Marsden said. "There aren't any mountains, only hills and fields."

"It . . . it's not that kind of Valley." Garrett turned his head to stare at Dubric. "Don't you want to live forever? Don't you want eternal life?"

"No one lives forever," Dubric said.

"The sisters did! It's what they found! Don't you see? The Valley of the Soul! It's there, between the mountains!"

"I thought you said they were dead," Marsden said.

"Two are. They were murd—er, killed during the war, by mage killers. But they'd lived nearly four hundred summers! And their sister, the one who lived, came here. They said she couldn't be killed, that she was the one who'd found the Valley. That she's *still here*."

* * *

No one was dancing.

Lars and Jess sat at a round table with the head archer, Werian, and his very pregnant wife; the head accountant, Jelke, and his companion, a big-bosomed woman named Gwennie, who spent the meal fawning over him. Lars had endured the entire meal forced to remember his failure at archery every time he looked at Werian, and being bored senseless by the administrative conversation between the adults. He hesitated to be the first on the dance floor, where Lord Brushgar—and possibly every other person of power in central Faldorrah—would see. Better to stay put, stay quiet, and hope Jelke and Werian would bore themselves to sleep.

Jess also looked bored. Sleepy. *She's supposed to be having fun. Not sitting here falling asleep.* Getting sleepy himself, Lars put his arm over the back of her chair and looked around.

Two tables to the right, Lord Brushgar laughed and drank ale with titled performers from the faire. Physicians Rolle and Halld sat at the next-closest table with their wives, along with Friar Bonne and the head scribe. Lars nodded to Bonne and Rolle, wishing there were open chairs at their table.

Lars looked to the left, and immediately met Lord Talmil's chilly stare. While the new herald and his wife chatted with Squire Fultin and Eamonn the mapmaker, Talmil leaned over to speak to the ferrotypist, his eyes fixed on Lars. Smiling and his eyebrow raised in a slight challenge, Talmil sat straight again and sipped his wine, his gaze never leaving Lars's.

Aren't nobility supposed to be on Brushgar's right and officials on the left? Why are you in the wrong place? And what's the ferrotypist doing up front? Faire vendors are farther back. He's not even wearing formal attire.

"They're dancing," Jess whispered, pulling Lars's attention back to their own table.

"Good." Lars offered his hand, helping her rise.

The other dancing couples were decades older, all castle nobility or village officials, and they gave the young couple confused looks as the pair walked onto the dance floor. After a brief hesitation, Lars and Jess slipped somewhat uneasily into the quadrille with Sir Neworth and his wife.

Their quadrille turned and Lars nodded politely to Lady Neworth as he became her partner. She had to be nearly fifty, but she blushed like a girl at his lead. Another set of steps, another turn, then Jess again, their raised palms almost touching.

"You're a better dancer," she whispered as she matched his hop-step and twirl, an embellishment he hadn't attempted with Lady Neworth. "I think she's a bit smitten with you."

They eased their bodies close then backed away, their hands remaining a breath apart. "That's too bad, because I'm smitten with you."

Jess giggled, their palms touching for a whisper of time, then the quadrille turned again and Lars led Lady Neworth through the end of the dance.

They danced another quadrille with a different pair, then a calm gallopade, as staid and predictable as the quadrilles. As Lars drew Jess in precise curves across the dance floor, he tried to dismiss the stodgy dances, the dull table conversation, and even the age differences. He thought only of her, her hand on his shoulder, the beckoning curve of her waist, and the taste of her lips.

Lars glanced to their table, expecting to see Werian and Jelke still discussing finances, and nearly tripped. Talmil was sitting in his chair, Jerle Dughall in Jess's, and they were passing what looked like ferrotypes around the table.

He felt Jess's fingers on his cheek, turning his face to look at her. "Off duty, remember?"

"Sorry," he said, drawing her near. The distance was

technically too close for the particular dance, but he didn't care.

"I'm having a good time," she said, her hand sliding from his cheek to his collar, a fingertip lingering on his neck.

He eased her closer and received a few tsk-tsks from nearby couples. "Do you think we might have a better time if we left?"

"We might," she said. "Fyn told me that minstrels play in the northeast corner every faire."

"Let's go see," Lars said. He guided Jess out of the structured dance and back into the supper crowd. A few minutes later, they passed through the east tower and into the night.

* * *

"I get caught away from my post, it's gonna be my ass," Serian muttered as he pounded on Bacstair the baker's door. The dog sat beside his feet, its ears perked. "C'mon," Serian said. "I can hear you in there."

The door flew open and Bacstair peered out, wobbling, an open whiskey bottle in hand. He smelled of bread and old booze, and looked like he'd been crying. "What?" He wiped his nose with his sleeve.

Serian pushed past him. "Where's Otlee?"

Bacstair took a swig of whiskey and stared at the dog as it followed Serian in. "He died a moon ago. That sick bastard killed my bright little boy."

"He's not dead," Serian said.

"Not his body. His soul." Bacstair drew a shaky breath. "He was supposed to have a good life, make something of himself, but he's gone. My boy's . . . gone."

Serian stomped farther into the suite. He found the

other children asleep in their beds, their mother sitting just inside the bedroom door with a willow switch in her hands. She glared at him, her cheek twitching.

"Where is he?"

She pointed across the hall. "I didn't beat him. Didn't need to."

Serian turned and opened the door, but it hit something soft. He pushed, gently, until he could just squeeze through. Otlee lay curled on the privy room floor, his knees to his chin. He was deadly still, his eyes wide open, and bloody bandages were tangled around his wrists.

"Aw, damn," Serian said, kneeling. "C'mon, little guy," he said, trying to lift Otlee. "Let's get you out of here."

Waking from his strange trance, Otlee began to shriek and kick, his limbs flailing weakly. His eyes stared ahead, but didn't seem to actually see. "He's taking boys! Cutting off heads!"

Serian snatched Otlee up, restraining his movements. The opiate Gilby had given the boy had made him half-limp and difficult to hold. "I hear you," Serian said as he opened the privy room door. "Everything's gonna be okay."

Otlee's head rolled back. "It's not going to be okay. Never. Dubric's going to cut out his tongue."

The dog fell in beside Serian's heel as he strode across the suite. *The kid's drugged half out of his mind.* Serian opened the door, struggling to hold Otlee as he worked the latch, then carried him out without saying a word to Otlee's silent parents.

For being almost thirteen, the kid was awfully little. Too small, too thin. It was like carrying a child of only eight or nine summers. Otlee's head bobbing against his shoulder, Serian opened the door to his room and carried Otlee in. He didn't trust Otlee's roommates to treat the kid decently under the best of circumstances, let alone when he was medicated halfway to heaven. "Okay, here you go," he said, pulling back the blanket on Lars's bed. "You can sleep here tonight."

Otlee sat on the bed, looking around with a dreamy expression on his face. "This is Lars's room," he said as if it were the most miraculous thing he'd ever seen.

"Yep." Serian took off Otlee's shoes, then patted the bed, encouraging Lars's dog to jump up. The mutt leapt up and settled in beside Otlee. "And this is his dog, Kedder."

"Lars doesn't have a dog," Otlee said in an airy voice.

"He's got a dog now. I have to go back to work, but the pup's gonna stay with you, okay? You get some sleep."

"Sleep in Lars's room. Yes. Sounds fine." Otlee started to lie down then fell over, curling on his side. He immediately fell asleep.

Serian covered him. The dog snuggled close, his black muzzle resting on Otlee's hip.

* * *

Maeve bathed and readied for bed. She wished Dubric would come home, so they could talk, so she could see his face.

I don't know what's wrong with me, she thought as she put on her sleeping gown. *Was I like this with Braoin?*

It had been eighteen summers, a lifetime ago, when she had been pregnant with her son. Her hand fell to her belly, to its soft and rounded curve, not the firm, flat one she'd had at sixteen. She wondered if life had taken root there, if at thirty-four she could survive the birth, if . . . if she should marry him.

It seemed underhanded to agree to marry him then tell him she might carry his child. She was half his age and knew his steady slide into old age bothered him; the aches, the pains, the slow decline. Was he trying to regain a bit of his youth by being with her? Would he want a child? If she was indeed pregnant—at a whole phase late with her courses and her breasts feeling as though they had been lit on fire, she deemed it fairly likely—he would be in his mid-eighties when the child reached maturity. Would he even be alive? Would she? Young women handled the rigors of birth fairly well, but she was no longer young. What would that do to Dubric? To have a second wife and child die?

"Goddess, what a mess," she said as she sat on their bed and blew out the light.

He deserves an answer. She touched her belly again. *And he deserves to know the truth.*

She smiled. *I do love him. I love his grace and kindness, his responsibility, his strength, his certainty.* She lay back. *I love the way he smells, the way he kisses me, his touch, his laugh, how he always turns a cup around before first drinking from it, his refusal to eat beans, the way he mumbles in his sleep.*

She crawled beneath the covers, wrapping herself around his pillow. It smelled like him, like home. He was hale and healthy, other than a bit of arthritis in his knees and hands. He had all of his teeth, perfect vision, and a clear mind. There was no reason to think he wouldn't live another two decades, perhaps even three. *Long enough,* she decided. *Long enough to be happy.*

She smiled, snuggling in, then the smell of swamp

and ash hit her again. Not in the pillow but all around, as if she were drenched with it.

She opened her eyes but otherwise held perfectly still.

Clackclackclackclack

Then cold, dead breath on her cheek.

She didn't have time to scream.

CHAPTER

17

†

It was near midnight when Dien and Dubric left their horses in the stable and trudged to the castle with Yaunel's head in a sack. All around them, parties and late celebrations filled the courtyard with music, revelers danced, and faire workers called out for late night games of chance.

The ghosts floated ahead, but Dubric barely saw them. He had too much on his mind and too many worries in his gut. Garrett was misled, an eager child romanticizing a horror. He was not their killer. But Dubric had seen the rooster head, detached from its body yet still alive. Something had kept it alive when all reason stated it should be dead. Someone in Quarry Run practiced shadow magic. If Garrett was not responsible, then who?

* * *

The dance finished and Jess laughed as she fell against Lars, the back of her head thudding against his shoulder. "Once I catch my breath, I'll need another cider."

"Me, too." He wrapped his arms around her waist and leaned his head back against the cool stones of the outer wall. They'd found plenty of minstrels playing for coins and dances, but had soon decided the best were in the northeastern corner of the courtyard, near the cooper and the wheelwright.

The three men played lively music that was perfect for dancing, if exhausting. About a dozen young couples and a few singles danced in a loose and hopping group, nobles and commoners alike. Bells of music and dance and laughter in Jess's eyes.

The minstrels chose their next song and began playing. It sounded like a hop-hop-slide-turn tune, a modified couple's redowa. And a fine thing it was. Like flying.

Jess turned in his arms and grinned, her necklace glowing softly as she wrapped her arms around his waist. "You want to get that cider or bounce around some more?"

"Cider," he said, lifting the glowing ball and letting his knuckles drag across her skin. The moonstone shone like its namesake from within its delicate cage, its shimmer more silvery than he had expected. It felt cool to his fingers and he let it fall, watching it roll below her throat and illuminate the glimpsed curves of her breasts.

Her eyes grew soft and drifted closed when she kissed him. "Cider," she whispered as they both drew a breath. "Then another dance?"

"My whole night is yours," he said, kissing her again.

A cider merchant had set up a booth perhaps fifty lengths away, handily between the minstrels and a group of game vendors. Lars bought two ciders, but instead of returning to the dance he led Jess away from it. "Let's take a walk," he said.

Hand in hand, they strolled and sipped their ciders,

pausing occasionally to observe a game or watch an acrobat earn a few last crown. "Have you had a good time?" he asked.

"Oh, the best!" she said. "The whole day's been wonderful."

Good. They looked over some scarves in one of the few remaining vendor booths. "Even the dinner?"

She winked at him as they walked to the next open booth, a man selling little glass goblets. "The food was good but I like these outdoor dances better, I have to admit."

"Me, too." They walked along, watching a farm boy win a copper pot at a ring toss game, and Lars tried to settle his hammering heart. "There's something I . . ." He took a breath and said, "Would you be my intended, Jess?"

She stopped in mid-step and turned to look at him.

He grasped her hand. "I love you, and I'd be honored if you'd be my intended. Just me, just you. Every dance, every event."

Her eyes searched his, questioning. "We've only courted a moon. My dad—"

He kissed her knuckles and grinned. "I've already asked your dad."

"Intended to become betrothed." She set aside her mug on an empty vendor's table and moved close. "How does that change things?"

He put his mug beside hers. "I had planned to wait and ask you before I kissed you, but that fell by the wayside last night."

"Yes, it did," she said softly.

He swallowed, feeling her breasts press against his chest, her belly and hips against his. "Maybe I could touch you?" he asked, tentatively letting his hand slip downward, off the small of her back.

Her eyes closed slowly then opened again. "Touching is good."

Yes, it is. He glanced down at the inviting curves crushed against his chest. A pale vein was just visible beneath her faintly freckled, translucent skin. He swallowed and moved his hand on her back a little lower, holding her against him. "This is all right?"

"It's fine," she said, her voice soft.

He kissed her, one hand caressing her bottom, the other cradling her head, and he almost cried out as her lips parted beneath his and he tasted her tongue.

She clung to him as they stumbled against a cool wall. He could barely breathe and she, too, seemed to have trouble finding air as he explored her cider-sweet mouth.

* * *

"Serian!"

Serian turned on his heel to see Dien coming toward him. "Yes, sir," Serian said. "On patrol, sir."

Dien yawned. "Have there been any catastrophes?"

"No, sir, nothing major. A few pick thieves, some drunks. The usual."

"What about Gilby? Otlee?"

"They're here. I've seen both. They're fine."

Dien's eyes narrowed. "What happened? Do you know what Rolle said about Otlee?"

"Um. Rolle's still at the formal ball, as far as I know. Gilby left him a note and I put Otlee in Lars's bed. Thought our suite might be quietest, with most of us gone all night."

Dien looked at a group of revelers dancing. "Most?"

"Moergan was off duty at midnight, but I've already told him about Otlee, sir. Made sure he understood no visitors. The boy needs to rest."

"Have you seen Lars and Jess?"

"Yes, sir. Several times. They've been moving from minstrel to minstrel, dancing. Seem to be having a lot of fun."

Dien chuckled. "Good. Glad someone's had a good day." His smile disappeared as he asked, "Where's Gilby now?"

Serian tried to keep his expression calm. Now would *not* be a good time for Dien to decide to talk to Gilby. "I don't know, sir. Probably enjoying the faire." As soon as the words passed his lips, Serian knew he was caught. He'd always been a shitty liar.

Dien's expression hardened even further and he took a menacing step toward Serian. "Is he with Fyn?"

Serian took a step back. "I don't know anything about that."

"Yes you do," Dien said, his voice falling low and dangerous. "Is Gilby with my baby?"

Another step back. "Honest, sir, I don't know."

Dien followed. "He wouldn't look me in the eye all day. Not that that's unusual, but it got me thinking. You see, I've heard a rumor."

Serian swallowed. Dien had backed him against the castle wall. "I don't know anything about rumors."

"He seemed awfully eager to bring Otlee home and leave us back in Quarry Run." Dien's head tilted. "Did he happen to meet my daughter?"

"Sir, really, I—"

Dien pushed Serian's chest with a single finger, accentuating each word. "Did that piece of worthless filth meet up with my innocent, underage daughter?"

Serian clenched his teeth and gritted out, "I can't say, sir. I've been patrolling the faire."

Dien loomed close, but movement must have caught his eye because he turned, blindingly fast for a man of such bulk. "Norbert," he purred, his voice low and deadly.

Norbert, another low-ranking junior page often assigned duties with Gilby, emerged from the crowd clutching an ale in one hand and rubbing his eyes with the other. As Dien spoke, he jerked to attention and dropped his drink. "I'm off duty!" he yelped, wavering slightly on his feet.

"Where's Gilby?" Dien asked, as sweet as honeysuckle nectar, his thick shadow immersing the boy in darkness.

Serian reached for him. "Sir, I'm sure if we went inside, you'd find Gilby goofing off somewhere."

Dien shrugged off Serian's touch. "Where is he, Norbert? I know you two are friends."

"We're not friends," Norbert said. He wiped his nose with the back of his arm and said, "Not anymore. All he wants to do is spend time with her."

"Who's 'her'?" Dien asked, his voice syrupy sugar and death.

Serian grasped Dien's shoulder and tried again. "Sir, really, he's probably inside. Let's just go take a look, okay? Norbert's drunk. He's got no idea."

"Remove your hand now or I'll cut you in half," Dien said.

Serian took a breath and held on to Dien's jacket, tugging the squire toward him. "Sir, please. Let's go inside."

Dien turned, a blur of movement, and shoved Serian backward against the wall. Serian's head smacked the stones and he slid to the ground, dazed. "You had your chance," Dien snarled.

He turned back to Norbert, his voice less sugar and more threat. "Where, you little shit? Where'd he take my daughter?"

Serian got his feet beneath him and started to stagger upright, then slipped back to one knee. *I can't let him find Gilby. He'll kill him.*

Norbert squawked in pain. Dien held him up by his shirt collar, his feet flailing a length or more above the ground. "The grain barn! They always go to the grain barn!"

Norbert fell to the ground, whimpering, as Dien stomped away. Serian lurched to his feet and stumbled after.

Dien shoved through a crowd of gamblers, pushing past them as though they were stalks of grass. Serian, trying to keep his eyes on Dien's menacing bulk, went around them and found Trumble leading a sloppy drunk toward the east tower.

"You're coming with me," he said, grabbing Trumble by the arm.

"What? Why? I've got three more drunks—"

Serian pointed to Dien. "He's heading to the grain barn and he's already knocked me on my ass once."

"Aw, piss," Trumble muttered. He ran ahead. "Sir!" he called out. "I have a question! There's a problem with one of the drunks. Do you know—"

Dien grabbed Trumble by the head, Trumble's face lost beneath his palm, and shoved him away.

Trumble landed on his ass, and Serian heard his teeth clack together. "Oh, he's furious," Trumble said, scrambling up again.

Dien reached the grain shed and ripped the door

open, tearing it half off the hinges. He stomped in, the two pages trailing like shadows behind him.

"Sir, please. Let us get him, okay?"

Dien headed for the stairs without a moment's pause.

Trumble ran ahead, placing himself between Dien and the loft steps. "Sir, we're asking you to stand down. Please."

"That lying little shit is with my daughter." One sweep of Dien's arm and Trumble fell aside, rolling against a stack of bagged grain.

A couple, naked and panicked, slipped past them down the stairs, clothes clutched over their privates.

Dien glanced to the left as he passed another couple hurriedly dressing between hay bales, and a third pair caught in the act of coupling.

Two steps later, Dien stopped and Serian heard all the breath fall out of him. Fyn and Gilby lay sprawled together in a cozy little nest between straw bales, naked and blinking awake beneath Gilby's cloak. Gilby sat upright and Fyn cowered behind him. "I . . . I've been meaning to talk to you," he said, his voice shaking.

Serian made one last attempt. Hoping to take Dien by surprise, he shouldered the big man from behind and tried to get between Dien and Gilby. But Dien was too fast. He knocked Serian aside as though he weighed nothing at all, then reached down and grabbed Gilby by the throat. Fyn screamed.

Two punches to Gilby's face, cracking bones, by the sound, then Dien flung him back, over Trumble and toward the stairs.

"I can't let you, sir," Trumble said as Serian got his feet beneath him again.

Dien just snarled and tossed Trumble into the bales.

He charged after Gilby, Serian right behind him, then kicked the naked page down the stairs.

* * *

A scream rang through the air and Lars pulled back from Jess's lips. "Did you hear that?" he asked, holding her close.

"Yes," she said, nodding against his throat. Crashes, then another scream. *"No, Daddy! No!"*

"That's Fyn." Lars grasped Jess's hand and dragged her away from the wall. "Where is she?"

"I . . . I don't know!" Jess said.

As they came out from between two vendor tents, Lars saw people running toward the grain barn. "Piss!" Lars muttered. "Stay here." He ran, reaching for a sword that wasn't there.

Fyn's screams echoing in his ears, Lars yanked the sagging grain shed door open and leapt aside as Trumble slammed against the half-open door and tumbled into the courtyard. Something moved in the darkness ahead, something big.

A boy, dark-haired and covered with blood, flopped limply onto the stack of grain bags to Lars's left.

"Dammit! Stop! You're gonna kill him!" Serian screamed.

Dien's voice. "Yes, I am."

Lars scrambled around a pile of grain sacks and squinted in the dim light.

"Goddess damned son of a whore! Hargrove!" Serian cried as he slammed into the wall and fell. "Help me!"

"Stay out of this, pup." Dien grabbed Gilby by the foot and flung him aside, slapping him against the wall above Serian. The page left a dark, wet smear behind and Lars heard a bone snap. Gilby didn't make a sound.

Fyn crawled toward them, naked and speckled with blood. "Daddy, please," she begged.

Lars glanced at Serian, who was struggling to stand—*no help there*—then he stepped swiftly between Gilby and Dien, staring into Dien's crazed eyes. "He's punished enough. Stand down."

"The hells I will," Dien said, and he knocked Lars aside, hard against the bags of grain. Something in Lars's shoulder popped and pain shot down his arm and up his neck.

Serian growled, and jumped onto Dien's back, but Dien flipped the page off as easily as shrugging off a cloak.

Lars ignored his throbbing shoulder and ran between Dien and Gilby again. "It's done. Stand down."

"It isn't done till I say it is," Dien said.

"Oh, Goddess!" Jess cried to Lars's right, but he didn't turn to look at her.

"Get Fyn," he said. "Get her out of here."

"I'm not leaving without Gilby!" Fyn screamed, but Jess dragged her away.

"Get out of my way, pup. I've got business to attend to."

"You're done," Lars said softly. "And we're going to go inside and have an ale, maybe talk to Dubric."

"I found the shit naked with my baby daughter!" Dien bellowed.

"I know," Lars said softly. "But if you kill him, that's murder. You're not a murderer. Stand down."

"He raped my baby!"

His gaze resting on Dien's larynx, Lars took a step

toward him. "He didn't rape her. She was willing. It's done. Please."

Serian, bruised, battered, and bleeding, stood beside Lars. "We can't let you hurt him any more. I'm sorry, sir."

"He deserves to die," Dien said, wiping his mouth with the back of his hand. Behind him, in the dark, Lars saw Dubric, three soldiers, and Fultin approaching with ropes.

Relieved, Lars looked into Dien's eyes. "Fyn chose him a long time ago, and you know it. Please, back away. Let us tend him."

"You can't tend him if he's dead." Dien lunged forward but ropes looped through the air around him, encircling his chest and throat, pulling him back. Dien screamed, fighting, but in the end they dragged him down. With Fultin and the soldiers keeping Dien subdued, Dubric hurried past to check Gilby.

"Where's my baby?" Dien asked, struggling as the soldiers bound his hands. "Where's my daughter?"

Lars knelt beside Dien and removed his weapons with his working arm. "She's with Jess. And you, my friend, are under arrest."

CHAPTER
18

✝

Lars held Jess with his good arm and tried not to yawn. They waited, observed by two soldiers, on a bench outside the physicians' office while the victims of Dien's rampage were behind the closed door. Jess had no injuries, just Gilby's blood drying on her dress, but Lars had lost feeling in his left hand. His shoulder and chest on that side burned with constant pain. It seemed likely that he'd dislocated his shoulder. They'd been under guard since the incident, tucked quietly away, silent and hidden. Lars knew exactly what was happening.

Catastrophe containment.

Dubric had sent a lackey to fetch Rolle from the ball and, with luck, no one outside their small circle had heard what had happened yet. Not Sarea, not Gilby's father, and hopefully not Lord Brushgar. Dubric would keep the incident quiet as long as possible to clarify the situation before emotions ran rampant. Lars prayed it would be long enough. If Talmil or Lord Brushgar became involved before Dubric had everything straightened out, Dien would likely hang.

"They're going to be all right," he whispered to Jess. "Even Gilby. He was conscious when they brought him in. That's a positive sign."

She nodded, then sat upright as the door opened and Dubric came through with a sheaf of papers. He looked at Jess. "Wake your mother and tell her that Fynbelle had a fright and needs comforting, nothing more. Change your clothes before you wake her and do not mention Gilby or your father. Not yet."

"Yes, sir," Jess said, standing. She squeezed Lars's good hand then left.

"And me, sir?"

Dubric motioned for the soldiers to leave. When they were alone, Dubric stared Lars in the eye. "I want you out of your finery and in a working uniform immediately. Your holiday is officially suspended and you are back on duty."

* * *

Dubric entered his office and slammed the door, then tried to smooth out the papers he had crushed. He saw that Dien had calmed from rage to tightly focused fury. He had been shackled to the chair by his arms, legs, and chest, and he sat staring at the floor, his breathing hoarse, hard, and angry.

"You are damned lucky," Dubric said, walking to his desk and snapping through the notes. "Rolle tells me the boy will live."

"Not long, he won't," Dien snarled.

Dubric pushed aside a pile of Gilby's clothes then leaned against his desk. "Would you like to explain what happened?"

"My daughter is thirteen summers old!"

"Gilby is seventeen. She is young, true, but we have pulled younger girls from the loft."

"I don't give a damn about other children, just my own!"

Dubric sighed. "I sent you to ask Serian about faire

security. How did that lead you to beating Gilby nearly to death in the grain shed?"

"Gilby dumped Otlee on Serian then abandoned his post, and after all the messes he made today . . . He's a worthless, lazy shit, sir, you know that."

"I see, and when you saw him with your daughter you snapped?"

"Something like that," Dien muttered.

"What if it were Lars?" Fynbelle asked from the door, and Dien turned his head to look at her. "What if you found me with Lars instead of Gilby?" Her thin face shone with tears. "Tell me the truth, Daddy."

"It doesn't matter who it was. You're too young."

"I see." Fynbelle bit her lip. "Jess has liked Lars since she was little and not once have you tried to keep them apart." She sniffled. "They've only been courting a moon and you let her stay out all night. If you'd found Jess and Lars in the loft, what would you have done? He's not much younger than Gilby and Jess is barely a summer older than me. What would you have done, Daddy? Would you have beat Lars until he bled? Would you have thrown him down the stairs?"

"Lars wouldn't have done that! Can't you see, Fyn? Gilby's a frigging delinquent. Lars isn't that way."

"And neither is Jess. Right? She's planning on attending University and Lars will do whatever you say, so it's all right for them to court, even stay out all night. Is that what you're telling me?"

"No, it's not what I'm telling you. I'm saying that lazy little shit isn't good enough for my daughter, especially when she's thirteen summers old!"

Fynbelle raised her chin. "I'm already marrying age in Klandan and Gattol and Flisske and I don't know how many other places."

"Too bad. This is Faldorrah and you're not even courting age yet."

"I love him, Daddy."

"No you don't! You're only thirteen. This is just a passing thing."

"He's not a passing thing, Daddy! I've loved him for as long as I can remember! Why don't you like him? Why? What's he ever done that was so horrible?"

Dien took a deep breath. "He lies, Fyn. Cheats. Sneaks out of work and lets other pages take the fall for him. He gambles and drinks too much. Today he couldn't even look after Otlee when he was hurt. You can do so much better."

"I don't want to do better. I want Gilby."

"You don't know what you want. You're just a child."

"I'm not a child!" she cried. "I'm a woman! I've been having my monthlies for a whole summer now and I've fallen in love! Why can't you see that?" Tears streaming down her cheeks, she stomped to the outer office. "Stop treating me like a baby!"

The outer door slammed and Dien turned to Dubric. "You knew she was standing there, didn't you?"

Dubric looked up from the notes. "Your daughter has a sprained arm and several bruises. The boy has three broken ribs, a broken arm, nose, cheek, and a concussion. His jaw and left thigh are dislocated, and both of his wrists are sprained. That is just the beginning. Do you have any idea how much trouble you have caused?"

"No, but if his hip's dislocated he's not gonna be pegging my daughter again, is he?"

"Sir Talmil will call for your head. I cannot say that I blame him."

"You tell Talmil I'll bust his Goddess damned legs.

He and his worthless shit of a son can recuperate to-gether."

Dubric folded Rolle's notes in half, tucking them under his arm. Pulling his keys from his pocket, he un-locked one of Dien's wrist shackles and shoved the physician's notes in his hand. "You almost cost your grandchild his father. You might want to think about that before you resume your beatings."

* * *

Lars struggled to pull off his jacket without scream-ing. He bit his lip as he peeled the jacket sleeve off his bad arm. After a fumbling start, he managed to unbut-ton his shirt and work his way out of it. His shoes proved trickier, since bending over sent a wave of agony through his shoulder. His bad arm curled against his belly, he sat on his bed, then jumped up, turning.

Someone was in his bed with his dog. The person rolled over and Lars saw two pairs of eyes glittering in the dark as the dog thump-thump-thumped his tail. "Lars? That you?"

Lars stepped back, startled. "Otlee? What are you doing here? Why's my dog here?"

Otlee yawned. "Gilby took me to my folks', but Serian said I could stay here. I think. Everything's hazy." He yawned, his voice drifting away. "It's okay, isn't it? If I stay?"

Lars sat and struggled out of his shoes. "Sleep. I'm back on duty, anyway."

" 'Kay," Otlee said, his voice faint and far away.

Lars scratched Kedder's head before he stood, then walked barefoot to the privy. He closed the door and fumbled with the light, straining to hold the lamp steady with his left hand. He looked in the mirror and cursed. His shoulder was swollen and misshapen, and an angry bruise stretched from his biceps to his neck. Wincing, he watched his reflection as he moved his arm. He could bend his elbow, sort of, but he could hardly raise his arm at all, certainly not above his lower chest.

With a grimace, he bent to wash the blood from his face and hands.

* * *

Dubric reached the hall to see Fynbelle returning to Rolle's office and Lars heading toward him, one arm held across his belly as if he was nauseous, or pained.

"How bad is Gilby hurt, sir?" the boy asked.

"Badly," Dubric said. He paused, frowning at Lars. Other pages knew about Fynbelle and Gilby, so it only stood to reason that Lars knew as well. "He will live to be a father."

Lars sighed. "That's a relief."

"How long have you known?"

"About a moon now. Jess and me both." Lars looked stricken. "We've been begging them to tell Dien and Sarea, but they . . . I don't think they had the courage, sir, to be perfectly honest."

"Why did you not say something?"

"It wasn't my secret to tell. I couldn't betray Fyn's trust, not when I still had hope that they'd do the right thing."

Not my secret to tell. Dubric had uttered similar words the night before. Hearing them come from Lars sent a shiver down his spine. "Rolle examined her and reports that everything appears to be fine."

"Good." Lars nodded, looking relieved.

They both turned at the sound of hurried footsteps

and saw Sarea running toward them, on the edge of panic. "Where's Fyn? What happened?" She lurched to a halt and stared at Lars. "You're in uniform. And Jess . . ." She shook her head. "What happened to Fyn? Is she all right?"

"She's okay." Lars hugged Sarea with one arm as he led her toward Rolle's door. "Fyn's fine. There was an . . . incident, and she got a bit of a shock, but she's fine. Right, sir?"

Dubric followed. "Yes. She is fine."

"Then why are you two escorting me? What sort of incident? Where's Dien?"

They were interrupted by a shrill voice screaming, "I will kill that bastard. I will have his rotting head served to me on a plate, do you hear me?" Sir Talmil rounded the corner and stomped down the hall toward them.

Dubric turned to intercept Talmil. "Lars, stay with her."

Talmil reeked of liquor, pipe smoke, and perfume. "Where is my son? I demand to see my son!"

He tried to brush past Dubric, but Dubric held his ground. "You son is in surgery and I need you to remain calm."

Talmil shoved Dubric angrily. "My son's in *surgery* and you expect me to remain calm?"

"Yes. You will sit down, over there, and I will explain—"

"Gilby's in surgery?" Sarea asked, her voice cracking as it rose. "Goddess, what happened?"

Talmil tried again to push past Dubric. "Your beast of a husband tried to kill my son!"

"You liar!"

Lars said, "Sarea, please, let's just get Fyn, okay?"

"Go. Get the little tramp. Filthy whore, I'll have her

head, too, and I'll get that brat cut out of her womb, even if it takes an official order from Waterford."

"I want you to sit your rotted backside down!" Dubric said, nose to nose with Talmil.

Behind Dubric, Sarea wailed.

"Get out of my way, old man," Talmil snarled. He shoved Dubric, knocking him to the floor as Dubric's bad knee buckled. Talmil stomped past, then shuddered backward as Lars stepped in front of him, a sword aimed at the nobleman's throat.

"You all right, sir?"

"Yes," Dubric said as he stood.

"Okay, shit heap," Lars said, backing Talmil toward the chairs. "I've listened to your asinine drivel long enough and it's starting to bore me. You are going to sit down and keep your fool yap shut. Do I make myself clear?"

Talmil sneered. "You appear to be injured, Lord Hargrove, and I am armed. Can you stop me before I cut your throat?"

Lars said, "You're welcome to try. I've already taken your dagger."

"Liar."

Lars gave a slight smile. "Try me."

Talmil's eyes narrowed, but he backed away, stumbling to a chair.

Lars held his sword at Talmil's throat while holding an unfamiliar dagger in his sagging left hand. "Why don't you explain things to Sarea, sir. I'll keep him company."

"I will return quickly." Taking Talmil's dagger from Lars's shaking hand, Dubric watched as the boy curled his arm against his belly again.

* * *

The door opened and Otlee rolled over, squinting. "Lars?"

"Nope. Moergan. Go back to sleep."

Otlee lay back, hugging the dog. "Where is he?"

Moergan yawned and there was a rustle as he pulled off his shirt. "He was supposed to have the night off, but . . . Never mind. I'm just catching a couple of bells of sleep before I head back to it. Sorry to wake you."

Otlee slid his fingers through the dog's hair, repeatedly stroking sleek to scruffy, a repetition of texture and movement. The dog rolled over, exposing his belly and thumping his tail, but Otlee kept stroking his head, his neck. *Sleek to scruffy. Smooth to rough. Nice doggie. Lars's doggie.*

Otlee felt a slight bump where the fur changed, a thin raised line, so faint he thought he might have imagined it. He felt it all around the dog's neck. A demarcation line, separating the two types of fur.

Sleek to scruffy. Nice doggie.

* * *

"I'm fine, sir," Lars said after Dubric returned.

"Sarea is with Fynbelle, and you require medical attention. I can watch over Sir Talmil." Dubric paused and added, as an afterthought, "Until his son completes surgery."

"It's just my shoulder," Lars said. "I'm fine."

"It is not a suggestion."

Giving Dubric an exasperated glare, Lars sheathed his sword and walked to the examination room.

Trumble sat just inside, blood caked on his forehead and one eye swollen shut. He had a fat lip, a bruised wrist, and held one folded towel on his knee and another on his head. "I hear you're banged up, too," he said, the words thick and clumsy in his swollen mouth.

"Not too bad, though."

The injured soldier next to Trumble snored, his arm over his eyes and his nose flat and bleeding. Past him, Serian sat in his underdrawers, enduring stitches.

"Hey, Hargrove," he said, blinking away blood as Physician Halld worked on a gash across his forehead. "Thanks for coming when you did."

"Sure," Lars said. Sarea sat on a chair beyond Serian, her expression numb and desolate.

Serian laughed nervously. "Halld here tells me I've got a sprung knee, three busted fingers, and a concussion. Plus a dozen places that need stitches. Nothing a good night's sleep won't fix, right?"

"It's a bit more complicated than that." Halld finished off a stitch and asked Lars, "What seems to be the problem?"

"It's nothing," Lars said, pressing past. "Just a popped shoulder. I can wait."

He knelt before Sarea and grasped her hand with his good one. "It's going to be all right," he said.

She burst into tears. He held her as she cried for a few moments, then she swallowed her sobs and asked with a terrified whisper, "What's going to happen to Dien?"

"I don't know. You have to have faith that Dubric—"

"I don't trust Dubric," she hissed. "He's never once, in all these summers, considered how things affect our family, our girls, our life. Nothing is more important than the damned job."

Lars tried to quiet her. "Shh. You can't—"

"Yes, I damn well can. My underage daughter is

pregnant from a boy whose father has threatened to have the baby cut out of her. My husband is likely in gaol this very moment, facing a hanging. Our lives are in shambles and that old bastard didn't want to hear it so he sent you in to deal with me."

"Actually, he sent me in to get my arm fixed."

Sarea stared at him, unconvinced. "I don't trust him. Not for this. But I do trust you."

"Sarea, I—"

"You're a good boy. You've always been like a son to us, done your best for us. You're family, and we love you like you were one of our own."

"Thank you."

"I want you, need you, to watch out for Dien. I can't . . . I can't lose my husband, and my girls can't lose their father. Please. Don't let him die. Not for this."

Can I keep him from the noose? Is it even possible? Lars leaned forward to kiss Sarea's forehead. "I won't let him hang, and I won't let them hurt Fyn or her baby. I promise."

*   *   *

Dien sat beside Sarea outside the physicians' office, his wrist chafed from the shackles and his hand clenched in hers. "Tell me it's not true," he said, his voice breaking. His fury had left, leaving him empty and aching.

"I . . . I wish I could," Sarea said, mopping at her eyes with a handkerchief. "Fyn admitted it while you were in the office."

"How . . . how far?"

"Five moons, she thinks." Sarea hitched a sob and collapsed against him. "Our baby!"

But she's not a baby anymore. He held Sarea close,

stroking her hair, then looked up as the door opened. Sir Talmil stepped out, his face tight.

Talmil glared at Dien and Sarea, his dark eyes shining with fury. "Not only has your trollop daughter endeavored to entrap my son, you've tried to kill him. I'll see you twitching in the breeze for that."

Despite Sarea's clinging weight on his arm, Dien stood. "Your worthless piece of shit son molested my daughter."

Talmil took a single step forward, snarling and showing his teeth. "She saw an innocent boy, a noble, and threw herself at him, got herself impregnated by Goddess knows who—"

Sarea punched him in the face.

Dien stared, astounded as Talmil fell to the floor, his legs splayed in front of him. "Don't you dare say such things about my daughter!" Sarea screeched.

Rolle's door flew open and the physician stomped through. "Dammit, Dien! Stop this! I don't need any more injuries!"

"It wasn't me," Dien said. "Not this time."

Rolle looked at Sarea, who stood, shaking, her teeth gritted and her fists clenched. "The three of you had better face this like rational adults," he said. "You have two young people here—confused, scared children— who are going to have to grow up very, very quickly. Watching their parents insult and beat the stuffing out of each other is not going to help."

Talmil stood and straightened his brocade jacket. "My son is not going to claim a bastard commoner brat as his own. That is all there is to it. And you, *peasant*, are going to hang."

* * *

Dubric stumbled to his suite somewhere between three and four bells in the morning. Lars's arm had taken some pulling, but Halld and Rolle had returned it to its proper place then ordered him to wear a sling for a phase. Serian and Trumble were stitched up and had been sent to bed. The soldier had returned to duty. And Gilby . . .

Gilby would live. He had required eighty-seven stitches, two casts, countless bandages, and had had his jaw tied closed.

The thought of three bells of blessed sleep warmed Dubric as he opened his door to darkness. "Maeve?" he called out. "I am home."

Lachesis came running, meowing and wrapping around Dubric's ankles, but he could not hear Maeve.

Dubric maneuvered through the stacks of boxes to the bed. It was mussed but empty. "Maeve?"

No answer.

He lit a candle. Her clothes were draped over the back of a chair and her shoes were beneath. Lachesis jumped on the bed and begged for attention, but Dubric ignored him.

Her dressing gown hung on its usual hook. Even her slippers were where they were supposed to be.

His heart quickening, he called her name as he searched the suite. She was not in the bath chamber, at her loom, in the sitting room . . .

He stepped into the area that would be their new bedchamber and paused. Something stood in the shadows of the far corner.

"Maeve? Are you all right?" he asked, rushing to her.

She stood on a chair facing the corner, her hands stretched up to the ceiling. Stagnant water puddled beneath the chair and her nightdress was damp and filthy, smeared with ash. She was balancing on her toes, but her hand was still a good six lengths or more beneath the ceiling. "It's too high," she said, her voice barely a whisper.

Sleepwalking? A dream? Could she have been moving the mirror in her sleep and not remembering? He held up the candle. "What is?"

She pointed upward. "That."

He saw nothing on the ceiling except fresh paint. "Let us get you dried off and into bed," he said, reaching for her.

"Sounds fine," she said around a yawn. "Whatever you say."

He helped her from the chair and back to bed. "How did you get dirty? Why are you so wet?"

Her hand clenched on his arm, and she shook her head, then released her grip. "Sorry about that," she said softly as she disrobed. "I don't know what happened. I've done so much sorting and cleaning lately, maybe I tried to scrub out the fireplace in my sleep."

Dubric yawned, certain he could sleep until noon. "That is probably all it was. Just a dream."

"A dream. Yes." Nude, she climbed onto the bed and crawled toward him. "Joining me?"

So much for sleep. He grinned and removed his clothes. "Of course."

As he leaned over to kiss her, he paused, his brow furrowing. "Your eyes look green."

She smiled coyly and ran her fingers down his belly. "Must be that candle." Then she blew it out.

CHAPTER

19

†

Rubbing his sore shoulder, Lars glanced at the window as he stood—not quite dawn, so the pounding at the door surely wasn't Dubric telling them they were late—and rounded the settee.

Through Dien and Sarea's closed bedroom door he heard Sarea crying. Dien said something too soft to make out, Sarea sobbed louder, then the baby started crying, too.

Lars stared at the main door. Dubric had refused to put Dien in gaol, and only Lord Brushgar could overrule his decision. *So who is it? Soldiers? Lord Brushgar? Or is it just Talmil, come to threaten us?*

"Dammit, Dien, open this door!" Lars recognized the gravelly voice of Fultin, Lord Brushgar's squire. "You're not making it any better."

"Go ahead, pup," Dien said from behind him. He had emerged from his bedchamber without making a sound. "Let them in. They're just doing their jobs."

Lars glanced back to the family clustered together; Sarea and the girls crying while Dien remained steadfast, like a soldier prepared for battle.

Lars unlocked the door. "Morning," he said to

Fultin, wedging his leg behind the door to discourage it from being shoved open. "You're up awful early."

Fultin sighed. "What are you doing here?" There were four soldiers behind him and, down the hall, a grim Sir Talmil.

"I was about to ask you the same thing."

"Don't get smart, Lars," Fultin said. "You know why I've come. He's under arrest. Assault of a noble and attempted murder. They're capital offenses and I don't have any choice."

"You're not touching him without an official order overruling Dubric's decision."

"I know." Fultin pulled a scroll from his cloak and handed it to Lars as he lowered his voice. "For what it's worth, I'd have done the same thing if I found the little shit with my daughter. But you know how our lord is when a noble has a complaint, especially one as big as this."

Lars unrolled the scroll and read. He was no advocate, but everything appeared to be in order. Dammit. He rolled the scroll again. "Did our illustrious ass pustule make any rulings on trial or sentencing dates?"

"You're going to get demoted if you're not careful."

"What's not in the order?" Lars asked, his voice softening.

"Officially? He's hanging," Fultin whispered. "Unofficially, we all want to bust Talmil's skull. Tell Dubric I'll keep him informed as things develop."

"Keep *me* informed, too," Lars said. "Everything Dubric knows, I want to know."

"You have my word."

"Fair enough." Lars stepped back from the door.

Fultin entered the suite and pulled a set of wrist

shackles from his belt. "You going to give us any trouble?"

"No," Dien said. "Just let me kiss my girls good-bye."

Fultin raised a hand to halt the soldiers while Dien quietly conversed with his crying family. Sarea's chin quivered when Fultin locked the shackles on, but she otherwise stood fast.

Dien walked to the door with his head held high. Before he passed to the hall, he met Lars's gaze. Then he was gone.

Lars followed and watched as Dien marched steadfastly away. Talmil taunted him, muttering something lost to the distance, but a soldier brushed the nobleman aside.

Relieved, Lars turned back to Dien's suite to find Kia in the doorway staring at him with the baby clutched to her chest, her stony eyes smeared with tears.

"He'll be okay," Lars said, approaching her. She took a step back, tightening her hold on Cailin. He'd barely seen Kia since they'd returned from the Reach, and she looked different. Older. Jess said she barely spoke anymore and he'd never seen her care about the baby.

"You can't fool me," Kia said, her voice low and cold, and she turned slightly as if protecting the baby from him. "Don't think I don't know."

"Know what?" Lars asked, confused.

Her lips tightened. "Whose fault this is." She moved toward him, her face so furious that Lars retreated a step. "It's you. Again. It's always you. My family trusted you oh so much, Dad's little pup, but you just let Aly die when you should have been protecting her. Didn't you? My grandparents died because of you. And now here you are, letting them take our dad away to die like a criminal."

Startled by her hatred, Lars found he couldn't say a thing.

"And if you think for one damned moment that I'm going to stand aside and let you ruin Jess's life, too," Kia said, her voice rock hard and dangerous, "believe me, that's one more thing you've got wrong."

She turned away and slammed the door in his face.

* * *

Dubric marched into Brushgar's office. "Release Dien, immediately."

Head Accountant Jelke pivoted and dropped his ledger. "My lord, we're having a budgetary—"

Dubric pointed to the door. "I do not care if you have a rabid skunk shoved up your ass. Get out. Now."

Jelke gathered his ledgers and left.

Brushgar leaned back in his chair. "That was a bit harsh."

"You have incarcerated my squire."

"Yes. For committing a capital offense. A *hanging* offense. You're damn lucky I haven't tossed you in there with him for failing to arrest him last night."

"I want him released. Now."

Brushgar sighed. "I gave you permission to do what you needed to do in Quarry Run. Because of your zealous pursuits, I've endured days of complaints from one of my prominent landowners, and I've done my best to support your efforts and deflect Jerle Dughall's anger. But I do have my limits, Dubric. I cannot stand aside and let a commoner, a peasant, beat a noble boy nearly to death in my own castle."

"In order to locate and exterminate the mage in Quarry Run, I *need* my squire."

"You'll have to manage without him. He beat that boy nearly to death! Have you seen Rolle's report? Broken bones? Dislocations? Internal bleeding? It's a wonder the boy survived. How could that beast of a man do such a thing?"

"He found Gilby naked with his underage daughter."

Brushgar rolled his eyes. "He should've been thankful a noble bedded her. She could've been with a manure boy or swineherd."

"Gilby is seventeen, a man, and Fynbelle is thirteen, a child. She is not of courting age and I could prosecute him for rape."

"Why haven't you?"

Dubric ground his teeth. "Because they are youngsters in love and he did not force her. There was no crime other than youthful ignorance, and I have better things to do than pursue such meaningless charges."

Brushgar pulled a sheet of paper from the mess on his desk. "The boy's father doesn't think they're meaningless. In fact, he's insisting that he has just cause to have the child forcibly miscarried. He's claiming the girl seduced Gilby, knowing she was pregnant with some laborer's bastard, then, once she convinced the poor boy the child was his, blackmailed him into proposing marriage."

"That is absurd and you know it. Those two have been sneaking into corners and quiet rooms for seasons. I have no way of knowing if they have plotted marriage, but the child is Gilby's. Of that I have no doubt."

Brushgar tossed the paper back onto his desk. "I concur on the child's parentage and, Talmil's anger aside, there's no reason to have the infant killed. I also doubt the girl had malicious intent—simply because there are other more likely, less troublesome lads to ensnare than Gilby Talmil. But regardless of the girl's intent, an inopportune pregnancy does not excuse your squire's actions."

"He found a naked man with his thirteen-summers-old daughter. What would you have done in his place?"

"My daughter was raised better than that and she knew better than to associate with peasants. Why can't you see that the commoners you so adore are heathens at best?"

"I will not fault a man because of his birth."

"That is why you serve your betters. My decision stands. He's charged with assault of a noble with the intent to commit murder. Attempting to murder a noble is a hanging offense."

"I know the law." *I wrote the damn thing.*

"Witnesses have already informed me he repeatedly stated that he intended to kill the boy. I have no choice but to pursue punishment by hanging."

* * *

"He *what*?" Lars asked, hurrying alongside Dubric as he adjusted his sling.

Dubric ground his teeth and wished he could scream. "He intends to hang Dien for attempted murder."

Lars walked silently for a few steps then said, "I won't let that happen, sir."

Dubric glanced sideways at the boy. "I will not, either."

Lars nodded once, his mouth set tight. "What do you need me to do?"

Dubric explained what had happened with Garrett

and what he had learned at the sanatorium the day before, including the man who claimed to be from Galdet's army. "I need you to locate the missing patient. He may be named Klammer Felk."

"Yes, sir, but what if he's not a soldier at all, just a mixed-up man believing he's from the war?"

"He very well may be, but it is a lead that must be pursued."

"I'll find him, sir."

"And that boy's body is still missing. He is dead, decapitated like the others, but I want him found. We cannot allow a child to rot discarded in a ditch or field."

"Yes, sir. Anything else?"

Dubric gave Lars his notebook. "Continue the investigation as you see fit, especially concerning the sanatorium. I authorize you to take whatever support staff and supplies you need. I will attempt to calm the situation here."

He sighed and looked at his ghosts, two dripping from their severed throats. "Come back with your head attached to the rest of you."

* * *

Lars smacked Serian's feet, then Trumble's. "Get up. We're leaving. Where's Moergan?"

"In the privy," Trumble said, blearily. "Where we going?"

"For a ride." Lars kicked the closed privy room door. "Hurry it up!"

Otlee yelped, jerking upright, and Kedder leapt off the bed. "No! Not the dark! Please!" Otlee blinked, staring around, then sagged. "What happened? Why are you wearing a sling?"

"Popped my arm out of joint last night, and I'm getting ready to head out." Lars strode to his dresser, almost slipped in dog mess, then saw a large wet spot on his blanket. *No wonder it stinks in here.*

The privy door opened and Moergan sauntered through. "What's the rush? Can't a guy have a bit of quality time to himself? I mean, shit, Lars, I spent the night alone. A. Lone."

"It's a wonder you survived," Serian muttered.

Lars rooted through his drawer one-handed. "Get dressed. We're leaving. Consider it a combat situation."

Otlee said, "What can I do? Can I go?"

"You can clean up Kedder's mess," Lars said. "I don't want to sleep in dog piss tonight." He pulled three daggers from the drawer and dropped them on the top of the dresser.

Otlee rubbed his bandaged wrists and glanced at the other pages getting dressed. "No problem."

Lars added a pouch to the pile and slammed the drawer closed. "Thanks." He yanked open another drawer, retrieving a leather envelope and a larger pouch. "You're supposed to take it easy today, but you might try helping Dubric. He's going to need it."

"Why? What happened?" Otlee asked.

Wincing at the stress on his arm, Lars shoved everything into his travel pack. "Dien's in gaol. That's all I can say right now."

He glanced at his friends. *At least they're armed and dressed.* "Ready?"

"With a concussion and a few bells' sleep, I'm as ready as I'm gonna get," Serian said.

Lars flung his pack over his shoulder. "Good. Let's go."

* * *

Jess hoped she hadn't come too early. It wasn't that she was eager to sort packing boxes and old clothes, but she had nowhere else to go, nothing else to occupy her mind, especially with her mam and sisters crying. Lars was back on duty, classes didn't start for two bells . . .

She waited a minute or two after knocking, then decided Maeve must still be asleep. She was about to turn and walk away when the door opened.

"Oh!" Maeve said, stepping back. "Come in."

"Sorry to come so early," Jess said. "But I was just wondering if you needed any more help sorting things."

Maeve hugged her. "I'm sorry about your dad. Do you want to talk about it?"

"No. I just want something to *do*."

"Well, there's plenty here." Maeve led Jess through organized stacks and rows of belongings. "There are several boxes of clothes and things I started to put up in the attic, but I'm busy trying to get this bolt of fabric done by tomorrow. I'd really appreciate it if you could take them upstairs. As long as they're not too heavy . . ."

"I'm sure they're fine," Jess said. "Where do they go?"

"I started a stack yesterday, down toward the northeast corner. Boxes and boxes of fabric and a few of Braoin's paintings. You can't miss it."

The first box cradled easily in her arms, Jess made her way to the attic door and then up the stairs. She'd never been in the North Wing attic before. It was dusty and unused, full of decaying junk, and it looked as if hardly anyone had been up there for summers. She found Maeve's stack of boxes easily and carefully set the box she was carrying on top.

As she came out of the door at the bottom of the stairs, she saw Jelke the accountant hurrying down the hall, muttering to himself. He looked flustered. When he saw her, he stumbled, taking a quick step back. She nodded hello, but he just brushed past and continued on.

Another box retrieved, she returned to the attic and added it to the stack. She had just reached the stairs when the door below opened.

A man wearing the clothing of a castle official entered the stairwell, his face lost to shadow. "Why, Miss Saworth," he said, his voice low. "How lucky for us both. This is the only way out."

Then he pulled a knife.

Jelke. What? Why is he . . . Oh, hells!

Looking frantically around her, she backed away. Once she was out of Jelke's sight, she ducked behind a stack of trunks and old books. She crouched, snatching up a huge, dusty embroidery bag that lay on the floor.

"Oh, Miss Saworth," Jelke called, reaching the attic. "We have an account to settle."

Jess hid in a pocket of shadow, pulling brittle yarn and partially embroidered linens from the bag.

"What have you been up to in the attic? Stealing, perhaps?" he asked, his thin voice low and coaxing as he searched for her. "Commoner tramps like you can't store things here, and your Lord Hargrove is as poor as a church mouse. Did you know that? He has his modest wage and nothing else. The boy is a financial ruin, not the grand catch he's reputed to be."

Jess found an embroidery needle and held it between her teeth as she stuffed books in the bag. Looking up, she froze and held her breath. Jelke was moving past a space between the trunks, close enough to touch.

He chuckled and she heard him move on, searching.

"He nearly emptied his accounts to take you to the faire. Such irresponsibility. And you didn't properly reimburse him, did you? At least your sister knows how to repay a nobleman." He sniggered. "Or so I hear."

Jelke shuffled toward her again, never moving far from the stairs. "We need to talk, you and I. Come out and I'll be a gentleman. I promise. Look, I've even put my knife away."

Jess pulled the needle from her teeth and set it in her right fist, the pointed tip protruding between her middle and ring finger, and the rounded eye-end resting on the pad of her thumb, just like her father had taught her.

"I have something to show you," Jelke cooed as he moved through the clutter. "Tsk-tsk, Miss Saworth, there are events happening around you that you're unaware of. Let me show you. Let me help you plan for your future. You have much to gain and the risk is minimal."

He moved close again. Jess held perfectly still, barely breathing, her left arm through the handles of the embroidery bag and the needle held tight and hidden in her right hand. *He could keep me trapped here all day.*

Jelke walked past the nearby rack of dresses, past the crack between the trunks, all the while trying to coax her out. She waited and watched, silent, then she heard a crash.

"Where are you?" Glass shattered, then she heard a heavy *thwupp* as something big and flat hit the floor. "I cannot afford to lose precious time. It is money, after all, and the lord's monies must never be wasted." Another crash and a clang of metal against a wall.

Jess licked her lips, hesitating as she gathered her

courage. *Through the dresses then straight to the stairs. I can do this. It's maybe fifteen, twenty lengths to the left. Six good steps then I'm gone.*

She gasped as the top trunk flew away, crashing to her left.

"There you are," Jelke snarled, shoving aside another trunk, then reaching for her. "Hiding like a filthy thief!"

Jess bolted through the dresses, just past his reach, but then tripped over a broken trunk and fell, sprawling to the floor.

Jelke grabbed her leg with both hands, his grip painfully tight and hard enough to bruise. She squealed and rolled over, swinging with the heavy purse as she kicked.

"You're a feisty one," he said, grinning as he pulled her to him.

Jess slammed her free foot into his belly, knocking him back a step as he grunted and released her. She frantically scrambled away but slipped on more old junk. Jelke caught her around the waist and snatched her toward him.

"Let me go!" she screeched as he lifted her and turned away from the stairs. She swung again with the purse, and his grip loosened when she struck him in the face. She spun in the opposite direction, putting all her weight behind the twist as she slammed her elbow against his jaw.

His arms dropped and she sprang away, stumbling over the broken trunk as she headed for the stairs, but Jelke was too fast and he managed to get between her and the stairs again.

He pulled a thin-bladed dagger from his belt and wiped his split lip with the other hand. "No wonder

Lord Hargrove's so smitten with you. All this physical-ity is rather exciting." He turned the blade, flipping it in his hand.

"Let me go." Her eyes locked on his, she stepped out of the mess to surer footing. "Nobody needs to get hurt."

"Oh, you're going to get hurt." He held up his blood-smeared hand. "After this, you're definitely going to pay your due." He lunged, slamming her against the wall. He held the blade before her eyes, his free hand circling her throat, and he smelled like paper and ink and corroded coins. His fingertips were cool against her skin.

She spat in his eye, his right one, then kneed him in the crotch. He started to double over and she used his own momentum, her left hand clutching into his hair as she yanked his head forward, toward her right fist and the needle. She punched him square in the eye.

The needle punctured with a barely audible *pop* and a sudden release of pressure. Turning her fist, she ground into his softening eye socket, then let go.

He screamed. Hot fluid burst over her opening fist and he staggered away, taking the needle with him as clear fluid and blood streamed between his fingers. "You bitch! You cursed, sneaky bitch!"

Jess ran down the stairs and burst out the door. Behind her, she heard a crash from the attic and looked back over her shoulder as she ran—smacking headlong into doddering old Sir Knude. His cane clat-tered to the floor and skittered away.

"What's wrong, child?" he asked, clutching at her to keep from being bowled over by her frantic escape. At least eighty, he was a head shorter than her, a wizened chipmunk of a man. She'd never spoken to him before.

"He . . . he attacked me," she said, pointing. Shakes overtook her and her heart hammered a speedy staccato against her ribs. Her knees threatened to buckle.

Knude pushed her behind him and stared at the open door. "Who? Who'd dare to do such a vile thing?"

"J-Jelke," she said. "The accountant."

"Greedy wretch," Knude said. Leaving Jess where she stood, he tottered to the open door and peered up the stairs. Jelke's screams echoed down from the attic. "Whatever she did, it serves you right, you embezzling crook!" Knude slammed the door. He rummaged in his pockets and mumbled, "And to think I let him convince me I was mistaken about my deposits."

Jess struggled to stop trembling. "W-what are you doing?"

"Locking the door, child. Everyone in this wing has a key," he said. "Go fetch Dubric. I won't let the wretch loose."

* * *

"He's going to lose that eye," Rolle said as he sat behind his desk. "There's simply nothing I can do to repair it. How is Jesscea? Does she need medical attention?"

Dubric rubbed his aching eyes, but the ghosts remained. "She appears to be well. A bit shaken, a bruise on her neck, but otherwise unharmed."

"She's damn lucky," Rolle said, leaning back.

"He's calling to have her charged, claiming she tried to rob him."

"Dien's daughter? Nonsense. Does he realize when word gets out that he's a dead man?"

"No," Dubric said. "He thinks he can bluster Lord

Brushgar into believing she attacked him for keys to the coffers."

"Brushgar's favor or not, Lars won't care," Rolle said. "He'll just walk up and kill him. As would Dien, if he were free."

"I have already told Nigel that if he so much as utters one word against Jesscea, he will regret it to the end of his days. That girl is no more a thief than I am."

"This was not a random attempt. I believe he planned it." Rolle shook his head and reached into his desk drawer. "This fell from his pocket when the soldiers carried him in," he said, sliding a dark rectangle of metal to Dubric. "I thought you might want to see it."

Dubric lifted the thin metallic card. It was an image of Lars and Jesscea, cheek to cheek, grinning and happy. He saw a relaxed joy on Lars's face and Jesscea simply glowed. Especially her eyes.

How did Jelke manage . . . Dubric looked back at Rolle. "Does he know that you have this?"

"No. He was rather distracted at the time."

Dubric frowned, staring at the picture and swallowing back the taste of bile. *Not now. Not again.*

Rolle sighed and opened a low drawer in his desk. "As for other matters, you bring me the strangest things," he said, removing a jar. The rooster's head floated within, still moving. "I have absolutely no explanation why is it alive, yet it obviously is. Where did it come from?"

"The same village where we found the bodies and the dead sheep."

"How is this possible?" Rolle asked. "It defies all reason."

"Shadow magic does not have to be reasonable. Can

you tell me anything about it other than it is impossibly alive?"

"The substance appears to match what you brought in on the sheep." Shaking his head, Rolle pushed the jar aside. "What madness are you going to bring me next?"

"I have no idea." Dubric looked at the ferrotype again, at Jesscea's white and glowing eyes. He ran his finger over the shining top and right edges of the ferrotype and frowned. They had been cut after chemicals had created the image. "Do not allow Jelke to leave these rooms. Restrain him, medicate him. Whatever you have to do."

* * *

Lars dismounted at Constable Marsden's office and motioned for his men to follow. Moergan and Trumble fell in side by side, Serian in the rear. All were well armed.

"Oh, good, you're here." Marsden stared at Lars's sling. "What happened to your arm? Where are Dubric and Dien?"

"They can't come today," Lars said. "Castle business. And my arm's fine." He introduced his friends. "Have any other bodies turned up? Any new developments?"

"Not yet, no. A bunch of us spent the night looking for Raffin but we had no luck. Jerle's already been here this morning to insist I release his son, along with Verlet, too drunk to walk and looking to kick your ass over his brother's death. I sent them both home. Oh, and Garrett's been bawling like a baby." Marsden chuckled and shook his head. "He pissed his pants last night when Dien had him on the ground. I haven't bothered to fetch him dry ones."

"Won't hurt him any to be a little damp. If you don't mind, I'd like to take a look at that tattoo."

* * *

"I didn't kill him, did I?" Jesscea asked, walking with Dubric to the stairs.

"No. He will likely lose the eye, though." Dubric watched his ghosts float ahead. "You are quite resourceful."

"Dad always told us a small, sharp object held in a fist can punch a hole in someone. He suggested keys, but I didn't have any."

"Your father was correct." Dubric descended a few steps then glanced back at her. "Did you enjoy your day at the faire?"

"Yes, sir, very much."

"I do not suppose you and Lars did anything unusual, did you?"

"I wouldn't call the day 'unusual,' sir. We visited the booths, played some games, had ferrotypes made, ate too much . . . It was a lovely day."

"I did not know there was a ferrotypist here this season. That must have been expensive."

"It was, but Lars said he'd saved for it. We each got one. They're amazing, sir. I have mine with me. Would you like to see?"

"Certainly."

They stepped aside as a pair of floor maids clattered by with pails and mops. Jesscea handed Dubric the ferrotype. He saw their laughing faces, Lars looking directly toward the camera while Jesscea looked at him. All four edges were dark and rounded. "Your scarves match. Very clever," Dubric said, noting that Jesscea's eyes appeared normal. He had seen no scarves on the picture Jelke had dropped.

"They do?" Jesscea scowled. "That's odd. We took them off, I know we did. I can't believe I didn't notice that he gave us the damaged picture."

Dubric returned it to her. "Damaged picture?"

"Yes, sir. Lars paid for two, but the first one got dropped. The man said it was ruined, so he took two more. We took off the scarves for them, but not for the first one. Blast it!"

So they sat for at least three images. "I would not fret," Dubric said, descending again. "It obviously did not get ruined."

"But if I have the first picture, mine and Lars's don't match," Jesscea sighed. As they passed the second floor, she asked, "How's Dad? How bad is it?"

Dubric stopped, then turned to look at her. "I do not know. Much depends on the Council. I hope it does not come to that, that I can free him from the charges. But, at this point, I do not know."

Jesscea's gaze was hard and unflinching. "If you're trying to remove the charges, why are you with me instead of helping my dad?"

"Ah, but I am helping him," Dubric said, resuming his descent.

She followed without speaking until they reached his office. He motioned for her to sit, then opened the desk drawer where Oriana's dagger rested. He expected sadness and longing for Oriana at the sight of it, as he always had experienced before. Instead he felt a breath of fondness for her memory, much like when he saw a relic from his days at University, but nothing more. It was just a dagger, a thing.

Oriana truly was gone.

"Is something wrong?" Jesscea asked.

"No. Of course not." Dubric lifted the dagger and held it carefully, his fingers wrapped around the sheath as he came to sit beside her. "I want to show you something."

Jess looked at the dagger, looked at him, then back to the dagger again. "I saw it in your suite. Is it . . ." She swallowed and licked her lips. "Is it Oriana's mage killer dagger?"

"Yes. I need to tell you about its curse."

"A . . .curse?"

"Only women may use it," he said softly, drawing the blade. "The simplest twist, the slightest menace from the hand of a man will render him impotent."

"Sir? What? How?"

The silver blade shimmered and he showed her the engraving. "All magic, even the Goddess's, must draw from life to power itself. The purpose of this dagger is to consume the life of a mage, but the hunger is never sated. Women are blessed with the ability to grow new life and it regenerates along with the phases of the moon. Because they carry that potential within themselves, use of the dagger barely tires them. Men, however, only carry and discard the life's seed. The dagger pulls that aspect from them. Permanently."

He paused and stared Jesscea in the eye. "It not only makes men unable to become fathers, it removes the capability to lie with a woman as well. You, as a young woman, could routinely use this dagger in any aspect of your life and it would not harm you beyond an occasional yawn. If Lars, or any man, were to merely scrape mud from his boots with it, he would become a eunuch. Immediately and with great pain. Without possibility for a cure."

Jesscea blushed. "That's horrible! Why'd you keep such a dangerous thing?"

"Because it efficiently kills mages." He placed it in her hands. "I cannot keep it anymore and I want you to have it."

Dubric saw the orb at her throat pulsate softly with the beat of her blood, the light brightening as her fingers curled around the hilt. "I can't, sir. It's too valuable. Magical. It was your wife's."

He patted her knee and stood. "I am growing old and a young woman should have it. I have no daughters, Jesscea, no one to pass it on to. It will be safest in your hands."

She thrust it back at him. "I can't, Dubric. Please."

"Yes, you can," he said, harsher than he had intended. He softened his voice. "Please. Humor an old man. Keep it, wear it, use it. But mind its curse."

"Dubric, I—"

"Keep it. Think of it as passing on the light."

CHAPTER

20

†

"Let me go!" Garrett said, struggling in Serian's grip.

Lars wrenched the physician's head aside. "I asked nicely to look at it, and you refused." He found the tattoo and measured it against the ball of his thumb. "Who was daft enough to put this on you?"

Garrett clamped his mouth shut.

Lars punched him in the gut, then leaned close as Garrett sagged in Serian's arms. "Let me tell you about my problem. I have a good life ahead of me, see, plans, things I intend to do. The only way I'm going to be able to do them is if I find and kill this mage before he finds and kills me. You happen to stand right in the way of that."

Lars raised Garrett's chin and stared into his eyes. "Let's come to an understanding, shall we? I don't like you. You're maybe half a bell older than I am, yet you act like you're smarter and better than everyone. You're not. In fact, you're locked up, facing criminal charges, and stinking of your own piss.

"The way I see it, you can await trial quietly right here, with three squares and a cot—maybe even a conjugal visit or two if my friend Calder Marsden there is feeling charitable. Or you can really make me angry and spend your time flat on your back, wallowing in your own shit with your limbs busted and your balls floating in a jar of kerosene." Lars turned and pointed at a nearby shelf. "I'll put them right there so you can look at them every moment of the rest of your life. It's your choice."

"What do you want?" Garrett asked, flinching away from Lars.

"To start with, I want to know all about that symbol, and I want to know about a patient named Klammer Felk."

"Don't you say a Goddess damned word!" Tupper said from the next cell.

"You have something to do with all this?" Marsden asked, approaching Tupper's cell.

Garrett stared at Lars and pointed back at Tupper. "He did it. Put the mark on me. Put it on all of us."

"You ass-faced bastard." Tupper charged the bars separating the two cells, reaching through.

"We've spent these past moons looking for her," Garrett said, nodding eagerly at Lars. "Both of us, and a couple of others."

"Shut your Goddess damned mouth!" Tupper struggled to reach Garrett through the bars, while outside the cell, Marsden flipped through his keys.

"Who else?"

"One of the barmaids—Winni—and Yaunel Derk."

"I'm gonna slit your lying throat! You pegging bastards! Let me go!" Tupper bellowed as Marsden and Moergan entered and dragged him back.

Lars looked at his notes for a moment. "Derk's dead. Is that why? Because he was in on it?"

"No, he just died. Too injured, nothing to be done. By the time I saw him, he was already dead."

Lars had read Dubric's notes, but he wanted to hear Garrett's answers for himself. "Who's this 'her' you're looking for?"

"Fayre Sweeny." Garrett gulped. "She found the Valley of the Soul. She knew how to keep the soul alive forever. She knew the secret!"

"And you think she's here?"

"She was here—rumor is she died here, killed during the war. We'd been looking for where she died, where she lived, hoping to find the secrets of the Valley. But we didn't have any luck," Garrett spat, pointing at Tupper, "not until he found the heads. But he was too drunk to keep his yap shut about it."

Tupper's curses and screams were muffled by Marsden and Moergan holding him down.

"If you'd have kept your fool mouth shut, this all would've blown over," Garrett snapped. "We're all going to hang because of you. Master dowser, my ass. All you had to do was find the caves and keep quiet. But you can't even do that right, you Goddess damned drunk."

"We found the cave," Lars said, looking between the two men.

Garrett's eyes gleamed. "So you saw it? You saw the Valley for yourself? Saw the miracle?"

"No," Lars said. "The cave was empty."

The eagerness in Garrett's face fell, then he broke out in a grin. He started laughing.

"What's so funny?" Serian asked.

"Don't you see? She knew! She knew we'd found the heads, that you would see the Valley. She moved them herself. She's here, and she's still alive!"

* * *

After Jesscea left, Dubric sat behind his desk and sorted through the evidence he'd taken from the grain shed, describing and cataloging each item. He had no doubt that Talmil would question every aspect of the investigation, and Dubric wanted to ensure all the facts were in order and documented. The smallest detail could save Dien's life.

After completing his assessment and description of bloodstains on grain bags, Dubric folded them and carefully laid them in a box. Fynbelle's shoes followed. They had been crushed by a boot, likely Serian's, and Dubric made a note to confirm that supposition. Next, Dubric sorted Gilby's clothes.

They were the same stained and rumpled clothes the boy had worn while helping with the investigation in Quarry Run, and they stank of horse, sweat, grime, and lack of care. Dubric emptied the trouser pockets and listed each item. A bit more than seven crowns, mostly in small change. A steel toothpick. A rumpled, snotty kerchief, two pieces of rock candy, and a piece of cork.

He put all the items in an envelope, sealed and labeled it, and placed it in the box on top of Gilby's trousers. He found nothing in Gilby's shirt, but the jacket crackled a bit and the right front felt oddly heavy.

Curious, Dubric located a pocket inside the standard pocket on the right front of the jacket. It contained a small working timepiece and a tiny notebook. Dubric stared at the clock for a long time, wondering how the boy could afford one. Working timepieces were a rare and expensive novelty, mechanisms created by the ancients with industrial practices and materials that the postwar society had not yet perfected, even in Waterford.

Dubric smiled, fascinated despite his concern, as he watched the steady tick of the hands on the watch's face. He'd seen few working clocks before. A lovely specimen was kept under glass in King Tunkek Romlin's private office and carefully wound every morning by a man whose only task in life was to ensure the winding was done correctly. Yet Gilby, the lowest-ranked, least-trustworthy page Dubric had ever known, carried a working piece in his jacket. He suddenly wondered how, if Gilby carried time with him, he could be perpetually late.

Dubric left the watch open as he examined the tiny notebook. It contained an alphabetical list of common words, each followed by a different, equally common word. *Abandon—Contest. Access—Parody. Acquire—Table. Alternate—Deliver.* Hundreds of words. Dubric flipped through the book, and near the halfway point the edges of the pages were blackened with ink and the list began again, but opposite. *Table—Acquire. Deliver—Alternate.*

Why does Gilby carry a translation guide?

A sick twist in his gut, Dubric set the notebook beside the watch and lifted Gilby's jacket again, carefully feeling for other hidden pockets and items. It took him several minutes to locate the source of the crackling noise: four folded slips of paper held flat in pockets hidden between the front facing of the jacket and the lining. Each was sealed and three had names written upon them. Dubric recognized only one: Jelke.

Someone entered the outer office and Dubric hurriedly put the watch, notebook, and sealed papers in his desk drawer. Smiling, he looked up to see Otlee coming toward him.

"I . . . I'm sorry about what happened, sir." The boy entered the inner office and closed the door behind him. "It won't happen again. And I'd really like to help. Please."

Dubric rose and walked to the front of his desk. "Are you truly fit to work, to research?"

"Yes, sir, I think so, sir."

"I have to be certain, Otlee. I am too short-staffed, and there are too many crises, for me to assign you duties if you cannot successfully manage on your own."

"Research I can do, sir." Otlee licked his lips and swallowed, glancing away. "I need to do something."

Dubric wrote a list of topics on a piece of paper. "Tell Clintte the librarian I grant you full access." Dubric handed Otlee the list and the gold token. "I need answers today, by two bell if possible. Can you do this?"

Otlee read the list, his face going pale. "Yes, sir."

There was a knock on the door. "It is open," Dubric said.

Aghy the gaol master opened the portal and peered in. "Mornin', sir. Came to tell you he's wakin', just like you said."

"I will be right there." Dubric gathered his things. As he walked to the door, he patted Otlee on the shoulder. "It is merely research in the library. You will be fine."

* * *

While Fyn slept fitfully in the next bed, Jess fell onto hers with a journal, hoping to calm her nerves. She read:

2 6, 2216

I stepped through into a safe house in Deitrel precisely at midnight. All materials were present as requested. I dressed as a bard and arrived at the festival at a quarter past. I secured a street corner in the harlot district and played a selection of bawdy tunes, including Nuobir's favorite, "Dance With Me Darkly." The whores loved it, three sang along, and passersby tossed coins in my hat before taking away my backing singers, the bastards. Do they have any idea how difficult it is to find four women who can sing a dirty song in harmony? And not blush?

I don't suppose they cared. I wasn't there to sing, anyway.

The tower bell had struck one a while before I saw Amelie. She came from the alehouse on the arm of a plump man, her touch darkening his coat even under the street lamps. I kept singing—a delightful ditty called "Hard Up, Hard In"—and her gaze passed over me and moved on. As she walked away, she touched her prey's cheek, drawing blood with her fingernail, but he didn't notice. He had already slipped under her presence. She licked the blood from his cheek.

I sang until they passed from my sight, then two bars more to finish the song. I left the money where it lay, then I followed, into an alley, into the shadows, into the stink of blood with four pebbles held in my left hand.

I found the plump man easily enough. He stood in a shaft of lamplight with his back against a vine-covered wall. His pants lay around his ankles and Amelie's shadow knelt in front of him. The vines had encircled his wrists and throat, but he didn't struggle. He just grinned, his face turned upward, blood oozing from the cut on his cheek. His belly was already shrinking, his flesh starting to sag, his face now more oval than round.

I moved closer, then closer still, until I saw blood seeping between her fingers. She stopped every now and then to lick her hands, and he'd beg for her to continue. I never understood how men could feel so much pleasure from a mortal woman yet no pain when a blood mage tore their penises to tatters. They liked it, the wretches. Especially the fat ones.

Another step, and she must have sensed me, because I know I made no sound. She turned, hissing, her mouth a smear of blood and semen as she reached for the night. I pulled my dagger and dropped the pebbles, one for each phase of the moon, and the alley filled with white light.

"No shadows for you," I told her.

The not-so-fat man cried for her to come back, like an infant for a teat, but he was held fast to the wall by vines that withered and died in the holy light. His penis was a sliced and chewed mess, ravaged and bleeding. To finish him, to drink her night's blood, she needed to kill me first. I blocked her escape, waiting for her to come for me, and Amelie wasn't one to disappoint. Blood mages seldom are.

At least she went down fighting, teeth and nails and rotten sweet breath. The man fell when I stabbed her the first time. My dagger drank deep of her darkness, making her shrivel as her prey had. The four phases brightened as my dagger consumed her. I hoped no one else would come to see what brought the light, at least not until after I was gone.

Who would believe a saggy, once-fat man who claimed a fine, dark woman sucked him in an alley and another cut her apart with light and a bright dagger, all for him? No one, that's who.

"Why?" he cried out, reaching for us as I opened Amelie's belly. "A beautiful woman wanted me! Why can't I have her?"

Evidently his mangled prick didn't hurt. Bet it will next time he tries to piss.

Amelie's entrails fell to the dirt and I cut them free from her chest, letting his blood and fat and semen pour onto the ground. It was rancid and dark, like old vomit and shit, already half digested and empowering her.

Still she fought, still he cried. I had nothing to stop them, nothing to burn. I had to take her with me.

"Be glad you have your life," I said to the man as I removed Amelie's head. She snarled and tried to bite me, but I lifted her by the hair and held her face to the four phases.

"May the waters of life run deep," I said, then stepped backward, through the mirror and into Nuobir's workshop.

He got out of the way when I tossed her head into his hearth. Nuobir and I watched through the mirror as her body burned, then charred, then turned to ash and dust. The man saw what had happened to him and screamed. The four phases fell dark and the reflection faded.

So much for Amelie.

"A blood mage?" Jess sat up and stared at the book. Oriana hadn't mentioned one before. There had been many mind mages—they seemed to be the most common—fire mages, death mages, even a bone mage, but never a blood mage.

Leaning back again, she moved on to Albin Darril and the predawn assassination of a dark lord who had been breeding common people to feed mages. No commoners died, and all of the lord's soldiers were captured. Only the dark lord himself, a man named Nalrid Garrett, was killed. While Oriana and Albin's mage killer, Katarinne, had watched for mages, Albin alone approached Lord Garrett. They fought, but without Garrett's soldiers to protect him, Albin quickly opened Garrett's femoral vein, then, after Garrett fell to the floor, Albin slit his throat.

Jess read on.

There is a quality about Albin that commands respect. Maybe it's his focus, his unerring determination to see things done. Maybe it's the ease in which he leads his men—they are more like equals than pawns to be played upon a battlefield. He listens to them far more than any commander I've ever met, yet the decisions are his alone and no one questions them. Maybe it's his unfaltering adoration of Katarinne and the kindness he shows the farmers and villagers we meet. Maybe none of those things. For me, at least, it is his precision, his grace, his near invisibility when he kills.

I once saw him walk by our target on the way to a game table in a crowded alehouse. The target stood talking with several others, all of whom were armed in a room full of farmers and villagers. He alone was a mage, Katarinne and I were certain of that.

Albin walked away from us, passed a hello and a grope with a barmaid, gossiped with some hog farmers, then walked behind the target, dodging a maid at the same time. He said, "Excuse me," tapped his hat, and continued on to a dice game and his mug of ale. Before he finished his ale, the target fell to the floor, dead. Albin acted just as shocked as anyone else, even though he had cut the man's renal artery. The mage had bled to death internally while talking with his friends. He was dead

*from the moment Albin dodged the barmaid, and never
even noticed.*

That's talent. You have to respect that.

*I've seen him go cold. Seen him kneecap a man with
a flick of his wrist, question him until no answers were
left to tell, then open his throat and walk away. I've seen
him remove a man's eyes and leave him screaming in the
dark. I've seen him break a mage's legs so they couldn't
get away, then throw them to starving dogs. Tidy or
messy, you just never know with Albin. Katarinne and I,
we watch, we protect, and we let him work.*

*It's a shame he's married. I bet he gives Katarinne a
damn fine ride.*

Jess blinked at that last notation.

"That can't be right," she muttered, reaching for her
history textbook. She flipped through a few pages to
find Lord Darril listed among the war leaders. His in-
credibly short notation gave his birth and death dates,
then remarked, "Lord Darril faded from notice after
the war and died a drunken, carousing bachelor without heirs or lands."

Jess frowned. According to Oriana's diary, Albin
never drank anything stronger than ale, and was married. Were the texts wrong? Or did Katarinne die during the war and leave him a broken man?

She flipped to the next entry and continued to read.

* * *

"Morning, sir," Dien said, glancing up from a thick
book as Dubric and Aghy entered the gaol's cluttered
office. "Just catching up on my reading."

"So I see," Dubric said. "I thought we agreed that
you would maintain the appearance of incarceration."

Dien sipped his tea and chuckled. "I'm in the gaol, aren't I? I'd rather be almost anywhere else, but here I sit, in gaol, up to my ass in legal books, as I don't imagine Sarea wants me to hang."

Dubric glanced at Aghy. "May I speak privately with Dien?"

"A'course, sir," Aghy said, shucking up his pants. "I'll just go harass the pris'ners fer a bit."

Dubric sat. "We have a new problem."

Dien marked his page and closed the book. "What problem is that, sir? More ghosts? More bodies? Brushgar wanting to make my noose himself?" He leaned back, no longer joking. "Is Gilby worse?"

"No. He is doing as well as can be expected. The problem concerns Jelke. And Jesscea."

Dien's mouth hardened. "What happened?"

"He attacked her in the attic," Dubric said. "She is fine, though Jelke is not faring so well. You would be proud," he added, smiling despite himself. "But the most pressing matter is that Jelke carried this." Dubric passed the ferrotype Rolle had found to Dien.

"They do make a good pair," Dien said at first glance, then he looked up at Dubric. "What's wrong with her eyes?"

Dubric took a breath and forced his hands to unclench. "I think she may have handled Oriana's dagger when she was helping Maeve move our things, and it . . . marked her." He paused as Dien swore. "This morning I gave her the dagger. To keep."

Dien stood. "You *what?*"

"It cannot harm her. It is a woman's weapon and it offers many more protective measures than detriments."

"You gave my daughter a cursed weapon?"

"It is not cursed to her."

Dien shoved the ferrotype back across the table to Dubric. "It turned her eyes white. What do you call that? Fashionable?"

"No, no," Dubric said. "She has her normal eyes. Yesterday she and Lars had a pair of ferrotypes made, one for each of them. The ferrotypist took three images, though. One, this one, with a special lens. I believe they were looking for her."

Dien sat back down. "How? Why?"

"Ferrotyping is an efficient way to identify potential mage killers. Nuobir made an optic device that showed anything touched by the Goddess's magic as blazing white. When seeking new mage killers, we sent ferrotypists into villages to take images of the children. They viewed them through the lens, and if any girls had blazing eyes, we gathered additional information. Later, a recruiter would attempt to press the girl into service."

"Kidnap them, you mean," Dien muttered.

Dubric ignored the comment. "I believe that yesterday the ferrotypist followed a similar procedure. While using the identifier lens, he discovered she had been touched by white magic, likely Oriana's dagger, and made an extra ferrotype of her. He told Lars and Jess that their first image was damaged, so he took two more mundane images, when in actuality, the additional image was for magic identification."

"So some bastard with an image box is going to try to kidnap my daughter?"

Dubric turned the ferrotype in his hand, fingering the two shiny edges, top and right. "No. I believe Jelke followed her to the attic not to kidnap her, but to kill her." Before Dien could break the table in half, Dubric held up a conciliatory hand. "I told you we were still at war. Our enemies can ill afford a living mage killer, especially one I may possess. The ferrotype shows she is in Faldorrah, and identifies her." He held Dien's gaze as gently as he could. "No ferrotypist was scheduled to be here. That booth was supposed to be occupied by a flute and fife merchant."

"Is it true?" Dien asked. "Is she a frigging mage killer? What in the Goddess's name did you do to her?"

"Jesscea is not a mage killer, she merely has the potential to be trained. She is no different than she ever was. In fact, all three of your older daughters would likely qualify for training, and possibly your wife. They are female, were exposed to magic at a young age, are in good health—"

"But you're here about Jess."

"I believe her intermittent exposure to her grandmother's magic as a child, then handling Oriana's dagger soon after puberty has awakened her gift, yes. And unlike the others, Jesscea is prime. Recruiters preferred girls between the ages of eleven and fifteen, girls who had reached puberty but had not yet awakened sexually. They were . . . just stepping into their power. Many, like Oriana, left service after marriage or pregnancy, and no mothers were ever recruited. Only one mage killer remained active after giving birth." Dubric closed his eyes as he thought of Katarinne. *Five children and she never put away her dagger.*

He looked at Dien again. "Nothing about your daughter has changed, I swear. Not by my hand or another. She is the same young woman today as she was a moon ago, a summer ago. Think of it as discovering a talent with a musical instrument. Until the lyre is in your hand, you never know you have a gift. Jesscea merely picked up her gift."

"It's not a gift, it's a frigging death sentence. I won't let you have my daughter."

"I do not want to train Jesscea," Dubric said. "Even if I did, it is too dangerous." He reached into his pocket and pulled out a shard of taupe-colored quartz. "This, too, was found in Jelke's possession."

As Dien stared at the rock in puzzlement, Dubric reached into a different pocket and pulled out a similar gray shard. He tossed it to Dien. Dubric rubbed a concave facet of Jelke's stone with his thumb and it glowed softly. "Consternation," he said.

Dien jumped back, dropping the gray stone. "Goddess damn! What is that thing?"

The stone landed on the table, vibrating softly as if an insect were trapped inside. Dubric rubbed Jelke's stone again, and the gray stone fell silent. He laid both stones side by side. "They are communication stones. Every commander in the war carried one. They allowed us to deliver orders instantly across vast distances, pass information, and coordinate troops. Most were gathered after the war and were supposedly held in a safe vault in Waterford. That vault has evidently been compromised.

"The gray stone is mine from the war. My code word was *consternation* and any commander could contact me by speaking it into their stone. There were at least seventy stones, perhaps more, made during the war. I have kept mine for decades in case I needed to contact King Tunkek and I have no way of knowing what password activates Jelke's stone, or who else has one. I only know that he is a spy, for he is obviously not an ally. He surely attacked Jesscea because an image identified her as a mage killer." Dubric lifted the ferrotype and showed the shiny edges to Dien. "This was cut after the image was burned upon it, and I guess that it is but one quarter of the whole. Four pieces, four spies. All of whom are going to want your daughter dead."

CHAPTER

21

✝

"I need him alive and able to talk," Dubric said, walking down a dark hall of seldom-used cells that stank of decay and stagnant water. "Leave the rest for the hangman."

"Yes, sir," Dien said, beside him.

"Who's there?" Jelke's trembling voice cried from the dark. "Where am I? Somebody please help me!" They heard a splash of water, a grunt, and a whimpered curse, then a frightened wail.

"Piss, sir, he sounds like a scared baby. What'd you do?"

"Left him in the dark and told him he was going to hang." Dubric stopped at a cell and put his lamp on a hook beside the door. He fished the two stones from his pocket, activated his gray shard, then unlocked the cell door. He hoped the indirect light was dim enough to conceal the shard's true color.

Jelke paced across the cell like a trapped animal. One eye was covered with bloodstained bandages and he was already filthy, his fine clothes stained from dampness and mud.

"Who's there?" he asked, backing into a corner.

"I am," Dubric said as he stepped in. "With my squire."

Jelke panted, shaking his head. "No. Please."

"Hey, shit heap. Looks like you have some explaining to do."

"I never hurt the girl," Jelke said, turning his head back and forth as Dien and Dubric separated. "I barely touched her. I demand to see Lord Brushgar!"

"You're not seeing anyone," Dien whispered from Jelke's blind side, drawing Jelke's attention as Dubric moved close.

"Not after what we found in your pocket." Dubric grabbed Jelke's hand and slapped the gray stone in it, despite his struggles.

Jelke winced as the thrumming stone hit his palm, and threw it away. It clattered to the floor. "That . . . That's not mine."

"Then why was it in your pocket?" Dien asked.

"Four men were allowed to keep their stones after the war," Dubric said. "Two stones are in my possession and neither Tunkek's or Siddael's were that color." He smiled slightly as Jelke jumped and skittered away from Dien's threatening nudge on his blind side. "Where did you get it?" Dubric asked, his voice falling soft. "Who contacts you?"

"No one," Jelke said, his hands fluttering up to cover his bloody face. "It's just a rock."

"Then why's it buzzing like it's full of bees?" Dien asked, shoving Jelke toward the middle of the room.

Jelke stumbled and fell to his knees in a puddle of rancid water. "I don't know anything," he pleaded.

"You know enough to have a communication stone," Dubric said, kicking the stone to Jelke. "Answer it."

It buzzed against Jelke's knee and he lurched away. "I demand to see Lord Brushgar!"

Dien kicked him in the backside and Jelke fell face-first into the puddle. "You're a spy. Brushgar won't help you."

"I keep the lord's monies, guard his coffers. I'm no spy."

Dubric winced at his pained knees as he crouched. "And a trustworthy money counter just happens to attack my squire's daughter? Just happens to have a communication stone?"

"She . . . she was giving me the look at dinner last night. I thought she wanted to meet privately. And it's just a rock I found, phases ago, out in the courtyard."

Dien grabbed Jelke by the hair and held a blade across his throat. "You had a picture of my baby girl, a special picture, and don't you be lying about her giving you a look. The only look she'd give you is of contempt."

"Who took the ferrotype?" Dubric asked. "Who gave you your quarter?"

Jelke's pleading expression changed abruptly to one of gleeful contempt. He turned his face toward Dubric. "A *quarter*? Ah, Lord Byr, you can't see it, can you? I might have lost an eye, but you're the blind one." His voice threaded to a vicious whisper. "That girl's as good as dead."

"Shut up!" Dien said, shoving Jelke backward to sprawl on the wet floor.

"Seek the head and ye shall find the Valley." Jelke chuckled, his lip curling in a sneer as he rolled to his knees. "You're a fool, Byr. Do you really think we'd let you have them?"

The Valley? Again? "Them?"

"The master was right. You're blind to us. We've infiltrated every level of authority in the province. Watching. Waiting." He crawled toward Dubric. "Soon the dead will rise."

Dubric stumbled back from Jelke's maniacal grin.

"Quit talking in frigging riddles!" Dien snarled, kicking Jelke in the stomach and flipping him back onto the floor. "What pigshit fool told you to assault my daughter?"

"You're the fool," Jelke said, curling around his belly, "and she's already dead."

Despite their best attempts, he would say no more.

* * *

Arien's bed shifted as Haydon crawled up. "I made you a drawing but it's not so good."

She opened her eyes and ruffled his hair. "Of course it's good. You always draw beautiful pictures."

He shrugged and handed it to her.

The chalk colors had gouged the paper, almost tearing it, and the lines were heavy and thick, the shading rough. It looked like some other child's drawing, a child who had never held a chalk color before. "Is it a house?" she asked.

He turned it over. "You've got it upside down."

"A pig?"

Haydon sighed. "It's a *horse*, Mama. That man came again today, the one that helped me ride his horse. Remember?"

"Oh. Well, it's a beautiful horse."

"Is not. There's something wrong with my hands. They don't hold the colors right."

She sat up and hugged him. "You've been sick, and

you're still feverish. I'm sure they'll be fine in a day or two."

"They don't even look right." He held his right palm toward her. "What's this red mark? Like I got cut. I never got cut, Mama. And they feel too big. Clumsy. They break my colors. I never break my colors."

She looked at his hands and smiled. "They look just fine to me, sweetie." She hugged him again then rose from the bed and stretched. "Maybe it's a growth spurt."

Haydon didn't look convinced. "It's not just my hands, Mama. My feet itch and feel *cold*. How can they be cold? What's wrong with me?"

Arien walked to the table. It was littered with drawings, each as crude as the horse. None looked like they were made by her son and most of his precious colors were broken. She turned her head to look at him. "You're fine, just a little feverish. I'll get you more colors. Maybe some good paper. Everything will be okay."

* * *

Dubric dropped Jelke's quartz shard on Brushgar's desk. "We have a nest of spies in our midst, my lord."

Brushgar plucked the stone from the mess. "Who is it? I'll have the bastard's head."

"It is a nest, my lord, not one man. There are at least four spies, perhaps nine. Or more."

Brushgar clenched the shard in his fist. "Who?"

"Jelke, and he has likely funneled funds to his benefactor."

Brushgar stood abruptly, knocking papers and trinkets every which way. "Jelke? Bull piss."

Dubric ignored the interruption. "I have taken the liberty of requesting an accountant from Haenpar to examine your books. I dare not trust any of Jelke's underlings to do it. Kylton will send someone above reproach."

"You've made a mistake. Jelke's been my personal accountant for twenty-some summers."

"There is no mistake. Jelke admitted his part in a greater plot and, with his access to the coffers, he has surely spirited funds away. How much could he have embezzled in twenty summers, my lord? How many times has the budget come up short? How many times has he insisted taxes be raised or that there were no funds to purchase necessities?"

Brushgar stared at the stone. "Too many. Every few moons, it seems." His face stricken, he said, "He cannot be a spy. It's Jelke, for Goddess's sake. Surely there's an innocent explanation."

Dubric handed him the ferrotype. "This fell out of his pocket. He intended to kill Miss Saworth. He admitted that as well."

Brushgar glanced at the image then winced and turned away. "First mages, then spies, and now this? Are you creating these crises for your own enjoyment? For Goddess's sake, Dubric, we are no longer at war. There's no reason to seek mage killers."

Dubric snatched the ferrotype from Brushgar's hand. "The war continues and you know it. You've always known it. Your cowardice will not make the threat any less real."

"Cowardice? I am not a coward by wanting to keep my people safe from war!"

"Dark magic sniffs our shadows because I want it to come here. I can kill it here, in the north. If it grows in the south again, in the cities, the entire world will fall. Nuobir is dead and there will be no one to save us this time. It must come here. No one else is prepared to fight it, and I am growing old."

"You dare to bring corruption to my doorstep?"

"If you had done your duty to the crown, it would already be dead," Dubric snapped. "Because of your cowardice, your wife died, Siddael, Albin . . . even Nuobir. I have spent the nearly fifty summers since cleaning up a mess you made. I will not fail because you do not have the stomach for death.

"You have spent your life hiding from the truth, but I can no longer let it lie. Your failure in Pavlis, your refusal to bow to the greater good, nearly killed us all."

Forty-seven summers ago, Albin Darril had had a bold plan, a workable plan to exterminate every mage, every scrap of magic in the land. Only he could have made it work, only he could have discerned the truth from a web of lies. But because of Brushgar, it had not come to fruition.

"Albin was not fit to rule," Brushgar snapped. "He should never have gotten a single vote, let alone four. I expected blind fealty to him from Tunkek, but Siddael? Nuobir? You? Goddess, he was the least—"

"He was the best for the task," Dubric said. "If Albin had been able to wield the assassins at will, the last mages would have had nowhere to hide. Instead, because you were greedy and afraid, the crown fell to Tunkek. Tunkek is no strategist; he has no sense of subtlety. The last mages fled into hiding and he was blind to them. He still is blind to them. Tunkek is a good man, but not the right man."

"Albin Darril was a murderer. It's his fault Tunkek rules these lands."

"He was an assassin, not a murderer, you fool," Dubric said. "He and his Shadow Thirteen killed more mages during the war than your army and mine combined. It was his duty." And because of that, when the six remaining Royals had met in Pavlis forty-seven summers ago to choose a King, they had intended to select Albin to rule. Albin had been a good man, humble and above reproach. Power would never have corrupted him; he would have brought peace to Lagiern.

But Brushgar had voted for himself instead of Albin at the last minute. And Albin, always one to shy away from power, refused to accept the crown without a unanimous vote. "You thought only of yourself, and taking the crown for your own," Dubric said. "Your greed stopped Albin from ruling and forced the second vote."

Brushgar clenched his teeth, old anger burning in his eyes. "You could have voted for me, not Tunkek. You were all backstabbing bastards. Even Tunkek voted for Albin the second time instead of me, even though he knew it was a wasted vote."

"Because you couldn't see past your own desires, the rest of us risked our lives, our families, everything we had, to draw the mages out. We made ourselves targets because of you. We died because of you. And now that innocent girl has a mark on her head. We could have had peace, true peace! My wife could have lived. Your wife. Our children! Damn you, Siddael was only twenty-seven when he died. Nuobir forty-one. They were young men who could have lived had you done the right thing."

"I did do the right thing," Brushgar said, raising his chin. "If Albin Darril was man enough to be King, he would have accepted the initial vote. He didn't need my vote to be King. He just used it as an excuse to run away from his responsibility."

Dubric clenched his jaw. That barb stung. For all that Dubric had loved and respected Albin, Brushgar's taunt held some truth. Albin could have ignored Brushgar's spiteful, selfish vote, and taken the throne. He should have.

Brushgar's lip curled. "Face it, Dubric, he didn't have the balls to be King. Your precious Albin didn't have the stomach for battle. He commanded eleven soldiers and a single mage killer because troops intimidated him. He couldn't control a real army! He was no general, just a gossipmonger who went from murder to murder, then drowned his sorrows in a cup. He was weak. Cowardly. At least Tunek stood and accepted his responsibility after the vote. Four to two. The same numbers that weren't good enough for Albin."

"Are you finished?" Dubric asked.

"No. The only reason that your beloved squire's daughter is marked for death is because your arrogance, your refusal to obey me, has drawn attention to her. It's your fault, not mine. I forbade you and Albin to bring magic here decades ago. You ignored me. You both did. Now mages and spies and the corrupt are trying to take my lands away." He let loose a breath and added, "If I had been chosen King, none of this would have happened."

"You cannot rule a province or even keep a tidy office. How could you manage the entire kingdom? You are a figurehead, a garbage-collecting lout, and you are so unaware of your responsibilities that your head accountant is a spy and you trust the sycophantic whispers of prick-sucking nobility over the calm words of an honest common man."

Dubric stared Brushgar down. "I've ruled these lands in fact if not name since I arrived here forty-two summers ago. I stepped into a mess of treachery and posturing and, because of my careful hand, Faldorrah prospers. Not by your guidance. Mine. I have sacrificed my life and youth for Faldorrah and Lagiern. Hear me now. Every spy I find I will kill, regardless of their position in your court. I will rout and remove every mage and follower who dares to breathe. I will protect the common people. And I will not be subject to your whims, or the desires of your sycophants. The demarcation line is drawn. Keep your delusions. I'm freeing my squire and if you interfere with my work or my staff again, I will cut you open and piss on your cowardly entrails."

Dubric turned and walked away.

"What are you going to do about the girl?" Brushgar asked. "How can you save her if my lands are crawling with spies?"

Dubric paused at the door. "I will do the only thing I can."

* * *

"We're looking for a man Dubric needs to talk to," Lars said as he climbed the sanatorium steps. Dubric had said that he had searched the main halls, the areas containing the injured and sick patients, without luck. Only one wing remained. Lars cringed just thinking about it. "He's likely a mental patient who thinks he's a soldier from the war. He has to come back with us, if he's mobile at all, but we might have trouble with the staff. Be ready."

"If we find him, we're taking him, Hargrove," Serian said. "We'll make sure of it."

Lars turned toward the doors of the Mental Wing and swallowed back the acrid taste erupting in his throat. He thought of his mother, her hysterics, and hesitated, taking a few quick breaths before he reached for the door. "If he's here, I want to find him," he said, pushing the door open.

His friends following, Lars worked his way down the hall, checking every male patient's room for someone who fit the description Dubric had given him. They found nothing but drowsy patients, treatment rooms, offices, and a few staff members too busy to help them.

The fourth ward they checked held six men shuffling about the room or quietly sitting in chairs. One was youngish and dark-haired, as Dubric had described. Lars approached him. "Hello," he said. "What's your name?"

The young man grinned, showing his rotting teeth. "Nolan. Who are you? My brother come to visit?"

"No," Lars said. "Sorry. Have you ever met someone named Galdet?"

Still grinning, Nolan strained against the straps binding his wrists to the chair. "Had a cat named Galdee. She was tasty."

Lars took a step away and, from the hall, he heard Serian say, "Stay back, ma'am."

Lars hurried to the door.

Dubric's twitchy friend, Elena, graced Marsden and the pages with a smile. "Stay back? With all these new toys to play with?" She gave Moergan an appraising glance.

"They're not for playing with," Lars said, stepping through the doorway.

Elena clenched her gown in a random rhythm, drawing it tighter around her. "Lars! It's good to see you again. What brings you here?"

"Business. Have there been any new patients brought in lately? Say, the past couple of days?" Lars asked.

"Three of them," she said, looking oddly nervous. "One yesterday, two the day before."

Lars fished his notebook from his pocket with his good hand as he stepped around Marsden. "Where might I find them?"

"Not sure. Most folks get moved around." She paused, her eyes widening. "What the bloody hells happened to your arm? Are you all right?"

Lars's friends glanced at one another as she pressed past them.

"I'm fine," Lars said, confused. "I dislocated my shoulder last night. It's fine."

She muttered, "That damn Byr, letting you get hurt."

"It's just part of the job," Lars said, backing a step away. "I get hurt all the time."

Serian snorted. "Heh, not all the time, Hargrove. Mostly you get dirty."

"Filthy," Moergan agreed.

Elena stared. "Your name's Hargrove?"

"Yes, ma'am," Lars said. "My father's Lord Bostra Hargrove of Haenpar. Now, about those patie—"

"I'm going to kill him," Elena muttered. "As the Goddess is my witness, I'm going to kill the bastard."

Lars glanced at the others; they looked as confused as he felt. "Ma'am, we're here to ask about a particular patient. Is there anything you can tell us—"

"Are you treated well? When Dubric's not popping your arm loose or gettin' you filthy? Do your folks—"

"Yes, ma'am," Lars interrupted. He did not want to discuss his parents. "Now, that patient—"

She smiled. "How's your schoolwork? Have you got yourself a steady girl?" A stricken look crossed her face and she asked, "You got time for that, don't you? He's not working you half to death?"

"No, ma'am." Lars paused, his palm under his notebook getting sweaty. *Why's she so interested in me? And why'd she react that way to my father's name?* He remembered the taunting comments about his parentage he'd heard his entire life, and his heart beat faster. Lars knew he shouldn't encourage her, but he couldn't help but ask, "You don't know my father, do you? Bostra Hargrove?"

She fell silent for a moment, her lips tightening, then her expression changed to bitter amusement. "Nah, I don't know him." She laughed, her eyes wild. "Now, about that girl?"

Lars sighed, relieved. "Look, ma'am, I'm not here to talk about—"

She turned and stared at Trumble, towering over him. "He got a steady girl?"

Trumble yelped, startled, and backed into Marsden. "Yes, ma'am."

She returned to Lars. "What's her name? You kids got any future plans? When can I meet her?"

Lars looked her in the eye. "Ma'am, you can't meet her. Dubric might know you but I don't. *We* don't. Personal details about my life are none of your business. I'm here to ask about a missing patient and other matters concerning our case. Can you tell me anything else about the new patients?"

She backed away, her arm slapping against her side. "You're right. I'm sorry. I . . . I just . . ." She swallowed, stumbling as a spasm wracked her leg, then wiped at her eyes with the back of her hand. "I didn't mean no harm."

"The patients, ma'am," he asked gently. "Was one a young man with dark hair who says a lot of numbers?"

Elena looked down and tapped her good foot on the floor. "Klam? Is that who you're talking about?"

Lars tried not to appear too eager. "Where might I find him?"

"He's in a ward one floor up, near the sunning room. Least he was yesterday. Him and the other new guy, too." She paused, then added tentatively, "You gonna marry your girl?"

Lars glanced up, astounded. But in a moment of pity, he nodded. "Plan to."

He half expected her to proposition him, offer lessons or practice, but Elena looked into his eyes and smiled. "I'm glad. It's good to talk to you. Damn good."

She grasped his arm. "You're a good boy. I can tell. And you take care of your girl, whatever her name is. You hear?"

He patted her hand on his arm. "I will. I promise. And thank you for your help."

She nodded and stepped back.

Lars directed the others back toward the hall entrance. As he moved away he looked back. Elena was watching them leave. "Her name's Jess," he said softly.

Elena beamed. "Thank you."

Lars nodded, then turned away. He wasn't really sure why he had told her about Jess, except he couldn't help but feel that Elena had lied about not knowing his father. He also wasn't sure he wanted to know what that might mean.

* * *

I am so tired of mathematics. Jess's book bag lay open on the floor beside her at her usual table in the library.

She tried not to smile as her classmate Daphe doodled Serian's name on her graded assignments.

Jess wondered if Serian had any idea Daphe liked him, then reminded herself, *Mathematics*. She put her hands beside her eyes like blinders blocking her view of Daphe as she tried to concentrate. Homework just seemed so unimportant today.

Someone landed hard in the vacant chair beside Jess and she glanced over to see Deorsa scowling as he slammed his books on the table. "That damn Ruggins," Deorsa said. "He's assigned *another* oral report, third one of this term. It's due next phase!"

"Yep, he's awful," Jorst said without looking up from his book.

Deorsa groaned and slumped back in his chair. "The war's been over since before my da was born! Who cares about this battle or that general?"

"Ruggins," Jess said. "It's just War History. Endure it and move on."

Silence reigned for a short while, everyone focusing on their work, then Deorsa ran a finger up Jess's thigh and leaned over to whisper in her ear, "Speaking of moving on, you ready to dump your stinky suitor yet?"

Deorsa tried something like that every now and then. Jess flicked his hand away out of habit. "Nope. Perfectly happy, thanks."

"You wound me."

"You'll survive."

He slumped back in his chair again, tapping his index fingers like sticks on the edge of the table. "What's this?" he asked, leaning over to reach into her book bag. "You walking around armed now?"

Jess glanced over and gave him an exasperated look as she pulled the dagger out from beneath her books.

"Never mind it. I just didn't want to leave it around for Kia to find." She tucked the dagger beneath her mathematics book and settled in to resume working.

"Let me see it, Jess," Deorsa said, snatching it free. "It looks pretty old."

Jess tried to get it back but Deorsa held it away from her. "It is, and it's not a toy. Please. Give it to me." She stood. "I'm serious, Deorsa. Give it back."

Deorsa puckered his lips and made smacking noises. "Only if you give me a kiss first."

"You know me better than that." She held out her hand. "It's dangerous, and you need to give it back. Now."

"Goddess, Jess, it's just a dagger," he said, pulling the blade from the sheath.

"That's more like a little sword," Jorst said.

Jess swallowed when she saw faint white haze drifting along the blade's sharpened edges. "I'm serious, Deorsa. It's a mage killer dagger and it can hurt you. Bad. Put it back in the sheath, slowly, and hand it back to me. Please."

"It is not any such thing and you know it," Deorsa said, testing the edge with his thumb. "The whole mage killer myth was crea . . . ted . . . urgh!"

The white glow brightened as vapors of translucent smoke steamed off Deorsa and trailed into the dagger. "No, no, please," Jess begged, wrenching the dagger free and clutching it to her.

The dagger flexed in her hands as if it was breathing, and it *pulled*, the vapors getting thicker, more opaque. Deorsa choked, falling off the chair. Smoke twirled from his eyes and mouth, his throat, his chest, his belly, his privates, thickening and thinning in waves, rippling as if floating on a breeze.

Lilla bolted for the door but Daphe and Jorst just

stared, frozen in horror as Deorsa screamed in pain and fear. The sheath fell from his hand and it skittered around him, sliding quickly between chair legs, to lean against Jess's feet.

"Stop it!" Jess cried, but the dagger kept pulling.

Deorsa's face thinned, his lips and eyelids flapping like laundry drying on a breezy line, and he let out a low mournful wail.

Jess snatched the sheath from the floor and tried to shove the dagger in, but it was too big, too thick, the tendrils of light blocking the way as if they were substantial.

Deorsa writhed on the floor, his screams wavering as he seemed to slip in and out of consciousness. More students panicked and ran, leaving only a few remaining in the library. None looked at Jess or the dagger even though it glowed as bright as a full moon in the midnight sky.

Can't they see what's happening? The vapors snapped from Deorsa as if cut by an invisible blade. They finished their twirling trek to the dagger, then Jess slammed it home, back into the sheath, as the light faded.

Jess dropped the dagger on her chair and ran to Deorsa. He was twitching, barely breathing, and cold. She looked up to Jorst. "Get Rolle. Now."

Jorst ran.

* * *

Dubric entered his suite to find the curtains thrown wide and the room blazing with light. He heard splashing water. "Maeve?" he called out.

"I'm here," she replied from the bath chamber. "This is so strange."

"What is?" Dubric asked as he worked his way to the

new suite. The bath chamber door was propped open and Maeve stood at the washbasin, scouring something under water.

She glanced at him then resumed scrubbing. "I can't seem to get my hands clean."

"Your hands?"

She held them up, dripping wet. The creases around her nails were stained black. "I can't for the life of me remember getting them dirty."

"It was probably from something in the new suite. Perhaps you touched some varnish or wood filler and did not notice."

"I'd have noticed," she said. "You're home early."

"I am not really here," he said, "merely between tasks and hoping you could have a late lunch with me."

"Of course." She rinsed her hands and sighed as she pulled them from the basin. "How's Dien? Fyn? Jess?"

"I have released Dien from the gaol. I need my squire; Nigel can complain all he wants. Jesscea is fine and Fynbelle is resting, as far as I know."

Maeve dried her hands. "And the boy?"

Dubric leaned against the doorjamb. "He will heal and Rolle expects him to wake soon. I do not know if Dien will ever accept him as a fit mate for his daughter, or if Gilby's father will allow him to take responsibility for the babe. The boy faces numerous difficulties ahead, some more challenging than his injuries."

"Only time will tell, I suppose," she said, embracing him.

"You were rather wild last night," he growled, kissing her below the ear.

She giggled but made no effort to push him away. "Something happened last night? Surely it was your imagination."

He grinned and pulled down his collar to show her a bite-mark bruise near his collarbone. "This is not my imagination," he said, backing her out of the bath chamber. He waggled his eyebrows. "Would you like to give me another one?"

"I didn't do that!" Maeve squealed as he danced her across the empty room.

"How soon they forget," he said, laughing, then he stopped. "What happened to the ceiling?"

Maeve turned in his arms then gasped and backed into him. "I . . . I don't know."

A pile of boxes stood in the corner of the new bed-chamber and, above them, a strip of ceiling had fallen, the plaster and lath broken and shattered on the boxes and floor.

Dubric released her and approached the mess. Black gouges marked the subfloor of the attic above. He squinted. They looked like scorch marks. *Could there have been some sort of fire?*

"Forget about the ceiling," Maeve said, closing the curtains before she grasped his hand. "It doesn't matter, anyway."

He let her draw him away from the mess. "Does not matter? It could have fallen on us, on you."

"But it didn't." She grinned and started to unfasten the front of his trousers. "Let's rut. Right here."

Rut? "Here? There is no furniture, no pillows. Just a floor."

She opened his pants and teased him with her fingers. "So? Let's do it, anyway."

"You know about my knees."

"You can stand." She pushed his drawers down and winked up at him as she crouched.

"We have a perfectly good bed," he said, grabbing

her. Despite her squirms, he half carried her to the old suite.

"At least draw the curtains," she said.

He gave her one kiss, her hands taunting him, then he did her bidding. He closed the curtains, and turned back to find her nearly disrobed and climbing onto the bed. He unbuttoned his shirt. "This was not what I had in mind for lunch."

"That's too bad," she said, almost purring.

As he finished undressing, he glanced down and saw a paper-wrapped parcel peeking out from beneath the bed. "Did we receive a package?"

"Package? What package?" she asked, reaching for him.

Dubric soon lost all ability to talk.

* * *

Lars found four wards near the sunning room on the second floor, two on each side of the hall. All were filled with male patients strapped into their beds. An orderly hurried by carrying a chamber pot. "Don't think I've seen you gentlemen here before," he said.

"We're looking for Klammer Felk," Lars said.

The orderly nodded back over his shoulder as he entered a privy room. "Second room on the left. You claiming him?"

Lars stopped. "Claiming him?"

Privy dumped, the orderly returned and lowered his voice. "He's a charity patient and the bosses don't like having too many of those. If you're next of kin—hells, any kin—I'm supposed to send you downstairs to arrange payment for his treatments." He lowered his voice even further. "But if you don't claim him, you don't have to pay."

The orderly winked, then said at a normal volume,

"Yep, he's on down the hall. You be sure and let me know if any of you gentlemen will be claiming him." One more wink and the orderly continued on his way.

Lars walked to the dimly lit room and looked in. "Wait out here," he said to the others, then entered. Six men lay in their beds, strapped down by their arms and legs, with gags tied across their mouths. All but one were awake and watching him. Three were young, one elderly, and the sleeping man and one other were roughly Dien's age.

Lars stopped at the first young man, who struggled in his binds as Lars approached. "Are you Klammer Felk?" he asked softly.

The man arched, frantic and wailing in terror. He fought the strapping until his ankles and wrists oozed blood.

Lars moved on to the next man. He glared and lunged toward Lars, only the strapping holding him back. Lars asked the same question and the man growled from his throat and strained again, the edges of his gag fraying. Lars stepped back, then looked at the third, a man who was maybe a summer or two older than himself.

The young man stared straight ahead, his eyes glassy and his mouth sagging around the gag. His gaze rolled slowly, watching Lars.

"Are you Klammer Felk?"

Recognition glimmered in the man's eyes and he struggled to say something, but between his limp mouth and the gag, he made little more than soft grunting noises.

"You served under Herold Galdet?"

Confusion clouded the man's eyes and he shook his head. Lars paused then asked, "Jepert Galdet?" Dubric had told him to ask of Herold first, the elder brother who had served as assistant defense counsel while the younger, Jepert, had commanded an army in northern Lagiern. Herold's name was fairly well known, mentioned frequently in history texts, while Jepert had been a minor general, barely a footnote in treatises of the war.

The man nodded, watching Lars.

"At ease, Major," Lars whispered, pulling his dagger. "I serve under Lord Byerly. My men and I have come to rescue you."

Felk nodded, looking relieved, and closed his eyes for a moment. He watched, calmly, as Lars reached for his gag.

Felk turned his head aside as Lars cut the cloth and pulled it away. Once the gag was free, and the wadding pulled from Felk's mouth, his voice was soft and slurred as he said, "General Byr? Here? Word was, the Cudgel's in Fliskke."

"He came north," Lars said, cutting Felk's wrist strapping. "It's a secret. You can't mention anything about your mission here in Faldorrah until we meet back with Lord Byerly."

Felk's gaze turned hard and suspicious. "*Lord* Byerly?" he asked, grasping Lars's wrist. "That's an error, my friend."

Lars easily wrenched his arm free; Felk's grip was like a child's. "No, it's not. Dubric will explain. Until then you'll just have to trust me. Unless you'd rather stay here."

"I'll trust you. For now."

* * *

Jess's hands shook as she opened her suite door. The dagger felt cold and dangerous, no longer romantic.

Deorsa had not regained consciousness, but Rolle couldn't find a reason why. He had no apparent injuries, his eyes were reactive, his heart and breathing sound. But he wouldn't wake up and it was all her fault.

Goddess, what was I thinking?

She staggered in with her bag of class books then halted, almost dropping her bag. Her father lay on the settee with baby Cailin sprawled on his chest. Both were asleep.

Dad's home? But how?

She quietly closed the door and had taken a couple of shaky steps toward her room when Dien opened one eye.

"Ah, Jess," he said, turning his head to look at her. "I never got a chance to ask you. How was the faire? You and Lars have a good time?"

"It was great," she said, braving another step. "And we had a lot of fun. The lord's dance was stuffy, so we danced with the minstrels." She paused. "Lars asked if we could be intended. But I guess you already know that."

"I knew he wanted to ask you. I was afraid I'd ruined it." Dien sounded relieved as he closed his eyes again. "Glad to hear you had fun."

"So, it's okay? Me and Lars?"

He patted the baby's bottom. "He's a good lad, and you kids are fine. Just take it slow, all right? Keep your old dad from dying of heart failure."

"Okay, Daddy. We'll try."

She stood in the middle of the sitting room, stiff, until Dien opened his eyes again. "What's wrong? What happened? Did Lars—"

"No! Nothing like that," she said. "We're fine, everything's fine. Great, even."

Dien sat up, holding the baby against his chest. "What, then? What happened? Something's wrong."

Her hand shaking, she pulled the dagger and sheath from her books. "I . . . I took this with me to the library today. In my bag. I didn't want to leave it just lying in my room."

Dien stared at it then looked back at her. He stood, clutching the baby. "What happened? Did it hurt you?"

She shook her head. "No, it can't hurt me. It . . . it hurt Deorsa. Bad."

"*How* bad?"

She explained what happened, her voice shaking. "Dubric gave it to me and I know it's valuable and a generous gift, but I don't want it anymore. I don't want someone else to accidentally get hurt. It was horrible, Daddy, seeing it pull all that white stuff from him. I think it liked it, and I know that sounds crazy . . ."

Dien shuddered. "No, it doesn't sound crazy at all."

"Daddy, can you please, please, make Dubric take it back? Can you tell Dubric I can't keep it? Please?"

He stared at the dagger. "I can't touch it. I'm terrified of the frigging thing."

"It can't hurt you if you don't—"

"I'm not touching that thing. Ever. It's evil, and I'm not taking a chance with it." He frowned, then nodded. "All right. Wrap it in cloth—towels, maybe—then put the bundle in a sack. That should make it safe enough for me to carry."

* * *

Dubric groaned and rolled out of bed, grasping a bedpost to keep from crumpling to the floor. "I have to get back to work," he said, his voice cracking. His balance wavered as he grasped his pants and stumbled into them.

"Why?" Maeve reached for him, her touch tingling on his skin. "Don't you want to stay? With me? And play?"

He braved a glance. She crouched on the bed, on her knees, with a smear of blood, his blood, across her breasts. She had bitten his inner thigh, bringing an erotic mix of pleasure and pain, and he'd watched her lick the blood off him. They had tried things he had never thought she would do.

And he had liked it. Every bit, even if it had not been at all like the Maeve he knew. He wondered if she was being overly accommodating because he had been home so rarely the past few days.

"Just once more? Please?"

Think of the dead, the ghosts, Gilby. Dubric dragged his gaze away before he succumbed again. He had already lost most of the afternoon to sweat and lust. "I cannot," he said as he drew his pants over his hips and fastened them. "I must return to my duties."

She pouted, but he remained steadfast.

One of his boots had rolled under the bed and he knelt to retrieve it, grimacing at the stiff pain in his knees. The paper-wrapped parcel lay nearby and he pulled it out as he stood. It was long and thin, tightly wrapped, and tied with twine. It was also addressed to him.

He knew exactly what the package contained and he brandished it at her. "When did this come? By the King, Maeve, you know I have been waiting for this, especially now with the mage in Quarry Run!"

She shrugged and lounged back. "Does it matter? It's here, you found it. Now come back to bed."

"I will do no such thing." He sat on a chair to yank on his boots and snatched his shirt from the corner of the bed. "What has happened to you?" he asked, thrusting his arms into sleeves. "I never thought you would hide something like this from me."

He felt an icy weight fall behind his eyes. *Of all the times to endure a murder.* He glanced at the newest arrival; a young man who looked around with the blank eyes of an imbecile.

Maeve rolled her eyes and stood, flaunting her nakedness as she walked across the room. "I never thought you'd turn me down." She paused to wink over her shoulder at him. "Especially after the things I did." She pointedly licked her upper lip then turned away, tossing her head.

Dubric ached to follow her, but he choked down his desire and stumbled away, the slam of the door behind him doing nothing to quench the need to return to her touch.

CHAPTER

22

†

Tucking the parcel under his arm, Dubric opened the outer door of his office to find Otlee sitting in the waiting area.

"What are you doing here?"

"You told me to be here with my report at two bell, sir," Otlee said. "And it's nearly four. It's not like you to be late, sir."

"I was occupied. What do you have for me?" He entered his office and set the package on his desk.

Otlee sat and opened his notebook. "The first mention of the Valley of the Soul was in Lattalok, about four hundred summers ago. It was discovered by a mage named Kaza Hakneel. He claimed he had found the path to eternal life, to the fabled Valley of the Soul." Otlee glanced up. "Only it's not really a path, sir, it seems to be a concept."

Otlee looked back at his notes. "Hakneel discovered a way to cheat death, that if a particular part of the brain was kept alive—the part he called the Valley of the Soul—the person would stay alive. Information was sketchy, but it involved decapitation, like you suspected, and submersion of the heads in some sort of fluid. After the head was preserved in the fluid, a mage would use a secret process, perhaps a spell, that brought the person back to life."

Dubric tapped a pencil on his chin. "Was Hakneel a blood mage?"

"I don't know, sir, but he was believed to be killed by his wife, Fayre, who disappeared. I found no record of her after his death, but almost a century later a Fayre Sweeny appears in some Casclian records."

"That was the specific mage Garrett mentioned."

"Yes, sir. Again, there isn't much information available, but after some digging, I did find her listed as battling Galdet's army in Faldorrah, so she's possibly the same mage I found earlier, only now we have a name, which helped. And I located her death notice."

Dubric looked up. "She *died*?"

Otlee handed Dubric a rolled scroll. "Yes, sir, according to official records. But Galdet didn't kill her. Fayre Sweeny died forty-eight summers ago in a Faldorrahn village. She supposedly survived several battles but eventually a lone woman burned her to death."

Dubric unrolled the scroll and read. A scribe for the village of Cypress Swamp wrote of a woman who had strapped Sweeny to a tree then burned everything— Sweeny's mansion, her staff, and her family—before burning Sweeny. Burning powerful mages and their families was a standard practice of the war. Some mages could regenerate from their corpses, or pass their power on to a relative or associate. Burning everyone to ash removed both options. A burn removal was ugly work, but sometimes the only choice.

Dubric rolled the scroll. "Is Cypress Swamp near Quarry Run?"

"I found no records for Cypress Swamp anywhere else, sir. I also didn't find anything else about decapitation, or other blood mages in Faldorrah," Otlee said. "Quarry Run isn't mentioned anywhere but on maps, and only then as a village and granite mine." Otlee glanced up from his notes. "There's never been any noteworthy trouble there, as far as I can tell."

Dubric dropped the scroll on his desk and rubbed the itchy spot on his thigh with the heel of his hand. "What about the use of preservatives on corpses?"

Otlee flipped to a new page. "The ancients practiced a procedure called embalming. It was similar to our bleeding of a corpse, but they replaced the blood with a preserving fluid. It slowed the decay."

"But did not stop it?"

"No, sir."

Before Dubric could ask another question, Dien barged into the office with a stuffed pillowcase in hand. Glowering, he dropped the pillowcase on Dubric's desk. "I told you this was a mistake, and if you ever give one of my daughters a filthy piece of magic again, you can get yourself another squire. I've lost one to your schemes; I won't lose another." He leaned over the desk. "I'll leave it to you to explain to Deorsa why he'll never get it up again. He's in the infirmary, if you'd like to talk to him. I want you to remember he's seventeen frigging summers old. Think about what this means to his life, his future." Then he turned and stomped away.

* * *

Dubric rubbed his aching eyes as he left Physician Rolle's office. Deorsa had awakened and had not taken the news well, not that Dubric could blame him.

By the King, will this day never end? Dubric yawned

as he trudged ahead. He rounded the corner to see Lars and Serian helping a young man to a bench.

"You found him," Dubric said, hurrying to them.

"Yes, sir," Lars said around a yawn. "In the Mental Wing. He was strapped down, gagged, and heavily sedated."

"Still is," Serian said. "Was like riding with a loose sack of grain, but we got him here."

Klammer Felk looked at Dubric, wavering a bit as he leaned back against the wall. His voice was muffled and thick, likely from the medication. "They told me they were bringing me to General Byerly. Where is he?"

Dubric frowned and fished his keys from his pocket. "Bring him to my office."

Lars and Serian helped Felk to a chair across from Dubric's desk.

"Serian, you can go," Dubric said. "You are off duty."

Serian paused, looking between the three men, then yawned and shrugged. "Thanks, sir," he said.

Dubric locked the door behind Serian as he left and, motioning for Lars to sit, leaned a hip against his desk.

"Where is General Byerly?" Felk asked, looking worriedly at Dubric and Lars.

"I am he," Dubric said.

"That . . . That's not possible. I saw General Byerly once, about a summer ago. He's a young man."

"Do you remember tracking and perhaps facing a mage named Fayre Sweeny?"

Felk's eyes narrowed. "This is a trick. I demand to see General Byerly!"

Lars sighed. "It's him, I promise." When Felk turned to look at him, Lars said, "I'm Lars Hargrove."

"Reid Hargrove's younger brother?"

"No. Reid Hargrove's grandson."

Felk stood, tottering. "No. I know Reid. He's seventeen, for Goddess's sake, a summer younger than me. We trained together. He's not married and certainly not a grandfather."

"He died after the war, shortly before my father was born. He married Elise Grennere."

"What? The princess? That's impossible!"

"It's true," Lars said. "The war ended almost fifty summers ago. It's 2264, not 2215."

"It's the first moon of 2216," Felk said, looking panicked. "Winter, just after the solstice."

"Did it look like winter outside when we rode here?" Lars asked. "Do you recognize anything? Clothing? Buildings? *Anything?*"

Felk looked back and forth between Dubric and Lars, then sat. "So you're telling me we faced the mage, then I was pulled forty-eight summers into the future? Are you mad? Where are the rest of my men? Did we kill the bitch?"

"I was hoping you could tell me," Dubric said.

"You're crazy," Felk said. "Both of you. It can't be forty-eight summers in the future, for Goddess's sake! I have a wife, a child on the way—"

"The war ended, officially, in the summer of 2218, two summers after you faced Fayre Sweeny, but it quietly continues to this day. Did you kill her? Please, it is vital I know everything you can possibly tell me."

Felk's hands clenched. "This can't be true!"

"Why would we make it up?" Lars asked.

"I demand you return me to my unit," Felk said, glaring at Dubric. "Whoever in the hells you are."

"Your unit, all seven hundred men, disappeared. You are the only one we have found. Please, help us."

"Seven hundred and forty-two. And that many men do not just disappear without a trace."

"Our research indicates they did," Lars said.

"Research?" Felk asked, glancing at Lars. "For a battle that happened days ago? This is insane. I demand to see General Byerly!"

Dubric bent slightly to look Felk in the eye. "I swear to you that I am Lord Dubric Byerly, originally of Waterford, and you are in Castle Faldorrah of Lord Nigel Brushgar's demesne. It is now the first day of five moon, 2264, and we are facing a mage in Quarry Run who we believe is Fayre Sweeny. I swear to you that is true. If we have any hope of defeating her, I need to know what happened forty-eight summers ago. Please."

"How can I be sure you're not a mind mage trying to trick me? I've heard tales of mental torture, tricking soldiers into divulging battle plans and armament allocations."

Dubric leaned back in his chair. "I knew General Galdet personally. We were not close friends, but we boarded our horses at the same stable when in Waterford. He preferred a chestnut mare with one white stocking and had named her after his hometown of Ravenswood. He called her Rave."

"That is not proof, sir."

"No, but his nickname for her might be. When giving her apples and treats, he whispered to her often, calling her his 'Beauty Girl.' "

Felk hesitated, then nodded. "All right. What do you want to know?"

"Start by telling me everything you can remember of the battle."

"There was no battle. We separated from the main army at reports that she held no army on-site, nothing but household staff and other noncombatants. We snuck our forces closer, fighting weather. Mud and ice, mostly.

"It was the dead of night when we came upon the swamp. It was steaming, I remember that, and thawed. It smelled dead, sir, and our horses would go no farther."

He paused and took a breath before looking into Dubric's eyes. "That's when we saw her, sir, floating from the water like a green demon from the depths of the seven hells. The water rose up, slamming against us, just stink and slime and dead plants. A wall of swampy muck. She was laughing as the water pulled us under. Even over my men's screams I heard her laughter. And the water, milord, it seemed to last for eternity."

He took a shaky breath. "I thought I'd drown for sure, but I woke in the hospital bed. That was a day or two ago, best as I can tell. Everything before that was just swamp water."

"If we returned to the area, could you tell me where she came from when she floated from the water? And could you recognize her if you saw her again?"

"Yes, milord, I think I could."

Dubric stood. "Lars, take him to get something to eat and assign him a suitable suite. Tell the staff he is my guest and is to be cared for accordingly."

* * *

Jess sat on the slope of the North Wing roof and watched Lars as she kicked off her shoes. He looked tired and worried.

"Okay, we're alone now," he said. "Are you going to tell me why your neck's bruised, or not?"

"Just don't go crazy on me, okay?"

He flumped down beside her and pulled off his boots, then socks. "That depends on what happened and what you consider crazy." Barefoot, he leaned back onto his elbow, facing her, and grasped her hand. "What happened?"

"Jelke attacked me," she began, her voice beginning to tremble.

Lars remained silent through the entire tale, his fingers gently squeezing hers. "All right," he said when she finished. He kissed her wrist. "I'll take care of it."

"By killing him?"

"That's a definite option."

She sighed and leaned back on the slope. "I'm all right and he's in gaol, isn't that enough?"

He toyed with her fingers. "It sounds like he intended to kill you. When those boys attacked you back on the farm, they hurt you and I let them live. I should have killed them for what they did. I didn't, and I failed you. I live with that every day, and I won't make that mistake again."

"You've never failed me, and you can't go around killing everyone who looks at me wrong. Those boys on the farm didn't deserve to die. But Jelke . . . Dad says he's a spy and they're charging him with treason. He's probably going to hang, anyway. Right?" She leaned close to kiss him. "So, please, don't murder anyone for me. Let the Council decide, okay?"

She felt his smile. "Can I at least beat the tar out of him?"

"Only if you have to."

A couple of kisses later, he pulled back. "What else is wrong? There's something on your mind."

Hesitating at first, she told him about Deorsa and the dagger.

"He's a bully and it serves him right," Lars muttered after she finished. "But you're not hurt?"

"I'm fine. And Dad gave the dagger back to Dubric."

"Good."

Lars lay on the roof and Jess moved closer, nestling her head on his shoulder as they looked up to the stars.

"Which constellations are we exploring tonight?" she asked.

He yawned, running a finger up her ribs from her waist to her shoulder. "I have some ideas."

She giggled and brushed his hand away. "Not yet."

He yawned again. "Sorry about the yawns. It's been a long couple of days."

She reached for his battered spyglass and the blanket. "We have a bell, bell and a half before curfew. You just lie back and doze, and I'll see what interesting stars I can find." She spread the blanket over them. Once covered, she snuggled in again, her head pillowed on his shoulder and his arm around her.

CHAPTER

23

✝

"Are you dressed?" Dubric asked, unfastening his shirt. "We are going to be late."

He paused and gaped. Nearly every packing box in his suite was opened, the contents strewn about, and every light, lamp, candle, and lantern he owned was lit.

"I'm dressed," Maeve replied from beyond the mess.

He climbed over clothing and trinkets and boxes of books. All pathways were lost beneath the clutter. "What happened?"

Maeve sat on the floor in her new dress, with stacks of boxes all around her and four lights shining down from the highest piles. Her cheeks were blotchy and damp, her eyes puffy. "I can't find it!"

"Find what?"

Her hands shook as she reached for another box and opened it. "I don't know." Her gaze rolled up to Dubric and she looked terrified. "What's wrong with me?"

He winced slightly as he knelt and wiped a tear from her cheek. "I do not know. You are worrying me a great deal."

"I . . . I looked in the new suite first," she said. "In the corner, maybe above the ceiling. But it's not there. It *was* there, in the corner, but now it's not."

Did she damage the ceiling herself? Why? "What was?"

"I don't know!" Shudders ran through her and Dubric drew her into his arms. "I need to find it but I can't, no matter where I look. And I don't even know what it is!" she cried against his chest.

"Maybe you need to rest," he said, stroking her hair.

"No!" She pulled back and looked at him, begging, her brown eyes wide and terrified. "No, I can't! Please don't make me!"

"All right," he said, shushing her. "You do not have to rest. Are you well enough to come with me tonight?" He moved a lantern so he could sit beside her, and his shadow fell across her face.

He heard a clacking in her throat, like a suppressed cough, then she jerked out of his arms and back into the light. "Where are we going again?" she asked, panting as if pained. "You told me to dress nicely, but I don't remember where we're going."

"The temple. I told you, after the sword came—"

Even in full light, the hollows of her eyes darkened and angled slightly. "You're not taking me there, you filthy old shit!"

Dubric leaned back, astounded at the venom in her voice and words. "What is wrong?"

Maeve gasped a breath and reached for another box. "I have to find it, find it soon."

Dubric watched her search, his heart pounding as he rubbed the itchy place on his thigh. Crushing his alarm, he tried to reason through her change in personality. "Have you seen Brinna lately?"

Maeve shook her head. "No, not since right after you took the mirror away."

He looked around at the lights, the boxes, the black

smears on her fingertips. "Are you looking for the mirror?"

She shook her head. "No. Something else, something the mirror used. I have to find it."

"Why do you have to find it?"

Maeve's hands leapt in rough jerks. "Because. Just because I have to."

He heard the clacking sound from her throat again, but Maeve looked at him, silently pleading, and swallowed the sound away.

Dubric staggered to his feet and rubbed the bite on his thigh as the realization hit him. The blood she'd drawn, the aggressive sex, his own trouble leaving her side. *No. I cannot have been bitten by a blood mage.* He looked at Maeve and wondered if Sweeny, the mage whose presence lingered in Quarry Run, had followed him home. But if she had, if she was here in his suite with Maeve, who had killed the man whose ghost he had received that afternoon?

"Will you be all right here for a moment?" he asked, his hands shaking.

She nodded and resumed searching.

Ripping off his grimy shirt, Dubric staggered away. He pulled on a clean shirt and drew on a jacket as he hurried to the cabinet where he stored his extra gear. Behind a spare tent, under his old knapsack, he found a ragged coil of rope and pulled it out.

Do not think of what she may have done to you, do not think of anything but what you need to do. He unrolled a few lengths of rope and, with his left forearm through the coil, made a quick slipknot. He strode quickly to Maeve, making another knot beside the first. Holding the coil-side knot in his right hand, he came up behind her, on her right.

He saw the black stains on her fingers, like ash, but he knelt behind her and asked, "Were you able to get the stains off your hands?"

Maeve finished searching one box, then reached for the next. "No, I scrubbed them raw."

"May I see?"

"Of course," she said, glancing back as she raised her hand.

When she saw the rope in his hands, her eyes turned green and she hissed. The lights closest to them died, leaving only thin trails of smoke, then the others fell dark as well. Only the farthest remained lit, and they flickered, offering random illumination. Before she could extinguish those as well, Dubric lunged and knocked her forward, face-first into the box.

She bucked, fought, but he yanked the first knot over her hand to her wrist, and pulled sharply with his left arm, tightening it.

Maeve rolled beneath him and swung with her tied hand, snarling. She caught him across the cheek, ripping into his flesh. He felt her nails break his skin, felt the sting of blood on his face, then she sprang forward, pushing him back.

"I've tasted you, old man." Maeve laughed, vicious and sharp, as she climbed on top of him. She pinned his arms down and settled onto his hips. "Each bite, each taste, made me stronger."

She lowered her head and licked her lips, watching him as a cat might an insect. "It's a shame I couldn't just bleed you dry, but too much Royal blood after summers of starvation would have been lethal. For both of us."

She rocked suggestively on his lap and grinned at the result. "So I found other, slower ways to drain you."

She giggled as she aroused him, sending shivers down his legs. "You liked it, didn't you? Even the pain."

"Only because I love Maeve," he said.

"Maeve, Maeve, Maeve," she said, tilting her head back and forth. "She weaves, she sits at home. What's to love?"

"More than you might think. You can't have her."

She leaned forward until he could smell her breath, seductive even though it stank like ash and rancid water. "I already do." Her tongue flicked out, reaching for his bleeding cheek, and Dubric sat up abruptly, slamming his forehead against her face.

She fell back, startled and cursing as he shoved her legs away and moved between them. She kicked him, but he kept coming, pinning her down with his weight on top of her and his forearm across her throat.

"You're too weak to cast, aren't you, bitch?" he said. "Or should I call you Sweeny?" He grabbed her hip with his free hand, hooked one leg behind her knee, and, using his own weight, rolled her swiftly onto her belly. One yank on the coil and her right hand came to her spine. He sat on her back and held the coil, his grip tight on her bound wrist.

"Not after tasting you," she said, gnashing her teeth as she bucked beneath him. "Next time I'll drain you to a husk."

Her left hand was tougher to catch, but he had tied many prisoners during his summers as castellan. His head pounding and demanding to set her free, he finally grasped her wrist, then yanked it to her back and into the binds. Her left hand in the knot, he pulled the free end of the rope to tighten it. He used the coil to wrap her wrists, trying to shut out the sound of Maeve's voice calling him filthy, vulgar names as he crushed her against the floor.

He pulled out a few more lengths of rope and made a simple crossed loop, which he wrestled over her head and around her throat. "We are taking a walk, you and I," he said as he climbed off her, holding the rope at her throat.

"Back to bed?" she asked sweetly.

He nearly swooned to do her bidding. "No," he choked out. "The temple. And I am not averse to choking you to unconsciousness."

"She's mine!" Maeve snarled, her voice a gravelly husk through the strain on her windpipe. "You left the beacon open, you took away the lock. It's your fault, and the bitch is mine."

He shoved her forward.

* * *

Maeve stopped struggling and Dubric's ghosts disappeared the moment they passed through the Temple Wing doors.

She looked over her shoulder. "Dubric? What's happening?" She struggled feebly at her bonds, her eyes filling with confused tears. "Why is there a rope around my throat?"

"You are all right," Dubric said, gently pulling the loop over her head. He tried not to breathe the stench of the Goddess's incense, nor look upon the religious artwork on the hallway walls. "She cannot bother you here."

"She?" Maeve watched as he untied her wrists.

"Sweeny." He pulled the last knot free and wound the rope back onto the coil.

"Who's Sweeny?"

"I will explain later." He grasped her hand and tried to lead her forward, but Maeve refused to move.

"You can explain now. How did I get here? Why was I tied up? Who in the seven hells is Sweeny?"

"Now is not the time. You are in no danger here. You have to trust me."

She scowled. "The last thing I remember was putting on this dress. Somehow you tied me up and dragged me, unknowing, halfway across the castle, and now you want me to blindly trust you?"

Dubric groaned. "I believe that the strange things you have been experiencing in our suite have been caused by a spirit named Sweeny who died a long, long time ago. She began to affect your mind, so I brought you here, by force, to compel her to leave." He gently squeezed her hand. "There. Better?"

"No, not better at all. I think you've lost your mind. Or I have." She gave him a lopsided frown and touched his scratched face. "What happened to your face? Are you all right?"

Other than having been bitten twice by a blood mage? "I am fine, and we are late," he said, leading her through the temple doors.

Dien, Sarea, and their daughters sat on one pew; Physicians Rolle and Halld and their wives on another. Behind them, Trumble and Moergan sat with Flavin the stable master, Clintte the librarian, and other castle officials and prominent members of the staff. Dubric nodded to them all, scanning the room. "Where is Lars?"

"Serian went to get him and Jess," Dien said.

"You're not intending to tie the boy up, are you?" Rolle asked.

"No, of course not," Dubric said, tossing the rope

onto a pew. He led Maeve forward and helped her sit, swallowing back the taste of bile. He hated temples, hated the smell, the finery, the opulence built on lies. But sometimes sacrifices had to be made. He looked up to the round window in the roof and the panes separating it into the phases of the moon.

He grasped Maeve's hand and smiled at her. Surely everything would be all right.

* * *

Bleary and rumpled, Lars blinked, trying to wake up. Beside him, Jess yawned. Serian had dragged them from the roof and from sleep, explaining nothing as he herded them to the temple. Lars had no idea what they were doing there, or why there was such a rush. Surely it couldn't be good news.

Serian grimly opened the temple doors and pushed the pair through.

Everyone turned to look. Family, friends, teachers. *Everyone.*

Lars swallowed.

"You are out of uniform," Dubric said, to Lars's left.

Lars turned, startled. "I'm off duty." He'd never seen Dubric anywhere near the temple before, let alone smiling about it.

"Jess!" Sarea called quietly. "Come sit here with us."

Fyn waved for Jess and, beside her, Kia glared, her eyes narrow and cold. Dien smiled at him, looking far more proud than angry. Jess slipped away, and Lars didn't know what to think.

"Let me straighten your collar," Dubric said, and Lars turned back, confused. "I told you to get some sleep."

Lars raised his chin and tried to relax as Dubric made adjustments. "I did. Sort of."

"You will need it." A pat on the back, then Dubric sent him on his way to the altar.

Nervous and praying he wouldn't vomit, Lars managed to reach Friar Bonne. He glanced back at Jess and her family, and Dubric smiling beside Maeve, before he climbed the steps.

"Thank you all for coming," Bonne said, motioning to Lars to hurry up, "even if we are a bit late."

Late? For what? Lars reached the top and tried not to fidget as everyone stared at him.

"Kneel, son," Bonne said.

The room fell silent as Lars knelt. His mind churning, he barely heard the prayer but started at the sound of drawing steel. Bonne held out an exquisite long sword with silver engravings polished to a glowing sheen.

Lars lowered his head as Bonne's voice rolled over him. "Although you are still a boy, you have shown fortitude, bravery, and honor beyond that of most men." The friar touched Lars's left shoulder with the sword and a tingle ran through him.

"The King and Malanna's Holy Church have found you worthy. The petition on your behalf has been granted." The right shoulder this time, and another tingle of the Goddess's magic. "It is my honor, Lars Hargrove of the Grennere line, to anoint you squire."

* * *

After seeing Maeve to bed, Dubric returned to the temple. He paused and took a cleansing breath before he opened the doors.

Lars sat on a pew near the front of the empty nave, his head hanging.

"You wanted to speak to me?" Dubric asked.

Lars nodded but didn't look up. "You shouldn't have done this," he said, his voice cracking. "I failed archery. I don't deserve to be anointed."

Dubric sat beside him, noticing that Lars's hands were clenched so tightly that all the blood had left them. "Yes, you do. There is more to being a good squire than simply passing classes. I filed a petition on your behalf and both King Tunek and his high priest approved it."

Lars raised his head and looked at Dubric. "But you lied. I'm not a Grennere, am I?"

Dubric tried to keep his face passive, but the pained acceptance in Lars's eyes told him that he had failed.

"So it's true, isn't it? I'm a nameless bastard. I'm someone's dirty little secret."

"No," Dubric said, struggling against the tightening of his throat. "Not like you think."

"The son of a twitching whore, right?" When Dubric started to speak. Lars let out his breath in a hiss. "I saw her again, today at the hospital. I didn't realize at the time . . . I just thought she was crazy. I mean, wanting to know all this stuff about me, about Jess, fussing over my shoulder . . . but I couldn't stop thinking about it, how you must know her."

Oh, Elena. You could not help seeking out your bright boy all grown up, a man who would make you proud. He sighed.

"No wonder my father hates me," Lars said, looking away. "If he's even my father at all." He took a shaky breath. "Who is my real father? You?"

"No. I do not know who he is. Elena had no idea."

Lars nodded, his jaw clenching. "Figures."

How can I do justice to what happened? My part in it? "If you were my blood, I swear I would gladly claim you, but it is not my honor to take." Dubric laid his hand upon Lars's shoulder. "You have heard me speak of my friend Albin Darril?"

Lars nodded. "Lots of times. You were at University together, both of you were generals, and his sister Brinna married Lord Brushgar. But he died long before I was born."

"Albin secretly married Katarinne of Narles during the war," Dubric said. "He was the King's high assassin and she was a mage killer. They were particularly lethal and together killed more than ninety mages. After the war ended, mage followers systematically murdered every surviving mage killer, including my Oriana. Only Katarinne remained. Few knew she and Albin had married, and he kept her hidden, here, in Faldorrah."

Dubric gently squeezed Lars's shoulder. "Mages feared the possibility that a mage killer might bear children, and all Royals, all of the children of Nall, are partially immune to magic. If a Royal and a mage killer were to combine their bloodlines, they could potentially remove the mages forever. To protect his family, Albin had no choice but to keep them secret. Brinna may have suspected Katarinne and the children existed, but Nigel never did. After Oriana died, I came here to help protect them."

Lars looked up abruptly, but remained silent.

Dubric continued. "One winter, Albin went out to kill a pack of dogs that had been threatening local livestock. His horse returned without him. I followed the trail back and found a fresh crater with bits of burnt flesh and cloth scattered in the snow. I also found part of his hand."

Dubric forced his fists to unclench. "My lifelong friend, a man who had more honor and integrity than anyone I have ever known, was murdered while tracking rabid dogs. I rushed to Katarinne and the children, but they were already dead, slaughtered." Dubric shut his eyes against the memory. Katarinne, so brave and loyal, her head ripped from her shoulders and cast aside. The children scattered about, dismembered. Young Marcus, seventeen and as talented with a blade as his father, had killed six before he fell. Dubric cleared his throat and continued. "I buried them as they had lived, in secret. But I never found the youngest, Elena."

Lars's head snapped up at the mention of her name.

"I did not know if she lived or died or if she had been taken captive. I searched the woods for days to no avail, then spent summers looking for her everywhere I traveled, every road I walked. Then, sixteen summers ago, in a poor section of Waterford, I saw a street harlot who reminded me of Katarinne. I questioned her and discovered she was Elena, alive after all that time. She remembered me and I convinced her to come back, to come home, so that I could protect her. We were on the mainland a few short bells when we were attacked."

Lars nodded. "Go on."

"I lost three men and Elena was gravely injured. When she woke, she suffered her first seizure. Then another. And another. She endured more than seventy on our three-phase journey home. You have to understand, I had no choice. She could not live here in the castle, nor could she survive alone."

Lars turned, furious. "She was your best friend's daughter, you'd sworn to protect her, and you *had no choice* but to put her in that hellhole?"

Dubric pressed on. "It was the only way I could keep her safe. I sent a stipend every moon to ensure she received the best food, the best care. About a moon after she arrived, I received word she was with child."

The fury on Lars's face turned to horror. "I was *born there*?"

"I increased my stipend and arranged additional medical care. I was there, just outside the door, when you drew your first breath."

Dubric smiled past the tears blurring his vision. "You were so strong, so healthy, like your grandparents. I took you to Friar Bonne because I knew he could find you a good, safe home. I swear on my life, I intended you to be raised as a commoner. A miller's son, a farmer, a merchant. Anything where you could be safe and anonymous. But Jhandra Hargrove was here, visiting family, and she saw you, saw the baby she had so long wanted. There was nothing I could do."

Lars shook his head, horrified. "Nothing you could do?"

"I knew you were not safe in Haenpar. You were three summers old when I first requested to train you as a page. You finally came to me on your ninth birthing day."

"You knew," Lars said, grimacing. "All along, when I thought my father didn't love me, that it was my fault my mother fell into madness, you knew it was all a lie? You let me live my life thinking I was worthless, disposable? And, worse yet, you knew there was someone alive, someone who might love me, *family* who might want me, and not only did you keep her trapped in that awful place, you said nothing?"

"Elena wanted you hidden as much as I did," Dubric said sharply. "She could not care for you there. I hid you in plain sight and you have lived to manhood. Do you have any idea how impossible that seemed fifteen summers ago?"

Lars stood. "No, and I don't care. Goddess! I can't believe you waited this long to tell me."

"Now that you are grown, you deserve to know. And I did not lie about the sword, not when I had it created." Dubric released a shaky breath. "After you faced the mage in the Reach, I sent a private message to Waterford requesting a blessed sword for the Darril line. I merely neglected to mention your real heritage to Bonne before the ceremony."

"So you made Friar Bonne lie? To the Goddess?"

Dubric waved off Lars's concern. "Bonne's words are immaterial. It is far more important that you be properly armed, especially now."

"Why now? What else aren't you telling me?"

Dubric hesitated, then reached into his pocket for the ferrotype. "Jelke had this. I am so sorry," he said, handing it to Lars.

Lars snatched it up. "Jess? What's wrong with her eyes?"

"Mage killers' eyes glow white when viewed though a special lens. That is how we identified them. Jesscea may have awakened her ability when she touched Oriana's dagger."

"No," Lars snapped. "She's supposed to go to University, not become a killer. You can't do this to her. I won't let you." He looked at the picture again, his fingers dragging along the cut edges. "I saw sheets of nine at the booth. Oh, Goddess, no." He looked at Dubric. "Where are the other eight?"

"I do not know."

Lars grabbed Dubric by the throat, his grip painfully hard, and shook the image in front of his eyes. "Bull piss. You know every frigging thing that happens, you lying bastard. What happened to the other eight pictures?"

"Spies have them. I do not yet know who they are, or whom they serve. I swear to you that is the truth."

Lars shoved Dubric back. "So you're telling me that not only am I the grandson of some dead assassin and the son of a whore, but spies are out there trying to kill my intended?" Lars said, pacing.

"That is not all," Dubric said softly. "You are also the grandson of a mage killer. You and Elena alone possess both Royal and mage killer blood. If you and Jesscea were to have children . . ." He swallowed. "Just like Albin and Katarinne, the Ghost and his Blade, the most feared and deadly assassins of the war, again walk the land. It is not safe for you here. They will come for you, and Jesscea. They dare not let you breed."

Lars stopped pacing.

"You may need to leave. Hide. As Albin did."

"We can't run!" Lars said, flinging the ferrotype at Dubric. "She's fourteen! They have our frigging pictures! What do you expect us to do?"

"If it comes to that, if the danger comes close to Faldorrah again, I will help you," Dubric said. "I will help both of you." *And lose one of my most trusted men,* he thought. *And cost my squire another daughter.*

"Right," Lars snapped, his face twisted with rage. "The way you helped my mother? Or my grandparents? We're better off on our own." Dubric thought Lars might strike him, but the boy snatched up his new sword and stomped out of the temple, slamming the doors behind him.

Dubric tucked the ferrotype into his pocket and stood. He took a calming breath and looked up to the round window. He would do whatever was necessary to get them to safety. Just as he had always done.

* * *

Friar Bonne opened his door and smiled out at Dubric. "Of all the people in my parish, you are the last I ever expected to knock on my door." He stepped aside and bowed slightly. "Please, come in."

It had been more than forty summers since Dubric had been in the friar's home, a humble apartment tacked onto the Temple Wing. On his previous visit, Dubric had found blood on the walls and floor, blood that belonged inside Friar Esmund. There was no blood in Bonne's suite, only lived-in clutter. The place smelled of cheese and freshly baked bread.

"Would you like a glass of wine?" Bonne asked, brushing past. He wore a shirt and trousers, not the clerical robes Dubric had long associated with him, and his feet were bare. "You look as if you could use one."

Dubric followed. "I probably could."

They reached a small kitchen and Bonne slipped into a flour-dusted apron. He nodded to a pile of bread dough on a granite slab. "I bake. It relaxes me." He rummaged through his cupboards and produced two glasses and a bottle of wine.

"Haenparan red?" he asked, showing Dubric the bottle.

"That is fine." Dubric sat on a stool near a high table.

Bonne pulled the cork. "The Romlins keep sending me prime vintages," he said as he poured. "I tell them I need no thanks for having aided Risley, but they continue to send more wine, far too much for me to drink alone. They're an insistent bunch."

"That they are," Dubric said. Moons before, during the castle murders, Bonne had sent word to Lord Romlin concerning his son. Doing so had likely saved the lad's life.

Bonne set the bottle near Dubric. "To the Romlins and their most delightful wine."

Dubric raised his glass. It was a prime vintage indeed.

Bonne carried his wine to the granite slab then set to work kneading. "Whatever you've come to tell me, I'm listening."

Dubric stared into his wine. "Do you know anything about blood mages?"

Bonne flipped the dough. "Probably not as much as I should if the look on your face is any indication," he said. "Didn't they eat their victims?"

"Not exactly. They drained them," Dubric said. "All mages did in their own way; mentally, spiritually, physically, emotionally. But the blood mages kept their victims like a farmer keeps milk goats, drinking their fluids, sometimes directly from the victim." Dubric sipped the dark red wine, trying not to think about his own close escape. "Their victims enjoyed it, hungered for it until it became an addiction, and the blood mages often used the bliss of draining to force their human stock to maim, to kill, to steal. Whatever the mage wanted."

Bonne continued to knead. "Sounds horrid."

"Yes. It is."

Bonne sipped his wine. "You think we have a blood mage here?"

"I am certain of it. She is using Maeve as a storage vessel, and she has corrupted me."

Bonne looked up from his dough. "Excuse me?"

Dubric unbuttoned his collar and showed the bite bruise to Bonne. "She gave me this last night, then another, a worse one, this afternoon. On my thigh."

Bonne chuckled. "You dirty dog. I wondered why you brought such a young woman home. Ah, for the days when the ladies would leave bruises on my neck."

"No, no," Dubric said. "These are not romantic love bites." He paused to refill his glass. "All evening I have felt the craving for more. If she had bitten me a third time, I would not have been able to resist."

Bonne stared. "You're serious."

"Deadly serious."

Bonne turned the dough, curling it under itself until the top surface was smooth and round. He placed it in a large bowl then covered it with a towel. "Is that why you requested a rectory room for the night?"

"Yes. As I expected, the mage left Maeve when I dragged her into the temple hall. She needs to remain here, under Malanna's influence, until I find a way to save her."

Bonne removed his apron, washed his hands, and brought his glass to the table. "I'm half tempted to refuse you, after the grief you've given me these many summers."

"I know," Dubric said. "And I would not blame you."

Bonne hefted his bulk onto a stool. "But let us drink fine wine as we wait for my dough to rise." He took a sip and smiled. "Other than keeping her here, what can I do to help?"

Dubric's hands shook. "Are you trained for purging?"

Bonne met his gaze. "I thought you didn't believe in the Goddess's grace? All the things you've said . . ."

"I was once a castor of the white," Dubric said softly, his voice catching in his throat. "While at University, I served the Holy Temple as a bound knight." He closed his eyes then opened them again. "I apprenticed under Calladiere Bebhinn for two summers before duties called me to war. I . . . I have been marked."

Bonne gaped. "You?"

"It was a long time ago. Before Malanna and I came to an impasse. Before she saw fit to punish me."

"I never knew."

"No one does," Dubric said. "Although I know the rite, as a fallen I cannot purge Maeve. Even if she had not corrupted me, those powers are no longer mine to wield."

Bonne drained his glass in a gulp. "Whatever did you do to go from a castor to a fallen? What curse has she laid upon you? By the waters of Lake Culan, Dubric, how did you survive?"

Once the words came, they fell from Dubric as if they had been waiting at the precipice. "I married soon after the war. My wife, Oriana, was also a castor, and a mage killer. We lived in Waterford, but mage followers found her, trapped her, burned her. Alive."

He took a breath and looked up to Bonne. "I found her in the flames, praying, singing the holy lyrics, struggling to live. I . . . I couldn't save her. I tried. She was crushed beneath burning beams and when I tried to pull her out, her arm came off; it was cooked to the bone. But she was alive, trapped in her own magic." He felt tears sting his eyes and he blinked them away. "I could do nothing to help her. So I cut her throat, nearly removed her head. I murdered my own wife, a follower of the white, to stop her magic and stop her suffering. Doing so, I killed our unborn child as well."

"Surely, if she was a castor of Malanna's magic, she could have survived."

"Her flesh was charred! No white magic could repair that. At best she would have survived as a blackened husk, barely alive and in constant pain. I had no choice. I loved her too much to let her live."

Bonne laid his thick hand on Dubric's burn-scarred one. "And your penance?"

"I see death," Dubric said. "Since I killed the woman I loved, I see the souls that were not meant to die. I endure them until I bring them justice, either by man or Malanna herself." He paused and took a sip of his wine. "Because of mercy and love I was cursed, so I curse the bitch in return."

Bonne flinched. "You could ask for forgiveness. Absolution."

"Never. I committed the sin, I will serve the punishment. I have lived nearly fifty summers since then, and each glance in the mirror is a reminder of my compassion, each ghost a reminder of my curse. Contrary to rumor, I do not doubt the Goddess's existence. I see proof of her treachery every day of my wretched life."

Dubric took a breath then said, "After decades of loneliness, I have love again. I will not allow the dark to take her. Damn my ghosts, damn the bitch Goddess, and damn my own life, Maeve will not die. Not for this."

"You know, Dubric, you are a difficult man to help. Most men, when seeking guidance or a favor from a friend, do not insult their friend's profession."

Dubric drained his glass. "I am not most men."

Bonne smiled. "So I see." He poured more wine. "I've never participated in a purging. I've read of them, and I have the proper tomes and scrolls, but if she is possessed by a mage, what you need is a mage killer, not a priest."

"Therein lies my second problem." Dubric stood and reached into his trouser pocket for the ferrotype. He handed it to Bonne.

"The bitch provides with one hand and takes away with the other," he said, sitting again. "Jesscea is too young, untrained, and her father has forbidden it. While the potential is there, the reality is not. If I encourage Jesscea to the task, I will lose both of my squires. But if I ignore Jesscea's potential, Maeve will most certainly die. I will lose everything and gain nothing."

"Where did you get this?" Bonne asked, glancing up from the picture.

"From a spy, which leads us to problem number three. Do you see the cut edges? I believe the ferrotypist used a multiplier and took four images, or perhaps even nine, on a single sheet of iron. That is merely one corner. The spy had one piece, but how many others exist? How many of my enemies will learn I have a mage killer in my grasp? Even if they heard that she can never be used, they will not care. They will come to kill her or take her for their own. Her potential is too powerful to ignore."

Bonne laid the image on the table. "No wonder you're here."

Dubric nodded at the empty bottle. "And getting nicely drunk. Thank you for that." He drank. "My lover is possessed of dark magic, but the girl who carries the potential to save her cannot. Toss in murders somehow connected to the mage, my senior squire facing capital charges for which he yet may hang, and my younger page tottering on the edge of raving madness, I am in a bit of a bind. Tight enough that I need your aid."

Bonne stood. "I think we need another bottle of wine."

CHAPTER

24

✝

Four ghastly heads floated around Dubric as he rode to the Quarry Run ravine with Dien, Lars, Marsden, and Major Felk. With Garrett and Tupper in gaol, and Sweeny trapped with Maeve in the temple, he found himself without a likely suspect. The fourth ghost, the young man who had arrived while Dubric had argued with Maeve the afternoon before—*No, it was Sweeny who argued with me,* he reminded himself—had a bleeding, severed throat and screamed in mindless anguish. The ghost had the soft features and dull eyes of an imbecile, like so many he had seen trudging in the sanatorium's halls.

Dubric wondered who would murder such a harmless person. What purpose would it serve? He had been certain the mage had been killing in Quarry Run, but apparently he had been wrong all along. A person had committed the murders, not Sweeny, taking parts and pieces from people and animals, keeping some parts and discarding the rest. The substances Inek identified had healing properties. Was some sort of magical healing involved?

But why kill to heal? Why take such risks? Why use

magic and risk execution? Why kill to repair a leg, for King's sake?

He tried to reconcile the case with experience. Murders were typically committed for rage, lust, or greed; base human emotions and desires. In some ways that made sense. The boy, Raffin, was reviled in the community. Dubric could easily reason that the boy had been killed in rage or frustration. Higgle, the second ghost, had been reported to be a laggard and cheat. A multitude of reasons could have precipitated his death.

But none of the other incidents fit normal patterns. The first ghost, the corporal without a dripping throat, had been identified as a stranger. If he truly was a member of Nanke's army, why had it taken so long for his ghost to appear?

He had one ghost when the first remains were found. One, not three as the remains indicated. Higgle and Raffin's remains had yet to be found. Ghosts were potentially missing as well. And what was the connection between a murdered imbecile, dismembered sheep, and a rooster's living head?

Dubric looked over to Felk, who was gawking at everything as if he could not believe his eyes. How could the soldier be so young after nearly fifty summers? Even trapped in a spell of some sort, surely he would age.

It made no sense, and he had no idea how it connected back to Sweeny, to Maeve, to his hope of saving her. *I am missing the motive.* There had to be a connection between the clues. There had to be a *reason*.

Once across the bridge, they turned their mounts south and rode down to the marsh. "We weren't far from here when we first saw her," Felk said as the land flattened out.

Dubric glanced at the darkening sky, where rain clouds were forming in the northwest. "Let us dismount and walk, so that we are less likely to miss something."

The men dismounted and Felk led his horse to the tangle of brush near where the ravine emptied into the marsh. "I was here when I saw her," he said, his voice soft and awed. "I even stood upon this stone to see Colonel Marks on the other bank." He looked at Dubric. "How can this be, sir? To me, it was the dead of winter just days ago."

"That is what we are trying to discover," Dubric said. "Where did you see the mage?"

Felk pointed across the marsh. "Over there, near a tree."

Dubric squinted. He could see a man trapping crayfish, several willow trees, and the ghostly outline of a dead cypress.

"It looked a lot like that dead tree, sir. Had a few more branches, but it was that same size, that same twisted shape . . ."

Marsden tossed a small stone into the water. "Lots of the older folks fear this swamp and that tree. They were surprised when Gunth named his tavern after it."

Twisted and charred, with one living branch, the tree did indeed look much like the one on the sign hanging outside the Twisted Cypress Tavern. *Is that another connection? Did Inek not mention that the substance contained sap from an unusual tree?* "Did she appear on this side of the tree, or behind it?" Dubric asked. "I need to know exactly where she first showed herself. There may be a device, or a portal of some sort, that could lead us back to her." *There has to be something here to save Maeve.*

"This side, sir. I saw her reflection in the water."

"C'mon, pup, let's go," Dien said. "See if we can find the right place." He started along the bank toward the tree, Lars and Marsden following close behind. Lars's dog bounded ahead.

"How did she appear?" Dubric asked as his men walked around the marsh to the tree.

"Like she rose straight up out of the water to stand on the surface. She had her arms out, like this," Felk said, stretching his arms wide. "Then, when she clapped her hands in front of her like this," he demonstrated with a straight-armed clap in front of his chest, "the water lifted and came toward us."

I was correct to bind her hands. "Did you hear her speak?"

"No, sir. Just saw her hands move."

The men reached the tree. Yelling commands and motioning with their hands, Dubric and Felk directed them to the precise location. "That's it, sir," Felk said, pointing. "Right where Dien is."

Dien stood at the water's edge in a mass of cattails and sedge, not far from the tree.

"There!" Dubric called out as he and Felk approached the others to help search.

"I'm feeling something hard under here," Dien said, stomping a few steps side to side. "Maybe a hand's width or two beneath the surface of the mud." Behind him, Marsden poked a stick into the mud, pulled it out, then took a step to poke again. The stick never descended any farther than the initial wet mark indicated.

"I have an edge!" Lars said. He dragged one foot through the water and looked up at Dubric. "It's sticking out of the mud a bit here, feels like some sort of masonry. Maybe brick."

There is an underground chamber. "I am coming," Dubric said. But when Dubric was only fifteen lengths or so away from the others, Marsden yelped and disappeared, feet first, straight down into the mud.

* * *

The rectory room was perhaps twelve lengths on a side, with a bed, a dresser, a lamp, and a single chair. No windows. No books. Nothing to look at or do to pass the time. A room for sleeping, but Maeve had already napped. It felt like a prison.

"I'm going to go mad," she said, standing. She paced the width of the room for the umpteenth time, then sat, fidgeted, and stood again, grumbling in frustration.

Someone knocked on the door and she leapt for it. Friar Bonne stood just outside, a pile of books tucked in the crook of his arm and a bottle of wine in his hand. "I didn't know what you liked to read," he said as she motioned for him to enter. "So I brought some sonnets, a history book, a biography of High Priestess Louquinne—a wonderful read, by the way—and a story by Dunclaire. His prose isn't to my taste, but Clintte assured me his works are very popular."

In the back of her throat, Maeve tasted ash, dry and black and dead. She swallowed it away. "Thank you."

Bonne set the wine and books on the dresser, then rummaged in his pockets. "I also brought a pack of cards and a puzzle-pin game." He paused, raising his head as he sniffed. "Do you smell that?"

Maeve felt her brow furrow, a tightening in her forehead that brought a headache with it. "Smell what?"

"Mold or some such," Bonne said, still sniffing. "Musty. Wet."

"Swampy," she said, smiling.

"Yes, swampy," he said, nodding. "I shall have to tell the engineers we have a leak in the roof over this hall." Bonne rocked back on his heels and gave her a helpful smile. "I wish we had better accommodations, but if there's anything else we can get for you, please don't hesitate to ask."

Maeve stood silently, watching him, the same slight smile stretching her lips just enough to expose her teeth as the door behind Bonne quietly closed without being touched. The randy old fart had believed that proximity to filthy religious ornaments would trap her, but they only made her cautious and patient. She had remained quiet and hidden all night, but now, with a pious gift before her, and the privacy to do as she wished, she could barely contain her glee.

"Are you all right? Is there anything else you'd like?" he asked, his round face concerned.

"I'm fine," she replied, moistening her lips. "But there is one thing . . ."

He bowed. "Whatever you desire, my lady."

The lamplight flickered, then fell, leaving only a wisp of smoke. "You," she said, grasping his wrist and yanking it up to her mouth.

A flick of her teeth severed his skin, his arteries. As she drank deep, Bonne's startled gasp turned into a moan of pleasure. But it soon faded to a hiss of air, his last breath, as his plump arm and round soft body turned thin, then dry, then to a collapsing husk.

Licking her lips, Sweeny opened the door and stepped out to the hall, taking a moment to brush bits of friar dust off her dress. She'd almost forgotten how utterly delightful fat clergy tasted. Not quite as invigorating as Royal blood, but tasty nonetheless.

She nodded to a pair of altar boys as she walked

toward the castle doors, and stepped out of the Temple Wing with a sigh of relief. *I'm free!*

She turned around, sniffing, and looked upward. "Without all that dark magic above that old bastard's suite to call to me . . ." she mumbled as she shifted her focus. Grinning, she practically skipped to the west tower. Instead of passing through to the outside, she climbed the winding stair, stopping at the second floor to sniff the air before resuming her climb.

"Here we go," she said as she opened the third-floor door.

* * *

Sitting on her bed, Jess read,

4 32,2216
We'd waited for this night for moons. Faldorrahns celebrate the new moon after the equinox, some nonsense about the end of planting season. At my first entry to Quarry Run, the revelry was going strong. After securing the village, I returned to Nuobir while he repositioned the glass. He dropped me in Sweeny's bedchamber, almost two lengths above the floor. Thank the Goddess I didn't wake them when I fell. Judging from the stench of liquor and lust, the bitch had celebrated a great deal.

Jess bit her lip. *Oriana came to Faldorrah? The night of the spring faire?* Sick dread tainted Jess's stomach as she turned the page.

Sweeny lay in bed with three men, all young and fine, their numerous bleeding bites testament to her control over them. I slit their throats, quickly, quietly, then smothered her with sweet vitriol. She struggled, more than I'd expected but less than I'd feared. While she was unconscious I removed her tongue, broke and bound her hands, then carried her filthy body outside.

"Goddess," Jess whispered. This assassination wasn't quick and tidy like the others. She read as Oriana tied Sweeny to a tree then burned every thing, living or dead, that was connected to the mage, forcing Sweeny to watch. All that night and into the next, Oriana burned whatever she laid her hands upon. The second morning, she killed Sweeny then burned her body, leaving nothing more than ash and dust, which she salted. Purified.

Jess reread the final words of the entry: . . . *the Butcher of Quarry Run was dead.*

Not only dead, but erased from existence. *Butcher. Quarry Run.* She knew the name of that village. She'd heard her father and Lars mention it. Jess touched Fyn's shoulder, her hand shaking. "Fyn, did Gilby tell you anything about what he did when he went with Dubric a couple of days ago?"

Fyn tied off her darned sock and cut her thread with her teeth. "Yeah, they went to some village called Quarry Run. Sounded disgusting. Somebody up there's cutting up people. Taking off their heads. Why?"

Jess jumped at a knock on their bedroom door and let out a relieved sigh as her mother peeked in. "Jess, your aunt Maeve's here to talk to you."

Jess set aside the journals and stood as Maeve came in.

"What are you girls up to?" Maeve asked.

"Just reading, waiting for Lars to come home," Jess said. The horror of the journals faded for a moment as she beamed with pride. "Can you believe he made squire?"

"Yes, yes I can." Maeve's head jerked awkwardly as she looked around. Jess wondered if she had a stiff neck.

"That belt you're wearing," Maeve said. "I don't think I've seen it before. Is it new?"

"This?" Jess looked down to her waist, where she wore the belt she'd made from Maeve's fabric scraps and the old buckle Lars had found. "You gave me the fabric to go with the buckle, remember?"

"Oh, yes! It looks very stylish," Maeve said. "May I talk to you? In private?"

"Of course." Jess followed Maeve out of her parents' suite.

"What's wrong?" Jess asked as she closed the door and stepped with Maeve into the hall. "Are the men all right? Have they left yet?"

"They left this morning, as far as I know. Why?" Maeve walked toward the main stairs and Jess followed.

Jess looked about, but no one was near to overhear. "It's that village where the murders are. Quarry Run. Something happened that they need to know about. There has to be a way to send a message to them."

They descended the stairs, walking through a group of maids. "What happened?"

Jess waited until the stairway cleared. "I think the murders are connected to a mage that lived there a long time ago. They need to know."

Maeve continued past the second-floor landing. "A mage? Are you sure?"

"Yes. They called her *the Butcher*."

Maeve gave her a sideways glance. "That's not a very

pleasant nickname." They reached the main hall and stepped off the stairs. "How do you know so much about it?"

"From Oriana's journals." Jess followed Maeve around the stairs to the back hall. "I've been reading them. Remember?"

Maeve opened the hall doors. "And that interesting buckle? Where did you say Lars found it?"

They turned east, toward Dubric's office. "In the mud, in some ravine. I thought we told you."

"Mud. Yes." Maeve reached for the latch for Dubric's door.

"I think it's locked," Jess said. "He usually locks it if they're gone."

Jess almost thought she heard a faint crackle and hiss as her aunt grasped the latch and pulled. "Not locked," Maeve said, opening the door. "See?"

As they walked through, Jess's nose wrinkled. Something smelled alarming. Hot and sharp, like lightning in dry air.

Maeve continued to the inner office door and Jess frowned. Dubric *always* locked the inner door when he left the office. Her dad and Lars had keys, but no one else.

But the latch released easily. Jess stared as Maeve opened the door. *Dubric wouldn't leave the office, let alone the castle, without locking that door.*

Maeve hesitated in the doorway, her hand gripping the door frame, then she looked over her shoulder at Jess. "Are you coming, dear? What I need to show you is inside."

Dear? Jess's mouth went dry. Maeve's eyes were wrong. The shape, the angle, the color. Jess took a step back as she smelled that acrid, dangerous scent again.

Burnt. It smells metallic and burnt. "I'd better not," she said, glancing past Maeve to the lumpy pillowcase sitting on the floor beside Dubric's desk. Jess swallowed, wondering if Dubric had taken the dagger from it. She looked back at Maeve, anxiously noting the strange green tint to her eyes. "I'm not allowed past the waiting area without permission. Case files are in there. Confidential papers and things."

"It's all right," Maeve purred. "I just want to show you something, then we'll go." Her hand on the door frame darkened and the wood beneath it charred. Smoke curled between her fingers.

Jess ran for the outer door, but yelped and yanked her hand away. The searing-hot metal of the latch had sizzled the skin of her palm. She stared at the burn, horrified, her heart hammering. The pendant on her throat had turned ice cold. *I'm trapped. Goddess, no.*

Low laughter, *clackclackclackclack.* "What's wrong, dear? Get singed?"

"I'm not your dear," Jess snapped as she turned. "Where's my aunt Maeve?"

"Oh, she's here," Sweeny said, her head jerking like a bird's. Black char spread from her fingertips, up the backs of her hands and forearms. "Don't worry. She'll be fine. Until I don't need her anymore."

The skin on her arms crisped, flaking off, each movement of her joints making a *clackclackclack* sound as she stepped toward Jess. The charring rapidly spread like a greasy stain, burning her clothing and exposing blackened skin.

"What do you want with me?" Jess asked, her heart threatening to explode from her ribs.

Sweeny grinned, her throat and face darkening as her blouse charred and drifted away, leaving her nude.

Blood hissed out of her split cheeks and turned to bitter smoke. Her lips became cinders, then ash and dust, exposing her teeth. A puff of flame consumed her hair. "You have something of mine, and I want it back." She stared at Jess's belly and licked the crumbled ash where her lips used to be.

A sick feeling in her gut as she worried if Sweeny was going to burn her, too, Jess lowered her hand and covered the buckle at her waist. "And if I refuse?"

Sweeny's teeth, white in blackened flesh, gnashed together. Her brilliant green eyes stared at Jess from dark and skeletal sockets. Sweeny's head tilted in a sharp jerk, the neck bones slipping apart. "You have no choice."

"There's always a choice," Jess said, struggling not to panic. Sweeny smelled horrid, a stomach-churning stench of rot and stagnation and burning. "Oriana killed you. You're dead. Purified. Erased. You're just a ghost."

Sweeny moved closer, and Jess stepped to the side.

"Ah, but I'm not," Sweeny said, each movement cracking ash flakes from her body. "I live. I've always lived. Your precious Oriana made a mistake, little girl. She killed my body, but my spirit hid in my secret place. She burned everything she found, yes, but not all. I kept a living vessel hidden and safe, even from those like Oriana. I must admit Oriana was thorough, so thorough I had to kill my vessel to possess her. Even trapped, I was patient; I knew someone would come, sooner or later, and they did. But thanks to you showing that weaver my buckle, dear, I was shoved into that mirror. It took some doing, but now I'm trapped in this . . ." Sweeny gestured down at Maeve's body, "this pudgy thing, and I have to do this all myself." Sweeny gnashed her teeth again. "Now, just give me back my buckle and I'll be on my way."

"Why don't you just take it?"

Sweeny stepped sideways, blocking Jess from the entry to Dubric's office. "You'd like that, wouldn't you? But you're unarmed, dear." She glanced at Jess's hand, which was curled over the buckle at her waist, then back to her eyes. "You thought you were tricky, didn't you? Giving her the buckle so close to all that magic. So much magic, you thought I wouldn't notice when you took my buckle away."

"But you didn't notice, did you? I've had it for days. *Days.*"

Sweeny lunged forward, knocking Jess against the wall. Her breath smelled rotten, like stagnant water. "Once I found a way out of the mirror, this vessel, this Maeve thing, never left the rooms, never left the magic's light. She blinded me. And you did, too." She looked down, at Jess's waist. "It's mine and I want it back."

"No."

"Your choice," Sweeny said, and slammed her hand against Jess's forehead, knocking Jess's head against the granite wall.

Jess heard a faint sizzle and her vision wavered at the sudden burst of crushing pain. Everything turned gray, and she slid down the wall as her legs went limp.

"That randy old geezer taught me that," Sweeny said from the dark. "Hurts, doesn't it?"

Jess tried to hold on to the buckle, but Sweeny yanked her hands away, her touch sizzling hot. The stink of rancid smoke cleared Jess's foggy mind. Her fingers crushed into Sweeny's charred face, crackling with smoke as Jess struggled to stand. Sweeny snarled and ripped the belt off Jess's waist, then, prize in hand, she hurried away, even as Jess got her feet beneath her.

Jess's belt burned in a burst of flame, the glowing ashes floating to the floor like cinder snow. Sweeny dashed into Dubric's office and Jess stumbled desperately after her, holding her aching head.

She reached the door but was blinded by a flash of brilliant green light. She squinted through the brightness, seeing Sweeny at Dubric's mirror, the image in the glass diving forward then down, to a marsh and an ugly, dead tree.

"It's been a pleasure," Sweeny said, then stepped through, leaving a fruity scent behind, much like the one Oriana described in her journals.

Through the glass, Jess saw Sweeny jump down to the water, and the image wavered, focusing on the tree as she waded to it.

No, no, no! Lars is there! Dad!

The edges of the reflection darkened, its brilliance fading even as Jess watched. She scrambled for the pillowcase and snatched it up, then closed her eyes and fell through the mirror.

* * *

As Dubric followed Marsden's scream, he saw Lars disappear, scrambling down into the mud, Dien following close behind. The dog yapped, running frantic circles around where the men had gone. Felk ran ahead, then he, too, clambered down into what Dubric now saw was a large, rectangular hole about ten lengths from the tree's base.

His knee throbbing, Dubric reached the hole and peered in. A ladder stretched twelve or fifteen lengths down into murky water, and Dien stood thigh-deep in it, looking up. Behind him, a muddy cellar door hung, swinging slightly, just above the big man's head. "Marsden's all right, sir, just swallowed some water and got the piss scared out of him. You're not going to believe what's down here." Dien's face looked ashen and ill. Dubric heard someone retch, then vomit.

Dien moved to the left, sloshing outside the area visible from the hole, as Dubric descended. The ladder faced a masonry wall streaked with moisture, mold, and decaying webs. The air inside was cool and damp, with an odd, medicinal odor mixed with the stench of stagnation. Dubric felt an immense sense of space, like a vast cave had opened up behind him. Something in the water slithered past the back of his calf like a cold caress.

"There must be *thousands* of them," Lars said, awed.

Immersed in cold water nearly to his crotch, Dubric reached the bottom and turned around, slipping slightly on the slick stones at his feet. *The wall must be some sort of dam,* he thought, looking around. They appeared to be standing in a large cavern, a cool and dripping cave that disappeared into the dark. Straight ahead he saw the corpse of a little girl, decayed to moldy bones in a rotted dress and strapped to a raised platform. Roots punctured her head, plunging into her eye sockets and forehead. She wore a belt around her waist, the leather speckled with black rot and the buckle missing.

Dubric looked away from the corpse and up to a row of shelves, straight into a man's face, his severed head floating in clear fluid inside of a large, grimy jar. As Dubric stared, the man blinked.

Dubric scrambled back and slammed into the ladder, grasping it to keep from sliding into the muck. *How is this possible?* The jar stood among dozens of others on the shelf, one of a sea of jarred heads on shelves above and below. Some appeared to be sleeping, some stared straight ahead. Only a few floated crookedly and appeared dead. Three jars near the ladder were missing, with only muck-crusted rings marking the shelf where they once stood. Other shelves stood behind, and more shelves behind that, each filled with living heads. Hundreds of them, thousands, even on submerged shelves.

Dubric squinted into the dark, seeing soft glints of light reflecting on cobweb-coated glass, countless rows of shelving and jars reaching back into the recesses of the cave. The voices of his men echoed back at him, sounding cold and dead from the dark, like whispers spoken by the jarred heads.

Dubric shuddered. *I received fewer ghosts because their brains, thus their souls, are still alive!* He looked at Felk floundering in the water and felt his stomach clench. *Higgle suffered from head injuries, was about to die, yet I received his ghost. Shortly after, I first saw Felk in the bed Higgle had occupied.*

While Dien lit the lanterns hanging on the wall, Felk retched again, dry heaving. He spat into the mucky water then stood straight and wiped his mouth with the back of his hand. "These are my men," he said, gesturing to rows and rows of shelved heads in jars. Some barely protruded above the water, and others, above the partially submerged jars, were streaked with lines of dried slime that marked the highest water depths at roughly chest level. "That's Sergeant Tuttle. Privates Watson and Filbbe. Corporal Sanderhill. What in the seven hells happened to my men?"

Marsden was drenched, soaked to the skin and dripping with gray-green muck as he leaned against the masonry wall, shaking his head. "This is in my town? How? Why? How can this happen?"

"It happened before you were ever born." Dubric grimaced at the chilly stroke of a creature swimming against his legs, but he saw nothing but dark, cloudy water with clots of floating slime. He took a step toward his men, ducking beneath dripping roots, and sneezed at the stagnant stench. Away from the shaft of sunlight, the space seemed even larger, cavernous and aware, every sound they made echoing back at them.

A rotting severed head bobbed near Dubric's hip with an eyeless gray frog crouched in its eye socket. Dubric took another step forward. When the wave he created tilted the head, the frog hopped off, leaving a clutch of eggs behind. As it swam away, an eel brushed by Dubric's leg and dragged the frog beneath the surface.

Dubric looked about the dark, his heart hammering. Lars and Dien's voices echoed back, the softening repetitions creating a chaos of noise and dripping water. "Come with me to the light, Major. Please."

Felk wiped his mouth again then nodded and walked with Dubric to the bright area beneath the open cellar door. At Dubric's urging, Felk bent slightly so Dubric could examine the back of his neck. Dubric saw two marks, both doubled triangles, etched in black and red on Felk's skin near the base of his neck. And he saw a faint hairline scar running between them.

"What is it, sir?" Felk asked as Dubric traced the thin line around to his throat and across.

"I need you to *think*," Dubric said, drawing his hand away as *think* echoed urgently again and again. "How long were you lost in the swamp?"

"Forever," Felk said, staring at the jars as his hand

came up to his throat. "An eternity." He turned his head, gasping. "Goddess, no. I was one of them, wasn't I?"

Dubric grabbed him by the shoulders. "Think. Please. In all of that time, in that whole eternity, did you see anything, *anyone*, other than the water?"

"We found an empty workbench," Dien said, sloshing toward them from far past the shelves, Lars following in his wake. "Empty holes in the mud and mold make it look like there was a lot of stuff on it recently. Bottles, boxes, maybe a book or two."

The chilly water making his muscles cramp, Dubric returned his attention to Felk. "Please, for the love of the King, *think*. Did you see a man? A woman? Anyone?"

"No, no one. But I had a dream, not long before I woke, that a woman was talking to me. I couldn't hear her, not through the water."

A woman? Dubric looked at Felk. He had had no body. Higgle's head was damaged and useless, but his body was unharmed. Had Felk been given Higgle's body? Did the killer keep the good and discard the bad? Dubric nodded to himself. *Practical. The killer is practical.* He glanced at the other ghosts. The head of the imbecile, but no ghost of his body. The ghost represented the only part discarded. She, whoever she was, kept the body, used it . . . Maybe as she had used Higgle's to give Felk another chance at life. But why Felk? With all these other heads, why him? Was that a practical choice, too? Because he was near the ladder?

Dubric looked at Raffin's ghost, the boy's head still screaming and weeping in terror. The child had not been an imbecile. There had not been one thing wrong with the boy other than his attitude.

A thought echoed in his mind, like their voices across the cavern. *Keep the good, discard the bad.*

Dubric swallowed and took an involuntary step back. She had let the head perish but kept Raffin's body, used it, because another body, another child, was broken.

Oh, no.

All the men turned as a woman screamed from outside the cellar, then her scream was cut short.

"That's Jess!" Lars said, pushing past Dien.

"Can't be," Dien said, but his face had gone white. "She's back home."

"She would have no way to get here," Dubric assured Lars, "unless she convinced Flavin to lend her a horse and coerced our location from Otlee. She would not do such a thing." He reached for the ladder rungs and proceeded to hoist himself up. "It cannot be Jesscea."

From outside, a young woman screeched, "Give me back my aunt Maeve!"

"Jess!" Lars pushed Dubric aside, nearly knocking him into the water, then scrambled up the ladder, disappearing into the light.

CHAPTER

25

†

Jess fell, screaming. Miles, it felt like. Forever. A thick, spicy-sweet reek filling her senses. The falling continued, agony and fear without end, down, always down. On and on she fell, tumbling and screaming.

Then suddenly the darkness blinked away and she plunged headlong into marshy water, submerging completely, and slammed onto silt and mud.

Pillowcase in hand, she jumped up, breaking the water's surface. She gasped, sucking in the stink of spicy plums and green water. Her lungs and throat clenched at the fumes and she coughed, doubling over. A few lengths ahead of her, Sweeny walked through the water.

"Idiot child. You have no idea what you're stepping into." Sweeny glanced back then swept on.

Jess spat away mud, snatching open the pillowcase as she reached inside. As soon as her fingertips touched the dagger, her vision turned hazy, tendrils of white smoke teasing the edges. As she tore away the towel and wrapped her fingers around the dagger, clenching it tight, perfect clarity returned.

"Give me back my aunt Maeve!" She slogged through chest-deep water, her sodden skirt slowing her while Sweeny, naked and unencumbered, moved as if the water parted for her.

Sweeny turned, snarling a curse. A wide mark on her forehead oozed and dripped into her eyes. Sweeny's hand flicked across the water's surface as if intending a playful splash, but the droplets sprayed up and turned to hornets and dragonflies, green and glistening.

Jess ducked underwater, struggling to swim as her skirt tangled around her, hearing a faint buzz of the swarm above the water's surface. Using her dagger, Jess sliced her skirt above the knee then ripped and cut all the way around. The heavy, tangling weight fell away. No longer encumbered, she swam.

The water was murky and green, thick with plants and algae. She swam until she feared her lungs would burst, then surfaced to suck in some air. She immediately felt stings, sharp eruptions of fiery-hot pain on her face and scalp, and dropped beneath the surface again. Her dagger turned cold in her hand, and soft white light pulsed from the blade in rhythm with her thudding heart. She could see Sweeny's charred figure wading purposefully ahead. So close, maybe ten lengths away.

Another quick gasp, burning pinpricks on her neck, shoulder, and cheek, then under again. As Jess swam, the water level dropped until she had to crawl to remain beneath the surface. She scrambled close enough to touch Sweeny, then stood, leaping from the water to tackle her prey.

Sweeny squawked, surprised, stumbling as she fell to the muck. The insects disappeared in a curl of rancid green smoke.

Jess thrust her dagger down, aiming for Sweeny's

heart, but she missed, piercing only mud as the mage flailed and sunk deeper into the silt and muck.

Jess grabbed hold of Sweeny's neck to keep her still, but her adversary's weight was sinking too quickly into the silt, forcibly drawing down, and it pulled Jess off balance. She fell forward, on top of Sweeny, and her limbs were caught by the suction of the mud below. Dagger raised, Jess fought to keep her head above water and gasped for air as her left forearm, then her elbow, slid into the mud. She released her grip and pushed away with her legs, struggling to break free of the mud.

Jess heard growling, an animal charging through the water. Her arm slid loose and she fell back, gasping. Kedder ran to her, snarling and splashing as he scrambled to a stop, his hackles raised.

Struggling to stand, Jess heard a low thud, a beat, that rippled through the mud and water. She lost her balance and fell backward, her face slipping briefly under the surface, then sat up hurriedly, coughing and spluttering water. Dagger in hand, she staggered to her feet, tottering as another thud rippled the marsh, and wiped water and muck from her eyes.

Lars stood before her with his new sword drawn. "Are you all right?"

She took a step toward him, then stumbled, falling to her knees at the next rippling thud. "I was," she said as she tried to regain her footing, then slipped and fell backward onto her backside again.

Lars hurried to help her stand. "How did you get here? What happened?"

Jess grasped his hand and let him pull her upright. "I came through the mirror. She possessed my aunt Maeve and stole that buckle you gave me."

"Through the *mirror*? She who?"

Another shuddering thud, louder, but Jess managed to keep her balance. "Sweeny." Sudden silence surrounded them, so bright it pressed on her ears, and she felt the thud beneath her feet but heard nothing, not even Lars's voice as he said something to her. She shook her head and tried to knock the water from her ears. She could hear a low whine, a squeal like metal on metal, then her ears opened up again.

" . . .you home," Lars said, his hand on Jess's shoulder.

"There you are, you shit-eating bastard!"

Jess turned to gape at a drunken man screeching obscenities from the weedy bank to their right while three others stood scowling behind him with large hammers and a pickaxe.

Lars grimaced, his shoulders slumping. "Aw, piss, not now."

"That's right, you'd better be scared, you murdering son of a bastard whore," the man said, staggering into the water. "Marsden ain't here to save your mangy backside. You're all mine and I'm gonna do to you just like you did to Hewl."

"Dammit, Verlet, I didn't kill your brother!"

"The hells you didn't. I was there!" The others followed Verlet into the water. "We're gonna bust you up and leave you to die."

"I rather doubt that. You're all drunk and I'm better armed. Go home before you get yourselves hurt." Lars's head tilted slightly as another low thud rippled the water. "Do you hear that?" he whispered to Jess. "A woman's laughing."

Sweeny. "What do we do?" Jess asked, glancing over at the men as dark clouds gathered over them, blocking out the sun. "Where is she?"

Clackclackclack and a low giggle. "Asking me to play, dear? And you've brought presents!"

Lars turned. He moved in front of Jess as Sweeny's burnt, muddy from stepped from the reeds.

Verlet stopped his stumbling approach, but Sweeny curled a finger and he floundered toward her despite trying to scramble back and away. Her hand snapped out, clenching to pierce his throat, and she gasped with delight. Verlet went limp, releasing a soft orgasmic sigh as his flesh turned ashen, then dry and tight against his bones, then collapsed into dust.

"Oh, Goddess, no," Jess whispered, moving a step closer to Lars. She wanted to be sick.

Sweeny took a deep, contented breath and flung the last bits of the quarryman's clothing aside. "What a lovely snack. I think I'd like another." She stretched as if just waking from a nap then tore another man from the water. Wailing, he flew toward her and rapidly shrank into a dusty husk at her touch while the last two men ran screaming from the marsh. The mud covering Sweeny leached into her charred flesh, swirling into the buckle low on the front of her hips, as her form solidified to a charred and flaking woman. Sweeny glanced at Lars and licked her lips. "Why, thank you, dear. I see you've brought me lunch."

* * *

Dien was halfway up the ladder when the first pulse shuddered through the cave. Water coursed through cracks in the masonry, and he fell, knocking Felk aside and plunging them both into the water.

"What in the hells is that?" Marsden asked, struggling to stand while his question echoed around them. He stumbled against a set of shelves and clutched onto one for balance, scrunching his eyes closed and turning his head aside as dozens of jars tumbled off, crashing against him and one another.

"The mage," Dubric said through gritted teeth. The pulse had sent a sharp pain through the bites at his thigh and throat; they stung as if afire even as the ripples in the water faded.

Another pulse rattled the cellar and Dubric cried out in agony, slumping to his knees. The sudden shock of cold water against his chest took his breath away. Another crack appeared in the wall, burst open by rushing water, drenching Dubric's face.

"Sir!" Dien said, scrambling to him.

Severed heads floated in the water, some still in jars, others floating free, their mouths gasping like drowning fish. Turning his face away from the coursing leaks, Felk splashed forward to one of the floating heads and clutched it to him. Another pulse and he stumbled, nearly dropping it. The head in his arms stared at Dien and Dubric, its mouth forming words but releasing no sound. Felk sloshed forward and grabbed another head, and another, pulling them from the stagnant water as he wept.

Another pulse, a slam of pain in Dubric's throat and thigh. With Dien's aid, he staggered toward the ladder through rising water.

"The wall's cracking," Marsden said. "We're all going to drown."

"We must get out of here." Dubric reached for the ladder then fell back, crying out, as another pulse shuddered the cavern.

* * *

"My, he's a pretty one," Sweeny said, licking her teeth. "However did a nasty little girl like you manage that?"

Lars approached Sweeny slowly. "Stare her down, Jess. Dubric taught me mages can't hurt you if you concentrate. It keeps them from getting into your head."

Sweeny moved to the side, her gaze darting from his eyes to his sword to Jess. "That's good advice, boy," she whispered. "Best you keep on giving it."

"Shut up, bitch. You're already dead."

Sweeny laughed and licked her teeth. "That I am."

"She's not dead," Jess said, following Lars. "She's in Aunt Maeve's body."

Sweeny laughed, and held her charred hands out before her. "Oh, I'm dead, all right, little girl." She peeled off a black fingernail and tossed it aside before she took a step closer to them, moving to their left. "For now. A tasty little lunch and I'll be just fine, never you worry."

Jess clenched the dagger tighter and blinked away the soft white haze creeping over her eyes as she came to stand beside Lars. The haze swirled over Sweeny, briefly illuminating faint bones and organs before it flowed to the buckle. Jess seemed to see *through* Sweeny, almost as if she was partially transparent. She blinked and Sweeny was merely black and burnt again. "What do we do?"

"*We* don't do anything. I'll kill it."

"But Maeve! She's still there. Somewhere."

"Kill me, kill me, kill me," Sweeny chittered, tilting her head back and forth, her burnt flesh cracking and flaking off. "Is that all you can think about, boy? Killing me?"

"It's what I do to mages."

She took another step sideways, close to a hole in the ground. "This is a fascinating conversation, truly it is, but will you excuse me for a moment?"

She raised one arm as she took another sideways step, over the hole, then dropped straight down.

* * *

A charred, nude woman dropped through the hole, landing squarely on her feet in a slight crouch at the base of the ladder and effectively splitting Dubric's team in half. With no time to think, Dubric, Dien, and Marsden all hid, dropping into the dark water, as the woman stood straight and strode directly toward Felk, who was still struggling to hold the severed heads. Just past Felk, Dubric saw Marsden, his head a dark spot in the water, move against the shelving and slip backward between two racks.

"Didn't I already kill you once?" A flick of Sweeny's hand and Felk flew aside, slamming hard against shelving. The water-rotted wood crumpled beneath his body and collapsed, the loud cracks of wood punctuated by breaking glass and sloshing liquid. Felk and the heads plunged into the water, creating a churning mess of foam, glass, and clotting fluid.

Shivering cold with all but his head submerged, Dubric grasped Dien to hold him back. "No," he whispered, "she will kill you if you attack her, and we are trapped here. We must get out. Immediately."

"I'm getting Felk." Dien shrugged off Dubric's grip and crept forward through the water, moving silently between floating heads.

Sweeny continued on, rounding the row of shelving and disappearing in the dark.

"Go, go!" Dubric whispered to Marsden, and he crept forward to help Dien drag a gasping and spluttering Felk from the mess.

A low rumble sounded from the dark, trembling the water around Dubric's legs. As it grew louder, the rumble turned to a furious wail, endless and without breath.

"Go!" Dubric said, shoving Felk up the ladder after Marsden.

"Maybe we can lock her in here, sir," Dien said, urging Dubric to the ladder.

Both men turned their heads at a loud crash from where Sweeny had gone, then another. Other crashes sounded, fading into echoes.

"We can try," Dubric said, scrambling upward despite his aching legs, "but I do not know how much luck we will have."

"Where the hells is my book?" Sweeny screeched, then something else crashed, splashing into the water. "It was right here! I need my damned book or I'm stuck in this pudgy bitch!"

Dubric cried out and fell back—one hand grasping the bite bruise on his throat, the other reaching for his thigh—as stabbing white-hot pain flared from the marks.

"Shit," Dien muttered, grasping Dubric before he fell. "You're not helping, sir," he grunted, hefting Dubric over his shoulder and climbing up.

"You old bastard!" Sweeny screamed, sloshing toward them. "Where is it? What in Taiel 'dar's name have you done with my book? Tell me, damn you!"

A wrenching, ripping sensation tearing through his head, Dubric began to apologize, beg for forgiveness for his ignorance, but Dien shoved him up and through the hole to hands Dubric felt but didn't see. As he rolled onto his back, clutching his pained skull, the earth beneath him heaved upward in a blast of agony and greenish light.

*　*　*

Thunder booming across the sky above her, Jess reached down for her father. The water beneath him was roiling and greenish, like malignant boiling slime. Before she could touch him, it exploded upward, knocking her through the air. She landed hard on her backside in the marsh, her teeth clacking together.

"Daddy!" she cried, struggling to scramble to her feet. "Lars!" A vast and spewing hole had opened in the ground, a geyser of green water spouting viciously from its depths.

Sweeny, still black and burnt, rose from the noxious water, staring at Jess. "Where is it, you nasty little girl?" she snarled as water coursed and churned past her, flooding into the cavernous hole and draining the marsh.

Jess pulled the dagger from her skirt and took a step toward Sweeny, careful to keep her footing in the dangerously rushing current. The necklace against her throat was cold, an orb of ice, and her arm tingled all the way from the moonstone to her right palm. The dagger in that hand felt alive, hungry, and a confident calm fell over her, thrumming softly in the back of her head.

Take it take it take it. Kill her! Kill her now!

"Jess, no!" Lars cried, stumbling toward her, floundering.

"Where is it?" Sweeny asked again, striding forward

as if the rushing thigh-deep water was no obstacle, no weight.

"I don't know," Jess said, standing her ground. The dagger thrummed in her hand and white haze twirled around the buckle at Sweeny's waist, shooting inward and illuminating Sweeny's insides to her spine. *Kill her! Take it! Do it now!*

Far behind Sweeny, Dubric staggered to his feet and unknown men stumbled to the marsh's edge. Jess could not see her father. *Daddy, where are you?* She took a breath and braved a glance at Lars. "Any ideas?"

"Don't let her touch you." He swung his new sword with a snap, flicking water off the blade.

Jess swallowed. "I kind of figured that."

Sweeny stopped in mid-stride and smiled, the charred flesh at her cheeks flaking off. She reached down, crouching slightly, then flung her hands toward them. The water abruptly shifted direction, rising up in a sharp curl and charging back at them.

Lars grabbed Jess and wrenched her around, using his body to protect her from the wall of water. It slammed into them, knocking them both forward to their knees, their faces, shoving them into the silt and mud. Jess felt Lars's grip slip and she grabbed on, one hand digging into his arm, the other stabbing the dagger hilt-deep into the muck.

The wave surged over them, pushing them forward, then, just as Jess felt her lungs were sure to burst, the current shifted and pulled them back in an undertow. The dagger slipped free from the muck and, tangled together, she and Lars tumbled toward the gaping hole.

* * *

The dog barking wildly beside him, Dubric stumbled forward and cried out in anguish as water churned around Sweeny's blackened body. Dubric saw her draw a deep breath and straighten her spine. After she sent the wave over the children, she sagged slightly then staggered forward again.

She is still weak. The magic she uses drains her almost as fast as she gathers it. We must kill her soon, while we still have hope. But Maeve! I cannot. I cannot kill my love again.

Felk reached Dubric and grasped his arm. "What do we do, sir?" Behind Felk, Marsden stumbled out of the weeds and slumped to his knees.

Dubric wanted to say, *Serve her, lay with her, bleed for her, anything but kill her.* "Catch her and kill her," he forced out, choking on the words.

Desperate to get to Lars and Jesscea, Dubric moved forward again and nearly fell as Dien, blood-soaked and limping, thundered past them into the roiling water. Dien stopped mid-marsh and planted his feet, leaning into the surge. He staggered back a step, one foot locked in place, and let out a painfully deep bellow as water coursed up and over him.

Sweeny floated to Dubric. "He's trying to save his children. How very noble of him. We cannot allow that, now can we? Saving children?"

Kedder lunged at her, snarling and snapping, but Sweeny casually reached out and grasped the mutt by the throat. She blew Dubric a kiss as she turned Kedder into dust, the last fragments scattering on the wind. A delighted deep breath later, her dark gaze raked over Dubric with a knowing gleam. "Pull your dagger, my love."

"I'm not your love," Dubric spat. Sweet, succulent pain tearing through him, his hand fell to his dagger.

"Ah, but you are," Sweeny said, her voice a delicious torture in his heart. "You are. And you're mine forever."

* * *

Jess slammed into something solid and unyielding. As the wave started to twist her aside, she thrust her dagger into the firm mass, desperate to stop their churning descent to death. Lars clung to her and she clung to her dagger, her other hand reaching around to grasp whatever stalwart force had saved them. A leg, thick and warm. Horrified, she held on desperately, clenching down on the need to gasp a breath, as Lars climbed up her, then up the body of their savior. Her mind graying and her lungs shuddering in her chest, Jess felt Lars's feet slide beneath her belly, then hands gripped her by the waist and pulled her up, dagger and all.

She burst from the water and gasped a breath, her ears ringing under the volume of her father's scream.

He staggered back, falling beneath the force of the water.

Jess scrambled after him, screaming, "Dad!"

Lars ran past her, reaching her father first. "Help me!" he cried, falling back as he tried to lift Dien's limp and bleeding body from the churning water and mud.

Jess shoved the dagger through her skirt near her waist and hurried to help Lars tow him to the bank. "Dad?" she asked, glancing up at Lars. Her father lolled in their arms, dead weight as they dragged him through marsh grass and sedge. They managed to get him to solid, if damp, ground.

His eyelids flickered and he moaned, writhing, then opened his eyes. He looked up at them, smiled in relief, then closed his eyes again. "You're alive." Brilliant blood dribbled from the corner of his mouth, a nasty gash on his arm, and from the wound Jess had given him.

"Stay with him," Lars said, pulling off his shirt. "Use this. I'll be right back with dry bandages."

Jess looked up the bank to where Sweeny hovered near Dubric. "Be careful."

"You, too." Then, skirting the edges of the muck, he ran.

Oh, Dad. Jess tried to stop the bleeding, but Lars's shirt was soaked and did little to staunch the wounds.

Dien swallowed, licking the blood from the corner of his mouth. "You're okay?"

"Yes. Just rest." She looked over. Lars had reached the horses. "Lars'll be right back with bandages."

"You can't bandage this," he said, smiling slightly. "Busted up inside, but it's all right. Saves me from meeting the hangman." He swallowed again and opened his eyes. "That knife you stabbed my leg with . . ."

Jess winced. *What did it do to him? Oh, Goddess, did I unman my father?*

"Is . . . Is it that dagger Dubric gave you?"

She nodded. "Yes, Daddy."

"Can you kill it? Can you kill that burnt bitch?"

Jess looked over again to Dubric, who was still staring at Sweeny. "I think so, Daddy, but . . . But Aunt Maeve's in there."

Her father grasped her arm, drawing her gaze back to him. "Kill her anyway."

* * *

"My love, my love," Sweeny assured Dubric, glancing down as he unfastened the bond and grasped his dagger's hilt. With a flick of her hand she sent Felk and

Marsden crashing into the reeds. "But you were hers, too, weren't you?"

Rain fell and Dubric trembled, blinking blood-tinted droplets away like tears. "I still love Maeve, you bitch."

Sweeny laughed. "Not her, my pet. The other one. That unfeeling shrew who killed me, burned me, all those summers ago."

Dubric froze, his eyes widening as Sweeny leaned close and ran a finger up the front of his sodden trousers. The rest of the world disappeared and he fell into her eyes, warm and green and promising an orgasmic mix of lust and pain.

"Oriana," Sweeny whispered, smiling slightly, her breath rotten and dead on his face. "Fitting, don't you think, that the burning bitch died in a fire." She chuckled, teasing him with her hand, her voice soft and deadly intoxicating. "Charred to a crisp while carrying your child, is that right? And when she wouldn't die, you killed her."

Dubric struggled against the compulsion to pull his dagger, his hand shaking as he fought the need to draw the weapon, but the blade inched higher, a breath at a time, each moment more agonizing than the last. He tasted blood moments before Sweeny kissed him, her lips charred and blackened and dead. He whimpered as the blade snapped free and turned in his hand.

"That's it," she said, coaxing, one charred hand encouraging his arousal, the other a scalding grip encircling his wrist. "Right there." She eased the dagger forward, toward the buckle on her lower belly, and she grinned against his lips, char flaking into his mouth like bitter sand. "Do it again. For me. Kill your beloved and your child. Kill them both, my love."

Dubric's hand shook, the tip of his dagger denting

Sweeny's blackened flesh. *No! Maeve was pregnant? Why did she not tell me?*

Sweeny smiled against his lips, easing close and pressing against the blade. "You didn't know? How tragically delightful."

The blade crept forward, puncturing charred skin, as Dubric felt like his head would split in two. *No, please, not again. I cannot! Oh, Maeve!*

Another kiss, burnt and dead. "There you go, my love," she whispered, coaxing. "Kill your child, just as you did before. Let murdered Royal blood flow through my veins. Think of the power we'll—"

Startled, she gasped as white light burst from her shoulder. "Back again, dear?" she snapped, pulling her hands from Dubric as she turned toward Jesscea.

Flinching in a burst of light, Jesscea ripped her dagger away and ducked. On either side of her, Marsden and Lars both swung, Lars nearly lopping off Sweeny's arm.

Sweeny snatched out and grasped Marsden's wrist, his hand and lower arm turning ashen and dry. "You children want to play, we'll play."

Dubric was rooted where he stood, helplessly watching as Marsden wailed, falling to his knees as his cry turned from pain to pleasure. Marsden's fingers flaked off, his wrist collapsed like crushed paper, and darkness spread up to his shoulder like fire across a pasture. His head rolled back and he groaned, grinning, before slumping on his backside as Lars separated Marsden's desiccated arm from the rest of him.

Worthless limb in her hand, Sweeny screeched, twisting, knocking Dubric aside. Jess sliced toward her ribs, barely missing. Lars stepped rapidly to the opposite side and swung at her waist, char cracking as he buried his blade nearly to her spine. Thunder rumbled above and the wind quickened, driving the rain against their flesh.

Sweeny lurched toward the children, her wounds glowing green and sealing closed. As she stumbled, Lars and Jesscea turned and ran, scrambling up the bank and toward the ravine.

Snarling, Sweeny followed.

*   *   *

"Stay close," Lars said, lightning crackling in the clouds as he ran around an outcropping of earth.

"My . . . my dad . . ." Jess gasped, looking back toward the swamp.

Lars choked back stinging tears. "He'll be all right." He found a rock wedged in the bank and directed Jess behind it. "Stay down."

He crouched and slid the knapsack off his shoulder, wincing at his bad arm. It was throbbing and sore, but seemed to be in its socket. He ripped the knapsack open and reached inside. "Dubric said these explode on impact," he said, handing a marble ball to Jess. Dampened by rain, it slipped from their grasp, but she caught it and held it close.

Green gurgling water flowed upstream in a churning flood, bringing mud and plants with it as it pounded the banks. Sweeny followed, her charred flesh glistening with raindrops. "Where are you, dear?" she asked, and the opposite bank collapsed into the ravine, spewing up a cloud of dust, stones, and broken trees.

Lars and Jess leaned against their rock, their heads low. "Just a little longer," he whispered. Jess nodded and clenched her marble ball.

Another explosion of dirt, this one behind them and above their heads. Lars drew Jess beneath him, protecting her with his body as they were showered in grit and plants.

Coughing, he stood and flung his stone. He missed, as always—he was no better at throwing at a target than shooting one—but close was good enough. The marble ball hit the ravine bed near Sweeny's feet and exploded in a burst of yellow light. It knocked Lars back, staggering, and he fell on his backside as Jess, protected by the rock, stood and hurled her stone at Sweeny.

Hers hit the mage square in the chest in another yellow burst. Sweeny staggered, large hunks of charred flesh broken away to reveal blackened bone, but she kept coming.

Lars scrambled for the knapsack and flung another stone, as did Jess. And another. Sweeny stumbled, falling once to her knees, but she found her footing again and sent water crashing toward them.

They scrambled up the damp and slippery bank, away from the flood, but their protective boulder rolled loose, lost to water, and the knapsack rolled along beside it.

Jess clung to a clump of roots, her hair dripping in her eyes as she stared at Sweeny. "I have to kill her, Lars. I have to try."

"No. You can't become a killer. Please."

She looked over at him, her face tight and cold. "I have to."

Then she released her root and fell, sliding down the bank to the stream.

* * *

Explosions rocked the swamp as Dubric drew himself to his feet, his arm broken from Sweeny's crushing

grip and his bad knee throbbing mercilessly. He wanted
to follow Sweeny, wanted to lie at her feet and beg forgiveness for protecting Maeve and their unborn child,
but he pushed loathsome desire aside and staggered
to Marsden to help him stand. Another explosion
slammed from the ravine, the pressure from the thud
pounding Dubric's eardrums. It sent him stumbling
back, but, knowing Sweeny was still alive, he stepped
forward again, toward the noise, toward his love.

* * *

Jess stood as water rediscovered gravity and flowed
downhill as the Goddess intended. Dagger in hand, she
walked toward Sweeny with a smile on her face.

She's weak! Kill her kill her take it take it kill her! the
dagger cried in Jess's mind, white swirling light pouring
into the buckle at Sweeny's waist. "I'm going to kill
you," she said softly.

"Ah, back to that, are we?" Sweeny said, stepping
slowly sideways. Even drenched with rain, she crackled
with every movement and Jess saw several joints that
had no flesh left to cover them. "Shall I arm myself?"
Sweeny laughed and placed one fist over the other.
Drawing her hands apart, a sword formed between
them, the blade grimy and mossy green. She slumped a
bit then stood straight again. "Mine's longer than
yours, dear."

Jess's dagger felt cold. Alive. She clenched it tightly
in her right hand and an icy calm fell over her, thrumming like a soft hum in the back of her head.
Everything else forgotten, even her aunt Maeve, Jess
moved to the right, away from Lars, onto solid ground,
and bared her teeth. "Doesn't matter." Jess reached
a flat stretch of streambed, about five lengths from

Sweeny, and charged, head down, the blow knocking
Sweeny back a step.

Sweeny swung her hand, her charred fingers curled
into bone and ash claws. Jess ducked away, just beneath Sweeny's swipe, then ducked again when the
sword came swooshing toward her.

Jess rolled, getting a little distance between them,
then got back to her feet. She charged again and hit
Sweeny hard, tackling the mage as her father had taught
her, shoulder low with her weight and momentum behind it. Sweeny grunted and fell backward into the
water, her sword clattering away and dissolving in the
stream. Jess threw herself down after the mage and
slammed her forearm against Sweeny's throat, but the
ashen flesh just crumbled.

*She's dead, you idiot! You can't choke someone who's
dead!*

A ball of greenish light grew in front of Sweeny's
eyes. Jess swiped at it with her dagger, dissipating the
light in a bright, hot burst, and her blade gouged
Sweeny's face. A delighted cold shiver ran through Jess
and the white haze in her vision brightened.

Sweeny screamed, thrashing as white foam gurgled
from the wound, but Jess shoved her back, under the
water. She knelt on Sweeny's chest, then looked up at
Lars, the dagger vibrating in her hand, as he slid down
the bank.

Jess felt a tremor in the water. The light swirled
around Sweeny's buckle, then ran through to her
spine, illuminating everything in its path. *The buckle!*
the dagger whispered in the back of Jess's mind. *Get it,
take it, kill her. Do it now!*

Sweeny struggled, clawing and biting, but Jess
barely noticed. The mage was weak, unfed, and had

spent most of her power already. Nothing mattered to Jess but the buckle. Sweeny used it. Wore it. Right there in plain sight.

Take it, destroy it. Finish this, the dagger whispered. White light from her vision swirled around the buckle, making Sweeny's insides glow clear to her spine.

Jess drew her right hand back to strike, then paused. *This is too easy. Something's wrong. A trick? A trap?*

She squinted through the white haze of her vision, then took a sharp breath. *There, behind the buckle. That's what you're trying to hide.*

A nugget of brilliant white, tiny, a lumpy strip about the size of a tomato seed. In a womb.

"I'm no baby killer," Jess said. She swiped sideways, her dagger slicing beneath the charred brass and lifting the buckle from Sweeny's belly with a deft flick. It sprung loose and Jess caught it, the dagger's triumphant howl a delightful chill through her bones.

Sweeny screamed, her struggles turning frantic. White foam flecked with blood welled out of the wound but Jess didn't give it more than a passing glance. She slapped the buckle to the mud; then, holding it steady, stabbed down between her thumb and forefinger, piercing the buckle with Oriana's dagger.

Sweeny shrieked, arching beneath Jess as the buckle exploded. The flash of white light threw Jess back and the welcoming coldness left her, leaving only warm, black silence behind.

CHAPTER
26

✝

Lars flew backward under the burst of white light, his back slamming hard against the bank, then he fell down to the ravine bed and landed face-first in the rocks. Shaking, he pushed up to his hands and knees, then to his feet. Sweeny was gone. He sagged in relief and pain, wiping blood from his eyes with the back of his hand. "Jess?" he called out, staggering forward.

Silence. Nothing but the last remnants of a summer storm blowing through the ravine.

"Jess!" he called louder.

A woman lay nude and bald in the water, her legs floating but her torso safe on the bank. She had a deep silvery gash angling through her left eye to her cheek, a bruised scrape on her forehead, and a circular silver mark low on her belly. *Maeve.* Lars checked her—alive and breathing—then stood again. "Jess!"

Frantically searching, he finally located her in a mangled patch of weeds and brush, about halfway up the bank.

He fell to his knees beside her, tears burning in his eyes as he checked her for injuries. Some bruises, gashes on her cheek and bare legs, but he found no broken bones. He whispered her name as he lifted her onto his lap.

She lay limp in his arms, barely breathing, and Lars rocked her. "Wake up, Jess. Please, for the love of the Goddess, wake up." He kissed her brow, smoothed her hair, and tried to straighten her blouse, but it was bloody and twisted. Torn.

Something approached from behind. Lars snatched up his sword, then turned to see Dubric staggering to them, his scalp half peeled off, deep and flowing gashes on his arms, his legs, his chest, and one hand hanging crooked from the wrist. He had fresh blood everywhere, clotting in greenish swamp muck. Felk followed behind him, looking battered and bruised.

"You're alive," Dubric sighed, slumping in relief. Then he saw Maeve and ran to her, his horrible injuries not appearing to slow him.

Lars cradled Jess and stroked her cheek as he choked back tears. *Please wake up, Jess. Please.*

As if hearing his silent prayer, she drew a gasping breath and her eyelids flickered. Lars cried out with relief. He kissed her brow again and wiped mud from her bloodied cheek. "Praise the Goddess." He grasped her hand. Her fingers instantly curled around his.

"Lars?" Jess mumbled, her eyes opening then sagging closed again. "What happened? Are you okay?"

"I'm fine," Lars said, joy shining through him. "Everything's fine." He glanced back toward where they had left her father, and hoped he had told her the truth.

* * *

"Oh, Maeve," Dubric sighed, falling to his knees and sobbing. "Why did you not tell me you were with child?" He leaned over her, checked her throat, then looked back to Felk, his heart leaping. "Give me your shirt."

"Milord?"

"She is alive," Dubric said, pulling Maeve upright with his one good arm. "We need to get her to the sanatorium," he said to Felk. "I think I know who you saw in your dream."

"Who, milord? Can she repair my men?" Felk peeled off his sodden shirt and helped Dubric wrap Maeve in it.

"She would have to kill others to do so. I am sorry."

Lars and Jess stumbled down the bank. Both were battered and bleeding but whole, and Jesscea wore her dagger thrust through the waistband of her skirt. Two youngsters, untrained, had killed a blood mage. Dubric nodded grimly before turning back to Maeve. The Ghost and his Blade indeed.

"Help me get her to Arien," he said, struggling to stand. Then Lars was there, and Jesscea. The three men ported Maeve from the ravine to the horses, and, with Jesscea's help, managed to drag Dien and Marsden across saddles as well.

"Why Arien?" Lars asked, leading Dien's horse.

"I believe she is killing to repair the living." Dubric took another step, his knee throbbing. "She is our murderer. I heard she often performs surgeries and has easy access to the primary solvents for the preservatives and ointments. She has had ample opportunity, and enough talent, and I believe she has motive as well."

"Arien? Motive to murder someone? Why? I can't see it."

"Because of her son," Dubric said. "Raffin is the key.

She needed a healthy child's body to replace her son's broken one. She is repairing bodies, replacing parts. The details fit. The care shown to the victims, the cleanliness, the precision. The talent. I believe most of the first body we found was a practice specimen, a failed experiment, but the leg replacement worked and she discarded Sevver's ruined leg. The beheaded sheep, the living chicken head . . . even Kedder's odd black head was a clue.

"Somehow Arien stumbled onto Sweeny's magic. It is likely she took the book Sweeny so desperately sought, and set out to use it to save her son."

* * *

Lars ignored the shocked stares as he hurried down the hall, running ahead to secure Arien in her treatment room. He knew he was a bloody mess, but he'd had no chance to clean himself. *Alive, unharmed,* he reminded himself, opening the door to her waiting room. *Arien, the killer? Dubric can't be serious.*

One patient sat in the corner; a mindless, drooling woman. She tore at her hair with one hand while the other strained at the binds lashing it to the chair. She rocked, an endless repetition back and forth, knocking her head against the wall with each circuit. Looking at Lars, she grinned. "Geh!" she said, still rocking, and held her fist out to him. Scraggly hair poked out between her fingers.

He opened the treatment room door.

A man lay facedown on the table, unmoving, Arien standing at his head with a scalpel in one hand and a delicate, paddle-tipped applicator in the other. She looked up, blanching, and returned to her task. "Let me finish this. It'll only take a moment."

Lars moved away from the door and watched her work. The air smelled of the same medicinal tang as the sheep heads, and the man had two heads, neither fully attached.

Arien hummed, intent on her work.

His hand fell to his sword. *Secured. Unharmed. Piss.* "So it's you?"

Without speaking, Arien clamped a blood vessel in two places and severed it. She shifted the other head, daubing a vessel with the applicator before pressing two vessels together, then she counted, her eyes rolling up as she tapped her foot seven times. She removed the clamps, dipped her applicator in a dish, and moved on to the next vessel.

"I need to be careful with the blood flow, all right?"

"All right," he muttered. Watching the bizarre procedure was little different than watching Rolle work.

With the final vessel severed, she dropped one head on an empty instrument table. She glanced up at Lars as she plucked a larger applicator from the assortment of tools and set the scalpel aside. "Dubric send you to catch me?" she asked, spreading yellowish fluid on both halves of severed spine.

"I'm just supposed to keep you here."

"Well, it's about time," she said, glancing up again before she spread more fluid on the severed ends of clamped neck muscles alongside the spine. "I thought for sure he'd stop me after I replaced Sev's leg. With you fellas sniffing around, I almost didn't graft it. But the body was right there, it just took a few minutes, and I made sure Sev wouldn't be a cripple." She moved the head into position, counted, then removed the clamps.

"You stole a leg from a corpse?"

"He wasn't going to need it anymore. Can I finish

my last graft?" she asked, nodding to a pair of large jars like the ones from Sweeny's cavern. One was empty, but a youngish woman's head floated in the other. "That's Syrill. She had ruined kidneys. She also has a husband and two little kids who visit her every phase or so. She's twenty-two. Keeps a garden and sells bread for pin money. The woman outside is called Geh because it's the only sound she makes. She shits her pants, bangs her head, even in her sleep, and throws her porridge instead of eating it. She throws her shit, too. Someone dumped her here about fourteen summers ago and we ain't seen them since."

Arien dropped the applicator to clatter on the tray, then tilted the head back. She glanced at Lars as she plucked up a wired instrument. "I guess you're not gonna let me."

"I'm just astounded that you, of all people, are actually doing this."

Arien bent, prodding the man's gaping throat. "I'm just performing a service. Ah, there you go."

She stood straight and dunked an applicator in the dish. "Esophagus," she said, medicating the throat. "It never wants to line up." Wire in one hand, applicator in the other, she worked, then removed both and counted to seven.

"People like Geh have a right to live," Lars said, unable to look away. Seeing her reattach a throat with such matter-of-fact care was both intriguing and horrifying. "Who are you to decide they shouldn't?"

She attached the next piece. "Who are you to decide they should? Do you have to clean their endless filth? Shovel food in their maws? Get shit thrown in your face?"

"No, but—"

"Then don't assume that because the view's fine from your lofty perch that you know anything about this." She leaned back and counted again.

"My mother's a mental patient," he said through gritted teeth as he tried not to think of Elena down the hall. "Her illness destroyed my family. I have no home because of her insanity, so don't you talk to me like I'm an ignorant fool."

Arien shifted the head and fiddled inside the throat. "Would you fix her if you could? Make her healthy and whole again?"

"Of course I would!"

Applicator in and a quick count. "Then you do understand. Syrill's body was broken. Dying. Her mind was fine. Geh's mind is gone, but she's as healthy as a pack mule. Why not keep the working parts and discard the bad?"

"Because people are *people*. They're not gears and sprockets."

"Ah, but they are. I knew that the first time I saw the jars. Just pieces. All I had to do was figure out how to make the pieces work. But there was a book, see, and once I understood what it was trying to say, it was easy." She swiped the applicator, then slid the skin to the severing, shifting the two halves a bit to line up the incisions. "Almost done," she said as she walked to the cupboard.

"Why'd you do it?" Lars asked. "Just to prove you could? Just because you have some twisted sense of the value of a life?"

Arien pulled a vial from a shelf. "I did it for my son." She released a heavy sigh. "He kept getting sick, nearly dying, and sooner or later the medicines wouldn't be enough. He's a good boy, talented, and I couldn't let him die, not when I had the means to stop it. I never could get a mid-abdominal graft to work, but I started successfully grafting heads and limbs on small animals. Then dogs. Sheep. Finally people."

She returned to her patient, showing Lars a vial of cream-colored goop. "This ointment heals skin. The other works well on the inside, but it'll leave obvious scars."

Lars blinked, astounded. *She worries about scars?*

She opened the vial and poured a bit on her finger. "Want some? It'll seal those gashes right up."

He shuddered. "No. But Dubric wanted me to tell you about our other injuries."

Arien glanced up, concerned, but as Lars described them, she nodded. "As long as no one's dead. I can't fix dead."

"No one's dead, not yet," Lars said, looking down for a moment. "Whatever your reasons, it's not our place to tamper with Malanna's plan."

"Sometimes it is," Dubric said, helping Felk carry Maeve, Jesscea pushing Dien in a chair behind them. Dubric looked at Arien. "Can you help us?"

"One moment." Arien pulled a bottle of cleaning solution off a shelf and uncapped it, filling the room with the reek of ammonia. She waved the bottle beneath her patient's nose. "Come on, now. Let's wake up."

He jerked, then stirred, his eyelids flicking. Lars helped him stumble to the waiting room, then returned to find Arien stricken, shaking her head as she looked Maeve over, and Dubric cursing with words Lars had never heard before.

* * *

After they had returned to the castle, after Rolle had probed the gash across Maeve's face and somberly told Dubric there was nothing he could do, Dubric went to his office alone.

Dien was still unconscious. Maeve's wounds were cauterized, sealed, and scarred to the bone. His physician could not repair them, the mage healer could not remove them. Two quarrymen had died. Marsden had lost an arm. And Bonne . . . Dubric could not describe, even to himself, the empty ache he had felt when he had discovered how Sweeny had escaped from the temple. "You goat-raping bitch," he said aloud, glaring at the ceiling, "the pain and scars are supposed to come to me, not to the people I love."

His outer office door was stuck shut and he had to fight to get it open. The struggle fed his anger and he nearly ripped the door from its hinges. Once inside, he stopped and stared. The inner office door stood wide open.

Nothing appeared out of place except the mirror. It stood flat against the northern wall, its cover damp and rumpled on the floor.

He stared at his own reflection—his scars, the swampy muck, the ghosts milling about his head. Then he picked up a chair.

He dashed the chair against the glass, turning his head away from the burst of light and shards. He swung again, knocking the last shattered bits from the frame, then again and again and again, until the frame snapped and fell.

"You *are* cursed," he muttered, tossing the broken chair on top of the pile of glass and wood. "I fell into your seduction like so many others. If I had destroyed you summers ago, none of this would have happened. Maeve would not have been possessed and Jesscea would not have faced a mage. Bonne would still be alive. They were right all along. You are dangerous. But no more." He stared at the splinters and shards, just glass on the floor, then he turned, grumbling at a knock on the door.

"What is it?"

Rolle peeked in and handed Dubric a file. "Good news for a change. Gilby's finally woke. He may always limp, but otherwise should have a full recovery."

Dubric let out a breath, relieved. "I will be there in a few minutes."

Once Rolle had left, Dubric opened his top desk drawer, where he had hidden the items from Gilby's jacket. He put the timepiece and book in a small sack. After a slight hesitation, he sat and laid out the four sealed messages. He broke the seal on the note addressed to Jelke.

It read as gibberish, a couple of nonsense sentences, until he cross-referenced the note with Gilby's little book. Translated, the note read:

Four-thousand-crown payment required. Deliver to thirty-seven.

Dubric cursed and shoved his desk halfway across the room.

CHAPTER

27

✝

Folded notes tucked into his notebook, Dubric clenched down his anger as he entered Rolle's office. "Where is he? Can he talk?"

Rolle led him past Dien and his weeping family to a private treatment room. "His father's been insisting on taking him home, but I told him the boy was still in danger and needed to be kept for observation. I'll let you decide how long that needs to be." Just outside the door, Rolle said, "His jaw's tied closed. He can talk, but not very well."

"Thank you." Dubric entered, closing and latching the door behind him. "We need to have a little chat," he said, pulling up a chair. "About several things."

Gilby nodded.

Dubric opened his notebook. "I will try to ask yes-or-no questions so that you do not have to move your mouth very much. Some questions will require a more specific answer, so take your time."

Gilby nodded again.

"When Dien found you in the grain shed with Fynbelle, were you aware that she was pregnant?" After Gilby's nod, Dubric asked, "Did you intend to inform him of his daughter's condition?"

Gilby flinched, looking away, then nodded.

Dubric noted that as a maybe. "Have your injuries been explained to you?" Gilby raised his unbandaged arm and rocked his palm as if it were a boat on a rough sea. *Somewhat.* Dubric flipped back a few pages and read off the full listing of injuries and their expected prognoses. "Do you understand what has happened? The extent of your injuries?" Gilby nodded. "As a noble of rank, do you wish to charge Dien with assault with intent to murder?"

Gilby's eyes widened and he shook his head, giving Dubric an alarmed squeal.

"There is no need to worry for your safety. Dien has been gravely injured and cannot harm you anymore."

Gilby still shook his head. "No charges," he mumbled weakly, just his lips moving.

Dubric stared. "You do not wish to charge him, even though he nearly killed you?"

Gilby nodded. "No charges." He took a breath, swallowed, then said, "My fault."

"All right," Dubric said, noting Gilby's decision in his book. He reached into his pocket, into the sack he had tucked inside, and retrieved the timepiece. "Were you aware that this was in your pocket?"

Gilby just stared, his breathing deep and rapid.

"I shall ask again. Were you aware that this was in your pocket?"

Gilby took a shaky breath then met Dubric's gaze. A nod.

"And the book that was in your pocket as well?"

Another nod, Gilby's quiet stare holding steady.

"The notes?"

Gilby flinched, then closed his eyes for a breath of time before opening them again. He nodded.

"Who do you spy for?"

Gilby's gaze never wavered. "No spy."

Dubric took a breath to control his anger before he strangled Gilby. "You mean to tell me that you had those things in your possession, but that you are not a spy?"

"No spy." Gilby took a breath. "I swear."

"Did you bed Fynbelle to ply her for information, since she is Dien's daughter?"

Gilby shook his head, sharp and insistent. "No. Love Fyn."

"You love her so much that you are a spy against her home?"

"No spy!"

Dubric ground his teeth. "What are you, then?" he asked, brandishing the notes at the boy. "Is this why you are seldom at your post? Why you are always late? Why you have failed every assignment you have ever been given?"

Gilby glared at the notes and nodded. "Hate them. Forced to deliver them or he'd hurt Fyn." He turned his head and looked at Dubric. "I swear. I'm no spy."

Dubric's hand fell as the anger left him. "You were forced to be a courier?"

Gilby nodded. "Yes, sir."

"Goodness, lad, by whom?"

Relief shone in Gilby's eyes. "My father."

* * *

Dubric unfastened the peace bond on his sword. Beside him, Lars did the same, then stepped aside and pressed against the wall, out of the line of sight of the doorway. Dubric took a moment to settle himself, then knocked on Talmil's door. "It is Lord Dubric," he said to a crack between the door and its jamb. "I have just left Physician Rolle and I would like to talk to you about your son's injuries and prognosis."

He heard the door unlock, then Sir Talmil opened the door, dressed in a long shirt and sleeping trousers. "It's awful damned late," he said, stepping aside as he invited Dubric in. "Can't this wait until morning?"

Dubric dropped his hand to his sword as Lars shoved the door wide, knocking Talmil away. "I see no reason to wait to arrest a spy."

Talmil squawked in terror and tried to run, but Lars grabbed him by the scruff of the shirt and slammed him face-first against the wall, hard enough to bloody Talmil's nose.

Dubric calmly closed the door.

"Go ahead and struggle," Lars said as he yanked a set of shackles off his belt. "You've pegged with my family for the last frigging time. Calling Fyn a whore. I should geld you for that, you shit."

"I demand to see Lord Brushgar!" Talmil said, grunting as Lars slapped the shackles on his wrists.

"Brushgar's making your noose," Lars said, hauling Talmil from the wall as Dubric walked farther into the suite. "We've met your buddy Jelke, too. Too bad he didn't get the note you sent. I wonder if he ever paid the four thousand crowns of blood money."

Dubric hurried into Talmil's bedchamber, hearing the thud-grunts from the sitting room as he searched. He pulled open drawers and ransacked shelves in Talmil's bedchamber, but he found nothing more incriminating than a communication stone. Cursing, he returned to the sitting room before Lars could turn Talmil into bloody pulp. "Let him spend the night in gaol," Dubric said. "Perhaps then he will be more inclined to tell us who should join him on the gallows."

* * *

Dubric took a moment to gather himself before knocking on Dien and Sarea's door.

Dien opened the portal and took a startled stumble back. After nearly two phases of medical care, he had finally left the infirmary that morning and, despite the extended rest, he still moved weakly. Behind him, his family fell silent, all staring at Dubric's interruption of their welcome-home celebration. "Sir? Is there a problem?"

Lars stood. "Did we have another murder?"

"No murders today," Dubric said, stepping aside as he encouraged his companion forward. "Go on," he said. "It is all right."

Haydon hid, peering around Dubric's legs. "They're all strangers."

"I'm not," Lars said. He handed Jesscea his beverage and came to get the boy. "I'll introduce you."

Haydon hesitated, but let Lars take his hand and lead him inside. He was still a bit tottery on his feet, but improving every day. Dubric wondered when he would learn to run.

"Could I speak with you and Sarea? Privately?" Dubric asked, smiling as Haydon settled on the settee beside Fynbelle.

Dien and Sarea followed him to the hall. Dubric said, "There are several matters I need to inform you of. First, you will have no formal trial for assault at Council tomorrow. With Talmil facing a hanging and Gilby's continual refusal to press charges, there simply is no viable case for the advocate to present. Nigel mumbled about imposing fines, but I would not worry about that, either. It is merely bluster for bluster's sake." He smiled at the couple. "You are a free man, and I have cleared your official record myself."

Sarea sagged, grasping Dien's arm. "You're sure, certain, that this is over?"

"Yes, milady. If your husband is able, I would, however, appreciate his aide as Council bailiff tomorrow."

Dien grinned. "Been doing the job for twenty summers now. No reason to let a little headache stop me. Just don't expect me to do it very fast."

"Good. I have already assigned Serian to assist you, should you need it." Dubric paused and glanced through the open door. "There is one other matter. A favor."

"What is it, sir?"

"I must find a home for the boy."

Dien's mouth worked for a moment before he said, "Sir, I know you're trying to help, but we have four children, two future sons-in-law, and a grandchild on the way. We don't have *room*."

"The child needs a family," Dubric said. "His mother will surely hang tomorrow and I do not want to put him in an orphanage. I have no experience with children."

"Sir—"

"We'll take him," Sarea said, raising her chin. "We'll manage." As Dien turned to her, she said, "That woman loved him enough to kill for him. I won't make the tragedy worse by seeing him beaten or in a workhouse. It's just not right."

"Are you sure?" Dien asked.

Sarea smiled. "Might be nice to have a son."

* * *

Lars and Jess carried boxes and bags of clothing and supplies down the sanatorium hall. "You're sure this is okay?" he asked for the umpteenth time.

"I'm sure," Jess said, dodging a staggering patient. "A friend of yours is a friend of mine." She wondered why Lars was so nervous visiting someone who just needed a little help.

Lars stopped at a closed door and set down one of his sacks. "This is it."

Jess touched his arm. "Everything's fine. Relax."

"I'll try. Thanks for coming with me." He gave her a last worried smile, then knocked on the door.

"It's unlocked," a woman's voice said from within.

Lars took a deep breath then pushed the door open. Jess followed him in.

A blonde woman lounged on a worn mattress in a bright private room. She sat up, startled, as they entered, her left arm twitching. She started to speak but no words came out as she looked at Lars, then Jess, then Lars again.

"Good morning," Lars said, blushing. He returned to the hall for the sack he'd set aside.

"Hello," Jess said. "It's nice to meet you."

The woman nodded. Her left side shuddered and Jess politely kept her attention on the woman's face. It was pretty, if worn, the face of someone who had survived a hard life. The woman met Jess's gaze and smiled as she pulled a sheet over her legs.

Lars lugged in the last of the supplies, then closed and latched the door. "I know this is a surprise," he said.

"You might say that," the woman replied, sounding as shaky as Lars looked.

Lars carried the gifts to her and opened the boxes

and bags. "We brought clothes and utensils and bedding and soap. I wasn't sure what you'd need." He pulled things out, blushing at the undergarments, then quickly setting a blanket on top of them.

The woman looked pleased and surprised. "You didn't need to do all that."

He fumbled, muttering, "I know," then resumed unpacking.

Before nervous silence filled the room again, Jess asked, "Aren't you going to introduce us?"

Lars stood, startled. "Sorry!" he said. "Elena, I'd like you to meet Jesscea Saworth, my intended." A deep breath, then, "Jess, I'd like you to meet Elena Darril." He smiled at Elena and took Jess's hand. "My mother."

* * *

Dubric opened the door to his suite. The well-lit space was immaculate, everything in its place and the furniture artfully arranged for ease of use and foot traffic. "I am home," he called out, depositing his papers and keys on the table by the door.

"Back here!" Maeve replied.

He strode through the suite and found her sitting on the floor in front of open windows. Warm sunlight spread around her, illuminating the soft tufts of hair that had begun to grow back. She had two boxes before her and, as he approached, she pulled out a woven blanket, rubbing it between her fingers. "So soft," she said, bringing the blanket to her cheek. "Do you think the baby will like it?"

"I am sure he will," Dubric said as he sat beside her.

"What if he's a she?" Maeve turned to him, the scar

a silver gash across her face and through the empty socket of her left eye.

We are both scarred by the Goddess. He smiled and touched her cheek. *A daughter would be fine. Beautiful, like her mother.* "Then she will like it, too."

ACKNOWLEDGMENTS

In addition to my amazing editor, Juliet Ulman, many, many people helped me create this novel. I'd like to thank (and I hope I didn't miss anyone):

Frank O'Brien Andrew, Kelly Barnes, Gail Brookhart, Johnny B. Drako, June Drexler, Meg Godwin, Sam Godwin, Krista Heiser, Andrew Heward, Mary Hilliard, Doug Hoffman, Kathy Hurley, Barb Jebenstreit, Bill and Laura Jones, Peggy Kurilla, Michele Maakestad, Stuart MacBride, Anne Marble, C. E. Murphy, Carter Nipper, James Oswald, William Reiss, Joshua Rode, Terry Rowe, Jean Schara, Linda Sprinkle, S. L. Viehl, and Cassandra Ward.

I couldn't have managed this past year, or this book, without you!

ABOUT THE AUTHOR

TAMARA SILER JONES started her academic career as a science geek, took up graphic design and earned a degree in art, and now writes forensic fantasy full time. She's an avid baker and quilter as well as a wife, mother, and cat wrangler. Despite the gruesome nature of her work, Tam's easygoing and friendly. Not sick and twisted at all. Honest! Visit her online at www.tamara silerjones.com.